VOTE

A Vic Bengston Investigation

ALSO BY RICHARD J. SCHNEIDER

FICTION

WATER *A Vic Bengston Investigation*
Who Killed Porkchop? *A Key West Mystery*

VOTE

A Vic Bengston Investigation

A NOVEL BY

RICHARD J. SCHNEIDER

South Platte Publishing
Denver / Key West

Cover design by Vigil Design
Cover images © Bigstock.com / urfingus / ktsdesign
Author photograph © Clarissa Schneider
Book design by George Peabody

South Platte Publishing
P.O. Box 372338
Denver, CO 80237
www.richardjschneider.com

First Print Edition: December 2015

ISBN-10:0985931329
ISBN-13:978-0-9859313-2-2

P 7.2 122915

Dedication

To the Strnad sisters of Fox River Grove, Illinois: my mother, Jeanne Marie (Strnad) Schneider, who has always encouraged my writing, and in memory of her sister, my Auntie Midge (Strnad) Black, who inspired me with books and was an enthusiastic Vic Bengston fan.

Acknowledgements & Suggested Reading/Viewing follow this novel.

VOTE
A Vic Bengston Investigation

1

The tiny red light on his desk penholder told David Riley something breached the state-of-the-art security system guarding his house. This was nothing new. Autograph seekers, computer nerds, nosy journalists, homeless freelancers, and neighborhood dogs, penetrated the system two or three times a week. Denver Alarms, a tiny security firm he bought two years ago, was already on the job. They should be. The company only had one client. But David Riley always took precautions, especially when it came to the card.

A tripped alarm always triggered the same response from him. This time was no exception. He reached into his sport coat pocket and removed the tiny flat black micro SD card. It was already sheathed in thin clear plastic wrap, the kind his mother used when she made him a peanut butter and jelly sandwich for school lunch. Riley placed the tiny memory card on the desk in front of him, stood up and unzipped his pants, letting them collapse into a clump of Dockers khaki around his ankles. His even more practical white Fruit-of-the-Loom briefs trailed. Squatting, he ever so gently inserted the miniature package into his rectum, like a suppository. This card and its predecessors had traveled around the world like that, and no one else ever knew.

The discomfort was slight but worth it to hide the prize. The SD card and what was on it had to be protected and hidden at all costs. It was his "Precious."

It was also a Pandora's Box, so potentially treacherous that he could not even trust it to the U.S. Patent Office even though it was worth billions. Pants back up, thrift store leather belt re-buckled, Riley gingerly sat back down behind his desk. Carefully, he reached to his left and cracked open the top drawer providing quick access to one of his many Glock nine-millimeter automatics.

A muffled thump broke the quiet. The study door slowly and deliberately swung open.

"Don't move a muscle." The whispered command came from the silhouette in the doorway.

Riley placed his hands folded in front of him in the pool of light from the high-tech desk lamp. The rest of his study remained shrouded in darkness.

"Not a muscle," the shadow said. The voice was comical, high pitched and whiny, deliberately so. Not a girl's voice though. Riley recognized it, or thought he did.

"I heard you," Riley said, suppressing an urge to laugh.

"I don't want to hurt you," the voice said. "But I do have a gun."

"So do I," said Riley, peering into the blackest corner of the room, hoping his eyes would adjust to the darkness so he could catch a glimpse of a face, to confirm his suspicion. "Don't use yours. Please."

"I just want something from the safe," the voice said.

Riley shifted to his right cheek. He could only make out a faint outline of a figure. He thought he saw it up and grab something from a shelf on the other side of the room. "My secretary has the combination. We change it often." The combination had never been changed.

"Sure," the whisper said. "Just don't move. This won't take long."

The man, he knew it was a man, moved silently around to Riley's right and toward the mahogany file cabinet that matched the desk. There's nothing in there, Riley thought. Then he caught more shadow movement and heard sounds behind him. He started to turn around.

"Don't!" the whispered voice ordered in a burst through clenched teeth. Riley turned back. Something cold and hard was placed at the base of his neck. "I asked you nicely," the voice said. "No more fucking around."

"No more," Riley promised. He continued to listen.

"No one is coming, by the way," the voice said.

Riley's heart skipped. "How do you know?"

"I just do."

A "click" indicated the intruder had opened the short section of fake book spines behind him in the bookcase. This signaled access to the safe. Riley puzzled over the "no one is coming" comment. Was the house alarm disarmed? The safe alarm too? Did this intruder know which book to move after opening the fake book door? Apparently so.

Now, a feint whirr of the safe dial. Riley made a mental note. Install a safe with the voice command access instead of the old tumblers. Muffled tumbler ticks competed with Riley's tightly controlled breathing.

The silhouette, on the other hand, seemed not to breathe at all. Riley wondered if the gun was nothing more than a steel pipe. He could turn quickly, knock it away and run for the door. Maybe even get off a shot, something he had always wanted to do, actually shoot someone. No, he told himself, just wait.

The safe door opened and Riley felt the gun barrel or whatever it was jab at his neck. He heard the shadow's hand tapping at the insides of the safe. Then he heard the double click of the false back deep inside the safe. Silhouette was all the way in, Riley thought. So was the silent alarm call, he hoped. Something will happen. Something good.

In the darkness, a gloved left hand removed a thick accordion file and placed it into a bicycle courier pouch slung over Silhouette's shoulder. Riley knew what was in the file. It was the only thing inside the safe: a manuscript, three compact discs, and a six-inch long circuit board that fit into one of the internal slots of any personal computer. His shadow visitor has just swiped a poorly written draft of Riley's autobiography, three of his favorite Elvis Presley CDs, and a standard computer network card. Pleased with his decision years ago never to keep anything of importance in any safe, Riley squirmed and squeezed his sphincter muscles tightly around the object he was sure Silhouette was seeking.

"Sit still," the voice said, still fake, but oddly soothing. This was coming to a conclusion, Riley thought.

"I'm trying," he said. "Hemorrhoids."

"Life's a bitch. Try harder."

The shadow man's free hand then reached back inside the pouch and, in the dark stillness of the study, pulled out a brown heavy paper accordion file the same size as the one he had just removed from the safe. He slid the replacement file containing papers, three CDs and a network card back into the empty rear compartment.

Riley took in all the sounds, inventoried them, filed them away for later analysis. It seemed odd to him that Silhouette would put something back into the safe. He heard the door to the rear compartment of the safe close and latch, then thought, would whatever Silhouette put back into the safe mimic what was removed from it? Why bother?

More sounds to file away, if even for a few more minutes. The sound of the safe door being closed, the spinning of the combination dial, and the snapping shut of the fake books. As soon as the cops were here, and he looked at the safe contents, everyone would know it was all fake, Riley thought, unless?

A firm hand gripped his right shoulder. Something hard bumped his left temple.

"Apologies," Silhouette said. A blinding flash. Part of an explosion.

David Riley was no more.

2

The rhythmic sounds and rocking of the morning light rail ride lured Vic Bengston from the interview notes on his lap. Hypnotized, he just gazed out the train window as Denver whirred on by. His favorites slid past, the city's backside, the equipment yards, the loading docks, the rear doors of businesses with all sorts of things stacked up outside, used pallets, replacement utility transformers, heaps of rusty steel in varied sizes and shapes. Across the aisle, on the other side of the train, a matched set of tattooed skateboarding twenty-something males, iPod buds fused into their ears, both looked up when Vic's cellphone broke the spell and penetrated their respective walls of electronic noise.

"This is Vic."

"Vic Bengston?" the voice on the other end said.

"In the flesh," Vic said as he looked out the window to the west. The train was rolling past the heavy yellow, orange, and tagged Union Pacific diesel engines, parked in their rail yard and awaiting their next burdensome assignment.

"Les Vigil," the voice said.

"The Les Vigil?" Vic said. "The Editor Les Vigil?"

"Yes, the very one, Vic," Vigil said.

"I'm not giving anymore interviews," Vic said. He had tired of that and even turned down a book offer. He did not want to write books, at least not yet. He just wanted to be a reporter in spite of his age. Vigil had personally interviewed him after the Pulitzer and again after the death of the *Rocky Mountain Sun* for two pieces in the *Times*.

"I'd like you to write for the *Times*," Vigil said.

"What's left of the Voice of the Rocky Mountain Empire?" Vic said.

"It's still reputable," Vigil said. "And it's the only daily left in town."

"What about the *Denver Daily News*?" Vic said.

"A week-day free shopper?" Vigil said. "Give me a break. They're almost out of business too."

"So are you," Vic said.

"Not by a long shot."

"*Colorado Now*?" Vic said.

"Please," Vigil said. "Have you looked at their news hole lately? You need a magnifying glass to find it." There was a pause. Vic remained silent. Vigil filled the dead air. "They're a weekly. You're comparing the *Times* to a weekly?"

"Well, I'm sort of retired, Les," Vic said. "At least for a while."

"Bullshit," Vigil said. "Do you want to write for the *Times* or not?"

"Let me call you back, Les. Gotta get off the train." Vic tapped the End Call tile on his phone's touch screen and returned to mindless gazing out the window.

The light rail train began its slow squealing turn into the Auraria Higher Education Center, a sprawling complex built on the bulldozed remains of old neighborhoods that flanked the entire southwest edge of downtown Denver. Thousands of students now swarmed the classrooms of Denver Community College, Metropolitan State University of Denver, and the University of Colorado Denver, where Vic had earned his master's in Political Science a few years earlier. When the four light rail cars cleared the big curve and paralleled Colfax Avenue, they ceased their forward motion, permitting a torrent of students to flow off the train and flood the massive urban campus. Vic flowed with them. He headed toward the library to return a book, then to his part-time job on campus.

Vigil was right, Vic thought. The *Denver Times* was the only game in town. Vic had no desire to pull up stakes and relocate to some other city where a daily newspaper could stop its presses permanently at a moment's notice as the oozing internet monster continued to eat traditional print journalism alive. He called Vigil back.

"Well?" Vigil said.

"Sure," Vic said. "I'll write for the *Times*."

* * *

"Can you start right now?" Vigil said.

"Les, I'm tutoring students at the CCD Writing Center for the next two hours," Vic said.

"CCD?" Vigil said. "Are you at the Auraria campus now?" Vigil said.

"I am," Vic said.

"This can't wait, Vic," Vigil said. "Something important has happened. I need you here. Now."

"I can't imagine what could be so important that you need a perfect stranger to mach schnell right over to the paper," Vic said.

"Perfect stranger, my ass," Vigil said. "You've been in this town for centuries. You've got a Pulitzer in your hip pocket, for God's sake. Look, this is important, Vic. I'm offering you a job, a good one. And something big has come up."

"It's only been decades," Vic said, "But spread across two centuries." He wanted the job badly. "Let me tell them inside. I'll be right over."

Three other tutors were already there, enough to handle the student load for the next few hours. Vic made his apologies, explained the emergency and unexpected job offer to Dawn, who ran the Writing Center. She understood.

He headed out the door to walk the half dozen blocks to the *Denver Times*, the last standing daily newspaper in Denver, if you don't count the free *Denver Daily News*, which Vic did not.

"Hey, Dude," came a distant disembodied voice. Vic ignored it. "Dude!" Vic stopped and turned around. It was one of the tattooed twenty-somethings from the light rail, skating up on his board. The iPod earplugs were still buried deep in his ears, probably shortening his hearing lifespan by years.

"Dude," Tattoo said. "Thanks for the help on that paper. Like I got an A, man."

Vic raised his left fist, knuckles up, and the two pounded. Students recognized Vic by his near white frizzy spiked hair, a hairstyle adopted expressly for that very purpose. Then Tattoo skateboarded off to class.

* * *

Vic revolved through the oversized doors of the Denver Times building. He squinted at the familiar face behind the tall marble counter.

"Vic!"

"Joe?" Vic said.

"Yeah," Joe said. "They're waiting for you up on six."

"You survived the *Sun* burial, I see."

"Lucked out," Joe said. "Like you, I guess."

"Maybe," Vic said. "Jury's still out. How do you find Les Vigil?"

"Good guy," Joe said, sliding a clip-on security badge across the granite counter separating the guard station from the rest of the cavernous stone-lined lobby. "You'll need this."

"Hope you're right," Vic said. "How's Jane and, and—"

"Grace," Joe said.

"Grace, that's right," Vic said. "She still on the swimming team?"

"State record in the butterfly," Joe said, puffing his chest a bit.

"Awesome," Vic said, then jerked his thumb skyward. "Know anything about this?"

"Other than you're the new employee?" Joe said. "Not a thing."

"Okay," Vic said. "Here we go again."

* * *

For the second time since he shut down his public relations firm, Vic Bengston made the perp walk as a new employee across the sprawling city room of a Denver daily newspaper. The last time, at the now shuttered *Rocky Mountain Sun*, he was a gray-haired "rookie" returning to the newspaper game after years wandering in the corporate wilderness. He felt uncomfortable then, almost foolish. This time, though, it just seemed odd because this was where he started his search for a journalism job when he first hit Denver a long time ago. Only back then it was in the old Denver Times building, long since torn down.

Vic felt pretty good, the *Times* editor calling him. He did not even have to ask for the job like he did with the *Sun*, may it rest in peace. Of course, it helped to be walking in with a freshly minted Pulitzer Prize. That did not hurt at all. Playing to this minor celebrity, nose high in the air, Vic walked right past the glass-fronted windows that separated editor Les Vigil from the rest of the city room. He caught a glimpse of Vigil's olive face and sensed some movement on Vigil's part, like he might be getting up from his desk to run out and greet his new journalistic acquisition.

Vic maintained his pace, not worrying about Vigil, and sustained his march, passing what looked like the city desk in a commanding central position flanked by drab on drab sound absorbing cubicles. Technology guarded the worker bee spaces with multiline telephones and headsets, flat TV screens suspended from the ceiling, flat terminals on all the desks, wires dropping from above into the cubes, printers and copiers along a wall on one side of the city room and, on the other side, another wall, this one all glass and overlooking Denver's Civic Center Park.

He missed the clattering noise journalism made when he first signed on decades ago, dull gray and green metal desks scraping a hard sea of tile floors, slamming desk drawers that were always sticking, screaming phones, throbbing World War Two surplus teletype machines, squawking police and fire monitors, and the clattering of manual Smith-Corona and Royal typewriters.

An electronic chirp emanating from somewhere signaled radio scanners listening for fire, police, and emergency calls. As he continued his march through the city room, he felt many heads silently watching him, following him as he paraded past three more banks of mostly empty cushioned cubbies. In the distance, he could see a large banner hanging from the ceiling, declaring "*Denver Times* Sports." Avoid the sports department, he told himself, unless I need a score.

He halted at a chin-high cloth covered wall. A small rectangular sign, nothing as pretentious as the sports department banner, informed him he that was in the Features Department. Then he peeked around the corner.

"Hi Peggy," Vic said.

Peggy Mayer, eyes intently glued to her terminal screen, fingers flying across her keyboard, plapping out some feature story, looked up at Vic.

"I heard you'd been pulled in off the waivers wire," she said.

"I heard you finally got a job," Vic said.

"Deputy Features Editor," she said.

"Galas. Fad diets. Quilting. All that?"

"Then some," Peggy said. "Flint on steel."

"At least it has Editor in the title," Vic said.

"And you?" she said. "What are they calling you this time?"

"Associate Managing Editor," Vic said. "At least that's what I'm going for."

"Just like Bob Woodword," Peggy said.

"This is the *Denver Times*," Vic said. "Not the *Washington Post*."

"It's not the *Sun* either."

"May she rest in peace," said Peggy, another refugee from the *Sun*'s stunning demise.

She bowed her head in mock silence, then said, "Here comes Vigil. Saddle up."

Les Vigil looked like a retired Denver Bronco wide-out—wiry, six-two, athletic, fit, walking with a bounce. It would be nice to be that tall, Vic thought, glad that his walking, cycling, and eating less had finally started to flatten his belly. Vigil grinned. Vic hoped he was glad to see him and hoped even more that his hiring was not a directive from the ivory tower.

"Vic," Vigil said.

"Mr. Vigil," Vic said. "Les."

The editor had his right hand out. Vic took it. It was a good grip, dry and warm. It reminded him of an old farmer he knew.

"I need to send you right out," Vigil said.

Vic glanced over at Peggy, who had returned to her work on her terminal.

Vigil looked at her too, then said, "You two worked together at the Rocky."

"I thought she looked familiar," Vic said. "You know, you've got a pretty darn good editor there on the Features desk." Then thinking, why waste her talent on onion soup recipes?

"We think so," Vigil said. "We picked up a few others from city side at the *Sun*."

"You picked up mostly pundits, no reporters." Vic said. Peggy looked up, grinning at the mild shot across Vigil's bow. "It's all opinion these days, isn't it? Forget the facts, and the reporting? Just print the speculation."

"They had a following," Vigil said. "We had an obligation in a way, to the community."

Right, Vic thought. No Sale from that canned response. Vigil did not sound all that sold either, but Vic decided not to press the point, knowing that the Pulitzer would get him only so far. The *Times* would do anything to bolster circulation, even hire the opposition's top columnists, once the opposition was six feet under. Yet the *Times*' girth, circulation, and coverage was still headed south, even in the wake of the Rocky's closure. Now that Denver was a one newspaper town, comprehensive news coverage was merely an afterthought. Save that discussion for later, Vic thought.

Then, the editor shot back.

"We're not *Fox News*," Vigil said. "Or *MSNBC*."

He had a point, Vic thought as he glanced at Peggy. "You've got a few good enterprising reporters and editors," Vic said. "Like this one sitting here."

Vigil just took that in stone faced. Then he pursed his lips and nodded slightly.

"So what's this story you need me on?" Vic said.

"You haven't heard, then?" Vigil said.

"Heard what?" Vic said.

"Some nouveau riche high tech entrepreneur offed himself last night, one shot to the head," Vigil said.

"That's usually all they can get off, Les, just that first round," Vic said. "The second one is pretty tough, being dead and all." A suppressed laugh shuddered through Peggy's slight frame.

Vigil just shook his head. "Momma said there'd be days like this."

"Momma was right," Vic said. "So I'm to be a high profile suicide specialist for the *Times*?" Vic said.

"Well, just on this one," Vigil said. "It's sort of special."

"What do you want from me, Les?" Vic said, looking at Vigil, then down at Peggy.

She turned to him and said, "Your golf buddy's on the case."

"Driscoll?" Vic said. Peggy nodded and returned to her screen.

"That gives us a little leg up," Vigil said.

"On who?" Vic said. "The *Denver Daily News*?"

Vigil laughed.

"No," Vigil said, but try channels Two, Four, Seven, Nine, and Thirty-one. They all have news units."

Vic just shook his head and said, "Les, did you ever think it would come to this?"

"What?" he said.

"A major metropolitan daily actually considering local TV stations as serious news competition," Vic said.

"The times they are a changing," Vigil said. He handed Vic a piece of paper. "Here's the address. The carpool is down in the parking garage, level B3. They're expecting you."

Why did he ever leave this business, Vic asked himself, the juices starting to flow.

"Call the desk with anything you get," Vigil said. "Use your cell phone. We'll get you a *Times* phone once you settle in, but this thing is right now." Then to Peggy, "Peg, can you write down the city desk number on something for Vic?" She started to scribble on a paper scrap.

"I'd rather call Peggy," Vic said, knowing how much she detested the name, Peg.

"She works for the Features editor, not city side," Vigil said.

"Okay," Vic said. "If I stumble across a hot new yoga position I'll give Peggy here a shout." He emphasized her preferred name, Peggy.

"Here's the city desk number and my new cell number," Peggy said handing him the piece of paper. "Have you a notebook, little boy?"

Vic smiled and pulled a narrow spiral wire bound notebook from his back pocket and waved it at Peggy.

"Pen?" she said.

Vic patted his shirt pocket where his fountain pen resided.

"Go get 'em, tiger," Peggy said.

"And remember to call in early and often," Vigil said, sensing he was on the outside of an inside joke.

Vic started to walk back toward the elevators.

"You want the victim's name?" Peggy said.

Vic stopped and turned.

"Sure," he said. "Why not?"

"David Riley," Vigil said.

"Got it," Vic said, heart jumping. He spun to resume his march toward the exit, wondering if there were, in fact, special angels who looked after aging reporters.

When Vigil called him to offer a job at the *Times*, Vic was going over his voluminous interview notes with one David Riley, the reclusive Denver dot.com gazillionaire who had invented the first touch screen voting machine and who knew what else in the world of computers and software.

No angels, he concluded, unless he counted Peggy. She knew about the Riley interview, having learned about it from Vic over a steaming pair of venti Starbucks. She must have tipped off Vigil, and he wondered if that had triggered the job offer.

No matter, Vic thought.

With Peggy at least in the Times building, he felt like the Blues Brothers putting the old band back together.

3

Lt. Frank Driscoll looked down at the ten thousand dollar Navajo rug in David Riley's study. It had seen better days. A congealing pool of blood had dripped down from the desk and soaked into the natural fibers on the floor, ruining the traditional native pattern for eternity. Flies converged on the desk, searching for a spot to drop eggs. David Riley, head down like a schoolboy taking a nap, took center stage. No more dreams. No more thoughts of how the computer can be used to improve lives, control lives, shape lives, or ruin lives.

"What's with these people?" said the tall, well-dressed African American detective. He knelt down, careful not to disturb the scene and especially careful not to get any blood on his shoes, even though they were covered with anti-contamination booties. The detective leaned forward a few inches to observe the gaping chasm in the right side of Riley's head. "One shot, through the temple. God, I'm sick of this crap."

"Crap, sir?" said the anxious junior detective standing next to him.

"Crap, Willis. C-R-A-P. Crap. Guys like this have it all, and then they pull a stunt like this."

"Suicide, Lieutenant?" Willis asked.

"Good guess," the lieutenant said. "Look. This guy had more than a few bucks. Look around at this place. If it's worth a dime it's worth ten million. He's got money, cars, success, women, and probably a prescription drug habit. A little problem crops up, maybe a loan that's less than legal, or he does something stupid to save his business, who knows. Something comes up, and he checks out. Leaves us to clean up the mess."

"Sir, maybe he was clinically depressed or something like that," Willis offered. "You never know."

The detective started to lose his cool, but brought himself back, fast. He stood up straight, a head taller than Willis. He looked at his new assistant's short cropped hair, and black goatee guarding his chin. "You ever gonna shave?"

"I do every morning, sir," said Willis, a former MP.

The lieutenant just shook his head. "Well, at least you're not wearing one of those damn—you are! I don't believe it! What is that!"

"Diamond stud, sir."

"I don't even wear a ring, except this," the lieutenant said, holding up his left hand and displaying his plain gold wedding band.

"*Times* are different, sir," Willis said.

"Tell me about it," Driscoll said.

"Lieutenant," said a uniform who stuck his head around the bedroom door. Driscoll looked up. "Someone here to see you."

"Who?" Driscoll said.

"Me, cop," said another voice from the hallway.

"Great," said Driscoll, closing his eyes. "Now this. Just what I need."

Vic stepped into the doorway.

"Aren't we in a charming mood today," Vic said. "Nice suit, by the way."

Driscoll did not look up at Vic. Instead, he kept scanning his eyes over the body and the rug around him. "What in God's name are you doing here?"

"Your name came up in a conversation," Vic said.

"Where?"

"City Desk at the *Times*," Vic said.

"Don't tell me," Driscoll said. "They're nuts enough to hire you?"

"Something like that," Vic said.

"Something like that?" Driscoll said, this time slowly looking up.

Vic shifted his weight, but remained in the doorway. He knew Driscoll would have tossed him if he stepped into the room.

"Just thought I'd check things out," Vic said.

"Okay," Driscoll said. "You've checked them out. Now get the hell out of here. Go write one of your tree-hugger stories."

"At least someone is reading them," Vic said. "I didn't know you subscribed to Western Environmental News."

"It's a fine birdcage liner," Driscoll said.

"You don't have a bird, Frank," Vic said. "Mary has cats."

"And they make my eyes itch," Driscoll said, uncurling his massive six foot four frame up from a lineman's crouch. "Now, what are you really doing here, Bengston?"

"I'm here for the *Times*," Vic said. "Plus, I interviewed him."

"Riley?" the lieutenant said. "When?"

"About two weeks ago," Vic said.

The big man looked down at the body and quietly said, "Then you'll have some background for me won't you?"

"I'm not turning over my notes if that's what you're getting at, Frank," Vic said. "It was mostly business stuff anyway."

"Any business enemies?" Driscoll said.

"No comment," Vic said. "I thought this was a suicide."

"Suicide is still a crime," Driscoll said. "Anyway, you owe me, Bengston."

"For last week's drubbing on the golf course?" Vic said. "Or, that saving my life thing?"

"The latter," Driscoll said. "We could get a court order. I could arrest you right now as a material witness. Then you'd get to meet some real head cases down at the jail. Excuse me, down at the new Justice Center."

"You're just saying that to humor me," Vic said. "Anyway, arresting a journalist covering a story doesn't look all that good, especially for a police department with nonstop PR problems."

"Humor my you know what," Driscoll said. He swept his arms around the lavishly appointed room. "You see where the hell we are? Look at this place. Ten million bucks, if it's a penny. Presidents talk with this guy!"

"Talked, officer," Vic said, "Talked to him. He's speechless at the moment, in case you haven't noticed."

"Yeah, whatever," Driscoll said.

"What's your point, Frank?" Vic said.

The cop wound up.

"I'm gonna have every *Times*, *Gazette*, *Examiner*, *Tattler*, cable and TV station sniffing up my butt for the next six months over this," he said. "Look in the mirror, pal. The blood's not even dry and you're already here. I'm envisioning media tents outside City Hall."

"Admit it, Frank," Vic said. "You love the publicity."

Driscoll's face broke into that big grin, the same grin he flashed at the crowds in the old Mile High Stadium after crushing some unsuspecting quarterback deep in the backfield.

"I sure as hell do," he said.

"So, are you done here?" Vic said.

"No," Driscoll said. "Touhy's not here yet."

"Do you know what time it is?" Vic said.

Driscoll looked at his watch, then glared at Vic and said, "Yes, I know what time it is. I've got forty-five minutes until that appointment. Anyway, you know the drill. I don't leave until Touhy gets here."

Driscoll turned his attention back to the body, the blood, and the gun. He memorized the scene. He would not touch a thing until after Touhy finished up. Touhy the medical examiner. Touhy the brilliant forensic scientist. Touhy the neat freak. Touhy, the diminutive woman who must have chewed out Driscoll five or six times just for touching a body. Driscoll wised up. Now, no one moved a thing until Touhy was done. And for good reason. Since Touhy showed up, Denver's homicide conviction record climbed to one of the best in the nation. After combining the ME's office and forensic lab, Touhy and her special forensics staff handled all the crime scenes. The interns and the new hires handled all the routine deaths.

Touhy would definitely be here for this one.

* * *

"ME's Truck, sir!" It was Willis and his diamond studded voice coming from the first floor. Driscoll rolled his eyes.

"Quite the perky officer, your new assistant," Vic said.

"Yeah," Driscoll said. "But he's the best recruit I've ever seen."

"Tats?"

"A few, but all below the neck line," Driscoll said. "And you, Bengston, I'll see you later."

"Not if I see you first," Vic said.

"Get out of here, or we'll be late," Driscoll said.

"I'm going, I'm going," Vic said, abandoning his position leaning up against the study door jam and walking down the hallway toward the front door. As Vic stepped out onto the porche, he saw Touhy kneeling down and tugging light blue paper booties over her sensible shoes. Vic looked down at his own feet and the black-soled running shoes on them. They were the type of soles Vic banned from his sailboat because they left marks. They also left marks at crime scenes. Touhy glanced at the shoes, then up at Vic's face.

"Thanks," Touhy said. "You leaving, I hope?"

"Yes, I'm leaving," Vic said as he slipped by Denver's compulsive medical examiner. Touhy followed him with her eyes, closed them and just shook her head.

"No matter how many times I lecture the cops or scream at you reporters, everything's messed up by the time my office gets here," Touhy sighed. "You are a reporter, again, aren't you?"

Vic looked at his watch and said, "As of an hour ago."

"The *Times*?"

Vic nodded. Word gets around fast.

"Vigil never had much sense," Touhy said. She peered down at Vic's shoes. "What are those? New Balance, what number? Turn them around let me see. Five-fifties. Okay, we'll need to look at them. This just doubles my work. Look at all the imprints on the carpet. I can't even—" She glimpsed a uniform patrolwoman about to open Riley's front door. "Don't grab that doorknob!" The young officer stopped dead in her tracks and looked back toward Touhy, who was moving toward her quickly. "Dammit! I haven't even had a chance to look at this place and you guys are ready to cover everything up. Tape off this area and get back!"

Touhy tossed the young officer a roll of yellow crime scene tape. She looked back at Vic, pointed toward the ME's truck, and said, "Now get your sorry self over to my truck and tell that lady right there to make an impression of your shoe soles."

"I thought this was a suicide," Vic said. Touhy just scowled at him.

"Precautions," Touhy volunteered and then sternly waved him toward the lab truck.

The block began to fill up with cop cars as word of the Riley's death oozed out. Vic walked over to the forensics truck. A stunning dark-haired dark-eyed woman in a charcoal gray business suit was preparing sample bags and other equipment. Mature. Vic's age, or somewhere in the ball park, maybe ten years younger.

"I'm with the *Times*. Vic Bengston." A small name badge declared her to be Joan Keeler, Asst. M.E. "What does 'Keeler' stand for?"

"K." Her voice was wonderful, deep and strong.

"Touhy wants my soles," he said, sitting down on the curb next to the truck.

"Most of us just have one," Keeler said. A sense of humor is good, Vic thought.

"These," he said, lifting one foot.

"Take them off," she said. Nice smile. Then she shook her head just like Touhy. She pulled a shoe impression kit from the truck.

Vic sat on the curb and removed his shoes and handed them to her.

"Will this take long?" Vic asked, glancing at her left hand and seeing that the ring finger was naked and fresh. "Will it hurt?"

"Shut up, you brat," she said, like a girlfriend, not like an assistant medical examiner. She walked over to the open side door of the truck, grabbed an impression kit from a rack, and began her work. It took all of about five minutes. She wiped the bottoms of Vic's shoes as she walked back to him.

"I didn't feel a thing," Vic said. "You're good."

She handed him his shoes. "Now get out of here," she said as she turned and walked back to the other side of the truck. Her scent lingered.

Was he reading too much into this? Vic thought. Probably. He always did. Plus, he was too old. It was over in an instant.

* * *

Vic walked over to a shady spot on the narrow grass strip across the street from Riley's house. The Denver summer day was on a dead run to ninety. He sat down cross-legged, flipped open his cell phone and dialed a number.

"City Desk," said an unfamiliar voice.

"Bengston," Vic said, "for Peggy Mayer."

"Who the hell are you?" It was a gravelly old voice, one ruined by a lifetime of smoking.

"Vic Bengston. I work for the paper."

"Oh, that Bengston," the cement-mixer said. "You're on our team now?"

"Wide receiver," Vic said. "Who are you?"

"Veugler," he said.

"I know that name," Vic said. "George, right? Glad to meet you. I thought you were in sports."

"Sick of it, the travel mostly. Wanted a desk job."

"And they gave you the city desk?"

"Just fill in," he rumbled. "Nice break. I'll send you to Peg."

It was an uphill battle with the name thing, Vic thought. "Thanks."

"Mayer," Peggy said.

"Can you take notes?"

"Vic, you need to call the city desk," she said.

"I did. They rang me through to you."

"Pushing the envelope already?" she said. "I'm on Features."

"We'll include a sidebar on the dead guy's favorite salad dressing, okay?"

"What da ya got?" she said, sliding easily back into city desk mode.

"Hole in head, bullet-wise," Vic said. "Suicide, maybe. But they're treating it like a major crime."

"Riley is a major dude," Peggy said.

"Was a major dude," he said. "The guy has a major chunk of his brain missing."

Vic fed Peggy everything he had from the crime scene, including a detailed description of the study where Riley was found. The death occurred in the same room where he had interviewed the dead man a few weeks earlier.

"Can you work the story from there?" she said. "We'll dig for background back here. Unless Vigil fires me."

"Got an appointment," Vic said. "You've got everything I've got, except for the interview notes which are mine, by the way, not the *Times*."

There was a pause that lasted just a little too long. Then she said, "Sorry, I thought that might sweeten the deal."

"For whom? Me or the *Times*?"

"Both, really," she said.

"You too?" Vic said.

"Well, you think I want to spend one more minute covering some gawd-awful charity ball thrown by some fat cat who can't remember how any houses he owns?"

"You would if he was under indictment," Vic said.

"Well, that's different," Peggy said. "Anyway, that would toss the story over to cityside."

"Peggy, the *Times* doesn't get everything I own," Vic said. "I'll just have to have a conversation with Les about this. Notes from that interview are mine. No one else's."

"I thought *Wired* magazine assigned it," she said.

"Totally on spec," Vic said. "They don't even know I interviewed him. If they did they would have called me. I think I mentioned to them that I might take a run at Riley. It was a passing comment with one of their editors. We were talking about something else. Anyway, I've got to run, and no mention in any story about my interview, okay?"

"You know, you are working for us now, Vic," she said, sounding very city editorish.

"I know, but the notes are all mine, and this appointment I have I cannot break," Vic said. "Health."

"Is there a problem?" she said.

"No," he said. "It's just that these appointments are hard to get and, well, I just need to work on a few things."

"How long will you be?" Peggy said.

Vic glanced at his watch.

"Well, it's ten-thirty now," he said. "At least four hours, maybe five."

"Tests?" Peggy said.

"Possibly," Vic said. "I don't really know."

"It sounds serious, Vic," she said.

"It's not, but it's important, and it's been scheduled for some time."

"Somehow, we'll manage," Peggy said with a tone of finality. "Your byline will be on the story. I heard Les say that. It's all about that," emphasis on the "that."

"It's infotainment these days, Peggy," Vic said. "Celebrity."

"It's disgusting," she said. "They were absolutely beaming when you said yes."

"Hey, I'm sure the luster of a Pulitzer will dull once they get to know me," Vic said.

"You're right about that," Peggy said. "I didn't warn them, though. This place needs a little livening up anyway."

"Can Vigil send someone over to bird dog the developments?" Vic said.

"The desk already sent Broderick," Peggy said.

"Oh boy," Vic said. "Can he find Seventh Avenue?"

"The City and County of Denver hasn't moved it in the last century, have they?" Peggy said.

"Not that I know of," Vic said. "But the new bike lanes painted onto it might confuse him."

"He's getting better," she said. "Can I count on you for some background?"

Vic hesitated, reeled through the Riley interview in his mind, and said, "I'll think about it. But not for tomorrow's paper. Nobody has this interview. Nobody."

Peggy said nothing, turning the tables and waiting him out. Vic had already sequestered some of the interview comments for future investigation. He knew he could knock out six hundred words on general background, with a few quotes that would make it sound as though the *Times* were all over this story like a cheap suit. But the other stuff would stay in the vault, for now.

"I suppose I could write something, a general backgrounder," he said, tired of the silence. "But I'll need to write it tonight, not now. By the way, where are you sitting?"

"Across from Veugler."

"At the desk? Please explain."

"Can't," she said. "Your smart-ass comment must have resonated. Les just tossed me up here for the afternoon. Sort of a look-see."

"You belong on the city desk," Vic said.

"I know."

"If something critical happens, call me on the Bat Phone," Vic said.

"When will you be back in here?" she said.

"Give me till four, okay?" Vic said.

"That'll work," Peggy said. "Hit 'em straight."

"Am I that transparent," Vic said.

"You forget who you're talking to," she said, and hung up.

4

The midweek golf game was unusual. They booked it to sharpen up for an upcoming charity scramble on Saturday up in Broomfield. Vic had put together a team consisting of himself, Driscoll, Vic's favorite former client, and a long-time Denver radio and television personality who now co-anchors the morning drive time slot on KOA, Denver's fifty-thousand watt clear channel radio station. The practice round was uneventful. Both Vic and Driscoll raced through bogey rounds with a cart, finishing eighteen in a record three and a half hours. Both men had to get back to work, but not before a late lunch in the clubhouse.

One thing Denver's municipal golf course system could do was make a superb ham sandwich. Vic thought a beer would go good with it too, but his beer days were history. He washed it down with an Arnie Palmer. He watched Driscoll engulf two Arnies and a pair of sandwiches in record time.

"How can you do that without choking to death?" Vic said.

"Easy," Driscoll said. "The secret is in the follow through."

"Huh?" Vic said.

"You see how I stretch my neck by pushing my chin up?" Driscoll said. He tilted his head back and sucked down half a glass of the tea and lemonade mixture. "I saw some bird do it on the National Geo Channel."

"I'm glad to see you're involved with continuing education, Frank," Vic said. On the big TV, Tiger Woods sunk another birdie putt, a re-run of the 2001 Masters.

Driscoll's cell phone chirped. "Driscoll. No, I don't think so. Where'd you find it? Where? You've got to be kidding. What's it for?

How can we find out? No, don't inventory it yet. Don't tell anyone, you understand? Especially that sleaze Bengston from the *Times*. I'll be there in a half hour." He winked at Vic, then slapped the phone shut and dropped it into his shirt pocket.

"Do we have a lead?" Vic said.

"We?" Driscoll said.

"Well, we're sort of a team, you know," Vic said.

"Team, my ass," Driscoll said, glaring at him. "What do you know about computer chips?"

"They run everything," Vic said.

"No, I'm serious," Driscoll said. "What's the best way to find out what's on one?"

"Find a little old chip maker and asked him to hold it up the light and read off the ones and zeros."

"Very funny," Driscoll said, gathering his change off the table, getting ready to go.

"We're leaving?" Vic said.

"I am," Driscoll said as he stood up. "The ME found a computer chip."

"What kind of a computer chip?" Vic said.

"What kind?" Driscoll said. "Is there more than one kind?"

"Frank, you are so Twentieth Century," Vic said. "There are processor chips. They're pretty big, some a couple inches on a side. There are integrated circuits and erasable programmable memory chips. Then there are other kinds of memory chips that you slide into little slots of varying sizes. There's one right there on your cell phone."

Driscoll held up his phone and looked at it.

"Where?" he said.

"Here, give it to me," Vic said. Driscoll handed it to him. Vic pointed to a half-inch slot on the side of his phone.

"See this?" Vic said. Driscoll nodded. With the nail on his left forefinger, Vic pushed on the small dark edge of something that occupied the space. A tiny black object popped out about a quarter of an inch. He grasped it with his thumb and forefinger and pulled out a flat black chip about a half inch long and a quarter of an inch wide.

"This too is a memory chip, or card really," Vic said.

"Now I'm not sure what the ME meant," Driscoll said. "She said computer chip, then SD."

"It's probably like this, then, maybe bigger," Vic said. "This one's a micro SD card. They store data for phones, small computers, other electronic devices."

"I'll be darned," Driscoll said.

"You're funnin' me, right?" Vic said. Driscoll flashed his giant grin. Vic returned the chip to its portal on the cell phone and handed it back to the cop.

"You said the ME found this?" Vic said. "Where?"

"Down at the morgue," Driscoll said.

"No duh," Vic said. "Where on the body?"

"Off the record?" Driscoll said. "All this is off the record." Emphasis on the "all."

Vic knew it was fruitless to argue the point this early in the investigation, even for a suicide.

"Must it be this way always?" Vic said.

"Well, first, it's a little weird," Driscoll said. "And second. Just in case. We need to hold something back."

"Just in case of what?" Vic said.

"Foul play, of course," Driscoll said.

"Is that a possibility?" Vic said, sure that it was.

"Not from what I saw," Driscoll said. "And I've seen a lot of these, Vic."

"But just in case," Vic said.

Driscoll nodded. "He's too high profile, Vic"

"Yeah then, off the record," Vic said.

"The chip wasn't on his body," Driscoll said. "It was in it."

"In it?" Vic said.

"Stuck up his ass," the detective said.

5

Vic walked across Civic Center Park toward Denver's main library building. Parks and Rec workers were erecting a temporary stage, arranging hundreds of chairs, spiffing up an outdoor stand-up cocktail lounge, and fencing off the entire area to keep out most of the city and county's citizens, the ones who actually pay for the park.

Only those who paid an extra seventy-five bucks would be able to enter that portion of the public park during the weekend concert. Like many other cities, Denver was monetizing every aspect of its public facilities to generate cash for a dwindling treasury. Purists objected, arguing public parks should be free to the public. The cities countered by claiming they need the dough to keep the parks coiffed. Vic sided with the citizens. Maybe he would do a story on it, he thought. Denver Parks and Rec was the worst department in city government. Newly elected mayors parked all their campaign cronies there, which led to mischief.

Although the exterior of Denver's main library building at Fourteenth and Broadway had undergone a hideous facelift, the inside remained relatively intact, and Vic could still find his way around. He walked past the main information desk, nodded at one of the librarians he knew, and took the wide marble stairs two at a time up to the second floor. Vic's trek took him through several stacks of reference books, to the northwest corner of the building and an office marked "Reference Staff Only." He pushed his way through the door. The sticky sweet perfume indicated she was in. Vic walked around the corner and just stood quietly.

"What do you want?" she asked, not looking up, emphasizing the "you."

"You talkin' to me?" Vic responded. "Are you talkin' to me?" He stressed the "you" the second time.

"Cut the crap, young man, and sit your fanny down," she commanded. "I'll be done in a minute."

Dutifully, Vic sat, like a schoolboy ordered by his favorite teacher to sit straight and face the front of the room. He waited and watched.

Miss Raglin roamed somewhere in cyberspace, moving the mouse mostly, occasionally plapping something on the keyboard. She was always on the net. In the old days, she was always in the stacks.

"Like hell," she said to the screen. Then more plapping on the keyboard. Then another mouse move. And a click. On the other side of the room a laser printer whirred into action.

She turned to him and, looking over the top of the semi-circle reading glasses perched on her long, somewhat rounded nose, said, "Now, Vic, what can I do for you?" A salt and pepper tassel of hair fell across her face. She tossed it back where it belonged with a snap of her head.

"David Riley."

"We did Mr. Riley two weeks ago," she said. "Have you forgotten?"

"No, and you said there was more," Vic said.

"You're back for more then, are you?" she said. "Greedy little boy."

"He's dead," Vic said.

"No," she said, feigning disbelief.

"Yeah," Vic said, "Right after I interviewed him."

"You always were a killer interviewer," she said with a smile. "You'll want everything now, I suppose."

"Everything," Vic said.

"It's going to take a few days," she said. "The usual fee?"

"The usual fee," Vic said, getting up. She had turned back to the internet.

Miss Raglin was greedy too. So was the gas tank on her Piper Cub.

6

Vic wrote two stories for the next day's print edition. Both were loaded onto the *Times* website as soon as they were completed and edited. The first was a standard breaking news story on the suspected suicide death of David Riley, the who, what, where, when, why and how. Well, not so much "why," since nobody had a clue, including Vic, who was already wondering about the "how." He left out the part about the SD card inside the body. That information was off the record anyway and worthy of further checking.

The second story was a background feature on Riley based on Vic's interview. He had no firm commitment to run the piece from *Wired* magazine, just a "well, we'll take a look at it" from some young snot-nosed editor during a brief phone conversation when Vic pitched the story. To Vic, nothing in writing meant "no assignment." He blew off *Wired* and wrote the piece for his new employer, the *Denver Times*.

* * *

DAVID RILEY
The next Bill Gates?

Two weeks before his untimely death, David Riley was interviewed by Pulitzer Prize-winning reporter Vic Bengston, Associate Managing Editor of the Denver Times.

By Vic Bengston
Denver Times

David Riley, who died this week in what police sources described as a "possible suicide," was on the path to revolutionizing the way we elect public officials. Along the way, he was becoming another Bill Gates.

Since his Millenium Vote System was introduced in 2002, more than half of the states had signed on to purchase and use his voting software and touch screen-voting terminals, thirty-three foreign nations had licensed the system at the time of his death, according to company officials.

Manufacturing barely hit a bump in the wake of the entrepreneur's death. Riley's partner, NCC (formerly the National Calculating Company), is pumping out 5,000 units per month at its plant in Pueblo. Riley's design and software manufacturing facility in Boulder is producing a like number of software packages, all of which come with lucrative maintenance and security update contracts.

The beauty of the late entrepreneur's voting system is its simplicity. Riley's software runs on a standard personal computer with one security modification only available on NCC hardware, a marketing decision that has been challenged, unsuccessfully thus far, in three separate anti-trust lawsuits.

To many state and foreign election officials, the Millennium Vote System has been the greatest thing since sliced bread, especially in the wake of the controversial U.S. election in 2000 that put George W. Bush into the White House after a contentious ruling by the U.S. Supreme Court.

But to others, David Riley was little more than a one trick pony. For many years, he focused only on a single task to be done with a personal computer: vote.

In June of 1984, he sat in his shabby suburban

Denver office and stared at a 200-pound pile of new NCC computer equipment that had just been delivered. He said in a recent interview with the *Times* that he had "no idea" what to do with the gear.

Apple was already wowing school kids and hobbyists with its user-friendly computers. While the Apple machines were fairly small, the NCC system seemed to occupy about one-quarter of Riley's diminutive office. It was powered by software called DOS, an operating system that was being marketed by small start-up company called Microsoft.

However, the NCC computer was specialized. It included a laser videodisk player and a heavy color monitor that was sensitive to the touch. It had not even been made public yet.

Riley said he sat in his office for hours and poked at the screen, touching the hard glass surface and activating segments of a demo training program that came with it. The screen displayed primitive graphics and text. Occasionally, the system played video from a laser video disk. Everything was controlled by software inside the computer, which could even keep track of each user's progress.

It was the ancient times of personal computer development, and David Riley was about to start up a business to capitalize on this emerging technology. It had cost him nearly $20,000 to buy the NCC machine, which was designed primarily to deliver training programs to NCC's own employees.

It would be a few more years before this combination of text, graphics, video, images, and sound would be re-branded "multimedia" and another decade and a half before the technology matured into what everyone now takes for granted on their computers, book readers, tablets, and cell phones.

"I played with the machine until late in the

afternoon that first day," Riley said. "I remember, at one point I just leaned back into my chair and stared at the ceiling. Then it hit me. This would make a great voting machine."

To test the system out for voting, Riley hired a California computer engineer to develop a basic voting software program. The two made arrangements with the Denver Election Commission to set up three touch screen voting systems in a southwest Denver precinct on election day. The plan was to ask voters to cast test ballots on the machines after they had cast their real ballots using the old mechanical lever voting machines that had been around since the Forties. The votes on the touch screen systems would not be counted.

Riley said he was skeptical about his own machines.

"The image displays were crap," he said. "All we had were EGA graphics and they were very crude. Most of the voters in that precinct were elderly. I didn't even think they'd be able to read the screens."

One by one, Riley said, he invited voters to test out his touch screen voting machine after they had cast their real votes on the old system.

"One by one, they voted on the touch screen, and they loved it," he said. "They liked the way they could jump forwards and backwards and look at each race individually rather than on one giant ballot, the way the old mechanical machines were set up."

According to Riley, the elderly voters had no problem reading the screens or figuring out how to use the system, and nearly all of them said they preferred the touch screen computer system to either paper ballots or the old voting machines. "A few voters said they had used punch card systems in the past," Riley said, "And they stunk."

Then the school bell rang for lunch. The election

precinct was in a middle school.

"As the school children filed through the voting area, the colors on the computer screens caught their attention and each one of the three test voting machines were swarmed by kids," Riley said. "All I did was tell them the computers were for voting and the kids took it from there. Intuitively they knew exactly what to do and how to cast a vote. I knew I had a winner."

Some industry observers say this was Riley's first and last great idea.

If that was, in fact, the case, Riley certainly capitalized on it by creating an American-based enterprise that was generating annual revenues exceeding $10 billion at the time of his death.

-30-

* * *

Vic viewed the web version of the story on a terminal back in a temporary cubicle the *Times* had assigned to him. The story was set off with a headshot of Riley and an insert photo of the latest version of the Millennium Vote System, this one on a small laptop running off a car battery in rural Appalachia.

Vic chose to end the Riley story with the election commission demonstration and the current sales figure for the company, but that was far from the end of the David Riley saga.

What Vic did not report—what remained in his notes—was the story of a secret task force Riley had set up at a "semi-secluded" facility in the foothills west of Loveland. He had hired in the best computer programming geeks and hackers that he could find and tasked them to work on the next level of electronic voting, one that utilized the internet, cell phones, land line phones, satellites, game stations, cable television, home computers, laptop computers, tablet computers—virtually any electronic device that had a built-in communication system.

These special employees were granted anything they wanted or needed, within reason, and paid over-the-top salaries and benefits. If they were skiers or boarders, Riley bought them season passes to Colorado ski resorts. If they golfed, they got memberships at the nearby Mariana Buttes Country Club. If they cycled, he bought them the road or mountain bike of their choice, and even formed the Millennium professional cycling team. They got annual passes to Rocky Mountain National Park, a half-hour away. Fly fishers got memberships in the Wig Wam Club, an exclusive and private stretch along the South Platte River southwest of Denver. Whatever they wanted they got, provided they did not reveal anything about their work at the Loveland facility. In return, they would give Riley the tools he needed to give the vote to every citizen no matter where he or she was on the planet.

"How can you possibly safeguard the integrity of the election?" Vic asked Riley during the interview. "It seems easy these days to hack computers, cell phones—anything using software. The security failures are mounting each month. Sony, Target, Home Depot? NSA? Snowden? Wikileaks?"

Riley shot back. "That one, I've got covered." The wealthy entrepreneur leaned back in his chair, crossed his arms, smiled, and arched his eyebrows.

"But I won't talk about that," he said, jutting out a steely defiant jaw. "What I will tell you about, because I want this out there, is how political leaders are freaking out about this. None of those bastards want everyone to vote. Not one of them."

"Freaking out?" Vic said, writing the phrase in his notebook and underlining it twice.

Then Riley revealed two secret and separate meetings he had with the chairwoman of the Republican National Committee and the chairman of the Democratic National Committee. Riley said he laid out his vision for the future of the vote in the United States and globally. He predicted a nearly one hundred percent voter participation by Americans, not the thirty-six to sixty-three per cent voter turnout since the Sixties.

Vic had underlined in his notes how Riley described the reaction to the prospect of full voter participation. "They were absolutely terrified," one quote read.

Riley admitted to Vic he had been a "bit naive" to think the country's political leaders actually wanted everyone to vote. "I realized the major political parties could have cared less about voter participation, unless it was under their strict terms and only for their candidates," he told Vic, who was recording the interview on his cell phone, tucked neatly in his shirt pocket. "The Dems just want young people, college kids mostly, minorities, women, and as many naturalized citizens as possible registered to vote, because they tend to vote for Democrats."

"I had the feeling Democrats wanted everyone to vote," Vic asked, fishing for a particular response.

"So did I," Riley said, looking up at the books on the shelves in his dark study. "Well, I suppose it is natural to just round up only those who support you, but my observation is that the pols, or their leadership at least, are only interested in supporters who toe the company line, and that line is getting a little too socialistic for my taste. Too much nanny state."

"Bail outs?" Vic said. "Health care?"

"Banks?" Riley said. "Insurance companies? They put us in the tank, and we reward them with tax dollars? Car companies were a different story. They were crushed when the bankers destroyed our economy. No, those bailouts saved a lot of workers' jobs. Obamacare? Not sure. I'm still mulling that one over."

"Republicans do the same thing," Vic said. "It's what political parties do."

"I know that," Riley said. "But they seem to go out of their way to make voting tougher than it should be, almost as though they want to suppress some voters, or disenfranchise them."

"Well, that's the charge against them," Vic said.

"I like to say they just want to make it tougher by tightening the registration laws, or even challenging voters right at the polls," Riley said. "They think it's legal, what they're doing. The courts will have to decide, but there's just something I don't like about it. Getting rid of motor voter laws, restricting early voting, things like that."

"Voter turnout is low," Vic said, "but there isn't much evidence that what the critics call 'voter suppression' is having much of an effect."

"But we certainly are talking about it a lot, aren't we?" Riley said. "Republican voting legislation is sweeping across the country to protect us against voter fraud, only there is hardly a hint of voter fraud. I think they are trying to solve a problem that doesn't even exist. The bottom line is that I think what both parties are doing is undemocratic," Riley said.

"Small 'd' democratic?" Vic said.

"Yes, or small 'u'," Riley said, emitting a tiny burst of a laugh, then turning serious again. "But I am talking about small 'd' democracy. No matter what they say—these damn politicians—both sides have their grimy paws all over citizens and the right to vote. All they want to do is control and manipulate exactly who gets to vote and how they vote in a given election, rather simply getting every citizen to vote. This undemocratic thinking disgusted me. It solidified my resolve to press forward with the Universal Vote Project. We plan to set it up for the citizens, bypassing the politicians and their back-room handlers altogether."

"And where was, or is, this facility of yours?" Vic recalled asking him. "The foothills facility?"

"Doesn't matter," Riley said. "It's closed down anyway."

"You won't tell me where it is?" Vic pressed.

"No!" Riley shot back. "Is that a problem?"

Vic had let it go, interested in getting more out of the interview than prematurely ending it in a spat over a somewhat irrelevant fact, unless the facility was still in operation, or never existed at all.

* * *

Vic leaned back in the rickety office chair the *Times* had given him and reflected on the two hours he had spent with the late David Riley. The stories of a geek hacker compound tucked away in the foothills, the Universal Vote Project, and the professional politicians' fears about full citizen participation in elections all would remain in his notes for future use. Anyway, they needed to be checked out, he concluded.

Images of the gruesome scene at Riley's house drifted across Vic's now closed eyes, punctuated by painless but annoying jagged and vibrating black and white lines of an optical migraine, something that hit him regularly after a few hours of staring at a computer screen. He could not shake the impression that he was looking at a murder scene.

Like a tiny slide projector inside his skull, Vic once again brought up the image of Riley from the interview. All he could see was an enthusiastic, optimistic, energized, and passionate man proselytizing about the future of the "small-D" democratic vote.

He found it hard to believe he was looking across the table at someone who was about to blow his brains out.

7

"In my office," Driscoll said over the phone. "Tomorrow morning."

"Not even a hello?" Vic said.

"Hello."

"Ninish work?"

"Anythingish will work," Driscoll said. "Just be here. I need a statement."

"Still a suicide?" Vic said.

"No comment," Driscoll said and hung up.

Vic dropped the headset on his desk after the terse Driscoll call, then sprinted for the elevator before anyone else could collar him.

Outside, the setting sun bathed Civic Center with intense yellows. He walked across the park that put two city blocks of green between the Statehouse and City Hall. Vic did have an objective, the library. He slipped in just before the librarians locked up for the day and did whatever librarians did behind closed doors, then double-timed it to the reference section where Miss Raglin often remained until well after closing time, especially since the library commission cut back operating hours to save money. Her crystal blue eyes glued to the computer terminal, she just nodded toward a chair when Vic stepped into her surprisingly neat office.

"I don't think there's anything new here," she said with a note of finality.

"Anything?" Vic asked. "Or anything that you deem significant?"

"The latter."

She had a brain for categorizing, assessing, and synthesizing information. Based on every spy movie Vic had seen and every spy novel he had read, Miss Raglin would have been a perfect fit for the CIA or British Intelligence. She could sift and sort and prioritize data, a reporter's dream. And Denver taxpayers paid her salary. Vic's expense account covered the gas for her Piper Cub. Occasionally an analysis missed something, a tiny fact or two, crumbs brushed off the study table in the sweep of scrutiny, faint stains washed away as non-critical tidbits that became forever unseen because she thought them to be unimportant.

"There must be something new," Vic said. "There's always something new."

She looked up at him again, that look of hers, the one that said "Are you questioning the Queen?" Then the look changed to one of reflection, remembering, searching the memory banks. In a moment she spoke.

"There was a presentation," she said.

"A presentation?" Vic echoed.

"Yes, to an odd audience," Miss Raglin said.

"Why odd?" Vic said.

"It was a small group of Defense Department officials in the Springs six months ago," she said. "I found a small blurb in *Jane's Terrorism and Security Monitor* announcing the meeting and speech. It just said Defense Department officials would be meeting with David Riley on such and such a date. That's all."

"You get Jane's publications?" Vic said. "The library can't afford those, not these days, can it?"

She peered over the tops of her reading glasses at Vic, then smiled.

"I have my sources," she said.

"Well, what does that magazine cover?" Vic said.

"Mostly terrorism and counter terrorism issues," she said. "It's big business these days."

"Maybe it was about elections in the Middle East, using voting machines, how hackers might rig the results," Vic said, thinking out loud. "Riley was just into voting."

"Is that what your interview told you?" Miss Raglin said. "How long did you spend with him?"

"Hour and a half, two hours, over lunch." Vic said. "Nothing came up about defense or terrorism."

"Who was the interview for?" she said.

"*Wired* magazine," Vic said. "On spec."

"Well, everyone techie grabs *Wired*," she said. "It's one of the few consumer magazines that really covers the so-called Electronic Age, the trends, what's happening, what's going to happen, you know."

"Sure, yeah," Vic said. Actually, he had no clue. He just got lucky with a query letter and an assignment.

"Go back over your interview notes," Miss Raglin said. "Maybe there's something there."

"I have," Vic said. "Can't spot a thing." Since Miss Raglin failed to come up with the Riley story elements he was withholding from the paper, Vic assumed she knew nothing of Riley's meeting with the political party chairs, making that meeting with the country's top political Pooh-Bahs even more secret that the meeting with the Defense Department.

"Oh, did you know he had a library card?" she said.

"Who doesn't?" Vic said. "Isn't that mandatory in America?"

"When kids are replacing reading with cartoon movies, computer games, flashing lights, and rap?" Miss Raglin said.

"Texting is reading," Vic said.

"If you don't use vowels," she said

"The library card?" Vic said.

"He got it about a year ago, and that was the only time he used it. He checked out all our books on cryptography. He also inter-libraried in a few others including, a dissertation from Harvard."

"Codes?" Vic said.

"Codes," she said.

"You wouldn't happen to have a list of those items, would you?" Vic said.

"Weren't you around when Bush Junior was shoving the Patriot Act through Congress?" she said.

"Did you march with the librarians?" Vic said.

"No, but I organized a phone bank that crashed the White House switchboard," she said. "We didn't want the feds big footing us in here demanding to see what books our patrons checked out."

"Well, I'm not a fed," Vic said.

"I know. That's why I printed this out for you." She pulled a sheet of paper from a small pile to her left and handed it to him. It contained all the books Riley had checked out from the Denver Public Library and other collections, including the dissertation.

"Gee, thanks," Vic said.

"Gee, that's about five tanks of gas," Miss Raglin said.

"Gee, I'll get some cash," Vic said. "I'm good for it."

"I know you are," she said. "The library's closed. You'll have to duck out on the art museum side." She walked him to her office door. "Go down the stairs by the exit sign. Make sure the door is closed from the outside. You usually have to push it to latch." She patted him on the butt as he left.

As he wound his way out of the building, Vic thought less about what he had included in the Riley background story for the *Times*, and more about what had been left out—the vague outpost in the foothills west of Loveland, the universal vote project, hackers, geeks, the meeting with the political chiefs, now Miss Raglin's Department of Defense and cryptography leads, and what Riley may have shoved into a dark hole a few minutes before a bullet ripped his skull apart.

8

The next morning, Vic checked in at the city desk and with Vigil. He assured the editor that he would not turn over any notes to the police. After refusing to let the *Times* lawyer tag along, he walked over to the police department to give Driscoll as short a statement as possible about his interview with Riley. He managed to keep it to what they talked about, the invention of the touch screen voting system, how Riley got started, his family, hobbies, and that was all.

"That's pretty much the gist of it, Frank," Vic said.

Driscoll leaned back in his squeaky well-worn office chair. "Anything else you want to tell me?" He glared at Vic.

"No," Vic said, deliberately misinterpreting the detective's question. He did not want to tell Driscoll about all the material in his notes but not in the public sphere. Vic's nose told him these items were better left for another day, another story, maybe another Pulitzer Prize. If Elway could win back to back Super Bowls in his late 30s, maybe he could nab a second Pulitzer in his early 60s. Maybe it would say something about the value of baby boomers, who were being tossed onto the unemployment trash heap at unprecedented rates.

The interview was interrupted by a call from the city's human resources department. While Driscoll wrangled on the phone over his health insurance coverage, Vic sat quietly across the standard ugly gray on ugly green metal desk, still in good shape if you overlooked the spotty rust eating through the six-inch chrome plated adjustable legs. Green linoleum protected the top, or at least most of it, all but a five-inch square chip on one of the "guest" side corners and the three holes where a pencil sharpener once lived. Driscoll refused the high-tech integrated office system desk for his new office in the remodeled police headquarters building. He liked his old desk. Brought him luck, he claimed. Driscoll kept it messy. Vic liked that too.

As Driscoll listened to the drug coverage options, Vic scanned the papers and files that occupied the detective's immediate work environment looking for something that might spark a lead. His visual sweep was snagged by a small plastic evidence bag that contained a tiny black computer memory card the same size as the one in his cellphone. Riley's micro SD card, Vic concluded, with an adrenaline rush that flushed his cheeks.

"No, my daughter's on the policy and I need to add my son," Driscoll said to the phone. "June 26. Yes, that's the right year. He's 24. I want him on before the Republicans repeal Obamacare. Really? That much? Well, it's still cheaper than an individual policy, so let's go with it. It's just for two years or until he gets a job. Okay, Denise, fine. Thanks."

He hung up the phone and looked at Vic. "See anything you like?"

Vic shook his head slowly. "Nothing that I could use unless you've got a spare gun."

"Worried about prowlers?"

"These days? Sure. Especially cops."

"Well, go get your own. Have your pal Nelson teach you how to use it, though."

Through his internal office window, Driscoll caught a few caustic looks from the other detectives working cases in their new integrated office cubicles.

"Pricks," Driscoll said.

"That's plural so it can't mean me," Vic said.

"You know, the thin blue line," Driscoll said. "Me in here with you."

"Haven't we outgrown that yet?" Vic said.

"Afraid not," Driscoll said as he hit Ctrl-P on his terminal to send Vic's statement to a nearby laser printer. Driscoll told Vic once that he got a solid "A" in his high school touch typing class. Whenever he could he took notes on his computer. It saved time doing reports, Driscoll claimed. He had Vic's statement down verbatim.

A puffy whir signaled the laser printer's awakening, followed by a screech from an off-brand toner cartridge as it spit out the three-page document. The big detective reached over and grabbed the sheets, shuffled them together and handed them to Vic.

"That's got all the changes you made," Driscoll said. "Just sign it."

"Print another and you sign it," Vic said. "All three pages, okay?"

Driscoll was perturbed.

"It's for the lawyers," Vic said. "Just sign the pages."

"I still don't understand why the *Times* didn't send a lawyer with you," Driscoll said.

"They wanted to," Vic said, "but I wasn't an employee when I met with Riley, and my lawyer said the *Times* couldn't force the point."

"You have a lawyer?"

"No, but it sounds kind of cool, doesn't it?" Vic said. Actually, he did have a lawyer, and she did tell him to ditch the newspaper's lawyer because whoever it was, he would not have Vic's interest as a top priority.

"Whatever," Driscoll said, sliding the documents across the desk to Vic. "This is all pro forma anyway. Sign here and initial all the pages."

"Sure," Vic said. He signed and initialed the pages with his a fifty-dollar Waterman fountain pen from Office Depot. He put the cap back on it and set it down beneath his right hand on Driscoll's desk. When the detective looked down to put the statement into a folder, Vic's fingers scooted the pen beneath the nearest stack of papers so the Chief of Detectives could not see it.

"I gotta bolt," Driscoll said, grabbing his jacket.

"When are you back here?" Vic said.

"About five," Driscoll said. "I've got to sign some insurance papers down in HR and then update the Chief."

"I thought you were the chief," Vic said.

"The Big Chief," Driscoll said.

"Like the tablet?"

"Yes, like the tablet."

"Fat pencils, all that?" Vic said. Driscoll just stared at him. "Got time for a beer after that?"

"Maybe," Driscoll said, standing up. "Where you gonna be?"

"Not sure," Vic said. "I'll just walk over from the paper."

Driscoll hesitated. "Call."

"As you say," Vic said.

Vic stood up and slung the strap of his small computer briefcase over his right shoulder. Driscoll headed to the right, and Vic the other way. As his left hand brushed over the chipped corner of Driscoll's desk, Vic palmed the small evidence bag containing the micro SD card before falling in step behind the detective.

* * *

Halfway down the hallway toward the elevators Vic hung a sharp right into the men's room. Detective Greg Frakes was washing his hands at one of three basins. He looked into the mirror at Vic.

"Bengston," he said. It was a greeting.

"Detective Frakes," Vic said, another nervous flush hitting his face. "How are you?"

"I could do with a vacation," he said. "Other than that I'm okay, except for reporters being on this floor."

"Driscoll had to interview me for the Riley thing," Vic said.

"That's a switch," Frakes said.

Vic met Frakes two years earlier on the first day he had returned to journalism as a reporter for the now silent *Rocky Mountain Sun*. It wasn't a particularly elegant meeting, Vic tripping on a rock, as he recalled, then somersaulting down an embankment. He ended his tumbling exhibition sprawled at the feet of four Denver cops, one of whom was Frakes. They were at the edge of the South Platte River mulling over the discovery of an extremely dead woman who had been shot in the back of her head. Since then their relationship had been a notch above cool, professional most of the time, but once the two of them did break into milk-spitting laughter over Frakes' retelling of the Vic Bengston crime scene arrival story, now embellished over time, now an old standard in the lexicon of Denver detective bureau recollections about their foes in the Fourth Estate.

"I interviewed him a few weeks before he, uh—"

"Blew his brains out?" Frakes said.

"I was going to say died," Vic said.

"Or were you going to say killed?" Frakes said.

"No. Died."

"I guess that's generic enough."

"Generic?" Vic said.

"Just that it covers all the bases," Frakes said.

"Didn't the ME rule suicide?" Vic said.

"She hasn't ruled," the detective said. "Frank's still looking at it."

"I wonder if I'm a suspect or just a witness," Vic said.

"Either way, you're on the wrong side of the story, aren't you?" Frakes said.

Vic knew what Frakes was talking about. He should not be covering the story even if he had minor involvement such as the Riley interview just before his death. The *Times* already had acted on that facet of the story. After the day one, front page, above the fold breaking story under Vic's byline and the follow-up background feature, which ran inside, Vic was removed from day-to-day coverage for the very same reason Frakes had mentioned, the now completed witness interview with Driscoll. A familiar pattern, Vic thought, but for different reasons, recalling a similar decision to pull him from a major story after the first day made by the *Rocky Mountain Sun* because he had just rejoined the paper's staff after a twenty-five year break.

Before the stories on Riley's death ran, Vigil, *Times* Managing Editor Dale Whiteside, and Vic blew an hour hashing over the pros and cons of running the background piece under Vic's byline. Vic convinced them that since it was a suspected suicide, there wasn't much of a conflict of interest. He argued that the notes were his since he interviewed Riley before he went to work for the *Times*. Vic said he was going to publish the interview story one way or another, and then asked if the *Times* wanted the piece for free. The editors jumped on it. The story was picked up by every major newspaper, news network, wire service, and business publication around the world, all giving credit to the *Times*. Vic's recently acquired Pulitzer certainly did not hurt in his negotiations or with the viral spread of the story across the globe. However, they all agreed that Vic would not cover any future aspects of the story. This time Vic liked the idea. It gave him more time to investigate Riley's death without having to produce ongoing update stories. Vic enjoyed keeping bosses in the dark.

"I'm off the story, Greg," Vic said. "For those very reasons." Vic barely skipped a beat when he asked, "Do you think he was murdered?"

Frakes shook the rinse water off his hands and reached for a paper towel. The move gave him a few seconds to frame his response.

"That's for the ME to decide," Frakes said. "And the lab techs."

"What does your gut tell you?" Vic said.

"Just between us chickens?"

"That was a little below the belt, and unnecessary."

"How so?" Frakes said.

"We're all heroes in our own little ways," Vic said.

"Oh, the pen is mightier than the sword bullshit?" Frakes said.

"I don't want to press the point," Vic said. He did not. Frakes had two commendations. The cop was no chicken.

"I wouldn't," Frakes said as he headed for the door. The detective stopped and turned back toward Vic. "Yeah, I think he was murdered." Then he left the bathroom.

* * *

As soon as the door shut, Vic raced for a stall. He closed and locked the door, dropped his pants and squatted. He pulled a tiny netbook computer from his thirty-year old North Face soft nylon briefcase, a bag that while it had gotten dirty over the years had never busted a seam or a zipper. He bought it when he lived in Alaska for a year. After flipping up the computer lid and pressing the power button, Vic pulled a small one inch by one inch micro SD card adapter from a pocket in the briefcase. Then he retrieved the plastic evidence bag from his shirt pocket, opened up the self-sealing strip on the top and gently grasped the micro SD card by its edges with his thumb and forefinger. Vic inserted the tiny memory card into a small slot on the adapter card, then slipped the adapter card into a slot on the edge of his computer, which was now asking for his password. He typed in "CINDY," the name of his first family dog, an English setter. The computer began booting up, first the plain teal screen, then the photograph of a sailboat and small island in the Caribbean, and then the icons and files that occupied the desktop. When the computer detected the micro SD card, a window opened giving him a few options as to what to do with what was on the card. He clicked on "Open folder to display files".

Another window opened up and displayed a single file folder icon with a zipper over it, meaning its contents were compressed, or "zipped," into a smaller memory space. The title of the folder was "Art". Vic moved his cursor over the folder and held down the button that represented a left click on a computer mouse and dragged the zipped folder to his desktop. A dialogue window opened up telling him the computer was copying the folder from the chip to his computer and that it would take three minutes. The process was actually completed in a minute. Computers were lousy at estimating time.

As soon as the file was copied, Vic opened another folder on his desktop labeled "file cabinet", which was where he kept all his recent working files. A couple of dozen file folder symbols splayed out in a new window. He clicked on the folder labeled "ham", where Vic stored his ham radio hobby files. The "ham" window opened and displayed another pile of folder, document, and photo icons.

Vic renamed the "Art" folder "40 meter dipole" and moved it into a ham radio folder labeled "antennas", burying it yet one more level down in the hierarchy of computer files. He knew any savvy hacker, or his nine-year-old grandson, Devon, could find the folder from Riley's SD card fairly quickly, but burying and renaming it would keep it away from most people.

Vic ripped a few sheets of toilet paper from the oversized, covered, and locked roll and placed them on his knee. He removed the micro SD card adapter from the slot on his computer by pushing it in and releasing the spring-loaded lock. Then he pulled the micro SD card from the adapter using the toilet paper. He rubbed the tiny black memory card on both sides to wipe off any possible fingerprint partials and slipped it back into the plastic evidence bag, which he also wiped down with the paper. He kept one sheet to hold the evidence bag when he returned it to Driscoll's desk. He assumed the lab folks had already checked the chip for prints. At least, he hoped they had.

After closing the lid on the computer, putting it into hibernate mode, Vic stuffed it back into his briefcase on the floor next to him, flushed the toilet, pulled up his trou and pants as he stood up, re-tucked, re-zipped, and re-belted to make himself presentable for public display. He stepped from the stall, slung the strap of his briefcase over his right shoulder, the sore one, looked at himself in the mirror and tried to palm the evidence bag without touching it with his fingertips.

Heart pounding, he walked from the bathroom and into the hallway leading back toward the detective bureau and Driscoll's office.

"I thought you left," Driscoll said, as he walked out of the break room. The detective stuffed a protein bar into his shirt pocket.

"I left my pen in your office," Vic said. His palms were sweating.

"Go get it," Driscoll said. "I've got to get something from Sully over there, and then I'll walk you out."

Vic nodded, not wanting to talk, thinking his voice might crack. He sped across the squad room toward Driscoll's office. The dozen or so detectives at their desks, on the phone or talking with one another seemed to be paying no attention to him at all, which was fine with Vic. He did not see Frakes anywhere.

Vic walked into Driscoll's office and targeted the pile of papers where he had stashed his fountain pen. As he reached out with his left hand, he spread his sticky fingers, two of them holding the plastic evidence bag, letting it fall onto the desk as his fingers slithered beneath the papers and curled themselves around his writing instrument. He spun and walked from the office, stopping just outside the door and making a big deal about re-screwing the top onto the pen and sliding it into his shirt pocket. Vic walked back through the room and up to Driscoll who was holding the elevator door open. The two men stepped into the car which swallowed them up and headed down to ground level.

From the break room, Frakes leaned against the edge of a six-foot counter. He sipped on his cup of hot coffee and pondered what he had just witnessed. He had a good sight angle from where he was, through the partially opened door, across the detectives' bullpen, and through the windows into Driscoll's office. While he silently sipped his machine coffee, Frakes observed Vic's trek back to his boss' desk. The detective swore he saw something drop from Vic's hand as he reached in for the fountain pen. After Vic had left, Frakes casually walked over to Driscoll's desk see what that might have been.

9

Paxton Stone lived in an immense old brick house on a double lot at the base of South Table Mesa in Golden. A heavily patched cement driveway ran uphill from the street past the north side of the house and spilled into a wide gravel expanse, neatly graded, almost like a horse paddock, in front of a two-story, twenty-by-thirty foot garage building. Both oversized garage doors were open, the air filled with the tones of the King himself, his original track of Hound Dog. Vic transitioned from washed and tightly packed pea gravel to a polished battleship gray hot rod garage floor. No horses, but plenty of horsepower. Strolling past a red Shelby Cobra, not Ford's recent remake, but an original edition, Vic made enough noise to flush a head out from behind the car. The head positioned itself just above the vintage car and below an engine block suspended from a massive silver chained block and tackle rig secured to a thick eye bolt protruding from a steel I-beam that ran the length of the garage. Afternoon sunlight blasted in the garage doors, silhouetting Vic to anyone inside the building.

"Who's that?" came the familiar voice.

"Pax, it's me, Vic Bengston."

"Vic," Stone said, standing up, pulling a rag from his back pocket. He wiped the grease from his hands as he stepped into the center of the garage. Three hot rods in various stages of design and construction surrounded him. "How have you been?"

"Oh, I've been okay. If you don't count my mouth."

"What's the matter there?"

"I'm losing teeth. At least they're scheduled for removal pretty soon." For a moment, Vic beheld the flashy cars and the dragster over in the far bay. But he was not here for the hot rods. He was here for what was upstairs, above the garage. That was where Paxton Stone's computers lived.

"Too much sugar?" Stone asked. Gangly, gaunt, six-foot-three, with the glasses, light complexion and sandy hair, he looked more like a bookworm than a drag racing team owner who built custom-made street rods for yuppies with too much time on their hands and too much money in their offshore accounts. The cars kept him sane. The computers and the software upstairs drove him mad.

"Too much neglect, Stone," Vic said. "Too many years of avoiding the dentist. I fear pain, and I fear dental bills, especially big ones."

"Is there any other kind?" Stone said. "I lost a tooth once. It wasn't much fun as I recall. I'm still paying for it." He had finished wiping his hands, the reached out for a firm handshake.

"I'm losing about a dozen, and it was all preventable" Vic said. "At least that's what the dentists claim. Who knows what it will cost to replace them."

"At least your mouth will be healthy," Stone said.

"I don't want to talk about teeth," Vic said.

"Liz said you have a little problem that I might be able to help you with," Stone said.

"That's right," Vic said as he reached into his pocket and held out a small thumb drive containing the zipped folder from Riley's memory chip. "There's a zip file on this. I'm wondering if you can tell me what's in it. I can see the files, but everything is encrypted. I can't open them."

Stone reached out with a slender almost feminine hand and took the inch and a half long thumb drive from Vic. He held it up, looked at it intently for a moment and then cast his gaze on Vic.

"This folder, the one on here," Stone said. "It's not yours, is it?"

"No it's not," Vic said.

"Did you steal it?" Stone said.

"Borrowed," Vic said.

"Does the person you 'borrowed' it from know that you have it?" Stone said.

"Not really," Vic said.

"Is this a copy of the zipped folder?" Stone said.

"Yes, it is," Vic said.

"Do you intend to use whatever is in the zipped folder for your own financial gain?" Stone said. "Or anything that might compromise national security?"

"National security?" Vic said, mildly surprised. "That's not my intention. I'm just curious about what it is."

"Does this involve any criminal investigation?" Stone said.

"No," Vic said. He did not consider a probe into a suicide was really a criminal investigation, per se. Vic reasoned that the less he knew, the better off Stone would be if it hit the fan, so he did not even want to mention the suicide investigation. If the David Riley death advanced to something else, Vic thought, he might be able to play dumb about messing with the evidence, arguing that he thought it was merely a run of the mill suicide inquiry.

"I owe you one," Stone said.

"You don't, really," Vic said, sensing that Stone was about to agree to take a look at the folder.

"Yes, I do," Stone said. "And I don't want to know anything more about where this came from."

Stone gazed at Vic. Then his face broke into a knowing grin. He just nodded and turned to walk up the stairway to the second floor of his garage.

The two went back a long way. In the "old" days, Stone was known as the "Hacker's Hacker." The internet was just creeping into public consciousness. The personal computer was about to revolutionize the world. Vic was a young reporter writing for the *Rocky Mountain Sun*, and Stone was a brilliant graduate student at the University of Colorado.

The story was on hackers, and Vic's investigative trail led straight to Stone, who had demonstrated how to break into any computer system using the telephone network. The investigative series was powerful, since it centered on the theft of highly classified information stolen from the North American Aerospace Command buried in Cheyenne Mountain outside of Colorado Springs. The Justice Department pulled all the stops to trace the leak at NORAD.

Only there was no leak, something that became obvious after the third story in the series had run. What NORAD's computer system had was a more like a crack, a mar in its security veneer. Stone merely exploited the weakness to break into the computer system, giving him, and the *Sun*, access to the country's key security information. Nothing serious was made public. All the data was held under lock and key at the *Sun* and then turned over to the Feds after the story ran. Enough was published to show how vulnerable NORAD and other government computer networks were to attack.

Once the Justice Department realized it was dealing with a hacker and not a mole, investigators turned their guns on the newspaper. Vic was hauled into court and ordered by a federal judge to reveal his sources for the articles. He refused and was sent to jail for nearly three weeks until the U.S. Supreme Court, citing First Amendment rights, ordered him released. Stone's identity was never revealed. The series was nominated for a national reporting Pulitzer but Jim Risser from the Des Moines Register won it for reporting on corruption in the American grain exporting industry. Still, Congress appropriated a few billion bucks to overhaul the country's high security computer systems. If that was not a signal to stay in the journalism business nothing was, Vic thought. Too bad he did not heed the sign.

"Step up," Stone said as he entered a series of numbers on a small keypad next to the door to his upstairs "lab" as he liked to call it. "I've got a raised computer floor." A solenoid released the lock and a feint beeper sounded as the door opened, letting the two into an expansive room filled with computers and electronic equipment. They stepped up six inches onto the computer floor, beneath which ran thousands of feet of cable tying all the systems together. Stone walked over to an old Marantz stereo receiver mounted on a head-high shelf. He hit the power button, and Hound Dog went to sleep.

"Elvis fan?" Vic said.

"Elvis and hot rods are one in the same," Stone said. "My clients love it. Somehow they think—" He paused. "Well, I don't really understand what they think most of the time. They just like hot rods and Elvis. The Cobra owner was supposed to come over, but he was a no-show. I just picked up a couple of new CDs and thought I'd pop one in for him."

Now the prevailing noise was a steady hum of power supply fans and air conditioning.

"Coffee?" Stone asked as he headed for a corner kitchen area. "Bathrooms are over there." Vic did not have to go, but he spotted what appeared to be a comfortable area over in another far corner. Bookshelves, a nice Persian rug, coffee table, several easy chairs and a big overstuffed couch. Next to the couch sat a black Fender amp with a long cord attached to a guitar. Stone was also in a rock band, a pretty good one too. They played Thursday nights at the Little Bear in Evergreen up in the foothills west of Denver.

"Still drinking decaf?" Stone asked as he poured filtered water into a glass coffee carafe.

"Yes, I've managed to beat the caffeine jones," Vic said.

"Well, in your honor, I'll go with decaf today. I've got some great unleaded French roast from Starbucks. Fairly stout."

"That's fine," Vic said, settling into the couch and grabbing the guitar as if he knew what he was doing.

"Don't expect this kind of treatment in the future," Stone said. "Next time it's caffeinated coffee or water."

"I'll bring a teabag next time," Vic said.

With the coffee maker popping and wheezing, Stone walked over to a workbench, pulled a fresh pair of blue surgical gloves out of a box on the shelf above the bench, snapped them onto his hands, and then wiped the entire thumb drive with a sani-wipe he tore from a small package.

"Okay, I give," Vic said as he plucked a few strings on the guitar.

"This?" Stone held up his gloved hands. Vic nodded. "Fingerprints. Precautions, that's all."

"Understood." Vic set the guitar back onto its stand, wishing he had never given up on the sax and clarinet. He walked over to Stone, who held the thumb drive between his blue latex covered thumb and forefinger.

"I'm going to clean the outside of this and remove all the oils from your fingers and mine," Stone said. "Then, if you don't mind, I'll burn what's on this to a CD."

Vic shrugged.

"You really want to see what's on this bad boy?" Stone said with a grin. "You can always stop now. No harm, no foul."

"In for a penny, in for a pound," Vic said, resigned to the fact that he had lifted the original micro SD card from the lieutenant's desk. He wanted anything that might shed light on the death of David Riley.

"All right," Stone said. "You've been cautioned."

The lanky man walked over to another computer that had hibernated. He bumped the mouse with his right hand and the screen came to life with a detailed and beautiful photograph of Lopez Island in the San Juans off of Seattle. Vic knew it was Lopez because he recognized the small house set back from the rocky shore up in the trees. It was a summer home owned by Stone's family, and Vic had visited him and Liz the summer that photograph was taken. Vic had hauled his Venture 224 sailboat all the way from Denver to Seattle where he and his ex-wife, Erin, put in for a week of sailing. In retrospect, Vic concluded he should have just chartered a bareboat rather than dragging his own up there.

Stone slipped the thumb drive onto the end of a USB cable that was sitting on his desktop. A new icon appeared on the screen next to Stone's family cottage.

"Linux?" Vic said.

"Yes," Stone said. "How'd you guess?"

"Well, on my PC, Windows doesn't open a drive icon like that, like Tiger does on my Mac," Vic said. "I put Linux on one of my PCs once, the Ubuntu version, and it used similar icons."

"You've got a Mac?" Stone said. "I'm surprised."

"Well, I used it mostly for my photography and for off line editing video projects," Vic said.

"Doing much video these days?" Stone said.

"Not since Ben and I wound down the company," Vic said. "Actually, the economy wound down the company. We just locked up and turned off the lights."

"You wanted out anyway, didn't you?" Stone said.

"Yeah," Vic said. "Courting the corporate clients to get the work, then massaging egos while trying to actually do the job got old."

"My life at Genra-IC was sheer hell," Stone said. "But I learned a lot."

"More the other way around wasn't it?" Vic said.

"Sometimes," Stone said. "I still know their vulnerabilities. And my friends there let me know what's coming around the bend."

"Corporate America put my kids through school," Vic said.

"Corporate America put me in the hot rod business," Stone said.

"If I still drank, I'd drink to that," Vic said.

Stone hoisted his coffee cup and smiled. Vic did the same.

"A little decaf for the Man," Stone said.

* * *

"So what's on the drive?" Vic said.

"Let's see."

Stone swiveled around to face the computer screen. He moved the cursor over the thumb drive icon and double clicked, revealing the single folder icon with a tiny zipper on it. Stone dragged it over to his desktop, closed the thumb drive window, right clicked on the icon and selected "eject." After a moment, he pulled the small drive off the USB cable and set it aside. He grabbed the mouse again and double clicked on the zipped folder. An extraction program opened up and automatically unzipped the folder, creating yet another folder, no zipper icon over it, containing the uncompressed files. Stone double clicked on the new folder. It opened a new window and listed a dozen files, with gibberish names, all the same length, except for one.

"These look like randomly generated file names, letters and numbers," Stone said. "Except this one. It's a jpeg."

"Open the image," Vic said.

Stone doubled clicked on the file, "oriental.jpg." An image filled the screen.

"That's the Oriental Theater," Vic said. "It looks like a water color."

"I'd guess it's a photograph that's been Photoshopped to look like a water color," Stone said.

Vic could not fathom how many times he had driven past the Oriental, one of a handful of classic old neighborhood movie houses in the city that had thus far escaped the wrecking ball. The Oriental lived in northwest Denver and was now surrounded by neighborhoods madly redeveloping into gentrified new urban clots of mixed retail and living spaces, mostly condos and lofts, or into hipper "art districts" struggling to retain much of their original look and feel. Vic preferred the latter and from time to time frequented an indie coffee shop not far from the Oriental. The photo, which Vic also assumed was turned into a faux water color by some computer artist, set the pale yellow front of the theater off against a brilliant blue Colorado sky. The ridge of the building's face was trimmed with a white terra cotta strip decorated with multicolored inlaid designs. On either side of the blank marquee, narrow arches of brick trim stretched to the top of the building. The upper half of the long vertical "Oriental" neon sign pierced the heavens while the lower half guarded the front wall. At night, its glow invited nearby residents in for an evening of relaxation, real popcorn with real butter, and cinematic escape from the world outside. But that was long ago. Now the Oriental Theater protected its continued existence by hosting concerts for local or touring music groups, mostly rock and alternate rock, and selling booze. Occasionally, an independent film premiered in the theater.

"I wonder if that's in there on purpose or just by accident," Vic said.

"That one I can't answer," Stone said. "Let's see what's in one of these text files. I'm going to open it with a simple text reader program I use to analyze files."

He opened a command line and plapped on the keyboard to open one of the files. The screen filled with thousands of numbers and letters. Stone scrolled through it, which took a few seconds. At the bottom of the file, he just stared at the screen. He scrolled back to the top, then slowly displayed the characters screen by screen.

"I don't have a clue," he said after about five minutes.

"More gibberish," Vic said.

"Not necessarily," Stone said, continuing to scroll through the screens of numbers. There were nine or ten of them. Stone accessed a small menu from the top of his screen and then typed in a few text commands. When he hit the enter key, the screen flashed several times and then jumped back to the center of all the numbers and highlighted a single slash which floated like an island in a sea of numbers.

"You see this?" Stone said.

"What?" Vic said.

"This. Look." Stone pointed his mouse cursor to the highlighted slash. "The slash."

"Okay, I see a slash," Vic said. "What does it mean? Do we have a big fraction?"

"Possibly," Stone said. "Or two numbers."

"Oh boy," Vic said, thinking dullsville.

"This is the only non-numerical character in the entire file," Stone said. He stood up and walked over to his guitar, grabbed it and flopped down onto the couch. As he strummed a chord, Vic looked at the numbers and letters splattered all over the screen. They meant nothing to him. Eventually chords and licks emanated from the guitar. Stone was in Never Never Land.

Vic stretched out on the couch. In a few minutes, he was sleep.

* * *

Someone shook Vic hard.

"Vic. Look at this!"

Groggy, hands sweating, Vic looked at his watch. Two hours had had vanished.

"Wha—what?" Vic managed to get out.

"I've got it," Stone said. "At least I think I do."

Vic rolled off the low couch, landing on all fours. Crawling would be undignified, he thought, so he pulled himself upright and shuffled over to the computer where Stone had already sat back down to work.

"You know, first, I thought this might be a message, or some encrypted document," Stone said. "Like something someone was trying to keep secret or hidden." Stone turned around and looked up at Vic, who was standing behind him. "I don't really want to know the details, but was something extraordinary done to hide this file?"

"You could say that," Vic said. "I'll spare you the particulars. Any coffee left?"

"I'll make fresh," Stone said. "Let me run through this first."

Vic closed his eyes and nodded.

"Well, I figured that if this was an encrypted document, broken down into a series of files, it could take us forever to decrypt it," Stone said. "We'd probably never break in anyway, given today's encryption technology."

"So we're wasting our time?" Vic asked.

"I thought the same thing until I opened the first file and went back to the slash," Stone said.

"Slash?" Vic said.

"Each of these files contains a very long number followed by one slash, followed by another very long number, then a hyphen, then tons of jibberish, all letters and numbers, probably something encrypted." Stone said. "So I'm thinking that instead of some form of encrypted text, like a document, this file might be something else."

"Divided by the slash," Vic said, feeling very smart, but not knowing why.

"Only the two numbers are divided by the slash," Stone said. "So I proceeded on that premise. By the way, do you know that you snore rather loudly?"

"My backpacking buddy confirmed it," Vic said. "We pace off a hundred yards for tent separation when we camp."

"Well, it scared the hell out of the cat," Stone said as he walked over to another computer. "I took the first number, up to the slash, and copied it over here to see if, perhaps, it was a prime number."

"And was it?" Vic said, vaguely remembering something from high school math about prime numbers.

"No," Stone said. "I ran it through a prime number generator program I wrote. It took about fifteen minutes." Vic felt more in the dark than when he walked into the hot rod garage a few hours earlier.

"So I checked the other number, the one after the slash," Stone said.

"And?"

"That wasn't a prime number either," Stone said.

Oh boy, Vic thought. "Surely you did more."

Stone just stared at Vic and said, "Please don't—"

"Okay," Vic said, holding up his hands. "I won't call you Shirley."

The two laughed, and Vic said, "Carry on Herr Professor. You're quite mad, you know?"

"Just enough to be dangerous," Stone said. "So, while neither of the numbers in the first file were prime numbers, they each became prime when I added three to them. Then I opened another file, two more numbers, neither of them prime, but after some trial and error I found they became prime when I added five to them."

"How about the other files?" Vic said.

Stone grinned again.

"There are nine files," Stone said. "I just messed around for a while and turned them all into prime number pairs by adding the remaining numbers, one, two, four, six, seven, eight and nine."

"Clever devil," Vic said. "And why do we care about prime numbers?"

"The prime number thing is fairly simple," Stone said. "It's a number that can only be divided by itself or one. It can't be divided by any other number."

That was it, Vic said to himself, then to Stone, "Well, that I know. I was in high school Math Club, you know. Remind me why this is all relevant to our quest?"

"Prime numbers are often the basic tools used for encrypting and decrypting messages, documents, and all sorts of communications."

"So this is an encrypted something," Vic said.

"No, I think these are encryption tools," Stone said. "More precisely, these numbers might be used to create public and private keys."

Vic flopped back down on Stone's couch and began strumming the base guitar. "So what do you do with these keys?"

"Let me give you a little background," Stone said. "Back in the seventies, three guys from MIT devised a way to encrypt documents without having to distribute decryption keys, which was very costly. Actually, the Brits thought it up first, but they had to keep it secret, so the MIT guys got all the credit. Basically, the way it works is that you use two big prime numbers to create a pair of encryption keys. One is private, and kept secret at all costs. The other one is public. Anybody can get it."

"Like a phone book," Vic said. "So how do you scramble a message?"

"Okay. Say I want to send you a message," Stone said. "I look up your public key in the internet or you send it to me, and I convert the message into numbers and letters, scramble it, as you say. Now, this formula is essentially a one-way process. Once you encrypt the message this way, it's very hard to decrypt it."

"Very hard?" Vic said.

"Yes," Stone said. "If the private key is big enough, it would take so much computing power to break it that it becomes impractical."

"But not impossible," Vic said.

"No, not entirely," Stone said. "In fact, the NSA has been working on computers that use quantum theory to decode anything."

"Quantum physics now? My head hurts just thinking about it."

"Suffice to say, very powerful computers," Stone said, "Still theoretical, though."

"You hope," Vic said, then moving to refocus on the task at hand. "Okay, so how do I decrypt my message?" Vic said.

"Remember, these keys are paired when they are created. So your public key knows about your private key, but you are the only one who actually has your private key. When the message arrives, the one encrypted with your public key, only you can apply your private key to decrypt it. Bingo. The message can be read."

"How the heck can I explain that in a newspaper story?" Vic said.

"Think about a mailbox," Stone said.

"We used to blow them up with M80s when we were kids,"

"I think that's a felony," Stone said. "You ever get caught?"

"No. Lucked out there. All right. I'm thinking of a mailbox."

"Like a post office box," Stone said. "Anyone can send you mail. The postal clerk on the other side of the wall simply shoves the mail into the wide open gap at the back of your P.O. box."

"I get it," Vic said. "Only I can retrieve the mail from the other side, using my key. And it's all junk."

"But highly secure junk," Stone said, pointing a boney index finger into the air.

"I don't want anyone messing with my grocery coupons, including the NSA," Vic said. "Tell me, how does this actually work in the real world?"

"In the real world, it's happening all the time," Stone said. "Your email is transmitted this way, banking transactions, online purchases, passing along credit card info, things like that."

"But I've never created a private key or a public key," Vic said.

"Well, the server computers do that, the ones running your email service, or the bank, or whatever. When you sign up for an account, they create both public and private keys for you, using those big prime numbers and a step by step process to turn them into encryption keys."

"Step by step process," Vic said. "Isn't that an algorithm?"

"That's right. You were in Math Club, weren't you?"

"And don't you forget it," Vic said. "You never know when you may need help with some integral equations."

"You don't even know what an integral equation is," Stone said.

"Not a clue," Vic said. "So, where are the private keys kept?"

"They are kept right on those email or banking servers that created them in the first place" Stone said. "Securely, though, or at least until some hacker cracks the server codes and gets to the account information."

"So, they're secure but not really," Vic said, bracketing the word 'secure' with air quotes.

"Pretty much," Stone said. "That's why the security algorithms—you like that word, don't you? I can tell—the algorithms have to keep ratcheting up in size and complexity to keep these private keys secret."

"Does this file include both public and private keys?" Vic said, nodding toward the computer.

"I'm not sure," Stone said.

"So what you're saying is that I may have to find more keys to unlock something that may or may not even exist," Vic said, shaking his head. "And if I do that, I have to find whatever it is that these keys actually unlock."

"Assuming there is something to unlock," Stone said, as he stood up to stretch. "I'm still guessing. It probably is a key, or keys, to decrypt some other file or files. A written document, maybe, kept somewhere, on another memory card, a computer chip, a CD, DVD, a hard drive, or on some server somewhere in the world. Really, I have no idea, but it's not all that bleak."

"Give me something I can use," Vic said. "A crumb. A morsel."

"How many crumbs make a morsel, anyway," Stone said.

"I think about a hundred," Vic said.

"No," Stone said, bluntly. "You give me something I can use, like the guy's name. Where did these files come from?"

"I'm not sure about this, Pax," Vic said. "Won't that cross a line for you? I don't want to cause a problem for you and Liz."

"Don't worry about me or Liz," Stone said. "We'll be all right. I've done enough favors for different folks. I don't think it'll be a problem."

"David Riley," Vic said.

Stone stood up and stared down at Vic. "You have got to be kidding."

"Not kidding," Vic said.

"He's dead?" Stone said.

"Exceedingly," Vic said. "Don't you read the papers? Or, in Denver's case, paper?"

"Good God, man, you could have picked somebody a bit more obscure. I mean he's not Bill Gates, but darn close."

"I shouldn't have mentioned the name," Vic said. He did not want to drag Stone into this story if it blows up in his face. "I'm drawn to the big names like a moth to a compact fluorescent light."

"It's a flame, Vic, that attracts many moths," Stone said. "A flame that will cause your combustion if you get too close. So, let's see. I know. I'll tell you what not to say to me."

"Such as?" Vic said.

"Like I said earlier, I do not want to know how you came to possess these files, okay?" Stone said.

"Done," Vic said.

"I might be able to find his public key on the internet," Stone said. "It is public after all. Go back to sleep."

Vic hit the couch again. Stone sat back down at another computer and logged onto the internet.

"What are you doing?" Vic said, picking up a Time magazine, Riley's headshot on the cover. He was about to ask Stone if he even reads the rags that make their way into his office, but he decided to let that one lay for a while.

"Just searching a few server databases," Stone said after a few minutes. "Public keys are relatively easy to find."

"Don't we need the private keys too?" Vic said. "I thought those were almost impossible to get."

"Well, the impossible just takes a little bit longer," Stone said.

* * *

After a half hour, Stone pushed back from his computer consoles and said, "Riley's been busy."

"Doing what?" Vic said, tossing the comic book that Time had become onto a pile of hot rod and computer magazines.

Stone held out Vic's thumb drive. Vic took it from him.

"Creating encryption keys and using the internet," Stone said. "There are fifteen public and private key pairs on there. One of them might open what you are looking for."

"Whatever that is," Vic said.

"That's your problem," Stone said.

"Wait a minute," Vic said. He held wagged the thumb drive at Stone. "Did you say private keys?"

"You don't tell me where you got the files," Stone said. "I don't tell you where I got the private keys, okay?"

"Okay," Vic said.

"There is a file named 'readme' on your thumb drive. I jotted down a few notes on how you might use the keys."

Vic looked at Stone, cocked his head, raised his eyebrows.

"What?" Stone said.

"The 'readme' file," Vic said. "Isn't that traceable to you?"

Stone smiled. "Not to me, but—"

"To me," Vic said, shaking his head. "Sweet."

"If you run into problems, or if you find your holy grail, give me a call, but only ask me a question about a hot rod, nothing else," Stone said. "Then stop by later that night, after dark. I'll make sure I'm working on a car till midnight."

"No all-nighters?"

"Not anymore," Stone said.

"Sounds like fun," Vic said.

"Fun, right," Stone said. "Try not to be followed. Do some dodgy things like they do in the movies."

"Now I have to scour the earth to find out what this might unlock," Vic said, holding up the small gray thumb drive.

"Now you know why I prefer to build hot rods," Stone said.

10

A few minutes past ten at night, the city room at the *Denver Times* was dead quiet. Only the overnight crew haunted the place. Everything still looked too clean to be a newspaper.

Cliff Sparks, balding and paunchy, had eyed Vic all the way as he walked the length of the city room. From his throne behind the desk Sparks kept his eyes trained on him.

"You know what I think of freelancers," Sparks said dully.

"You know what I think of night city editors," Vic replied, even duller.

"Can't keep a job," Sparks said. "Can't hit a deadline."

"Can't write a lick," Vic said. "Don't play well with others."

"Sorry excuse for a reporter," Sparks said.

"Couldn't edit his way back to dayside on a bet," Vic said.

"I thought you and your daughter were coming by last weekend," Cliff said.

"She had to study for finals," Vic said. "And I was squeezing money and information out of a cop who can't play golf to save his soul."

"Hell, Bengston, Frank was supposed to come over too," Sparks said. "What am I, chopped liver?"

"That's why I stopped by, to apologize," Vic said. "We realized our faux paus on the seventeenth hole."

"Well, I hope you double bogeyed," Sparks said.

"As a matter of fact, I birdied out from there," Vic said. "We'll make it up to you."

"Okay," Sparks sighed as he snatched a stack of obits sitting in front of him and tossed them across the desk toward Vic. "Make yourself useful now that you're an employee. An editor at that."

"Assistant Associate Deputy Semi-Executive Managing Editor," Vic said. "And don't you forget it."

Vic sat down at a city desk terminal and logged in as Alfred Packer, the generic login name used since computers invaded Colorado newsrooms a few decades earlier. He looked at the top sheet and began writing obits.

"I need to talk to your pal at the cop shop," Vic said, after writing "She was survived by her cousin, Beth." Not much of a family, Vic thought.

"Dammit, Vic, you know I've got to be careful with that guy," Sparks said. "What about your golf buddy?"

"He'd never go for it, Vic said, and wrote, "Donations can be given to the American Cancer Society."

"What do you need to do?" Sparks said.

"I need to search a crime scene."

"Oh hell, and I bet I know which one," Sparks said, shaking his head. "You can't get in there. You shouldn't get in there. You're not even on the story."

"I know, I know," Vic said. "But there's something missing and I've got to find it."

"Let the cops do their job," Sparks said.

"I need to do my job, Cliff," Vic said.

"I should bust you with the boss," Sparks said as he turned to his computer screen to read a bulletin that had just moved on the AP wire. All Vic could see was the headline, "Islamist Radical Attacks NYC Cop with Hatchet." Now comes the homegrown jihadist, Vic thought.

"Look, Cliff, I've got a—"

"Don't tell me a thing," Sparks said. "I don't want to know about it. How sure are you about this?"

"Well, the thing might be found by the cops, but even if they do, they'll probably never be able to figure out what it means," Vic said while writing, "Like The Graduate, he got into plastics early, and built one of the city's leading manufacturing firms." Then he crossed out "Like The Graduate". Humor in obits probably wouldn't fly.

Sparks opened the center drawer of his desk and pulled out an old yellow pencil mottled with a hundred tiny bite marks. He carefully removed a yellow sticky note from the pad positioned next to a tape dispenser. He wrote down a phone number and a word, and then handed the sticky note to Vic.

"Redcloud?" Vic said.

"Jack will know what it means," Sparks said. "Don't be surprised if he turns you down."

"Okay," Vic said as he took the note. "Thanks."

Sparks opened his center desk drawer and grabbed a packet of nicotine gum. He tore it open, shoved three squares into his mouth and began chewing. It was the only way he could get through the night shift without cigarettes, the evil that he had struggled to evade for years.

The two wrote in silence for the next hour, polishing the final printed words about most of these people, and, for many, the only words ever published about them. They were born. They lived. They died. The night city desk wrote their obituaries and slotted them away for all eternity.

* * *

Jack Jenkins, a desk sergeant at the Denver Police Department's evidence locker, was not pleased to see Vic. In fact, the idea did not appeal to him at all.

"Let me see that," he said as he snatched the sticky note. "Cliff said Redcloud?"

"Yes, that's what he wrote," Vic said.

"Damn!" Jenkins said.

"Look, if you want me to try the lieutenant, I will," Vic said. "I just want to get a feel for the surroundings."

"Yeah, right," Jenkins said.

Jenkins wrote a security code on the sticky note Sparks had given to Vic. Then he handed him a key.

"This is the code," Hoffman said. "I'm guessing it's a standard security set-up. You'll probably have a minute after you open the door, but I'd punch in the numbers right away, under thirty seconds. This is the key to the back door." Then he glared at Vic. "You sure Cliff said Redcloud?"

"That's his handwriting," Vic said.

"Yes it is," Jenkins said. "This meeting, by the way, never took place."

Vic looked up at the dark glass hemisphere on the wall above the desk. "What about that?" Vic said.

"Busted," Jenkins said. "Cameras only work about half the time. Just be careful and don't take or move anything."

"I won't touch a thing," Vic said. "I just want to look."

What for, he had no idea.

11

Nelson swiveled around from his desk, leaned back, arms folded and stared at Vic.

"What?" Vic said, opening both hands.

"You've gone around the bend, my friend," Nelson said.

"Not really," Vic said. "We just go in, look around, get out. I've got the key and the security code."

"Why in the world would the cops give that to you?" Nelson said. "They'll probably be there waiting for you."

"Us," Vic said.

"No, you," Nelson said. Vic let it pass. Nelson always declined in the first round.

"It's a relationship the paper, or someone at the paper, has with a particular cop," Vic said.

"And how do you know that?" Nelson said.

"Well, the guy at the paper gave me a code word and the guy at the cop shop seemed to respond to it, like it really meant something," Vic said.

"Was there a decoder ring involved?" Nelson said.

"No," Vic said. It was a fool's errand, he told himself.

"Plastic badge?" Nelson said. "You're not a Secret Squadron member are you? They mess up all my missions. You know, Captain Midnight is actually a creep."

"Cut the crap," Vic said. "The cop asked me several times if my colleague really gave me the code word."

"You claim to have the keypad code and a key, correct?" Nelson said.

"Back door key," Vic said.

"That means you're going with me or without me, right?" Nelson said. Then he held up his hands and said, "Don't answer that."

Vic knew if he said he was not going, Nelson would feel guilty over scuttling his pal's plans. If he said he was going, Nelson would feel guilty about letting his pal go in alone with no backup.

Either way, Vic had him.

* * *

"We've got to go tonight," Nelson said. "Let's get it over with. Then get that key back."

"The guy said it was a copy," Vic said.

"Doesn't matter," Nelson said. "It's still probably inventoried. Get it back to him and make sure it's clean."

Vic trusted Nelson because Nelson knew what he was doing. All he really knew about the man was that he was military intelligence sometime somewhere, and who knows what since then. He was a friend and fellow backpacker who did not share Vic's love for boats, something about nauseating diesel fumes on his uncle's fishing boat when he was a kid. Taller than Vic, far leaner than Vic, and in better shape than Vic, Nelson was careful about everything he did, except in his relationship with Vic, who somehow was able to charm him into adventures like this one when drinking dark roast in a Boulder coffee house talking literature probably would have been more productive, and a whole lot safer.

"Am I going to be able to keep up with you," Vic asked, as he considered his swelling waistline, the one he swore he was going to work off by winter.

"We're just walking through a door," Nelson said. "How tough can that be?"

The two set some ground rules. Enter the rear door. Nelson would keep watch. If either one said the code word, Redcloud, they were to leave, no questions asked. Vic had suggested the code word.

"Redcloud?" Nelson said. "That's original."

"It was on my mind," Vic said.

"Be extra careful," Nelson said. "Don't knock anything over, reposition anything, or take anything. Just look."

Vic stared at him. That stare.

"You cannot take anything, Vic," Nelson said. "This is a crime scene."

"Technically, it is a suspected suicide scene," Vic said.

"Which is a crime," Nelson said.

"Whatever," Vic said.

"A high profile one to boot," Nelson said.

"Oh, high profile gets better treatment than low profile?" Vic said. "Where's the fairness in life—or death?"

Now it was Nelson's turn to stare. "I don't know why I do this," he said, shaking his head. "Now we're worried about equal treatment for dead bodies?"

"We've got to start somewhere," Vic said. "Live ones don't get much equal treatment these days. We can practice on the dead."

"All right, enough of your nonsense," Nelson said. "Listen. We exit the same way we enter. If the exit is blocked, use the front door and hope for the best. One more thing."

"Which is?" Vic said.

"No guns," Nelson said.

* * *

During the briefing at Nelson's "facility," he told Vic they would not lock the door or re-set the alarm behind them.

"It's a toss-up," Nelson had said. "Leaving it unlocked gives us a quick exit path if something goes wrong. The security system probably arms a few interior motion detectors. We don't want that. On the other hand, locking the back door keeps someone from coming in behind us, giving us time to split through the front door. Like I said, it's a toss-up. I like leaving them unlocked."

"You've done this before?" Vic said.

"No comment," Nelson said. "You know, we can call this off anytime. No skin off my nose. That's my preference anyway."

"No," Vic said. "I need to know more about—"

"That's enough," Nelson said, holding up his left hand. "I'm just getting you in and out, hopefully in one piece. I don't want to know what it is that you're after."

"Fair enough," Vic said.

Nelson walked over to a massive gun safe. He spun the dial and then turned it back and forth, entering a three-number combination. He opened the right-hand door. Vic spotted a half dozen long guns, the one on the left an old shotgun, probably a twelve gauge pump like his grandfather's Remington which Vic kept cased and unloaded in his front closet, along with Dad's semi-auto Remington twelve gauge. Next to the shotgun, Nelson had a few rifles, probably for deer or elk hunting, and a military-style semi-automatic rifle, the kind stirring up all sorts of mischief in Congress and in state legislatures.

"Is that an AK-47?" Vic said. "Semi-auto?"

Nelson said nothing.

"Auto?" Vic said.

Nothing.

"Semi?" Vic said.

Nothing.

Auto, Vic concluded.

Nelson pulled open the left door, revealing several shelves with various sizes of boxes or cases on them. Handguns, Vic assumed. Nelson reached up to the top shelf and removed a box about the size of a small microwave. He carried it over to a large workbench illuminated by a daylight color fluorescent shop fixture hanging from the rafters above.

"Come on over," Nelson said, "so we can adjust these puppies."

Vic walked over to the bench. Nelson opened the box and pulled out two pair of night goggles and held one pair up over Vic's head.

"Ever used one of these?" he said.

Vic shook his head. "We're not searching for Saddam."

"Look. This is what I know. You know I take precautions. No lights. Not even flashlights, except infrared, okay?"

"You're the boss," Vic said.

"No, you are," Nelson said. "I'm the cluck keeping you out of trouble." He lowered the goggles onto Vic's head. "You're a pumpkin head."

"Seven and three-quarters," Vic said.

"Like I said, pumpkin head," Nelson said. He was grinning. "Hold still."

He walked around behind Vic and expanded the headband on the contraption. "There, that might fit," Nelson said.

It did.

"Check the chin strap," Nelson said. "It adjusts on the side."

Vic snapped two hard nylon connectors beneath his chin, like putting on his bicycle helmet. He tightened the adjusting strap on the right side.

"Yeah, that's it," Nelson said. "That should work. Now flip down the goggles."

Vic reached up with his left hand and flipped them down.

"Careful with that," Nelson said. "Don't rip them off. That's eight grand worth of gear there, lad."

"And you've got two of them," Vic said.

"On loan," Nelson said. "They need to be returned intact."

"Another loan?" Vic said, "Like the night scope?"

"Which you nearly lost in that irrigation ditch."

"It came back with me," Vic said, eyebrows raised.

"Seventeen hundred in repairs," Nelson said.

"They were supposed to be waterproof," Vic said.

"Mil Spec isn't all that it's cracked up to be," Nelson said.

"I made it up to you," Vic said.

"A steak dinner at Elway's and a couple of drinks?"

"Ever priced an Elway steak?" Vic said.

"No," Nelson said. "I usually eat at Arby's."

"Well, we're close to even," Vic said.

Nelson shook his head, then grabbed Vic's right forefinger and lifted it up toward Vic's forehead. He placed the fingertip onto a button.

"Feel that?" Nelson said.

"Yeah," Vic said.

"Don't turn it on, but that's the on-off switch," Nelson said. He moved the finger again. "Up here is a focusing knob." Then he moved the finger to the front of the right goggle lens. "You can independently adjust each side, just like a binoc."

"I see said the blind man as he picked up his hammer and saw," Vic said.

"This is serious, Vic," Nelson said.

"I know," Vic said. "I know."

Nelson gently flipped the goggles back into the upright position, picked up the other set from the box, and the two stepped into the darkness outside Nelson's facility in a well-worn industrial district north of the old Stapleton airport. The two ran through the use of the night goggles enough for Vic to be comfortable with them. Then they went back into the workshop and Nelson brewed a fresh pot of coffee. They sat down over a pair of heavy white porcelain mugs and went over the plan to invade the home of a dead computer billionaire.

"There is one thing to be aware of, however," Nelson said after they had gone over everything a half dozen times.

"Prison time?" Vic said.

"Two things, then," Nelson said.

"All right, what's number one?" Vic said.

"Whatever company monitors Riley's security system might see the entry and call it in immediately," Nelson said.

"What are the chances that would happen?" Vic said.

"Well, if the company has been alerted to pay special attention to Riley's alarm, and if they are actually watching for it and not off slurping coffee or consuming donuts, then maybe there's a chance they'd call it in," Nelson said.

"So it's a toss-up," Vic said.

Nelson nodded, and said, "A toss-up."

12

The bulk of city life occurs in the alleys of Denver's older neighborhoods, especially Capitol Hill south of Colfax and east of the statehouse. Small dumpsters strategically positioned throughout each alley eased trash deposit duties for residents. The dumpsters replaced the old trashcans that had gathered like tired, dirty, and rumpled sheet metal gangs loitering behind each home next to decaying brick and cement ash pits, which had been outlawed decades ago. Most of the vintage houses had garage and yard access from the alleys, which turned the dirt, gravel, and concrete pathways into a bit of a secondary road system throughout the seasoned neighborhoods. Gardens often backed up to alley's edge, spilling flowers, vines, and vegetables over the fences. Kids played, biked, and triked in the alleys during the day. Adults fixed things back there, like cars, choppers, trucks, furniture, and bicycles. But at night these backside arterials turned dark, quiet, and spooky. Green vegetation turned black. Flowers furled until the next sun. Utility lights at each end hurled as much illumination as they could muster for as far as they could toward the obscure, mysterious, and shadowy interiors of the alleys.

The alley behind David Riley's renovated Victorian mansion was perfect for a burglar, or a murderer. The house, its attendant coach house, and lot ate up the center third of the block. No alley lights. The house behind it, directly across the alley, was about the same size, also with no alley lights or motion detectors that lit up backyards at the slightest nearby movement. Vic wondered about that, concluding that the big houses must rely on their extensive interior monitors and security systems to keep people like him, as well as criminals, at bay. Or was he a criminal too? he asked himself.

Nelson silently opened the alley gate and let Vic into Riley's backyard pathway created by two rows of chin-high hedges leading toward the house.

"Follow me," Nelson whispered from right behind him. Vic jumped. He had not heard Nelson close and re-latch the gate or walk up to him. The two moved in single file toward the house. They emerged from the cement sidewalk and hedgerow path and spilled onto an expansive brick patio.

"Watch your step," Nelson said as they walked up the three wide stairs to the back door. A speck of a red light inside one of the glass panes in the back door indicated the security system was armed. Nelson took out a thin flashlight that shot a focused beam through the window and onto the wall inside. He moved it around a bit until the tiny beam settled on the security keypad.

"Notice anything?" Nelson said.

"No."

"No crime scene tape."

"Is that good?" Vic said.

"Damned if I know," Nelson said. "Give me the key. Vic held out his hand, palm up, with the key in it. He felt Nelson's latex covered fingers remove it from his sweaty hand.

"Put your gloves on," he whispered. Vic's pulse quickened over the lapse.

"Sorry," Vic said, reaching into his right pants pocket to pull out his pair of latex gloves. He stretched them over his hands and then with the edge of each hand chopped between the fingers of the opposite hand to get rid of as much trapped air as possible. "Okay."

Nelson pulled out another pen like LED flashlight

"I thought you said no lights," Vic said.

"For you, no lights," Nelson said.

"I am rated on a flashlight, Nelson," Vic said.

"Chill, would ya?" Nelson said. "No names. Audio could be monitored. And I need the light to check the security components."

He poked around the perimeter of the door and adjacent window twice with the flashlight.

"I don't believe this," Nelson said. "There's nothing on this window."

"Maybe he trusted people," Vic said.

"There's at least one person he shouldn't have trusted," Nelson said. A chill ran up Vic's spine.

"What makes you think that?" Vic said.

"Just from what you told me," Nelson said. "You think the suicide thing stinks."

"Yeah, I know," Vic said. "But it sounds weird when someone else says it."

"Let me open the door and de-activate the security system before you come in," Nelson said.

"Okay," Vic said.

Nelson inserted the latchkey, held the doorknob tight, turned the key slowly and opened the door. The red light flashed and the keypad emitted a steady tone. In the dimness of reflected moonlight, Vic saw Nelson's hand cover part of the backlit keypad. His fingers punched in the code and the blinking red light turned to a solid green as the tone went silent.

"Step lightly past me," Nelson said. Vic followed orders and stepped in a few feet, then turned around. With his left hand on the doorknob and his right hand on the upper part of the latch stile, Nelson slowly but firmly closed the door with a muffled click.

Vic's heart pounded. He had not broken into an empty house since he was a kid.

* * *

From across the alley, Detective Greg Frakes stood motionless in a dark shroud of thick shrubs keeping a close eye on the rear of David Riley's house. When the two men stepped through the back gate, he checked his watch. 10:42 p.m. He heard them enter the back door. Then his stomach got the better of him. Frakes pulled a protein bar from the black pouch attached to his belt, removed the wrapper and consumed the first food he had eaten since lunchtime. He rolled the wrapper quietly in his hand and stuck it back into the pouch. Then he pulled out a small bottle filled with water and sipped a few ounces.

After replacing the water bottle he sat down on the ground and hunched himself deeper into the dark bushes to wait for the two men to return to the alley. He expected them to go out the same way they went in. Predictable, he thought, and muttered under his breath, "Redcloud. What a couple of dunces."

*   *   *

"What are you looking for," Nelson asked after checking the front part of the house to make sure no one was outside.

"I don't know," Vic said.

"Great. You've got fifteen minutes not to find it. Then I'm outta here."

"I know. I know."

Vic began searching around the desk. It was strange to see furniture, objects, everything really. It was all there, but in a green monochrome world. Just shades. No laptop, although if there had been one, the cops have it now. Maybe what he was looking for was on the laptop. If so, that lead was shot. Stone had said it could be something stored on a CD-ROM, a hard drive, a memory chip, or even in paper form. He was just guessing anyway. There may be nothing at all.

He stumbled around the room for ten minutes, pulling books out from the bookshelves, then replacing them, checking desk drawers, opening cabinets, finding nothing out of the ordinary. The desk drawers and cabinets were empty. Then, his mind dragged him back to the books, hundreds of them. It could be inserted in anyone of these, he thought. He knew he would never find it, if "it" even existed.

"Five minutes," came the loud whisper from the front room.

What a waste of time, Vic thought as he turned toward the door. His left hand caught the edge of a table blanketed with about a dozen small picture frames, probably family photos. The bump was just enough to start a small chain reaction as the frames toppled into each other.

"What's that!" The loud whisper again.

"Pictures," Vic responded. "Stay there. I've got them."

"Four minutes," Nelson said. "Hurry hurry!"

"Omaha," Vic shot back as he fumbled his way around the tabletop.

He could see things with the goggles, but his depth of field was messed up. One by one, he returned the family portraits to their spot on the small table, or at least where he thought they were on the table. Who would know?

Defeated, he just stood for a moment behind the desk and looked around the room once more at the books, the furniture, the lamps, all in the eerie monochromatic shades created by the night vision goggles. He panned across the walls, candle sconces, artifacts, and paintings.

A familiar shape stopped him cold. Something pegged to the wall between two of the bookcases. A marquee, a long vertical sign. Vic ripped the goggles off his head.

"Nelson!" Vic whispered as loud as he could. "Get in here."

Just outside, Nelson stepped around the corner and said, "Two minutes. Your time is up. We've gotta go!"

"Give me your flashlight," Vic said.

"No, we're going," Nelson said.

"Well, you can," Vic said. "I'm not."

"Amateurs will be the death of me yet," he said, pulling out the small flashlight. He turned it on.

"Put it up on the painting," Vic said. Nelson complied.

The blues of the sky set off the pale yellow of the theater's façade broken by the browns of the narrow brick arches and the detailed terra cotta trim.

"The Oriental Theater," Nelson said.

"That wasn't a photograph on the SD card," Vic said. "That was a photo of this water color."

"What in hell are you talking about?" said Nelson.

"Never mind," Vic said. "I'm taking that painting. Think we can find one about the same size to stick in its place?"

"We need to get out of here, pal," Nelson said.

"Not until I get something to stick up on the wall right here," Vic said.

"Sheese," Nelson said, blowing out his breath. "Pull it down. I'll go look."

"And no more foul language," Vic said.

As he reached up to remove the painting, Vic heard Nelson run up stairs. He retrieved the watercolor, which was in a glass-covered dark metal museum frame, black maybe, but he was back on night vision goggle light again and everything was green on green. A burst of thumps signaled Nelson's sprint back down the stairs.

"Here," he said as he entered the room. "This should fit."

It was a sketch of something that looked like a man's head. Vic handed the theater artwork to Nelson, grabbed the replacement artwork and managed to hook it in place on the first try.

"Go go go!" Nelson whispered. He was standing just inside the back door.

* * *

Frakes stood up again when he heard the back door click open. He watched the same two men step out onto the patio. The taller one reached back inside the door and re-armed the security system, then closed the door quietly and walked toward the alley with the shorter one. Frakes wondered if Bengston always operated like this.

Sucking in his breath, he pressed backward into the bushes and disappeared into their blackness. The two men emerged from the alley gate and again the taller one reached back and closed it without making a noise. Rothenberger was good, Frakes thought.

The two men stood for a moment and then the tall one motioned with his right hand to walk toward the south entrance to the alley. At Seventh Avenue, they turned east and walked two more blocks to Nelson's car, which he had insisted on using.

Frakes stepped from the shadows in the backyard across from Riley's and looked at his watch. 11:01. At least they were pretty efficient, he thought, pulling out his cell phone. He dialed a number and waited.

"They're out," Frakes said. "I thought so. Only fifteen minutes. Bengston was carrying something. Looked like a picture, in a frame. Oh, maybe two feet by something over a foot. Not real big. South, on foot. To their car I'd guess. Yeah, it was Rothenberger. Bengston's been over at his place twice in the last two days. If you want. Well, my car's too far away. They're in the wind. But they're probably going to either Bengston's or Rothenberger's warehouse. They're amateurs. Well, Bengston sure is. All right. I won't. I'll call you later."

Frakes flipped his phone shut. He stepped into the alley and jogged north to get his car, which he had parked in front of the Ace Hardware on Ninth Avenue just west of Corona. He needed a quarter-inch rubber washer for a leaky faucet so he picked it up before the stake out. He grabbed dinner across from the hardware store before taking a leisurely walk around the neighborhood. When the golden evening had turned to night, he walked over to set up the surveillance of Riley's house.

Frakes planned to make a night of it.

13

The King Soopers grocery store at Ninth and Corona occupied the heart of Denver's Capitol Hill neighborhood, home to some of city's most expensive restored mansions, older brick apartment blocks, and an eclectic jumble of students, elderly, goths, artists, writers, musicians, students, hookers, millennial professionals, the poor and homeless, the latter two groups rapidly being shoved out by the steady march of gentrification. It was the first food store in the city to stay open all night, largely to accommodate its unique clientele, many of whom led their lives more on Paris time than on Rocky Mountain time.

Just after midnight, a stocky man clad all in black sauntered from the supermarket tossing a baseball sized organic Granny Smith apple up and down with his right hand. He stopped in the parking lot. The tossing stopped too. The stocky man took a huge bite and resumed his walk, south on Corona, as he consumed the fruit with crunchy abandon. He crossed Eighth Avenue and turned east, walking a half a block before turning south into the alley. As he silently passed through the alley gate of David Riley's house, he was unaware that he was following the identical path taken by Vic and Nelson an hour earlier.

This time no one from the Denver police department was watching the Riley house from across the alley.

14

Baker danced inside as Vic leaned the painting up against the outside of the house. He unlocked and opened the back door. The dog shot past Vic and bolted for the back fence, but stopped midway through the yard to squat and take a leak. Baker never did learn how to lift a leg.

Vic flicked on the stove light, squeaked across the restored pine plank kitchen floor, flipped on the dining room light and wrestled the painting onto the dining room table. He reached for the Swiss army knife in his back pocket, but then decided to take the painting apart downstairs on his workbench. He picked it up from the table and maneuvered it under his right arm, then returned to the back door to get Baker. The black dog emerged from the black night and followed Vic downstairs.

Man and dog entered the ham shack, a basement room where Vic kept his amateur radio equipment, books, parts, and tools. Baker curled up on his tattered rug in one corner, and Vic stood before his electronics workbench where the painting lay face down on a soft towel. He carefully unscrewed the corner anchors on the back of the metal frame, pulled off the side, the top, and bottom rails, then lifted the backing off of the Oriental Theater watercolor. The artwork was affixed to the back of the mat with a single thickness of manila masking tape, except in the lower left hand corner where a second layer of tape secreted something small, something about the size of a micro SD card.

Vic teased up one corner of the extra tape with the tip of the small blade on the red Swiss Army knife he kept in his back pocket. Gently pinching the tape between the blade and his thumb, he peeled it back and revealed a black micro SD memory card stuck to the glue. He freed the card with a narrow silver tweezers normally used for handling small electronic components. Vic's heart screamed to see the treasure.

He fired up his small netbook computer, slid the micro SD card into the same adapter he used to read the card from Driscoll's desk and inserted the adapter into the slot on the computer. A few mouse clicks revealed a single folder labeled "Stuff" on the micro SD card. He left clicked on it, held down the mouse button and dragged the icon to his desktop. The netbook took a minute to copy it over.

When the copying process was completed, Vic removed the tiny memory card from his computer, grabbed a paper towel, wrapped the card and rubbed it between his thumb and forefinger. Then, using the tweezers again, he set it back into the impression left on the sticky side of the masking tape patch and returned the patch to where it was on the back of the painting. Then he reassembled the artwork and frame.

Vic had no idea what he was going to do next, so he went to bed.

*　*　*

Frakes sat in his car outside Vic's house waiting for him to show up. The detective used the small monocular he always kept in the glove compartment to check out the house, but it was all dark. Finally a light popped on, indirect, probably the kitchen, Frakes thought, assuming Vic had driven up his own alley, garaged his car and entered through the back door. Then the center of the house lit up, dining room maybe. He had never been inside. Driscoll could fill in the blanks, Frakes thought.

Still, the detective could not see all that much. Solid translucent blinds covered the windows, although the tops of the blinds were lowered part way. Frakes could see Vic moving around inside, but only his head and shoulders. It looked as though Vic set something down, possibly on a dining room table, something large or awkward enough to require both hands. The painting, Frakes assumed. Then Vic seemed to be talking with someone, but he was looking down at the floor. That would be the dog, the detective concluded.

Vic disappeared from view for about a minute. When he returned, it looked as though he picked that something back up and carried it out of view. A basement window behind a scraggly bush lit up with a yellowish light. Frakes pressed the monocular to his left eye and peered through the bush and into the basement window. He saw Vic's head pass by once, but that was all. He thought about creeping up closer but his instructions were to stay in the car, just observe the house and follow Vic if he went anywhere. Frakes did not like this.

After a half hour, the basement light went dark. Vic reappeared in the uncovered part of the dining room window, seemed to set something down on the imagined table and then exited stage left. The dining room went dark. In a few seconds, a light went on in an upstairs room. The same color shade covered that window, but completely this time. When the upstairs light went out ten minutes later, Frakes jotted down the time in his notebook, flipped open his cell phone and hit a speed dial number.

"I think he's in bed," Frakes said. "He did something, probably with that picture. Looks like he was in his basement for a little while, about a half hour. I couldn't see much, really. The shades blocked a clear view. I'd say whatever he was working on in the basement, he brought back upstairs and set it on his dining room table. At least I think that's his dining room. Middle of the house? Kind of behind his living room? Okay. Well, then he cut the lights and went upstairs. It's all dark now. About an hour. No, I watched him all the way. He had to get his car at Rothenberger's. They just stood outside and jawed. Then he left. Want me to slip in there and take a looksee? I'd say we have probable cause. All right. Mañana."

Disappointed and anxious, Frakes drove home.

15

Detective Greg Frakes set the venti Starbucks cup on the edge of his desk. A pink sticky note on his terminal screen caught his eye.

"See me now. D."

Frakes grabbed his coffee and headed for Driscoll's office. He looked at his watch. 7:30 a.m. The boss was in early.

The blinds all around Driscoll's fishbowl were down and closed. The door was closed. The blind on the door was down and closed. Frakes knocked on the glass door.

"Come in," Driscoll said. When Frakes had the door half open, Driscoll said, "Close the door."

To Frake's immediate right, tucked into the corner of Driscoll's office, Vic sat quietly. The painting of the Oriental Theater lay on Driscoll's desk.

"What's he doing here?" Frakes said.

"Answering a pang of conscience," Driscoll said.

Frakes locked eyes with Vic.

"Give me a break," Frakes said. "Have you booked him?"

"No," Driscoll said. "That's what we need to talk about."

"Why not?" Frakes said.

"Those are the kind of questions I get to ask, Greg, not you," Driscoll said.

"Sorry, Boss," Frakes said. "This guy and his buddy Rothenberger are tampering with evidence, messing up a crime scene."

"He's also finding evidence that your team missed," Driscoll said to Frakes with his I'm-not-too-pleased-with-you-either look.

With that same look, said to Vic, "But breaking in and finding it is another matter altogether."

"We didn't really break in," Vic said. "We had the code and a key."

"Something else I need to take up with you," Driscoll said. "I don't suppose you'd like to tell me who gave you those items?"

Vic shook his head, glad he was able to find Jack Jenkins to slip him the key to Riley's house before he walked into Driscoll's at 7:15 in the morning with the painting of the Oriental Theater. Guilt over the late night caper and complete lack of sleep got the better of him.

"Well, we'll leave that for another time," Driscoll said. "For now we've got bigger problems."

Vic and Frakes looked at each other. Neither one had any idea what Driscoll was leading up to.

"Frakes, when did Bengston and Rothenberger go in the back door, precisely?" Driscoll said.

Frakes flipped open his notebook, shuffled through a few pages and said, "10:42 p.m."

"You were following us?" Vic said.

"For two days," Frakes said. "Mostly you."

"My editor will love this," Vic said.

"You won't tell him," Driscoll said. "Or, her, if your pal Mayer is working this with you."

"What makes you so sure?" Vic said. His heart did not like this either.

"That's a negotiation and it involves felony charges," Driscoll said. "Just hear me out."

To Frakes, Driscoll said, "And they left?"

"At 11:01," Frakes said.

"Did they use the keypad and the key?" Driscoll said.

"That's all we used, why?" Vic said.

"I'm asking Frakes," Driscoll said.

"I couldn't see all that well," Frakes said. "But there was no special effort. Looked like they just walked in, and it seemed like Rothenberger reached back in to set the alarm when they left."

"You followed Bengston home?" Driscoll said.

Vic did not like this at all.

"Not directly," Frakes said. "I had to go get my car. It was a couple of blocks away. But then I drove right to Rothenberger's, picked up Bengston's scent and then followed him home."

Vic felt violated, but given his little foray into the Riley castle, he figured it was karma evening up the score.

"How long were you there?" Driscoll said.

Frakes looked at his notes again.

"Got there around twelve. Stayed a little over a half hour," Frakes said. "Then I called you."

"What about Rothenberger?" Driscoll said.

"I drove back by his place, the warehouse, saw a light inside and his SUV was parked out front," Frakes said.

"Did you see him?" Driscoll said.

"Rothenberger?" Frakes said. "No."

"Bengston, did you and Rothenberger toss the place?" Driscoll said.

"What do you mean?" Vic said.

"I mean toss it," Driscoll said, showing a little impatience. "Bust into Riley's safe. Yank the drawers. Empty them on the desk and floor. Books all over the place. Entry through a window. Security system disarmed. The whole nine yards."

"What's going on?" Vic said.

"I'd like to know too, Boss," Frakes said.

"I got a call from Billings, 1:30 in the morning," Driscoll said. "Pretty much wrecked my beauty sleep. A security drive-by spotted a light in Riley's house. The guy actually got out of his car and walked up to the house to check it out. He spotted the hole in the window, nice little glass cutter job, and called it in.

"All I did was swap out the paintings," Vic said. "We didn't touch a thing. I didn't even know there was a safe."

"Much as I'd love to bust this guy, Boss, I've got to go with his story," Frakes said.

"Thanks, Greg," Vic said. "I still won't sponsor you into the country club."

"Kennedy's a public course," Frakes said.

"Can it, both of you," Driscoll said. He pushed a sheet of paper across his desk to Frakes who spun it around and looked at it.

"What's this?" Frakes said, scanning the document. "Oh, from the security company."

"You can see where the Hardy Boys went in and then went out again," Driscoll said.

"That jibes with my times," Frakes said.

"None of the rent-a-cops were watching the place," Driscoll said. "Both the in and out were registered by the system but those security guys were off watching TV or who knows what." To Vic, Driscoll said, "When did you leave Rothenberger?"

"We went right to his place," Vic said. "I had to get my car. I think he said he was just going to crash. He's got a tiny pad in there. We talked outside for a while, and I went home."

"What was he driving?" Driscoll said.

"A black Chevy Tahoe," Vic said.

"Where was it parked?" Driscoll said.

"Right outside his front door," Vic said.

Driscoll looked at Frakes who nodded.

"He still might have had enough time to do it," Frakes said.

"Do what?" Vic said.

"Go back for a more thorough search," Driscoll said. "He had to break in the second time, because you had the key. The one you have back to Jenkins this morning, right?"

Vic just stared at Driscoll, then glanced over at Frakes, who shrugged his shoulders. So much for Sparks' inside source at the Cop Shop, Vic thought.

"We're simply not as dumb as you think we are, Vic," Driscoll said.

"Or I'm just too much of an amateur," Vic said.

"I'll second that," Frakes said. "What about Rothenberger? He's the pro."

"Give me a break," Vic said. That could not be true, Vic thought. "What about Jenkins?"

"No, it wasn't Jack," Driscoll said. "He's in enough hot water over this. But you do owe him an apology, Vic. And all this stays right here, understood?"

Vic nodded. He would have to tell Sparks what happened, but without spilling the beans.

"Frakes?" Driscoll said.

Frakes stared at Driscoll, then said, "Yeah. Okay. Stays here."

"Where's Jenkins now?" Vic said.

"I sent him home to do some hard thinking," Driscoll said.

"You're not going to fire him are you?" Vic said.

Driscoll stood up and leered down at Vic.

"Against my better judgment, and with your cooperation, I'm going to keep this under wraps while we get through this investigation," Driscoll said. "Then I'll decide what to do. Frakes here is my witness, so now he has something on me and on you. See what a sticky situation this is?"

"Something on me?" Vic said, ringing an imaginary halo above his head with a forefinger.

"Look through the blinds toward the break room," Frakes said.

Vic got up and stuck is index finger through the metal slats and pulled a few down into a snappy "V". He could see right into the break room.

"Okay, so what?" Vic said.

"I was standing there stirring my coffee while you pulled your little trick with the pen," Frakes said. "I saw the evidence bag drop down out of your hand."

"You think we'll all just laugh about this someday down at the retirement home?" Vic said.

"I doubt it," Driscoll said. "I seriously doubt it."

"You think Riley was murdered too, don't you?" Vic said.

"Possibly," Driscoll said. "But I still need to know everything that you know."

"I don't know very much, Frank," Vic said.

"That's an understatement," Driscoll said, holding up the evidence bag with the micro SD card inside it. "You saw what was on this chip? And the chip inside the picture frame?"

"That card I saw," Vic said, nodding toward the evidence bag. "By the way, it's a card not a chip, Frank." Vic wondered if a computer geek could figure out that something had been copied from the SD card inside the painting. "I saw the lump on the back of the painting, felt it. Thought I better bring it in."

"What did you make of this?" Driscoll said, holding up the

evidence bag.

"A bunch of files with numbers in them and an image file with that on it," Vic said, pointing to the watercolor of the Oriental Theater. "Gibberish. I have no idea what any of it means."

"What did you do with the picture?" Driscoll said.

"I just took it," Vic said. "I figured it might have something to do with what was on the memory card."

"Did you copy the stuff that was on the chip—the card?" Driscoll said.

"You have my computer, Frank."

"This is evidence, Vic, material evidence in a suspicious death investigation," Driscoll said.

"So it is officially a murder then?" Vic said.

Driscoll sighed and folded his massive forearms across his chest. "No, not yet. Suspicious death. Did you copy anything?"

"You have my computer right there," Vic said, nodding toward the netbook computer resting on the desk in front of Driscoll. "And whatever is beneath that lump of tape on the back of the painting."

"Again, did you copy anything?" Driscoll asked again, leaning forward.

"I copied that one," Vic said, pointing at the evidence bag, then to his netbook. "To that computer right there."

When he had gotten up that morning, Vic backed up everything on his small traveling computer, mostly photos of his kids, grandkids, landscapes, ham radio adventures, notes on building radios and making antennas, and an outline for a feature film script. He erased all his reporting documents, which he backed up routinely on a full size SD card that fit in the same slot he used to copy Riley's smaller micro SD cards. That backup card was in his pocket, but none of Riley's files were on it. They were on a CD that Vic had consigned to the *Times*' safe. It was a good one. No cops allowed.

"Does the *Times* get a copy if you decode it?" Vic said.

Driscoll just glared at him.

"Are you confiscating my computer?" Vic said. "Want to search my house?"

"The last thing we need is to drag your newspaper into this,"

Driscoll said, shaking his head. "Anyway, I'm sure your copy or copies are secreted away at the paper. Keep them under wraps, would you? And if you figure out what is in the—what do you call it? The folder. If you figure it out would you kindly give me a call?"

"Maybe," Vic said. "They're probably just sensitive financial records, Frank."

"I doubt that," Frakes said. "Somebody is picking up your breadcrumbs, pal."

"Watch my back?" Vic said.

"Well, we're not gonna," Frakes said. "You're on your own."

* * *

"So we are all supposed to mind read here and guess if Riley's house is a murder scene or not," Vic said.

The big cop slammed his right hand down on his desk. Both Vic and Frakes jumped. "It doesn't matter," Driscoll said. "It's not a public park."

"And?" Vic said.

"And what?" Driscoll said.

"And is it a murder scene?"

"We're leaning that way," the chief detective said.

"That's why I came down this morning," Vic said. "I figured if I was smelling murder, you were too."

"Oh, giving us a little credit now, are we?" Driscoll said.

"Sometimes I get a bit obsessed with these cases, Lieutenant," Vic said. "I've told you everything I know."

"No, you have not told us everything you know," Driscoll said. "You never really told us what did you do with this painting after you got home last night?"

Vic thought for a moment. He assumed Frakes parked out on Holly Street and watched him. The top-down-bottom-up shades were lowered a third of the way down a little from the top his windows, Vic recalled, so he could not have seen very much.

"Nothing much," Vic said.

"Nothing!" Frakes said. "I saw you doing something at a table, maybe your dining room."

"Well, I was looking through my mail," Vic said, now convinced that Frakes could have only seen the upper part of his body.

"You disappeared for about a half an hour before you shut things down for the night," Frakes said. "You were in the basement. It looked like you took the painting with you."

"I did," Vic said. "But when I saw the little lump of tape, I had second thoughts about swiping the painting. I decided I'd better just bring it back. Why didn't you just come on in for a cup of coffee, Greg? Take a load off. Settle this once and for all."

"Fun-ny," Frakes said. "What were you doing?"

"Well, the whole thing was getting to me," Vic said. "I'm not cut out for some of this stuff."

"What?" Frakes said. "Evidence tampering?"

"I brought it back," Vic said.

"How about breaking and entering?" Frakes said.

"The Denver Police Department gave me the code and the key," Vic said. "Key as in Keystone Cops."

Frakes began to rise from his chair. Driscoll held up his hands. "Greg!" Frakes sat back down.

"Let me arrest him right now, right here, chief," Frakes said. He was trembling.

"Here's how the story will go, Greg," Vic said. "It'll be along the lines of incompetent police work, failure to secure evidence, some of which was buried in a nest of papers on Frank's desk, and then failing to secure the crime scene. Something along those lines."

Frakes took a moment to regain his composure, then said, "You swiped this painting, took it home, took it into your basement, and did something with it."

"Right, Greg," Vic said. "I was a bit shaken. I took it downstairs, but I did something else."

"What?" Frakes demanded.

"I worked in the shack on a radio project for a while. To chill out."

"Radio project?" Frakes said. "Shack?"

"He's a ham radio operator," Driscoll said. "Half nerd. The shack is where he keeps his radios."

"CB?" Frakes said. Driscoll fidgeted because he knew what was coming. Vic turned and leaned toward Frakes.

"Vic!" Driscoll said. Vic just held up his hand toward Driscoll.

"No, not Citizens Band," Vic said. "Amateur Radio. The FCC-licensed Amateur Radio Service."

Driscoll clasped his hands and leaned back to await the conclusion of the coming mini lecture.

"We have to learn and understand how radio communication actually works," Vic said. "We have to pass federally administered examinations to prove it. We also have to learn Morse Code, or at least I had to learn Morse Code. I had to copy twenty words per minute. I passed four separate written exams and three separate Morse Code exams before earning my Extra Class Amateur Radio license, the highest level FCC Amateur Radio Service license."

Driscoll looked up at the ceiling and mouthed Vic's final phrase, "highest level FCC Amateur Radio Service license."

Frakes looked at Driscoll and said, "Did I say the wrong thing?" Driscoll nodded.

"Then what's CB?" Frakes said.

"Citizens Band radio was offered to all the other people who wanted to use radio communications but were too lazy to get a ham radio license," Vic said.

"That's a bit harsh," Driscoll said. "I used to run a CB rig in my RV."

"Ten-four, good buddy," Vic said. "That sort of illustrates my point."

"What point?" Frakes said.

"Not really sure, detective," Vic said. "At any rate, I'm building a three-band transceiver to take with me camping or just traveling. CW only."

"What's that?" Frakes said. "CW. Citizen What?"

"Continuous Wave," Vic said. "It is a radio emissions mode, that—well, suffice it to say it is used mostly for transmitting Morse code."

"So why isn't it MC or something like that?" Frakes said.

Vic turned to Driscoll and raised both his hands. "Frank, can't you just throw a flag or something? End this will you?"

"You never did explain to me what that meant," Driscoll said.

"CW."

"It's just a mode of radio emission, used for code. That's all."

"Dit dit dit?" Frakes said.

"Yes," Vic said. "All that and dahs too."

"So that's what you are telling us?" Driscoll said. "You were in the basement working on a radio?"

"Yes," Vic said. "You know I do that, Frank. My nerves were shot. They needed settling. Radio does that for me. How long did you say I was gone, Greg?"

"Half hour," Frakes said.

"A half hour," Vic said to Driscoll.

"All right," Driscoll said. "So you did nothing with the painting?"

"I felt the tape lump, and decided to bring it back," Vic said, leaving out a few intermediate steps, like pulling out the SD card and copying its contents onto his ham shack computer.

16

The car show was small, occupying one corner of a strip mall parking lot. Vic parked his Jeep across the street in front of a local furniture store and walked over to the show under the theory that he needed to get in as many walking steps per day as possible and, thus, reduce waist measurement and gross tonnage.

The hot rods were cool, but restorations drew him in more than the customizations. A teal over white 1954 Chevy convertible with a black ragtop caught his eye. He circled it for a few minutes admiring the nice leather upholstery, the white sidewalls, the brilliant chrome, and the perfect hand-polished paint finish. He figured it would be fun for him to drive this around for about five minutes. Cool cars attracted him, probably a genetic thing, but he never needed one, never really wanted one, never wanted to be the gray-haired guy in the fifties or sixties car. Hobbies always looked better from the outside.

Vic's oldest son, Sean, was a different story. So far he had not shown up at his house with a trashed out rusty hulk of an old car that would occupy the family garage for the next two years while he restored it. Instead, Sean sold insurance to the guys who fixed up these vehicles. His insurance company peddled a special policy tailored for collector cars. It was a nice little niche, one of several Sean had developed as he built his agency.

Vic ambled down the main aisle toward Sean's display table, starting with the Chevy, then passing a 1965 red Mustang convertible, a white 1960 Corvette, a brand new Mustang Cobra, a fully restored green 1932 Ford pickup, and a few other vehicles that either did not interest Vic at all or simply flopped in the curb appeal department.

"Pop, wassup?" Sean hollered from behind his table, which was covered with the company's "Collectible Choice" insurance brochures. Sean was wearing a Collectible Choice golf shirt and a Collectible Choice hat. His face was not painted in Collectible Choice colors of chrome and brilliant red.

"Wassup?" Vic said, "How's biz?"

"Not bad," Sean said. "Better than I thought it would be. Looks like two new clients for sure, one of them has twenty-three cars in a huge metal farm building out near Byers."

"Did he restore them all?" Vic said.

"Every one," Sean said.

"I don't get it," Vic said.

"They don't get ham radio," Sean said.

"Point taken," Vic said.

"The boys will be here in a little while with Jenny," he said. Sean took pride in his family and what he had built for them. He puffed when he said "Mom and our boys and I did this" or "we did such and such with our boys." It felt good for Vic to hear that, but he knew when Sean's boys turned into teenage axe murderers for a few years, he would be singing a different tune while he and Jenny navigated those unsettling waters. Payback is a bitch, Vic thought, then grinned.

"I'm not sure how long I'll be here," Vic said. "Have you seen Paxton Stone?"

"He was here earlier," Sean said. "I'm not sure where he is though."

"Is that going to work out for you?" Vic said.

"Oh yeah," Sean said. "I've already been over to his garage. We're doing a whole small business package, Collectible Choice on the cars, P and C on the house, extra for all the computers, life insurance for him and his wife, uh—"

"Liz," Vic said.

"Liz," Sean said, nodding. Then to a forty-something guy with jet black hair who just walked up, he said, "Hey, bud, where have you been? I hope you brought your car."

"I did," jet black hair said.

"Dad, over there," Sean said, pointing toward the LaMar's donut shop. Vic looked over and saw Stone walking into the store.

"I've got to catch him," Vic said. "Later."

"Later," Sean said, and the salesman in him turned and riveted his attention onto the man with the jet black hair.

* * *

It had been a week since Vic had managed to hand a thumb drive with the contents of the second Riley micro SD card on it to Stone without Driscoll, Frakes or anyone else from Denver police department observing him. The kerfuffle over Vic's incursion into Riley's house seemed to have died down for now. Nelson, not very pleased with either Vic or the cops, laid low. Driscoll had delayed release of the medical examiner's report and told the media the police had reclassified Riley's death as "suspicious" and that they were investigating several leads. Since Riley's wealth exceeded the magic one billion dollar mark, the national media sharks slathered all over the story. Nobody in the media had yet to mention the secret facility Riley had set up in the foothills or his conversations with national political leaders about Universal Vote. Vic was not about to bring it up until he had a better idea of what was on the two micro SD cards Riley had hidden away.

Despite the national media attention, the *Times* had taken Vic off the story. They wanted their Pulitzer winner to get back to his energy and environment roots. Vigil assigned him to look into breakthroughs in renewable energy sources. Vic successfully argued that he should instead investigate the growing controversy over hydraulic fracking and the impact the country's new oil and gas boom would have on water and air quality. He had pointed out to the editor that it would take quite a bit of time to delve into the energy story, months maybe. Vigil said to keep him updated. Vic promised, glad for the breathing space he bought for himself to chase down the Riley story even though someone else was covering it, technically.

As he entered the LaMar's, the last thing Vic was thinking about was energy. He was obsessing over what was on that memory card he found taped inside the painting he swiped from David Riley's house.

"There you are," Vic said as he walked up to Stone who was standing in line, three from the counter.

"Here I am," Stone said. "What do you want?"

"Black coffee and a plain old fashioned donut," Vic said, patting his shrinking tummy. "Got to watch this."

"Not hard to miss," Stone said. "Go get a table"

"Skinny braggart," Vic said. Stone just smiled and nodded.

Vic grabbed four napkins from one of those new dispensers that make it nearly impossible to actually extract a napkin, some bean counter's idea, no doubt. He snagged a corner table with windows on two sides. It offered minimal privacy. About five minutes later, Stone sat down with the coffees and the fat pills. Vic figured Stone could eat his weight in donuts without showing it.

"How's Liz?" Vic said.

"She says 'hi' and she's doing great," Stone said.

"Where is Liz?" Vic said. "I thought she'd be here."

"She split," Stone said. "Two minutes and she's done with cars. We always drive separately to these things. She had to go over to Bandimere anyway. She likes the track."

"Still running your dragster?" Vic said.

"Yeah, but I don't drive it anymore," Stone said. "My reflexes are shot. Liz got some young guy from Lakewood. An up and comer. I just build them, tweek them, and fix them now."

"Which car's yours?" Vic said.

"See the powder blue chop job over there?" Stone said, just looking up and raising his eyebrows. "Behind you."

Vic turned around and beheld the kind of street rod he lusted for as a kid, spurred on by Frankie and Annette movies. As he aged, the lust waned. Ham radio took over.

"Thirty-six Chevy in there somewhere?" Vic said.

"Absolutely," Stone said. "Somewhere."

"It's sweet," Vic said.

"Say, I've got to tell you, I really like Sean," Stone said. "And he loves the cars. I know I'll build him a rod someday. You know, he's already saved us about a grand a year on total premiums."

"That's what he loves to do," Vic said. "Protect families and save them money."

"Well, I want to thank you for getting us together with him," Stone said. "Now, I know you want to know about Brand X."

It was the code word they had agreed upon to refer to the second SD card from Riley's house.

"Anything?" Vic said.

"Quite a bit," Stone said. "The folder contained two more files of big prime numbers and then another large encrypted file. I'm assuming the prime numbers are part of the private key. I'm hoping that with those numbers, and with the numbers from the first folder, I can figure out the key to decrypt the bigger file. And I've found more public keys that Riley scattered all over the world."

"So you don't know what's in the big file then," Vic said, not pushy, just matter of fact.

"Not yet, but I've got a computer crunching the public keys and the possible combinations with the prime numbers," Stone said. "Something may hit."

"May?" Vic said.

"No real assurances," Stone said. Vic nodded.

"Have the police contacted you?" Vic said.

"No," Stone said. "Should they?"

"They might," Vic said. "I told you they followed me to your house that first time."

"Well, I haven't noticed anything," Stone said. "They can't get into my computers anyway."

"You sure?" Vic said.

"No one can," Stone said. "They can't bug the place either."

Vic wondered if Stone knew Nelson. Two paranoids in a pod.

17

The text message arrived when Vic was in the shower. He had been working in his garden most of Sunday afternoon cleaning up his ever-expanding mini vegetable farm, adding compost to the soil and organizing the yard for the upcoming growing season. Hot, dirty and stinking, Vic hit the shower just before five. After drying off and tossing on a tee shirt and shorts, he picked up his cell phone and saw the message notice icon. It was from Stone. He pulled it up.

"Nd to meet asap re brndx. 6 pm co rr museum gardn trn display. No calls."

Vic had just enough time to get across town to meet Stone. He stepped into his tattered canvas deck shoes, covered his bristly gray head with a dark blue Newport Beach Yacht Club sailing cap, and, since he would be driving west toward Colorado's intense setting sun, and snatched his polarized sunglasses to cut the glare that seemed to bother his eyes more and more each year.

A half-hour later, Vic rolled through downtown Golden, its quaint Main Street snugged up against the foothills in the northwest corner of the metropolitan area. For a short time right after statehood, Golden was Colorado's capitol. Now the old capitol building was a restaurant on the main drag while the real one stood high on a hill just east of downtown Denver.

He turned right onto 10th street, passing by the unassuming main offices for the Coors Brewery where the road turned into 44th Avenue, taking him the last mile to the Colorado Railroad Museum, an odd locale for a meeting, Vic thought. This mystery alone might soon be unraveled, or re-raveled into an undecipherable knot of trains, hot rods, software, cryptography, the vote franchise, and "suspicious" death.

Vic felt like he was inside a Marvel comic book.

* * *

The museum was a vast complex of both indoor and outdoor railroads, ranging from small tabletop model railroad layouts to the real thing. Full sized operating railroads included several miles of track, spurs, a roundhouse, and stations. Vic and his kids discovered about every aspect of railroading imaginable at the museum, even a Galloping Goose, a Frankenstein amalgamation with the body of an old Buick, Pierce-Arrow or bus attached to a boxcar with steel railroad wheels and a cowcatcher on the front. The Rio Grande Southern came up with those oddities to keep mail and supplies moving to Colorado mountain towns when steam powered trains became too expensive to operate profitably.

Two grown men decked out from head to toe in denim railroad work clothes occupied the center of the sprawling outdoor display of garden railroads. One of them was Paxton Stone. He even wore an engineer's cap and had a red bandana tied around his neck. The man had managed to drag the childhood love of model trains and the teenage lust for hot rods well into adulthood. The layout consumed an area the size of a small city lot. Technically, the trains were G-gauge, which meant they ranged in scale from about one to twenty or one to thirty-two in scale depending on the country and the train manufacturer.

Up stood Stone, a modern day Gulliver towering over this diminutive world, surrounded by ogling children, parents, and grandparents. He said something to his fellow railroader and then gingerly stepped his way across the miniature world toward Vic.

"Hot dog?" Stone said as he re-entered the true to life scale world where people died of gunshot wounds to the head.

"Why not?" Vic said. He had not eaten since noon.

They walked over to the concession area where massive quantities of burgers, dogs, chips, fries, custard, and soft drinks flew over the counters and into the hands of the ravenous mob. The two small talked while awaiting their delicacies, Stone opting for a hot dog and Vic going with a burger. Their conversation covered model railroading, a hobby Vic had dabbled in off and on over the years, finally scaling everything down to a single almost microscopic Z-gauge railroad that he set up during the Christmas holidays. Vic spent the bulk of his hobby time with ham radio.

Stone confessed he had gotten rid of all of his trains long ago and only volunteered at the museum to scratch the model-railroading itch. He thumbed his denim overalls bib and grinned proudly. They sat at a wooden picnic table painted the red, yellow, and green of the Denver and Rio Grande Railroad.

"Now, you need to get rid of this," Stone said, pulling a small gray thumb drive from the right breast pocket on his overalls. He set the small device on the table in front of Vic. "I erased this from my drives. Actually I pulled the drives and destroyed them."

"What is it that I've got?" Vic said. His fingers rubbed moist palms.

"A time bomb," Stone said. "You don't have any other SD cards, anything else physical, do you?"

Vic shook his head.

"You need to reformat any drive or memory device that these things were on," Stone said. "I mean a deep format, from the ground up. You need to wipe your drives. Better still, dump them off your sailboat in the middle of Cherry Creek Lake. Grind them up first."

"Seriously?"

"And then some. This thing scared the hell out of me, Vic. I shake whenever I think about it."

The sweaty stench of paranoia wafted across the table to Vic.

"Tell me more," Vic said.

"Well, we finally came up with the right combination of prime numbers and public and private keys to decrypt the big file in the second folder you gave me," Stone said.

"We?" Vic said. "More people know about this?"

"I had to enlist some help," Stone said.

"From whom?" Vic said.

"That I can't tell you," Stone said.

"Local guy?" Vic said.

"Can't tell you that either," Stone said.

Now him, Vic thought. Nelson was bad enough with his secrecy crap. Vic cupped his hand around his mouth and leaned on his right elbow, a tell he learned not to use when he played poker at the Press Club. He too kept secret sources, he admitted to himself, but to no one else.

"I understand," Vic said, not liking it, but understanding it.

"This thing is either all the good in the world stuffed into a single algorithm," Stone said.

"Or what?" Vic said.

"Or all the evil," Stone said.

"I never like the evil part," Vic said.

"It's all a matter of perspective," Stone said. "We unlocked the big file. That was easy once we found the right combination of public keys and the prime numbers."

"So what was in the big file?" Vic said. The "we" really bugged him.

"A white paper," Stone said.

"Like the white papers I used to write for Atlantic Richfield?" Vic said.

"I thought Big Oil was the enemy," Stone said.

"My brush with evil," Vic said. "I had a few clients on the dark side."

"What did you write for them?" Stone said.

"Oh, papers on their readiness for clean-up in the event of a spill, how they were helping whale research in the Beaufort Sea, protecting the North Slope tundra, stuff like that," Vic said. "Policy positions."

"Was it bullshit?" Stone said.

"Not really," Vic said. "They seemed sincere. And the checks cleared."

"Well, this is something like a policy paper," Stone said. "Almost like an academic research paper, about a discovery."

"Discovery?" Vic said.

"Math," Stone said.

"Arithmetic?" Vic said.

"Advanced theoretical mathematics. Fractals."

"Weren't you into fractals once?" Vic said. "It's a vague memory."

"I still am," Stone said. "They're an intriguing way to describe geometric and biological shapes."

"I just remember the psychedelic pictures," Vic said.

"Well, they involve patterns, but they explain a lot about the universe," Stone said. "Tell me, does the word *Sundial* mean anything to you?"

"Other than the time telling devices we see in gardens, no," Vic said. "Why do you ask?"

"It's in the header of this document," Stone said. "Like it's a project code word."

"Can you net it out for me?" Vic said.

"Unless we're mistaken," Stone said, "Riley developed an approach to computer encryption that's virtually unbreakable. And unless I am mistaken, it's the holy grail of computer security technology."

*　*　*

"There's that 'we' again," Vic said. "Makes me nervous."

"These guys, well there are some gals too, are the best in the world," Stone said.

"Best at what?" Vic said.

"Hacking, security, encryption, code writing, you name it," Stone said.

"You started with hacking," Vic said. "Is that what they really do?"

"Mostly. But they're on our side."

"On our side? Is this a game?"

"No, it's a war," Stone said, dead seriously. "A cyber war."

"Isn't there a new book out on that?" Vic said.

"Richard Clarke," Stone said. "Former presidential advisor."

"I saw him on Charlie Rose. I thought about getting the book."

"Remember the guys from MIT?" Stone said.

"Public key, private key?" Vic said.

"Right," Stone said. "That was just the start. I mean codes and encryption methods have been around for a long time. Some guys from Stanford really advanced the ball in the Fifties, got us to mid-field."

"That's only halfway," Vic said.

"Then a team at MIT put us into the red zone," Stone said.

"Are the Broncos playing today, Pax? The Buffs?"

His thin staid face broke into a smile. Then he laughed. "We preferred the sports analogies, over the war analogies," Stone said. "When we hacked, and then when we designed software."

"Okay, you're in field goal range," Vic said.

Stone turned serious again and said, "Yeah. That's where we are now. With public keys and private keys—that's what those guys from Stanford and MIT came up with—we can kick field goals all day long."

"Field goals only?" Vic said.

Stone nodded and said, "Even the most sophisticated encryption codes can still be broken, especially with today's computer power."

"So the holy grail gets you into the red zone and scoring position," Vic said, having fun with this analogy.

"Better than that," Stone said. "The goal is the perfect encryption system, one that can't possibly be broken."

Vic's six-decade-old heart pounded his sternum. "*Sundial* is the touchdown?"

Stone nodded again, but this time said nothing, just raised both his arms skyward, like an NFL ref dressed up in a train engineer outfit.

* * *

"You've got to get rid of it, Vic," Stone said. "It's too dangerous to have this."

"Riley may have been killed for it?" Vic said.

"I thought it was suicide," Stone said.

"I'm pretty sure that's just the cover story," Vic said. "They're really dragging their feet downtown, buying time. It's a big case"

"Either way, Vic, this is a hot potato," Stone said, poking a long boney forefinger at the thumb drive lying on the picnic table.

"How can you be so sure?" Vic said, knowing Stone might be right, turning over in his mind the cops' slow walk on the medical examiner's report, the break-in and search after he and Nelson had been inside Riley's house, and the growing realization that he was not just chasing a story. Vic possessed the very thing the killer was chasing, *Sundial.*

18

"The document, the *Sundial* paper, has the algorithm in it, or at least a preliminary run at a new encryption system," Stone said. "We took a test document, the U.S. Constitution, encrypted it using the system in the paper, and came up with something that we can't break into. We've been at it for a week."

"A week doesn't sound like much," Vic said. "Besides, don't super computers crack these things routinely?" He was guessing wildly.

"Vic, with the internet we have a super computer," Stone said. "Thousands of machines linked together."

"A hacker's network?" Vic said.

"Sure, you could call it that," Stone said. "Look, when I gave two guys and a gal the encrypted paper, Riley's public keys, and the prime numbers from the two chips, they busted out the decrypted file in about five hours. I used the algorithm in the paper to encrypt the test document and then turned it over to the entire network to hack open. That's about twenty-five hundred people and a lot more computers."

"So twenty-five hundred people know about this now?" Vic said.

"No, just the first three," Stone said.

"The two guys and the gal," Vic said. Stone nodded.

"I told the others I was just testing something out and asked them to crack it," Stone said. "The winner gets five hundred bucks. I also said the stuff might just be gibberish, but I want to see a crack."

"They still went for it?" Vic said.

"Hackers love a challenge, any challenge," Stone said.

"You think I'm in danger?" Vic said.

Stone did not say anything at first. He wiped his brow with his red engineer's bandana and looked out over the G-gauge model railroad layout. "You might be." He paused again. "No. I'd assume that you were." He nodded his head. "Me too, and—"

"The two guys and the gal," Vic said.

"Yes," Stone said.

"Who else?" Vic said. He already knew one answer. Nelson. Then he thought about the person who searched Riley's house after Nelson and Vic had been there. Whoever it was might be in danger, Vic thought, or Riley's killer.

"This is just software," Vic said, embarrassed the moment he uttered the words, knowing how naive he sounded.

"For starters, every major government on the planet will want this," Stone said, nodding toward the thumb drive. "Look at what WikiLeaks did with the State Department cables. Snowden on the NSA stuff. Transparency's one thing, Vic. Destabilizing parts of the world gets people killed, embarrasses others. *Sundial* prevents all that."

"Keeps stuff secret?" Vic said.

"Yes," Stone said.

"Before," Vic said. "Why did you use the word evil?"

"Well, would you want the United States to have this technology?" Stone said. "Or our enemies?"

"Enemies," Vic said. "Now there's a relative term."

"Enemies," Stone said. "The ones who want to kill us. Also, competitors. Rivals. Even allies. They all want to keep tabs on each other, and especially on us."

"What if everyone has it?" Vic said. "Doesn't that level the playing field? That was Reagan's theory on his Star Wars deal."

"Not really," Stone said. "*Sundial* offers a way to encrypt and decrypt information. It doesn't tell you much about breaking the code."

"You're telling me *Sundial* is the perfect encryption scheme?" Vic said.

"Essentially, yes," Stone said. "I mean, nothing's perfect, theoretically, but it looks like the *Sundial* team figured out how to rapidly change private keys in a way that outpaces the code-breakers. It's kind of bizarre. A bunch of keys are nested so that whoever came up with the first key has to be a player in actually decrypting any message or data."

"But it still all begins with that key, though, the one the initial person has," Vic said. Stone just shook his head.

"This is where it gets really freaky," Stone said. "The *Sundial* paper calls it a Cyborg Key."

"Cyborg?" Vic said. "Like Robo Cop?"

"In a way," Stone said. "A combination of mechanical, or artificial, and biological."

"Biological?" Vic said.

"It could be a DNA sequence, a pattern generated by an iris reader or a finger print reader, I don't know," Stone said, slumping down a bit, the hacker in him looking defeated.

"Like the human genome?" Vic said.

"Something like that," Stone said. "Or, a part of it. Or none of it. Or some other genome. There are millions of them. Let's say it was or all or part of some DNA sequence that was selected as a key. Numbers and letters are somehow connected with a genome sequence."

"All right, let's say," Vic said, not sure what was being said.

"Why does it have to be human?" Stone said. "We've identified a few million different plant and animal species. There could be a hundred million yet to be discovered." Then he just looked out at the foothills to the west, his eyes losing focus. "Or a molecule, a sequence of atoms, a sequence of atoms with one removed. The possibilities are infinite and random."

"Doesn't any key resolve itself down to a number, though?" Vic said. "That number exists somewhere."

"No, that's the beauty of *Sundial*," Stone said.

"What?" Vic said, truly confused.

"You erase the private key as soon as it's used to encrypt," Stone said. "Then through an entirely other mechanism, which includes another series of encryption routines, you come up with this combination of artificial and biological keys using fractals, and the damn thing changes with time or space or both. We think the algorithm is able to calculate backwards in time and space, or both, to find the key and decrypt the data. But everything keeps changing. One second it could be a frog. A second later, a pinworm. Another second later, a human."

"Sounds almost too complex," Vic said.

"Not when it's set up right," Stone said. "That's what the *Sundial* paper explains, how to do it, or at least the rough outlines of how to do it. There was enough there for me to encrypt the Constitution into an unbreakable file, and I just used the rudimentary parts of the theory."

"So, who else might want this?" Vic said.

"Wall Street," Stone said. "Banks. Switzerland. Russia. China. Major corporations. CIA, NSA, DIA, FBI, any power, anywhere."

"The mob?" Vic said.

"Anyone who wants to keep its communications and business secret," Stone said. "Wise guys, drug cartels, para-militaries, Al-Qaeda, Putin, radical forces anywhere, you name it."

"Some of those are evil, some are not," Vic said.

"Given the choice, humans seem always to pick evil," Stone said.

* * *

Vic looked down at the thumb drive, then back up at Stone. "Do you have a copy of *Sundial*, Pax?"

He stiffened. "No, I do not. I told you. I destroyed all my hard drives. It's gone. All of it."

"And I have a copy of *Sundial*, correct?" Vic said.

"Right there," Stone said, nodding toward the thumb drive. "That drive contains everything you gave me."

"What about the hackers?" Vic said.

"All they have is an encrypted copy of the U.S. Constitution with a challenge," Stone said. "I can just say I worked up an encryption tool and screwed it up. There are dozens out there."

"So there's this copy, and maybe the Denver Police Department has a copy," Vic said.

"Yes," Stone said. "And at least two others."

"Who would that be?"

"Well, there's the person who created *Sundial* for Riley," Stone said. "You can assume he has a copy."

"Or she?"

"Or she," Stone said.

"And then?"

"And then, maybe the person who shot Riley in the head," Stone said, deadpan. "Assuming he didn't actually kill himself."

"But the odds are that person, the killer, didn't get *Sundial* since Riley had it uppa his U.S., so to speak—"

"Then he, the killer, still wants it," Stone said.

"Or she," Vic said.

"Or she," Stone said. "Anyway you look at it, you, some people inside the Denver Police Department, and the creator of *Sundial* are in mortal danger."

"Mortal danger," Vic said. "That seems a bit melodramatic."

"Not when you consider that *Sundial* might be the most significant advancement in encryption technology since Cleopatra first sent that runner out with an encoded message five thousand years ago," Stone said as he tipped his engineer's cap.

19

After playing the Elvis CDs three or four times, his interest in them waned. Some "king," he thought. Reading the titles, listening to the lyrics, nothing sent him a message. He tore apart the CD cases, the liner notes inserts, read them several times, looked at the blank backs, and nothing. Nothing. He had read the autobiography twice. It was boring. The chapters on the electronic voting system were useless. There was no reference to ciphering or encryption, just a mention that voters liked to use touch screen voting machines. It cut off two years earlier anyway.

He had hoped the material in the safe would have been more helpful, more valuable. Did he miss a clue buried within it? Or was there no clue at all? Was it just too easy to get to the safe contents? Was that last meeting, when Riley casually asked if the stuff he planned to put in there looked innocent enough to fool an intruder? "It's all here," he recalled Riley telling him. "Hidden in plain sight." Had Riley conned him, setting up the safe as a ruse? As he massaged his thick calf, the one on the right, the one that always gave him trouble, a shadow of fear netted him. His customer would not be happy, and there went the sale down the drain. Riley was now dead, and he was no closer to finding *Sundial*

He knew he had to act more decisively with Bengston.

20

"I know a guy," Miss Raglin said.

"Who doesn't?" Vic said.

"No. This guy is a retired courier."

"What did he curry? Horses?"

She just looked at Vic and shook her head. "Vic, you come to me, hat in hand, jabbering about MIT, Stanford, codes, encryption, keys, you name it. You need to learn about couriers and keys, and—"

"You know a guy," Vic said.

"Vic, I was going to say, I am trying to help you," Miss Raglin said.

"And fill the tank on your plane," Vic said.

"And fill the tank in my plane," she echoed. "Can you be serious for a moment. I know deep inside that you are a serious man."

Vic waved his hand down across his face, wiping the smile to a serious look.

Raglin shook her head again. "Like I said, I know a guy."

"A courier," Vic said. "Of what?"

"Computer stuff," Raglin said. "You'll find out."

"For?"

"Banking. Intra-company messages. Inter-company messages. Government messages. Anything sensitive."

"He's a programmer?" Vic said.

"No," Miss Raglin said. "I told you. He was a courier. A very smart guy, but he made his living as a courier. Vic did the dog stare. "Ask him how he lost his job."

"This sounds, well, I hate to say it, cryptic," Vic said.

"It's meant to be," she said, turning slowing back to her computer screen. Late afternoon darkness began to seep into the crack of a window the library allowed her to have. "I can't do all your work for you."

"And to unravel this cryptic message?" Vic said. "The cost will be?"

"One tank for the Piper Cub," said Miss Raglin, her back to him, she moving on to some other research task. "I'm not greedy."

21

Not many metro areas boast of a Flying Saucer RV Park.

Denver is the exception. Still awaiting visitors from some other galaxy, the park hugs the south bank of West Hampden Avenue, the east-west thoroughfare that cuts through Denver's southern suburbs, in this case, Englewood. Despite the name, the RV park residents were all from the third rock from the sun. Vic had driven past it hundreds of times, either heading to a southwest suburb or the mountains. His image of the place consisted of a cheesy sign with a pair of aliens dancing beneath a UFO, a sheet metal saucer in a small playground, lots of trees, and row upon row of RVs. Laborers, retirees, houseless wanderers, and travelers anchor in the dirt and stay indefinitely for five hundred bucks a month.

So, for the first time in all his decades in Colorado, Vic left Hampden and entered the Flying Saucer RV Park, which was the home, according to Miss Raglin, to one Albert Haggerty, a retired courier. "A courier of what?" Vic muttered to himself as he entered the office to find out where Haggerty's flying saucer was docked.

"Right down that main road there," the middle-aged black-haired woman said, pointing out the front window of the main office. "Turn left just past the UFO. You see it down there right by that little blue shed. You turn left, then Al is down three, no four, stalls on the left. He's number four-oh-four. You got that?"

"I do," Vic said, wondering where she was from. She pronounced "right" as though it were spelled "rot." With the office door open, Vic hesitated and turned back toward the woman. "Okay if I leave my car here? I'll walk down to Al's."

"Sure you can," she said. "It'll be all rot."

* * *

A nicely maintained mid-seventies light blue Ford F250 pickup was parked next to a rather new travel trailer, about a thirty-footer, screaming the name "Denali" on the its leading edge. A slide-out expanded the interior space. Vic walked past the truck and a small picnic table flanked by a compact Weber "Q" grill and a small Rubbermaid outdoor cabinet. He placed his left foot on the first of two steps, rubbed his sore left knee, then rapped on the door.

"Don't want any," came an old, but determined voice from inside. "Wait! That you Janey?"

"Mr. Haggerty," Vic shouted. "I'm not selling. Frances Raglin sent me over. I need to speak with you."

"Frances? From the library?"

"Yes. I'm a friend of hers."

Rattling at the latch. Then the door opened inward. A stooped main with a full head of hair, glasses straddling a pointed nose, peered out. Vic heard a cane bump one of the cabinets inside the RV door. The screen was still closed.

"Ask me," Haggerty said.

"Ask you what?" Vic said.

"Are you sure you know Frances?"

"Yes, that's why I'm here."

"Then ask me."

Vic racked his brain, convinced his short-term memory was going. Then it hit him.

"I want to know how you lost your job," Vic said.

The screen door opened.

"Then come on in," the old man said. With the aid of the cane, he awkwardly turned his back on Vic and returned to one end of the sofa that occupied part of the slide-out section of his compact living room. Vic stepped into the RV. Haggerty grabbed a remote control, pointed it at a television mounted up on the wall and the screen went silent. "Sit down. Sit down. Make yourself comfy. Grab a cup of coffee. Just made it. Mine's okay. Just get what you need. Cups are above the sink on the right."

Vic began to make himself at home, or at least as best he could in someone else's home. He found a Dell Computer cup, one of many amidst a tastefully mismatched set of mugs loaded with all sorts of company logos, filled it with coffee from a built-in drip system, and slid into one of the bench seats of the dinette facing Al Haggerty, retired courier.

"You gonna record this or just scribble notes?" Haggerty said.

"Record if you don't mind," Vic said, pulling his small silver digital recorder from his shirt pocket.

"Won't record it," Haggerty said. "But you can take notes."

Vic slipped the recorder back into his pocket and pressed the record button. "All right, I'll take notes."

"Put it on the table, open her up, and take out the batteries."

"Fine," Vic said, spreading out the open recorder and two triple-A batteries on the table.

"I'm going to tell you how I lost my job," the old man said, and he hoisted his coffee cup as though he were hefting a tankard fill of mead to toast King Arthur at the Round Table.

* * *

"Your dad in the war?" Haggerty said.

"World War Two?" Vic said.

"Yup."

"He was," Vic said. "A photographer. Almost shipped out to the south seas when the war ended."

"Well I was in England," Haggerty said.

"So was my uncle."

"Codes?"

"No. He flew bombers."

"Seventeens?"

"Yeah."

"Poor bastards," Haggerty said. "Sitting ducks."

"He flew twenty nine missions," Vic said.

"Into Germany?"

"Yeah."

"Then he was a lucky bastard, wasn't he?"

He sure was, Vic thought, and he had a certificate to prove it, membership in the Lucky Bastard's Club after twenty-five missions. Vic teared up, then nodded.

"It was a good thing he did," the old man said. "What'd you say your name was?"

"Bengston. Vic Bengston."

"Vic. It was a very good thing your uncle did. Your dad too. Would have gone over if the war dragged on. Two lucky bastards in your family."

Who was this guy? Vic thought. "What did you do? In England."

"Bletchley."

"Where they broke the codes?" Vic said.

"You bet," he said, all grins, and he hoisted his cup again. Vic returned the toast.

"Where Turing broke the Enigma machine," Haggerty said.

"With his computer," Vic said.

"His electromechanical computer," Haggerty said. "Brilliant guy, but I built the other one."

"Computer?" Vic said.

"The very first electronic computer," he said.

"What?" Vic said. Had the UFOs landed? Vic thought. Had Raglin tossed him a red herring?

"I helped," Haggerty said. "A lot."

* * *

"I thought the first computer was built here in the U.S.," Vic said. "UNIVAC?"

"Close," the old man said. "No, UNIVAC was one of the first. Biggest name though. First real one, well the one that got credit for being the first, was ENIAC. Electronic Numerical Integrator And Computer. That's how they got the A in there, with the And."

"UNIVAC stands for what?" Vic said.

"Universal Automatic Computer," Haggerty said, then sipped from his mug. "They used Automatic to get their A. Basically the same folks built both, at least the main brains were the same. ENIAC people split up. Beef over patents. One went with ENIAC, the other with UNIVAC. But ENIAC was first, or so they thought."

"So ENIAC or UNIVAC were not the first computers?" Vic said.

"Nope. I worked on the first one. With Tommy Flowers. At Bletchley. He was a genius, Flowers." The old man expelled a raspy old cough. Vic recalled a farmer he knew who coughed like that, after years of smoking and eating dust. "To Colossus," Haggerty said and he raised his IBM coffee mug in another toast. Vic followed suit.

"Colossus?" Vic said.

"That was the first one," Haggerty said. "ENIAC, UNIVAC. Doesn't matter. We did it three years earlier. To win the war. To break the German codes. Oh, the krauts had their Z3 for making and breaking codes but that monster used relays, electromechanical. No, ours was all electronic. Used tubes, or valves they called them over there, like water valves, turning flows of electrons on and off. They were tubes. Electronic tubes. Thousands of them. Tommy, well, I told you he was a genius, invented the thing to break codes. Against orders too. The High Command wanted to stick with the mechanical calculators they were using. Tommy went off and built Colossus anyway. After the war, they made him destroy all the machines we built, and the plans."

Haggerty locked his eyes on Vic's. The old man was just warming up.

"Colossus was a weapon," Haggerty said. "It could break codes faster than anything anyone had. Military controlled it. Worked with the universities, but they controlled it. Like the bomb, the Manhattan Project. Colossus could win a war. We didn't want that in the hands of those damn Reds."

"They got it anyway," Vic said. "Didn't they?"

"Everyone's got them now," the old man said. "Back then, we knew what was coming after the war. Another war. This time with the Soviets. When the shooting war ended, there was such a mad scramble, you wouldn't believe it. For territory, for scientists, for rockets, for bombs."

"And for computers," Vic said.

Haggerty raised his now empty coffee mug in another toast, and Vic clinked it with his cup.

* * *

"What did you do on the Colossus project?" Vic said.

Haggerty wagged his empty mug at Vic, who grabbed it and stepped over to the coffee maker for a refill. Vic handed it to the old man and sat back down.

"I built them," Haggerty said. "Or, I really trained and ran the team that built them. Oh I spent long days and nights soldering circuits together. This thing filled a big room mind you. It was a lot of work. And we built more than one. Built ten of them."

"Flowers," Vic said. "This Tommy Flowers was your boss?"

"You bet. Good man. He had the brains. The designer. Laid it all out on paper. Oh, I knew the math too. I started with the math, working on breaking the codes with the mechanical calculators. That's how I got in there. At Bletchley. Married an English gal after the war. Flora. She was a real beauty." He looked down into his mug. "She died a long time ago. Been a bachelor ever since." He looked back up, tears glistening his ancient eyes. "Could never replace Flora. We were so— oh, I don't know. The way we met during the war. The bonds were so tight back then."

Vic nodded. He had sensed those bonds, those feelings with his father and uncle. There was something about those war years, probably any war that solidified beliefs inside humans beyond anything most of us experience in our day to day lives.

"So, you're a computer nerd," Vic said, wanting to break through the nostalgia and get back on track.

"A ninety-three year old computer nerd," Haggerty said with a smile. "I can still program them, build them, and run them. Got a couple back there in my bedroom. Internet. Whole nine yards."

"So how did you lose your job?" Vic said, wondering what job they were going to talk about.

"Okay, young fella, jump ahead a few years, into the Fifties, and the coming computer age," Haggerty said. "I started engineering these things. Went with the UNIVAC crowd. Became Remington Rand, Unisys today. Enjoyed that for a while, then, uh, well, Flora passed away. I got restless."

Vic made notes, not sure where this was going.

"I took a little vacation," the old man said. "Back to England, where we met, Flora and I. Even drove out to Bletchley. She didn't work there. I met her in town, off hours. She was a seamstress, patching up uniforms back them, but she made beautiful dresses. Made her own wedding dress. God, it was beautiful." He stared off, losing focus, out the window.

"Did you leave Remington Rand?" Vic said.

"Yup," Haggerty said, taking a sip. "But not right away. I felt rootless, so I decided to take advantage of that and start a business around it. I was going to be my own boss, my own employer. That was going to be my job."

"Courier?" Vic said.

"Courier," Haggerty said.

* * *

"When I took that trip back over the England, first time since the war, I happened to bump into a local banker in a pub," Haggerty said. "We got to talking. He flew fighters in the RAF. I told him I held down a desk job in England. Boring. Filed papers. We all signed agreements not to talk about anything at Bletchley."

"Anything?" Vic said.

"Not one thing," he said. "Like I told you. Colossus. Bletchley. Colossus was like the bomb. Bletchley too. They were weapons of war. Zipped lips." He motioned with his right hand, did the imaginary zipper across the mouth thing. "But the banker liked to talk about his business, and I could talk about my work, or most of it, with Remington Rand."

"So you talked business, computers and banking," Vic said.

"For a couple of hours," Haggerty said. "More than a few pints too."

"And?"

"And, this banker said his firm was automating more, using wire transfers, special systems, phone lines, radio transmissions, teletypes, sending sensitive financial and business information around the country and now, because his bank was expanding, across national boundaries, even back to the states," the old man said. "That's when the light bulb went on." He glanced up at the ceiling of his RV.

Vic made more notes, nursed his cold coffee. Then Haggerty uttered something that resonated with *Sundial*.

"Encryption keys," Haggerty said.

* * *

"That banker was talking about encryption and decryption," Haggerty said. "Bankers needed to encode their transactions, their messages, their analyses of business documents, deals, you name it. To do business they had to send these messages all over the place and they had to be secret. Other companies, other industries had to do the same thing. So did governments."

"I certainly understand that," Vic said. "I spend most of my time trying to unlock secrets."

"Yeah, but you have to pull them out of people, like me," the old man said. "You don't have to break codes to get the information. Now, breaking a code is one thing. That takes a lot of time."

"And a Colossus," Vic said.

"Yes and may she rest in peace," Haggerty said, raising his cup. Vic did the same. Then the old man said, "No matter how you did it, by breaking the code or by design, to decrypt any coded message, you needed a key, that one thing that will lock and unlock the words and numbers so whoever is on the other side, business associate, ally, even the enemy, can read the message. I have to pee."

Vic laughed and said, "I need more coffee."

* * *

As Haggerty ambled back to his spot on the couch, Vic struggled to frame a question based on what he knew so far. He just blurted it out. "So you have something to do with public and private keys?"

Haggerty laughed. "No. No. That came much later."

"Then I'm still not quite following you, Al," Vic said.

"Okay," Haggerty said. "Imagine this. You write a message to me and put it into a box, then padlock it so no one can intercept the contents. The key, you slip into your pocket. Then you send me the box. Now I've got my message, but I can't read it."

"Because it is inside the box which is locked and I have the key," Vic said.

"Precisely," the old man said. "You need to hire some trustworthy soul to take that key from your pocket and deliver it to me so I can unlock the box and read the message."

"And that's what you did," Vic said.

The old man nodded. "Acme Special Services."

"You couriered encryption keys," Vic said.

"All over the world, for hundreds of customers," Haggerty said.

"Acme," Vic said, thinking about Wylie Coyote's source for explosives and other gadgets employed in vain against the undefeatable Road Runner.

"Wanted something that didn't stick out all that much," the old man said. "I had about two dozen couriers working for me. Men and women. We traveled all over the world to deliver encryption keys for banks, companies, and governments."

"Were they written down?" Vic said. "Little black books?"

"Naw. We developed sealed envelopes, all sorts of things, stuff we picked up from the war, so if they were not opened correctly, they would self-destruct. Used invisible ink a few times. My couriers traveled on regular airlines, in cars, buses, trains, taxis. Briefcases handcuffed to their wrists."

"Anyone ever get hurt?" Vic said.

"You know, no one ever did," Haggerty said. "That surprised me. They were trained in self-defense, though."

"So how did you lose your job?" Vic said.

"Some smarty-pants named Diffie did me in," the old man said.

"How?"

"Well, no one could figure out how to securely distribute encryption keys around the world other than with couriers," Haggerty said. "I mean no one. None of the old Bletchley crowd, Tommy's team, Remington Rand, ENIAC, UNIVAC, no one. Everyone, even the best mathematicians, thought it was impossible to devise a key that could be transmitted without someone intercepting it."

"Until Diffie," Vic said.

"Right, but it wasn't easy for him either since no one bought into this obsession of his. He was convinced there was a mathematical way to do it," Haggerty said. "He found a couple other dreamers, university types. They figured it out. They could send keys by wire, or phone, or radio. Now the internet. Anyway, that finished me off, but I got a lot of miles in before the end."

"Was it a good business for you?" Vic said, wondering how much he made for himself considering his RV park living style.

"I gave nearly all of it away, a few million bucks," Haggerty said. "For cancer research."

"Is that what your wife died from?" Vic said.

Haggerty nodded. His eyes glistened. He looked out the window again and said, "I would have traded it all for just one more day with my Flora."

* * *

Passing on the offer for a fresh pot of coffee, Vic gave Haggerty his card and thanked him for his time. He walked back to the office, told the RV park manager that Al was "all rot," fired up the Jeep, and headed back downtown to the paper. Colorado Public Radio's FM classical station came up playing the Winter movement of the Four Seasons. He thought about Haggerty, now in the Autumn of his life, maybe the dead of Winter in the not to distance future. He lived one hell of a Spring and Summer, Vic thought. Bletchley. Colossus. Codes. Encryption. Keys. Couriers. All necessary to keep the world's secrets.

And *Sundial* trumped them all.

22

Vic was not sure he should have brought his father along with him on the drive. Dad was not feeling all that well. He had just gotten over a tough bout with the flu and seemed to be having more and more trouble breathing. Still, his small oxygen tank puffed away and he seemed delighted to get out of the house and into the countryside. They had thrown the cameras in the back. Dad had loaded a fresh roll of Kodacolor print film into his Nikon, an 8008 single lens reflex with a Nikkor zoom lens.

"I thought I might find a nice landscape for your mother to paint," Dad said. "She wanted me to keep an eye peeled."

Vic had the same camera, except his had a data back on it that he could use to store information about each shot he took. He never used the feature, but it looked cool. Both cameras were bought used from a dealer in Atlanta, one vouched for by Bob Scott, a former AP photographer Vic worked with over the years. Most of his and his father's gear came from the Atlanta outfit, which did a good job of grading used photographic equipment and always offered a fourteen day no questions asked return policy. Vic brought his Nikon digital single lens reflex camera with him, but it was locked in the trunk.

Dad rested his film camera on the floor between his legs. He grew up in the photography and photo finishing business, an enterprise started by his father, Vic's grandfather, in the northern suburbs of Chicago. Vic doubted whether Dad would ever shoot a digital image. Having studied once with Ansel Adams, Dad was a diehard film man. Vic's father learned photography at an early age, making good money at it through high school. World War Two dominated those years.

Busting to enlist, to follow his older brother into the U. S. Army Air Corps, Dad signed up right after graduation in 1944. Once the Army spotted his photography background, they immediately ran him through intense aerial photography training. As he was about to ship out to the Pacific Theater, the United States leveled Hiroshima and Nagasaki with Little Boy and Fat Boy. The war ended. With tens of thousands of other GIs, Dad was turned loose overnight.

Although the world's most devastating military war had ended, another one raged on fiercely, eventually paralyzing hundreds of thousands and killing many. All feared polio, which had crippled but not stopped the most significant leader of the Twentieth Century, Franklin Roosevelt. The polio virus roared loudly in Crystal Lake, Illinois, cheating some of the small Midwestern town's residents of their ability to walk and even breathe. Vic's grandfather, proud, tall, of Norwegian descent, who had survived German mustard gas attacks in the muddy trenches of France during World War One, found himself trapped in this horrible web of disease only a few years after World War Two.

Polio launched its assault on his grandfather in 1949. Endless battles involving whirlpool therapy in giant swirling baths at Elgin's Sherman Hospital where Vic was born and sweaty curse-filled struggles to walk once again with the use of painful leather and steel braces, wooden crutches, and handrails ended in defeat and permanent confinement to a wheelchair. Vic's memory of his grandfather was not the war against the invisible enemy, but rather its aftermath, with Grandpa in his heavy leather, stainless steel, and rubber wheelchair. To young Vic it was a toy that he would play in when Grandpa was in bed. To his grandfather it was a persistent symbol of defeat for the man who had started the family photography business. Six decades later, the subtle metallic clicks of Grandpa's wheelchair brake engaging and disengaging still ricocheted inside Vic's memory banks. Images lived there as well, scenes of his Dad and uncles running Grandpa up and down the wooden ramps they had built to get him in and out of the house, his sons loading him into a car to go off to dinner or an evening of canasta or bridge, all of this simply routine parts of day to day family life. Vic never viewed his grandfather as handicapped. Grandpa merely lived in that wheelchair and the big bed moved downstairs into the dining room for practical reasons.

Yet as Vic viewed this medical disaster as a normal part of his childhood, it profoundly affected his father's life. Grandpa's paralysis laid the groundwork for Dad's future, forcing him to choose between heading off to college or remaining in his hometown to take on the daily operation of the family enterprise. His younger brother was just starting high school, and his older brother extended his heroic wartime B-17 pilot career into the cold war era with the new Air Force and the Strategic Air Command, piloting B-47 Stratojets. Dad triggered his GI bill so he and Mom, married right after he mustered out of the service, could build their post-war starter house at the edge of town for ten thousand bucks, raise a family, and run the photo business.

When his folks moved to Denver for their retirement years, Vic took possession of his father's eighth grade autobiography, something that many public school students in Illinois were required to write. The small book, handcrafted by his father toward the beginning of World War Two, revealed that the man who raised him had thought seriously about becoming a math teacher, but also held an abiding love for photography. It was a good thing too, because thanks to polio, the photo business became his life.

"There are some interesting bluffs and rock formations just west of Loveland, Dad," Vic said. "A lot like the hogback that runs across the Front Range down near Denver. Maybe looking east with the sun low behind you. It might give you some decent light. Bring out the red in the rocks. One of the ridges is pretty weird. The Devil's Spine. You'll see why they call it that."

The two had gotten a late start. Vic spent the morning prepping a new planting bed in his garden. He turned a pickup truck's worth of compost, peat moss, and sand into three new four by four foot raised beds. It was backbreaking work, but his buddy Nelson convinced him to do it by hand, to keep working the body as much as possible now that he was past sixty. Gardening, at least the heavy work of soil preparation, provided just such an opportunity. Nelson was walking proof of the theory. A rock climber, Nelson kept himself trim and fit. Even though he had a few years on Vic, he could easily pass for a much younger man.

Vic picked up Dad just after noon. They drove north through the flat farmland east of the mountains on U.S. 85, then headed west for a pleasant ride toward Loveland, backdropped by the subtle blacks, greens, and browns of the foothills. Even higher, the regal Continental Divide lorded over this hilly kingdom. Still crowned in white from spring, the high country patiently awaited the warmer days and nights that triggered the gradual conversion of frozen water to liquid, saturating the ground, charging aquifers and springs, filling the brooks and streams and then the rivers and reservoirs and diversion canals and tunnels, all to slake the thirst of humans down below so they could water their lawns, flush their toilets, give life to their gardens and their bodies, wash their cars, take their morning showers, cook pasta or beans, and water their crops and livestock.

Just before they crossed I-25, Vic and his father stopped at Johnson Corners, a much visited stopover for travelers and truckers crisscrossing the country. They ate club sandwiches and drank coffee, talked about the Broncos and the Bears, the Rockies and the Cubs. Vic filled his gas-guzzling Jeep Cherokee Grand Laredo. The two men ordered coffees to go after lunch and drove toward Loveland, a few miles away. South of town, Vic caught County Road 18 which turned into 14th Street as they crossed the city limits and then headed north onto U.S. 287, the main northbound drag through the heart of old Loveland.

"Have you ever seen the old Loveland Grain and Feed?" Vic said.

"Only your photographs of it," Dad said.

"It's over at Third and Railroad Street," Vic said.

"Drive by," Dad said.

Vic navigated a few blocks over to the crumbling building that once served the vibrant agricultural community that surrounded Loveland, rapidly becoming another bedroom community for Denver to the south and Fort Collins to the north. The main structure stood about four or five stories and stretched at least a half a block along an old rail spur. The mishmash of buildings, additions, sheds, silos, and work yards teamed up years ago to store, mill, and redistribute the grains produced by the area farmers. Half brick, half wood, old rusty metal roof, covered with peeling white paint, the ancient Loveland Feed and

Grain escaped the wrecking ball when preservationists, local government, and Loveland's burgeoning art community formed an alliance to save the agricultural compound and reshape it into a workspace for artists and community activities.

"It needs a lot of work," Dad said.

"I think they're still raising money," Vic said.

"They better hurry up," he said, aiming his Nikon at one of the rooflines.

They circled the rundown complex at least twice. Dad found a good angle with light coming in from the west, and he stepped out of the car to take a few shots. He walked slowly, conserving energy in his oxygen deprived body.

"Your Mom might like to make a painting of this," Dad said, snapping a few frames, bracketing the light. He eased himself back into the car, set his camera down on the floor, and reinserted the cannula into his nose. The oxygen tank let out a soft gasp. "Okay."

Vic drove a few more blocks north to U.S. 34, Eisenhower Boulevard, and drove west along the southern shore of Lake Loveland, a small body of water surrounded by nice homes and small boat docks. Just west of town, a hogback leapt up from the plains. Once the shore of an ancient sea, the geologic structure heaved skyward when the Rocky Mountains were formed. Rivers and streams cut their way through the formation, carving out routes for migrating animals and, eventually, wandering humans.

Vic took one of those migration routes, swinging north onto County Road 29, Waterdale Drive according to the road sign. Waterdale ran along the west side of small creek that had formed a narrow valley running north and south behind the hogback. About a mile up from U.S. 34, Vic pulled the car off to the side of the road and pointed east.

"Check that view out," Vic said. A broad green field of spring grass spread out before them and stretched into the yellowing reflection of the afternoon sun. On the far side of the field, the water-etched bluffs of the hogback soared up a few hundred feet setting the yellow and red and brown rock off against a brilliant Colorado blue sky. The scene propelled his father, camera in one hand and pulling the oxygen tube from his nose with the other, out of the car and onto the gravel shoulder. Dad held the Nikon to his eye like Vic had seen him do with countless cameras, including the old Speed Graphic, thousands of times in the past. The old man framed the scene in the tiny viewfinder and fired three times, one shot with the light meter, then bracketing, one stop down, one stop up. He zoomed the lens back to a wide angle and fired off three more. The movements, the actions, the bracketing, the firing of the shots, everything flowed naturally to the man who took to photography like a natural, and who read mysteries and books on mathematics for recreation. It would be a gem, expertly framed, impeccably balanced, with enough light range to produce a perfect photograph. Vic just stood outside his car door on the driver's side and watched his aging father do what he loved to do most.

As they got back into the Jeep, Dad handed the camera to Vic who put it on the back seat. His father sat back down, adjusted the oxygen tube and belted himself in. They drove further up Waterdale Drive, which curved tightly past a handful of foothills homes, crossed the creek and then twisted back toward the north.

A few miles up the road, as the valley between them and the rising hills began to widen into a small pleasant looking pasture, Vic spotted what looked like relatively new construction, a number of low buildings, with shiny green metal roofs and heavily landscaped surroundings. Two empty horse corrals, also looking very new, snugged themselves tightly up against the ridge to the west. It looked like a modern ranch, but then again it did not look like a modern ranch. It had a hint of conference center to it, with a broad asphalt parking lot and smaller buildings that looked almost like dormitories flanking the larger structures.

When Vic saw the massive vertical slab of Colorado sandstone signaling the entrance to the ranch-like complex, he slammed on the brakes, startling his father, who uttered, "What the?"

"The sign," Vic said.

Chiseled deep into the rock were the words "Sundial Ranch."

* * *

"This looks interesting," Vic said. He turned left onto the gravel road. It took them through a tight S-curve, over a narrow bridge, and delivered the two men back to a tight tree-lined path on the west side of the creek.

"What is this place?" Dad said. He adjusted his oxygen tube.

"I'm not sure," Vic said. "But I think it might be owned by David Riley."

"The dead computer fella?" Dad said.

"Yeah," Vic said.

"Wouldn't that make this private property?" Dad said.

"It would," Vic said.

"Hand me my camera, would you?" Dad said.

"Sure," said Vic as he reached into the back seat and grabbed the Nikon. He gave it to Dad, who ripped off two quick shots of the stone Sundial Ranch sign.

As it emerged from the old cottonwood trees, the road straightened out and ran for about a hundred yards before it hit the asphalt parking area. Vic rolled slowly toward three buildings, all sort of an expensive looking neo agricultural style with brick, stone and heavy timber exteriors, broad gently sloping green metal roofs hinting of Frank Lloyd Wright's prairie style homes, but not really. These buildings were not homes, Vic concluded. The trio of structures stood in formation around the wide tarmac that was big enough to land a helicopter or park about thirty cars. Only there were no cars.

"The place looks deserted," Dad said.

Vic pulled up to a central circular patio that connected to stone walkways for each of the three buildings. Dad's glasses rested on his forehead. He brought the camera back up to his right eye, aimed at the heavy wooden door on the central building, and snapped a shot.

"I'm going to take a look," Vic said.

"I'll wait here," Dad said. Then he watched his gray-haired son step out of the Jeep and walk up to the front door of the building on the right. From behind, Vic reminded him of his younger brother, stocky, big shoulders, thick muscular legs, ten years younger than him, a decade older than Vic, almost like Vic's older brother, but really his uncle. He liked to remember his brother as he was, the bright, funny, smart, sandy-haired grinning jester, not the bloated hulk created by kidney failure in the waning days of a life surrendering to a metastasizing lung cancer. The view of Vic blurred with tears. He pulled his red bandana handkerchief from his pocket and wiped his eyes. Then he put the Nikon back up to his face, pressed halfway down on the shutter release to focus the lens on his son, now peering into a window next to the locked front door and snapped a frame.

Vic looked into what was once a very nice work place with massive wood beams that open all the way up to a shallow vaulted ceiling, stone floors, desks, cubicles and office equipment, abandoned, unused and gathering up a thin layer of pervasive and annoying Colorado dust. Vic thought of the coal dust and soot that built up on their window sills when he and Erin lived in cheap Chicago apartments while she worked and he finished up at DePaul University. The coal dust was worse, he recalled.

Looking back toward the car, Vic could see is father taking pictures. It looked like he was shooting all the buildings. Vic waved and then jogged over to the building on the other side of the tarmac. He found the same thing, expensive digs, evidence of work once happening there, and abandonment. When he saw the flashing red and blue lights coming down the road toward him, he walked quickly back to his car. The driver's window was open.

"Put the camera down between your legs, Pop," Vic said. Dad lowered the Nikon quickly.

Vic pulled out his wallet and removed his press card and his driver's license. He was glad to have something that identified him as someone other than a burglar. Holding one card in each hand, keeping both hands clearly visible, Vic walked slowly toward the approaching car, which was a white late model SUV. The sheriff, he thought.

Only it was not the sheriff.

*　*　*

The SUV stopped about twenty-five feet from Vic and through a PA system, a vaguely familiar voice said, "That's far enough, son." Vic halted. "Just what you doin' out here?"

"I'm a reporter," Vic shouted, waving his press card. "*Denver Times.*"

"All right," said the voice. "I assume you have an ID with you."

Vic waved both cards this time.

"Just stay right there for now, son" the voice said. The driver's side door opened and out stepped a younger version of Wilford Brimley, reflective aviator glasses, a regulation full cowboy mustache, thinning hair up top, some sort of a uniform shirt sheathed with a tan western vest. Below the door, Vic could see cowboy boots. Wilford reached back into the SUV, pulled out a Stetson and positioned it square on his head. The man remained shielded behind the open door. Vic saw his right elbow up, his right hand probably resting on the butt of a holstered sidearm.

"Do you have a weapon?" Wilford said.

"No," Vic said. There went the old heart. Pounding. What had he gotten his father into?

"All right then," the man said. "Listen up. This is a federal reservation. But seeing as how the designation just came down this morning, we don't have any signs up as yet indicating such."

This guy was right out of central casting, Vic thought. But he had a gun. It wasn't a prop either. Suddenly Vic felt awkwardly exposed, unaccustomed to confrontational scenes like this. He knew that if he had had a gun with him, the present situation could become much worse, yet he reconsidered Nelson's offer to teach him a few basic self-defense skills, which, for Nelson, always included a handgun of some sort.

"I'm just out on a drive with my dad," Vic said. "I thought I knew who lived here."

"As you can plainly see, son, this ain't no residence," Wilford said.

"Honest mistake," Vic said. "Any chance we can end this little standoff?"

"You bet we can," the man said. "Now here's just what we're gonna do. First, you're gonna stay put. You stand right where you are until I say otherwise. Understand?"

"I do," Vic said.

"Fine. Second, I'm gonna step out from behind this door and I will have my weapon out of its holster and trained on you. Do you understand that?"

"Yes," Vic said. "This isn't necessary."

"Oh, it is," the man said. "It is. Now, number three, when I tell you, you're gonna walk slowly toward my car here. And your hands are going to be out to your side, where I can see them. I want you to keep your IDs in your hand. Then you're going to lay those cards down on the hood of my vehicle here after which you're going to put both your hands on the hood, palms down. Is that clear?"

"Right," Vic said. "Just tell me when to move."

"Oh, I will," Wilford said. "I will."

The man stepped further to his left, out beyond the SUV door. Both hands gripped a handgun shoulder high, sights trained on Vic, who just knew the weapon had to be aimed right at his hammering heart.

"Okay, reporter, walk up to the car, slowly," the man said.

Vic walked forward gradually. He squinted to see what was on the SUV door. The logo was just two large red letters, "RS," and below it, the words, "Ralston Security." A rent-a-cop, Vic thought. Then he looked up at the gun and Wilford.

"ID's first," the man said. "Just lay them up there on the hood where I can see them."

Vic laid the driver's license, a *Denver Times* ID card, and his press card high on the hood, just below the windshield wipers.

"How about my Denver Public Library card?" Vic said.

"We can dispense with the humor right now, son," the owner of the gun said. "Now your hands, palms down, spread out. And don't move."

Vic assumed his father was watching all this. It worried him, because of his dad's fragile state of health.

"Okay, who's that in the car?" Wilford said.

"My Dad," Vic said. "For Christ's sake, he's seventy-eight and he's on oxygen." He wanted to say more, but he held his tongue.

"Anybody else with ya, son?" the man said.

"No," Vic said. "You know, the 'son' thing is getting old. I don't think I could be your father, but give me another ten years and who knows."

"Well, son, we don't need no smart-ass comments at such a

contentious time like this, so just keep it under wraps, okay?"

"Sure," Vic said. His heart let him know how he really felt.

"Is this some sort of joke?" Wilford asked.

"What do you mean?"

"This," he said, holding up Vic's press card.

"So it's a little old," Vic said. "There are no expiration dates on them."

"You're kidding me? Is this you or your son?"

"Me," Vic said. It was Vic's press card issued by the Colorado Press Association back when he first worked for the now defunct *Rocky Mountain Sun*. Vic's hair was all dark and he was in full beard. "A few years ago."

"More like a few decades ago," the security guy said. "No matter, son, these other two cards'll do the trick."

"You can call my editor," Vic said. "His name is—"

"That's all right, son. I already know who you are. Radioed in your plates before I came down."

That was a quick turn-around, Vic thought, then wondered if it was a little too quick.

"Maybe you ought to just stick to the paved roads next time you take your ailing father out for a little ride, son," Wilford said. That was it. Vic had had it.

"Where the hell do you think we are?" Vic said. "Alabama?"

"Oh, so there still is a little fight in you," the man said.

"We turned off a public road into an open driveway," Vic said. "There were no signs indicating that this was a, what did you say it was? A federal reservation? What the hell is that and who the hell are you?"

"Relax there, fella," Wilford said. "I'm just doin' a job and that job is detain' you at the moment."

"Don't screw with my dad," Vic said.

"Nobody's gonna screw with anyone," the man said. "Just do as I say so we can all get back to a point in time when no one's in danger."

"You mean get to a time, in the future," Vic said. "We all were safe a few minutes ago."

"Have it your way, son," the man said.

Vic wasn't sure what this guy was up to, but he knew he had few if any options, other than to play along. Wilford had parked his SUV so he could watch Vic's Jeep while he checked Vic for a weapon.

"Put your left hand behind your back," the man said.

Vic complied. He felt a strong hand grab his wrist. Then with a sudden thump, Wilford snapped Vic's face onto the hood with his forearm.

"Now the other hand," the man said. Vic moved his right hand as best he could. He felt the man fumbling around with nylon handcuff straps. With a feint zipping sound and a shot of pain, Vic's hands were pulled together.

"I'm not going anywhere," Vic said. "Boy."

That brought a second thump to the back of his neck and another sudden collision with the hood. Vic tasted salty blood inside his mouth.

"Just keep kissing that white hood," Wilford said. "Stay right there and don't move. I won't hurt your father."

Vic heard the man walk back toward the Jeep. He strained his neck to try to see his father but he could not see a thing.

"Sir," Vic heard Wilford say. "Would you mind stepping out of your car there for just a minute?"

Vic heard his father say something, but he could not make it out.

"He's hard of hearing," Vic yelled at him.

"You just stay put," Wilford said. "We're gettin' along just fine over here."

After a few minutes, Vic heard the man walking back toward him. He was talking on a radio.

"B-E-N-G-S-T-O-N," he said.

"Okay, give me five," the tinny female radio voice said.

"Make it two," Wilford said.

"Is my dad okay?" Vic said.

"He's fine," the man said. "I told him this was just routine, not to worry."

"Can I get up?" Vic said.

"No you cannot," Wilford said. "I'll let you know when you can."

The radio chirped, "Fourteen."

"Fourteen," the man said.

"I just spoke with Mr. Bengston's boss, a Les Vigil," the radio said. "He's the editor of the *Times*. He said Mr. Bengston is not on any assignment, but vouched for him. He does work for the paper."

"You can also call Frank Driscoll," Vic said. "Chief homicide detective at the Denver Police Department."

"You know Driscoll?" the man said to Vic. "Now I'm impressed." Then to the radio, "Can we clear him?"

"Stand by," the radio said.

"Roger," the man said.

"Fourteen," the radio said.

"Fourteen," the man said.

"He's clear," the radio said.

"Roger," the man said.

Vic felt something snip his hands free.

"Come on up, son," Wilford said. "Rub those wrists a bit. Get the circulation goin' again. Here."

He handed back the ID cards which Vic stuffed into a front pants pocket, then massaged his wrists.

"Sorry about that, Mr. Bengston," the man said, pointing toward the small bloody crack at the corner of Vic's mouth. "However, I do think a lawsuit would be pointless."

"Just doing your job?" Vic said.

"We can do without the sarcasm," the man said, holding out his hand. "I'm George Pendleton."

Instinctively, Vic grabbed the man's hand and squeezed hard.

"You know who I am," Vic said. "And now you know my father."

"Nice man," Pendleton said. "He gave me this."

He held up a yellow and black metal canister of Kodak thirty-five millimeter color print film, the kind Vic's dad liked to shoot on their rides through Colorado farm country or up in the mountains.

"That's private property," Vic said.

"That's correct," Pendleton said. "My private property. It's a small price to pay. Let me tell you."

"For what?" Vic said. "Trespassing on an imaginary federal reservation?"

"Now, there goes that sarcasm again," Pendleton said slipping the film canister into his shirt pocket. "Nope, Mr. Bengston, you need to read up on your Patriot Act regulations. This, in fact, is a federal reservation. Doesn't matter when the designation was made. Just so happens this one was made about eight hours ago. We don't need any signs, or any prior warning. But there will be signs and chains up across that driveway entrance up there before the day is out. And that's just the way it is. So what do you say we just chalk this up to a misunderstanding and part friends, okay?"

"I'll reserve the friend part," Vic said.

"I thought you might, "Pendleton said. "Tell your father goodbye for me. I'll just wait here as you both drive on out."

"Who does Ralston Security work for?" Vic said.

"Well, I'm sure you'd be able to find that out eventually," Pendleton said.

"My boss is going to want to know," Vic said.

"U.S. Department of Homeland Security," Pendleton said. "Now, you and your dad have a nice day."

He leaned on the SUV next to the open driver's door and kept a sharp eye on Vic as he returned to his car and drove away from the abandoned facilities at the Sundial Ranch.

*   *   *

"I'm fine," Dad said. "I am. The man was very courteous."

"I can't say the same," Vic said.

"I noticed he was a little less deferential to you," Dad said.

"A little less?" Vic said, rubbing his tongue over the new cut inside his cheek. Dad just smiled.

They were out on Waterdale Drive heading back the way they came. Vic was shaking. Dad seemed relaxed.

"He said something happened there and a federal agency had to investigate it," Dad said.

"Did he say what?" Vic said.

"No, just something," Dad said. "And he asked me not to talk about it."

"He took your film," Vic said.

"Well, he took the film that was in my camera at the time," Dad said.

"What do you mean?" Vic said.

"He didn't take this one," Dad said. Vic looked over and his father was holding an identical Kodak film canister between the thumb and forefinger of his right hand. "This is the one with all the pictures on it."

"Nice move, Dad," Vic said.

"I've still got a couple left," he said. His oxygen tank gasped.

23

Vic thought Les Vigil might have a problem reaming out a Pulitzer Prize winning reporter who was fifteen years his senior. Not so.

"I could fire you right now," Vigil said.

"On what grounds?" Vic said.

"Passing yourself off as a *Times* reporter on assignment when you were taking a joy ride with your old man," More said.

"Well I was acting as a reporter," Vic said. "That property was owned by David Riley."

"You weren't on any assignment," Vigil said. "It was your day off. You were taking a ride in the country."

"So I have to have an assignment in order for me to be on the job?" Vic said. "A note from my teacher? What?"

"Well, no—"

"No is right," Vic said. "What if I heard something at a cocktail party, or stumbled across something relevant to a story when I was on a day off, or had a hunch?"

"Was this a hunch?" Vigil said. "Quartermaine was not pleased to get a visit from Homeland Security. Let me tell you."

Quartermaine owned the *Times* and a string of other smaller newspapers. He was building a mini-me version of Rupert Murdock's media empire and was just busting at the seams to get his hands on a local television station.

"That must have rattled his cage," Vic said.

"More than that," Vigil said. "He wants to have lunch with you. And me."

"Lunch?" Vic said. "Today?"

"Now," Vigil said.

"It's eleven fifteen," Vic said.

"He eats early," Vigil said. "This is a no option deal, Vic. We're going to meet him at the restaurant."

"Fine," Vic said. "I'll have to reschedule an appointment."

When Vic left private sector public relations to re-enter the world of journalism, he knew he would be trading one set of over-the-top corporate egos for another set of journalism egos, generally materializing in the form of editors, publishers, owners, and the occasional reporter. The switch was worth it. While corporate work paid the bills and helped the kids with college, the chase of the newspaper story could not be beaten.

He had met Quartermaine only once, very briefly, a week before Scranton Media shut down the *Rocky Mountain Sun* where Vic had worked a quarter of a century ago and, more recently, when he returned to the newspaper business. The *Times* was in partnership with the *Sun* under a joint operating agreement that combined all business operations except the newsrooms.

Vic always wondered what role Quartermaine played in the death of the *Sun,* Denver's oldest and best newspaper.

* * *

"Subway?" Vic said. "I thought you said a restaurant."

"Well, technically, it is a restaurant," Vigil said.

"Well, technically, it's a hole in the wall, Les, through which unseen hands shove submarine sandwiches at you."

"That's a little severe, Vic, and please keep that to yourself, will you?" Vigil said. He was stiff and nervous. "Anyway, Quartermaine eats here every day when he's in town. Orders the same thing."

Vic and his editor stood outside on a dirty sidewalk. The Subway sandwich shop was in a seedy little retail strip at Monaco and Evans. Its neighbors included a liquor store, a vacuum cleaner repair shop, a martial arts studio, a neighborhood sports bar, and a drive-up psychic who occupied a tiny yellow and green shed in the middle of the crumbling asphalt parking lot.

"Subway," Vic said over the din of midday traffic on Evans.

"Yes, Subway," Vigil said. "Here, he gave me these."

Vigil handed Vic a one dollar off coupon that carried the grinning faces of happy skinny twenty-somethings, now the de facto national symbol for weight loss.

"We're buying our own lunches?" Vic said.

"Always," Vigil said. "We even buy our own food during editorial board meetings."

Suddenly, Vic missed client lunches in the PR business.

"Where's Quartermaine?" Vic said.

Vigil looked at his watch and said, "He'll be here in seven minutes. See that guy over there?"

Vic looked through the window and saw a middle-aged Hispanic man working on a sandwich, but at a separate cutting board, one that wasn't part of the typical Ford Motor Company assembly line Subway used to piece together its food products.

"Sure," Vic said.

"He's building Quartermaine's lunch order," Vigil said.

"He calls it in?" Vic said.

"He owns the franchise," Vigil said. "They just start the sandwich ten minutes before he blows through the place."

"What if he's out of town, or otherwise indisposed?" Vic said.

"Then it's delivered," Vigil said.

"Anywhere on Earth?" Vic said.

"Anywhere on Earth," Vigil said. "Where there's a Subway."

As they entered the tiny sub shop, Vic wondered whether he was going to meet with a Rupert Murdock wannabe or a Howard Hughes in training. Vigil ordered a ham and cheese on whole wheat. Vic went with the tuna salad on sour dough. Both men grabbed bags of the original Frito chips, paid, and their filled empty paper cups with iced tea, Vigil's sweetened, Vic's unsweetened.

When their derrieres hit the booth bench, Quartermaine walked in.

"Ola, Mister Quartermaine," called the sandwich maker from behind the counter. He handed a wrapped sandwich, a bag of seven-grain chips, and a capped and strawed drink over to the owner of the *Denver Times*. Quartermaine grabbed his lunch with two hands, said "Gracias, Leonard," and strolled over to the booth and slid in across from Vic and Vigil.

"Les," Quartermaine said.

"Ned," Vigil said.

"Bengston," Quartermaine said.

"Mr. Quartermaine," Vic said.

*   *   *

A small fit-looking man with short graying blond hair and sparkling green eyes, Ned Quartermaine flashed a big smile. Vic put him in his mid-fifties. The newspaper owner methodically pulled his sandwich, chips, and napkin from the standard issue plastic Subway order bag. He unwrapped the sandwich and carefully folded the top and bottom of the paper into a neat rectangle that fit squarely in front of him. Grabbing the top of his chip bag with both hands, Quartermaine pulled the upper seam apart. He dumped the chips into a pile next to the sandwich, and set his drink on the upper right corner of the makeshift placemat.

Vigil had the Subway assembly line toss everything onto his sandwich, so he already had a disorderly pile of olive pieces, lettuce slivers, and sliced pepper rings lying in front of him. Vic managed to prevent a glop of tuna salad from oozing its way out the opposite end of his bun, so he looked rather buttoned up and tidy in front of the newspaper's owner.

Quartermaine took one neat bite out of his sandwich. Nothing fell to the tabletop. His eating area looked like a photograph out of Haute Cuisine magazine.

*   *   *

After taking a second measured bite of his sandwich and a sip of whatever it was he was drinking, Quartermaine said, "I'm glad to be an American. What about you, Bengston?"

This was not what Vic had expected. He thought it might be more along the lines of, "Are you onto a good story?" or even something like, "What possessed you trespass in the name of the *Denver Times*?" Or, "You're fired."

Screw it, Vic said to himself and threw a hard left hook. "What kind of a dumb assed question is that?"

Quartermaine's right hand, halfway up to his mouth with a single multi-grain chip, froze in midair. He looked Vic in the eyes.

"What did you say?" he said.

"You heard me," Vic said, feeling a bit shaky, but caring even less.

"This is what you hired for me?" Quartermaine said to Vigil.

Vigil said nothing.

"I'm over here, Quartermaine, and yes I'm what you hired," Vic said. "You can fire me right now, but don't ever ask me a bullshit question like that again."

"What do you feed your guys in the city room, Les? Raw buffalo meat?" Quartermaine looked at Vic and said, "No, I'm not going to fire you."

"Yet?" Vic said.

"Yet," Quartermaine said.

"That sounds like an honest comment," Vic said.

"I'm an honest man," Quartermaine said.

"That question wasn't honest," Vic said. "It's the kind they ask on Rupert's Faux News Channel."

"Faux News," Quartermaine said, smiling. "I like that."

Quartermaine's suspended lunch bite resumed its flight to oblivion. Vic felt Vigil fidget next to him.

"My statement about me was true," Quartermaine said. "I am glad to be an American. And I don't want to see harm come to us. I love this country."

"Don't we all?" Vic said, reveling in the notion that he was not financially dependent on this odd little man sitting across from him, while churning over in his mind the two standing book offers he had from major publishers. Those were his backstops if the journalism thing did not work out. Vigil, on the other hand, Vic thought, was probably mortgaged to the hilt, driving one of his two cars, and still puzzling over how he and his wife would send his two teenage children to college. "What did you want to talk to me about?"

"Well, your little adventure up near Loveland caused quite a stir down here," Quartermaine said. "I had a visit from Homeland Security and the FBI."

"For turning off a county road onto a ranch driveway in Larimer County?" Vic said. "They do pay attention to details down at the federal building."

"For turning onto a property owned by the late David Riley," said Vigil, who showed signs of reviving after Vic's verbal tête-à-tête with their boss.

"Like I told Wilford, what was his name?. He gave me his card."

"Pendleton," Vigil said. "George Pendleton."

"That's right, George, from Ralston Security," Vic said. He had Googled Ralston as soon as he got home from the ride with Dad. Colorado Secretary of State corporate records revealed that the firm was an LLC formed only three months earlier, in January. It had two "members," as the principals in limited liability companies were known, James Willaby and Sanders Rutherford III, names that triggered no recollections. "I told George there were no posted signs. It was an innocent visit."

"Not according to the feds," Quartermaine said. "They showed me some photographs of the buildings, the doors and windows."

"My dad takes pictures," Vic said. Pendleton had confiscated the wrong roll of film. The roll that Dad had pulled from the camera showed Vic peering into the windows, checking the doors, and his confrontation with Pendleton, evidence for a slightly stronger trespass case. The replacement roll contained a series of innocent looking shots of the buildings and the surrounding landscape. Vic was proud of that move by his father. "He has all his life. By the way, did you ask for my dad's film back?"

Quartermaine shook his head. "I didn't know your father shot any others," he said. "Anyway, I doubt if they'll return whatever they confiscated."

"So much for the Fourth Amendment," Vic said. "Do the feds want your complicity in violating the First Amendment as well, because we love our country and all that?"

"All right," Quartermaine said. "Let's put that behind us. No, I'm here to find out what sort of a story you've dragged my paper into."

The veneer seemed to be cracking. Maybe there was a bit of humanity behind this obsessive-compulsive façade, Vic thought.

Quartermaine took another dainty bite from his sandwich, sipped his drink, and carefully wiped his lower lip with a paper napkin that he unfolded and refolded with each use.

"No story," Vic said. "I was just curious."

"How did you know that place was owned by Riley?" Vigil said.

"I didn't," Vic said. "Somewhere I heard the name *Sundial*. I can't even remember where."

"Maybe from David Riley?" Quartermaine said. "From your interview with him?"

Vic shook his head. "No. Everything relevant in my notes went into the story." That was true, he reasoned. The material that did not go into the piece was not relevant, at least for now.

"Could we see your notes?" Vigil said, knowing the answer.

"Hell no," Vic said. "That interview was done by me, on my time and well before you guys hired me."

Multi-grain chip number two vanished into Quartermaine's petite mouth. He crunched, swallowed, and then said, "Well, now we know where we stand."

"And where is that, besides you not trusting me?"

"We can't count on you to disclose your sources to us," Quartermaine said. "That puts our relationship in question and possibly puts the paper in jeopardy."

"In jeopardy of what?" Vic said.

"Being sued for one thing," Quartermaine said.

"Sued by whom, the federal government? That won't even get to first base."

"We're not that kind of paper," Quartermaine said.

"What kind of paper?" Vic said.

"The kind that takes on—"

"The government?" Vic said. "The *Times* used to be that kind of paper."

"That's not what I mean, Bengston," Quartermaine said. The bite number three routine had been severely disrupted. The sandwich went up but only made it to the chin before Quartermaine put it back down. "I mean if there's something that we know, that you know, something that might be important to national security—"

"Turn it over?" Vic said. Quartermaine nodded, then completed the sandwich bite sequence. "Let me ask you something, Mr. Quartermaine."

"What," Quartermaine said.

"Have you ever been a reporter?" Vic said.

"No," Quartermaine said.

"An editorial writer?" Vic said.

Quartermaine shook his head.

"What then?" Vic said. "What were you when you entered this business?"

"A distribution manager," Quartermaine said.

"A paper boy?" Vic said.

"Vic!" Vigil said. Quartermaine held up a hand.

"No, Les, it's okay," Quartermaine said. "That's where I started. Then printing plant management. Then advertising. Then ownership. I'm not ashamed of it."

"Shadow me for a day at the statehouse," Vic said. "You might learn something."

"Dammit!" Vigil said. Now he was standing next to the booth.

Quartermaine laughed.

"Relax, Les," Quartermaine said. "Sit down. He might have a good idea there."

Then Vigil laughed, nervously, relieved that the tension was broken for now.

"As I see it, Mr. Quartermaine, you have one problem," Vic said.

"What's that?" Quartermaine said.

"You're too satisfied," Vic said.

"I'm not sure what you mean," Quartermaine said.

"There is no hope for the satisfied man," Vic said.

"You might have a point," Quartermaine said. "I like that phrase."

Vigil was silent. He just looked at Vic and shook his head.

He should like it, Vic thought. It was carved into the stone above the front door at the old, now demolished, Denver Times building in downtown Denver.

It was a quote from the newspaper's founder.

24

Vic figured his days at the *Times* were numbered, especially after his Subway lunch with the owner. Book offers were on the table. An agent or two showed some interest. Even so, he liked reporting, covering the statehouse, the courts, and government. Politics was okay, but politics in America had turned into a foul food fight, and there were no signs of that letting up. He really liked covering crimes, something he did not do at all his first time through the journalism profession a few decades earlier.

Vigil was not too happy after the luncheon but was surprisingly open during their drive back downtown after the Subway meeting. He even told Vic he did not want to uproot his family again to go off and find an editor's slot at some other daily newspaper, the numbers of which were dwindling each year. The editor admitted he did not relish the idea of tweeting, Facebooking, and blogging with the younger set either, quickly becoming the norm for what passed as journalism these days. Despite his age, two decades Vic's junior, Vigil was a traditional journalist, a dying breed in the age of the internet.

"I need to know what you're working on," Vigil said after his confessional. "I'm not opposed to enterprise work, but you're pretty far off the books with this one, aren't you?"

As they walked and elevatored back to Vigil's office, Vic pondered the hot story smoldering in the ashes of Riley's questionable death. He liked working on his own, but he also liked the resources of a newspaper behind him, provided the newspaper did not chicken out.

"I have yet to figure out what the hell that meeting was about at lunch," Vic said. "Where is Quartermaine in this?"

"First we need to define what 'this' is," Vigil said.

"You're starting to sound like President Bubba," Vic said.

"You know what I mean, Vic," Vigil said. "Is there a story? If so what is it? And what is it that you are chasing?"

Vic had to decide whether he was going to throw in with this editor, who at times seemed more worried about losing his job than anything else. During his eighteen months at the now defunct *Rocky Mountain Sun*, the publisher turned out to be a real newspaperman, backing Vic all the way when he marched on the state's top water lawyer, bringing him down and eventually winning the Pulitzer for his effort. That work would not have been possible had the newspaper ownership yielded to the pressure from the state's political elite to downplay the water lawyer story or even spike it.

"They backed me at the *Sun*," Vic said.

"The *Sun* has set," Vigil said. "It will not return with the dawn."

"Did Quartermaine kill it?"

"No comment," Vigil said. "Don't go there. We have other problems to deal with."

"Homeland Security?" Vic said. "FBI?"

"Denver cops?" Vigil said. "Breaking and entering?"

Vic paused. "What?" he said.

"Cliff briefed me," Vigil said.

"Does Quartermaine know?" Vic said.

"No," Vigil said. "And he's not going to know."

"Look, Homeland Security and the FBI are already poking around, and I have hardly done a thing except write the initial story on Riley's death and that sidebar," Vic said. "If they're that hot already, there must be some kind of a decent story lurking somewhere."

"Lurking in your notes, Maybe?" Vigil said.

Vic looked across the editor's desk at Vigil, wondering if he would protect Vic and his sources? Or would he worry more about pulling his kids out of school? How much pressure could Vigil and Quartermaine withstand?

"I have trust issues," Vic said.

"Don't we all?" Vigil said.

"A lot with Quartermaine," Vic said. "A bit with you."

"All right, let's start with me," Vigil said.

"You're afraid for your job," Vic said.

"I checked on your history, Vic," Vigil said. "There was a time when your four kids were little that you quit a decent government job to go freelance. How smart was that? I know you worried about the same things back then that I do now."

"No," Vic said. "Quitting the government job was the correct decision. We were a part of the governor's office, pretty free and easy as I recall. The bureaucracy had us surrounded, and they would have absorbed us by the next legislative session. No, my first big mistake was leaving journalism, and my second one was not getting back in when I left the governor's employ."

"You don't have my kind of family worries now?" Vigil said.

"No I don't," Vic said. "The kids were grown and doing well, but family is family, Les. They're all here, their spouses, their kids, my ex-wife, and my folks, so things can happen, and I have serious emotional obligations to them. I'm not a total Lone Ranger."

"But darn close," Vigil said. "I've got three generations here. That's why I want to stay. I was lucky enough to work my way back from Cleveland. Okay, so we've both got some level of family stuff going on. We all have that. What are you worried about then, with respect to the paper?"

"That the *Times* will lie down," Vic said.

"The *Times* won't do that," Vigil said. "Not on a legitimate story." He just stared at Vic. "Do you have a legitimate story?"

"We're not up to that question yet," Vic said. "I really don't trust Quartermaine. Aside from being weird, I don't know where he stands on actually pursuing a tough story."

"Is this a tough story then?" Vigil said.

"Tough?" Vic said. "You've got a dead billionaire, a cop shop dragging its feet for some reason, and when I make a wrong turn on a country drive we get Homeland Security and the FBI up our rear ends with LED flashlights." Vic used the stare, crossed his arms and aimed at Vigil. "What about that does not sound tough?"

"Quartermaine is solid," Vigil finally said.

"How do you know?" Vic said. "I've got to know how solid

Quartermaine is before I can go any further."

"He wants to create the *Washington Post* of the West," Vigil said. "That's all he's talked about since I met him."

"And when was that?"

"I first met him ten years ago at a conference on the future of journalism," Vigil said. "He hired me two years after that to run the *Times*."

"How do you know he won't run away from a good story, a really good story, and one that might embarrass powerful people?" Vic said.

"Or governments?" Vigil said.

Vic nodded.

"I've seen him in action," Vigil said. "We had Defense and Justice brass in here when we started turning over rocks down at Fort Carson. They didn't want to see anything in the paper about the increased murder rates down there, the suicides, or the piss poor psychological care our returning GIs were getting. One of the guys, an assistant U.S. attorney, threatened to derail Quartermaine's plans to buy up some of the smaller dailies in the region."

"What was Quartermaine's reaction to that?" Vic said.

"He told them to go to hell," Vigil said. "Literally."

"Well, I saw the stories," Vic said.

"And were they good?" Vigil said.

"First rate," Vic said. Vigil remained silent, waiting out Vic this time. "All right. All right. But not here."

"Where then?" Vigil said.

"The Satire Lounge," Vic said. "In two hours."

"Are you kidding me?" Vigil said. "I've got—"

"No, I'm not kidding you," Vic said. "Look, you made me eat lunch with the owner in a Subway shop. Two hours, at the Satire, and I want you to bring my new partner with you."

"Partner?" Vigil said.

"Yeah," Vic said. "I don't want to work on this alone or just with you and Quartermaine, if he's even going to be involved," Vic said.

"Oh, he's going to be involved," Vigil said. "Assuming there's even a story here."

"There's a story," Vic said. "A good one." At least he hoped there was.

"Who's this partner you want?" Vigil said.

"Peggy Mayer," Vic said.

"Your old boss from the *Sun*?" Vigil said.

"Yes," Vic said. "She was a young boss, by the way."

Vigil pushed back from his desk. "She's the deputy Features editor," he said.

"Where her talent is totally squandered," Vic said. "She is one hell of a journalist, and you know that."

"Well, we slotted her over there to get her into the swing of things here at the *Times*," he said.

"Les, don't take this the wrong way, but the *Times* isn't much of a newspaper anymore, especially since the *Sun* folded."

Vigil jutted his chin out and leaned forward. "That Pulitzer on the wall doesn't make you God's gift to journalism."

"It's one more Pulitzer than you've got, Les, and Peggy has one more nomination than you've got," Vic said, wondering if he had taken things a bit too far. Vigil backed off, leaned into his chair and took a deep breath.

"All right," Vigil said. "I'll bring Peggy."

"See you at the Satire." Vic stood up and walked straight out of Vigil's office, wondering if the editor's heart was thumping as hard as his. Laying out his cards, or most of them, was the best way to go, Vic told himself, although he knew he did not have much of a choice.

The *Denver Times* was the only player in the Mile High City.

25

Vic stepped out of the brightness of East Colfax Avenue into the dank, stale beer obscurity of the Satire Lounge. He stood for a moment to let his eyes adjust before advancing. Since he was early, he would pick the booth. Vic walked to the back and slid into a corner job that let him see the front door.

He recognized three faces on his trip through the bar, a young lawyer from the Legislative Drafting Office, the Speaker of the Colorado House of Representatives with a lobbyist, no doubt, and a state senator from Aspen. A half dozen suited thirty-somethings, short hair, trendy three-day beards, tight jackets, open collars, had pushed two tables together and were downing tequila shots in celebration of a recent and rare victory by the Colorado Rockies. Half the tables, booths, and barstools were occupied by either Capitol Hill yuppies or drunks from the statehouse further west on Colfax Avenue. The jukebox spoke alternate rock. Happy Hour was getting underway a bit early. It was a good place for a private conversation.

The front door flashed open and two figures emerged from the whiteness outside. Vigil and Peggy both bumped into the first table before hesitating to get used to the dark bar. Vic waved a few times and caught their attention. They slalomed their way through a maze of chrome, Formica, and vinyl toward him.

"Vic," Peggy said.

"Peggy," Vic said. "Hi Les."

"Good afternoon," Vigil said. "Or, good happy hour."

"Happy hour," Vic said. "What are you drinking?"

A thin young girl with dark cropped hair walked over to them. She may have been Goth, but it was still too dark for Vic to pinpoint the precise look.

"Hi, kids," she said. "What are we having?"

"We are having a Fat Tire," Vigil said. "Peg?"

"White wine," Peggy said. "Les, it's Peggy."

"I'll get it one of these days," Vigil said. "Sorry."

"She won't let up until you do," Vic said, then to the waitress, "Decent coffee?"

"I'll make a fresh pot, just for you," the waitress said.

"Great," Vic said.

"I appreciate this, Les," Vic said.

"What?" Vigil said.

"Your support," Vic said. "I don't want to do this alone."

"I'm not sure if you've even got a story," Vigil said.

"That's how stories begin," Peggy said to Vigil. He nodded. He remembered.

Vic decided to lay out his theory. He welcomed the help from Peggy. She was solid. He would take a flyer on Vigil, going with his gut instinct that the guy was a straight player and interested in good journalism.

"I think Riley was murdered," Vic said.

"Hullo, where have you been?" Vigil said. "Sealed coroner's report? What else is new? I've had my, our, police staff chasing that down ever since they found the guy."

"Yeah, but do you have any reason why he might have been killed, or by whom?" Vic said.

"Of course not," Peggy said, again looking at Vigil, who just fidgeted in his seat.

The waitress arrived and set two chilled glasses of white wine in front of Peggy and a pair of Fat Tire bottles in front of Vigil. "Coffee'll be ready in a minute," she said to Vic.

Vic nodded. Vigil gulped his beer, Peggy sipped her wine. The duo formed a tiny rapt audience.

"I thought it had to do with Riley's electronic voting technology at first," Vic said. "Well, it still has something to do with that, but it's a little different now." Vic pinched the bridge of his nose. Vigil and

Peggy each took another gulp and sip, respectively. "Actually, it's a lot different."

"I don't follow you," Vigil said.

"There are a few elements to Riley's story that haven't been made public yet," Vic said.

"Did you have this before you wrote the backgrounder on him?" Vigil said.

Vic knew what Vigil was getting at. He wanted to know if Vic had withheld anything important to the story. Vic knew he had, but he did not want Vigil thinking that.

"It didn't seem relevant or even supportable at the time," Vic said. "And yes I had it before. My notes, remember?"

"But is it relevant now?" Peggy said.

"Sure," Vic said and then told them about the special facility Riley had set up in the foothills west of Loveland.

"I don't really see how putting a bunch of hackers on his payroll led to his death," Vigil said. He took a slug of beer. "Is that the place where Homeland Security busted you and your dad?"

"Well, a rent-a-cop working for Homeland Security roughed me up and swiped Dad's film," Vic said, hoping Vigil was simply playing dumb. "The Brimley look-alike."

"Huh?" Peggy said.

"The guy reminded me of Wilford Brimley, the actor," Vic said. "Private cop. Even dressed liked him. Sounded like him too. I was afraid he might pitch me on adult diapers or diabetes test strips once he saw my gray hair."

"What's this about, Les?" Peggy said. Vigil ignored her. "We're really out of the loop back there in Features."

"Crepe Suzettes and party decorating tips not cutting it for you, Peggy?" Vic said.

"Not really," Peggy said. "What did you find at this place? Sundial Ranch."

"Nothing," Vic said. "It was emptied, and it seemed as though it had been cleared out well before Riley was killed."

"Or died," Vigil said.

"He was murdered, and you know it," Vic said.

"Why do we care about these hackers?" Vigil said.

"Because one of them might be a murderer," Vic said. "Or, might lead us to the murderer."

"Lead us?" Vigil said. "Since when are we a police department?"

"Les is right, Vic," Peggy said. "There has to be more to this story than that."

"There is," Vic said. "Let me 'splain it to you. First, you both need a mini history lesson."

"I've got to get home," Vigil said, looking at his watch and launching into Fat Tire number two. Peggy still had no one to get home to.

"It won't take long," Vic said. "It's about codes, or ciphers, and encryption technology. Riley needed security for his voting system because he wanted to make the vote universal."

"The vote is universal," Vigil said. "At least in the United States."

"No it is not," Vic said. "And you of all people, Les, should know that. Much as they wrap the flag around the right to vote, our two major political parties want to control the voting process at every turn. Each party wants a solid dependable core that will vote lock step with them every time, no questions asked. There is nothing universal about it."

"Their party bases," Peggy said. Vigil nodded with heightened animation, the Second Beer Effect, Vic presumed. Then Vigil waived at Goth girl who was on her way over with Vic's coffee.

"Here's your coffee, dear," she said. She was Goth. Vic could see more metal strategically placed about her head. "Another round?"

"Yes," Vigil said.

"Not for me," Peggy said.

"Be right back," the waitress said.

"Okay, yes, that's the base," Vic said. "The party controls that. There also is a component of the so-called independents, on the right and on the left, which each party controls as well. Most of those independents are not independent at all. They'll vote the party line ninety per cent of the time. The parties now spend hundreds of millions of dollars to keep those alleged independents leaning with them and to convince the real fence-sitters to vote for one side or the other."

"Nothing new there," Vigil said.

"That's true," Vic said. "Republicans also spend a great deal of time, energy, and money keeping poor people, old people, and minorities out of voting booths. Their sharpie lawyers set up shop at voting precincts and challenge voter credentials as they come in to exercise their right to cast a ballot. They either walk away not voting or they have to cast a provisional ballot, which often gets counted last. On a grander scale, Republicans demand photo IDs to vote and they repeal laws making voter registration easy whenever they gain control of a state. They cut back on the number of polling places. All this is designed to discourage people who tend to vote with Democrats from actually voting."

"All right," Vigil said. "We know the Republicans try to suppress the vote, but the Dems aren't all that clean either."

"No they're not," Vic said. "They want everyone to vote, whether they can read or not."

"Fog on the mirror test?" Vigil said. Both Vic and Peggy laughed.

"Just about," Vic said.

"So they try to register everyone and get them to the polls," Peggy said. "Sometimes they cross the line there."

"Like with ACORN?" Vigil said.

"That was never proven," Peggy said.

"Doesn't matter," Vic said. "There were still a lot of bad registrations. Dems dump tons of money transporting people to the polls on Election Day, tons of money, like a machine. It's all a matter of numbers, nothing else. Most Republicans take themselves to the polls. Many Dems have to be dragged there, and you cannot tell me the party regulars aren't whispering the Holy Gospel of the Democratic Party into their ears on the way."

"So when the Ds register someone, they want to make sure they'll vote with them," Peggy said. "That seems logical. The Rs want the same."

"The parties hate close elections," Vic said. "Look at 2000. How many Democratic voters were tossed off the voter registration rolls by Republican credential challengers?"

Peggy was about to answer, but Vic held up both hands and said,

"Quite a few. And how many those disenfranchised voters could the Democrats have counted on to cast ballots in Florida? Probably quite a few. It's all part of the game played at election time."

"A presidential election decided by the Supreme Court is sick," Vigil said, halfway through his third beer. Vigil likes his beer, Vic thought.

"No matter," Vic said. "You can see how the major parties want to tightly control the vote process from start to finish, even down to the lawyers in Florida and the Supreme Court ruling that stripped the state of its constitutional obligation to count the votes."

"Putting the shrub in the White House," Peggy said.

Vic glared at Peggy. "Shrub? This is the president of the United States, or was."

"You spent too much time in graduate school studying this crap," Peggy said.

"It's about the best system there is," Vic said. "Worts and all. No. No. It is the best system. We can probably make it better."

"Are we getting a lecture?" Peggy said.

"No," Vic said. "Let's get back to the 2000 election. The Supreme Court settled it and we elected George W. Bush. The shrub."

"President Shrub," Peggy said.

Vigil burst in with, "Nader pretty much messed it up for Gore."

"So the Democrats say," Vic said. "Nader and the Green Party upset the 2000 apple cart in at least two states, making the election so close that Florida and the Supreme Court wound up making the final decision. Heck, Ross Perot messed things up for Dole in ninety-six, not enough to swing the election for Dole, but Perot did take more than eight per cent of the vote."

"Those bastards," Vigil said, slamming down a third empty beer bottle.

"Now, imagine a nation of many Green Parties, along with the two major parties," Vic said.

"Chaos?" Peggy said. She was only halfway through her first glass of wine. Their waitress checked in with them.

"Top it off?" the waitress said to Vic. He nodded and she poured from the glass pot she was carrying. "Anyone else?"

Peggy waived her off, and Vic said, "I think we're okay." She left in search of more orders and tips.

Vic took a good slug of coffee. "More than chaos," he said. "Every presidential election would wind up in the House of Representatives because it would be very hard for any one candidate to get a majority of the Electoral College votes."

"The loons in the House would be choosing our president?" Vigil said. "'scuse me?" The editor got up and headed back even deeper into the darkness of the Satire to find the men's room.

"He's wasted after three beers?" Vic said, thinking the Satire might not have been such a good idea.

"I saw him go four once," Peggy said. "After the Democratic Convention. I know his wife. I'll take him home."

"You know how I feel about this," Vic said, nodding toward the men's room. Peggy stared over her half empty wineglass, the full happy hour clone sitting alone and untouched in front of her. "I stopped wasting my time talking with drunks a long time ago when I quit."

"He's just a short-hitter," Peggy said. "He's got a good rep."

"Anything I say now will have to be repeated tomorrow," Vic said. "I can't trust his judgment let alone his news judgment. Crikey, I feel like the designated driver once again."

"Not with me you're not," Peggy said. It was a sharp retort.

"No, but with him," Vic said. He changed the subject. "Was your Features assignment punishment for working at the Rocky?"

"I don't really know," Peggy said. "They wanted to make sure I was *Times* material."

"Oh, they gave me that crap when I first got to Denver," Vic said.

"On your prairie schooner?" Peggy said, taking a quick sip of wine. Vic finished his coffee and caught their server's attention by waving his empty cup. She held up one finger and then flew into the kitchen.

"Yeah, my prairie schooner, a sixty-three Ford Fairlane my father-in-law gave me in a car-swap," Vic said smiling. "So, did I save you from the dark side of the paper?"

"You may have," Peggy said. "Here he comes."

Goth Girl stepped into line with Vigil as he returned from the head. The two marched together up to the booth, Vigil flopping back down into his spot, she reaching out to refill Vic's cup, then doing an about face and shooting off to do battle elsewhere in the bar.

"We're going to have to finish this up in the morning," Vic said. "I've got to go work on a radio building project with one of my grandsons this evening. How about breakfast?"

"Early," Vigil said, almost too easily.

"How early?" Vic said.

"Six-thirty," Vigil said.

"Tomorrow?" Vic said. He looked at Peggy, who raised her eyebrows. "Six-thirty?"

"Make it seven," Vigil said.

"Stop Inn," Vic said. "Monaco and Evans."

"That's right near Quartermaine's Subway," Vigil said.

"Quartermaine doesn't eat breakfast there does he?" Vic said. Vigil shook his head and said, "Stop Inn, seven."

"I'll take you home, boss," Peggy said.

"Naw, I'm okay," Vigil said.

"I'm busing it, Les," Peggy said. "Give me your keys. I'll drive."

The editor dug his car keys out of his pants pocket and laid them gently in Peggy's outstretched hand.

"You need a ride later?" Vic said.

"I'm okay," Peggy said.

"Can you make the breakfast?" Vic said. She nodded.

After Peggy and Vigil left, Vic finished his coffee paid the tab.

Vigil blew it, Vic thought, which might work to his advantage.

*   *   *

The 'Choke Café' was one of Denver's breakfast joints that actually cooked everything fresh, well almost everything. Nothing was organic and plate presentations did not resemble displays from the Museum of Modern Art. Coffee came from Bunn coffee makers and round glass pots which waitresses carried from table to table topping off the tolerable hot brown liquid. Hash browns came from real potatoes that had never been processed into frozen stringy shreds that often arrived at the table brittle and stuck together in some sort of microwave monstrosity. The place's real name was The Stop Inn, but one of Vic's clients renamed it to honor the two-ton biker who chocked on a fried chicken bone and fell to the floor at the client's high-heeled feet. After minutes of chocking, gagging, turning blue, and a quick visit from conveniently nearby EMTs, a Heimlich, a cleared throat, and a refusal to go to a hospital, the biker tumbled back into his chair to finish his daily special.

Vic arrived a half hour early and selected the corner table under the flat screen television that droned CNN's Headline News. The position offered the most privacy, which was not much. Ursula said hello, flipped his coffee mug and filled it. Vic walked over to the newspaper bin behind the cash register. With one less daily in town, he was stuck reading what was now his newspaper, the *Denver Times*. An interesting wire piece from the *New York Times* grabbed his attention. It was a sidebar to a main piece on the latest embarrassing revelations from Wikileaks, a website that specialized in publishing undisclosed government and industry information under the theory that exposing these secrets was better for the public dialogue than keeping them hush-hush. The sidebar explored methods used by the U.S. State Department to encrypt its secret cables to keep them from prying eyes. The gist of the story was that private industry seemed to do better than government agencies at keeping sensitive information secret and that the systems in use today, mostly numeric cipher techniques developed and managed by the Department of Defense, were too easy to crack.

That might explain why Homeland Security and the FBI paid a visit to Quartermaine, Vic thought, as he saw Vigil and Peggy wander in the front door. Eddie looked over at Vic, cocked his head toward the couple and raised his eyebrows. Vic nodded. The manager handed them two menus and pointed toward Vic's corner table.

No maître de escorts at the Choke Café.

*　*　*

"Sorry about last night," Vigil said, pulling up a chair. "I haven't slept much all week. Olivia's been sick, and, well, it's been a tough one."

"All nighters?" Vic said.

Vigil nodded and said, "Two this week, and I'm too old for that."

"I say the same thing, every time I pull one," Vic said.

They ordered breakfast. Vigil opted for bacon and eggs with hash browns and a large orange juice hoping the cold liquid would wash more of the previous night out of his system. Peggy ordered a fruit cup, cottage cheese and one poached egg to accompany her coffee. Vic had what has become his usual, a bowl of oatmeal with fruit on the side.

"Is that what I've got to look forward to?" Vigil said to Vic when the food arrived.

"That, and a swollen prostrate," Vic said. "Start with the oatmeal now, Les. You'll thank me later."

Peggy picked at her food.

"Where did I leave off last night?" Vic said, deciding to let Vigil identify precisely where he had descended from coherence and understanding to a lackadaisical alcohol-fueled milieu.

"You were going on about voting," Vigil said. "And how the parties, well the Republicans and the Democrats, wanted to control everything. Tell me something I don't know."

"Let's go back to Andrew Jackson," Vic said.

"Must we?" Peggy said, looking up from her plate. "History lesson?"

Vigil gulped his orange juice.

"Yes, and let me tell you why," Vic said.

"I thought you might," Vigil said. "By the way, I called in 'well' today. So take your time."

"I thought only reporters did that," Vic said.

"Hey, take a number," Vigil said. "Editors have lives too."

"Who's tending to the Voice of the Rocky Mountain Empire?" Vic said.

"Jameson," Vigil said. A worthy deputy editor, Vic thought.

"If you'll recall, the United States began by extending the vote only to male landowners," Vic said.

"White landowners," said Vigil. "Wealthy."

"Essentially," Vic said.

"No doubt you have firsthand knowledge," Peggy said to Vic. "That was before my time."

"Mine too," Vigil said.

Vic ignored them both.

"Andrew Jackson is largely credited with spawning the expansion of the vote franchise, when a number of states broadened the right to vote to include white males of some means and not simply landowners," Vic said.

"Was this before or after his face was put on the twenty?" Peggy said.

"A little before," Vic said. "This also marked the beginning of the Democratic Party, which has been largely associated with expanding the right to vote."

"It was still just white males," Peggy said.

"Yeah, but that was the start," Vic said. "Some of the constitutional amendments after the Civil War told states they couldn't deny the right to vote based on race, color, or indentured servitude, then sex, and failure to pay a poll tax."

"Not all at once, either," Peggy said. "We gals didn't get to vote until 1920. I'm still steamed over that."

"Don't look at me," Vic said. "I could vote from day one."

"You're age is showing," Peggy said.

"Poll taxes," Vigil said. "That's how they got at blacks and my people." He was a proud Latino.

"Devilish, those crackers," Peggy said.

"Northerners did their share too," Vic said. "But hey, Andy Jackson was one of those crackers. Elvis too. Watch your tongue."

"Elvis Costello was a cracker?" Peggy said. "I thought he was a Brit."

"You're incorrigible," Vic said.

"And don't you forget it," she said.

Vigil kept stuffing his face, then through a mouthful said, "Literacy tests."

""Yeah, boss," Vic said. "When the poll tax amendment didn't stop them, they came up with literacy tests."

"Okay, so that dragged things on for years," Vigil said. "I know all this."

"Let him set the table, Les," Peggy said. "I didn't know about the indentured servants. What about feature editors?"

Vigil just leaned back. He finished his orange juice, and then waved the glass at Ursula for a refill.

"The Democrats finally had to turn to legislation to finish off this war against African American voters," Vic said.

"Voting Rights Act," Vigil said. "Johnson."

"Sure," Vic said, "A century after the Civil War."

Vigil chomped on his breakfast, struggling to erase the night before.

"What's next, Teach?" Peggy said.

"Well, we eventually changed the constitution again to lower the voting age from twenty-one to eighteen," Vic said. "Something you might be able to relate to a little more closely, Peggy."

"Way cool," Peggy said.

"So what's your point?" Vigil said.

"The point is this," Vic said. "Everyone, every citizen that is, can vote in the United States. Now it's a matter of regulations, ease of registration, IDs, access to the polls, all that."

"And getting up off your lazy butt and voting," Vigil said as he wiped a light brown paper napkin across his mouth.

"The biggest problem of all," Vic said. "The parties depend on that because they want their hands on the levers of those who actually do vote."

"I'm assuming Riley is coming into the picture somewhere here," Peggy said.

"Very soon, I hope," Vigil said.

"Cool your jets," Vic said. "With computers, the internet, and voter motor programs, voter registration is getting easier, but legal forces, mostly financed by conservatives, work to make registration and voting a bit more difficult with tighter regulations, not impossible, a little more discouraging for the poor and minorities, sometimes elderly too."

"Who tend to vote for Democrats," Peggy said. "Them dang liberals."

"Correct" Vic said. "Whether it's trying to restrict organizations like ACORN, the League of Women Voters, or Jesse Jackson's Operation Push from registering huge numbers of eligible voters or by challenging voter credentials at the polls, or tightening down the ID requirements, it's basically a war against expanding the size of the voter pool. If some of the typical Democratic voters are discouraged from voting, it makes it a little easier for Republicans to win close elections."

"I still think ACORN shot themselves in the foot," Vigil said.

"They had a lot of losers registering voters."

"ACORN paid for their screw-ups," Vic said. "But the League of Women Voters? They are getting hammered in some states too."

"You can't get much more subversive than the League," Peggy said.

Vic and Vigil just stared at her.

"This is serious," Vic said.

"Lighten up, will ya," she said.

"There's a problem, though," Vigil said.

"Which is?" Vic said.

"This so-called voter suppression is turning out more Democrats, not less," Vigil said.

"To a degree," Vic said. "A reaction to all this new voter ID legislation. Tell me, Les, when was the last time the *Times* wrote a story on voter fraud?"

"Not since I've been here," Vigil said.

"At any time in your star-studded career, have you written such a story, or even seen one?" Vic said.

"Well no," Vigil said.

"So the states are passing all this legislation to solve a non-existent problem," Peggy said.

"Not quite," Vic said. "There are some cases, but very few."

"And the Dems want half of Mexico to move here and wind up voting for them," Vigil said.

"After they become citizens," Peggy said.

"But the fear, real or imagined, is that illegals will vote," Vic said. "That fuels the effort to impose more requirements on voters."

"I assume Riley was doing something to get rid of the roadblocks?" Vigil said.

"More than that," Vic said. "He was developing a system he called The Universal Vote. It would have started with his touch screen machines. He told me he planned to come out with a unit so cheap that even the poorest county in the country could afford a voting system."

"So he refined his voting machine," Peggy said. "Big deal."

"But wait, there's more," Vic said. "His cheap voting machine was just the start. Riley was going to take the vote to the cloud via wireless and cell phone networks."

"The cloud?" Vigil said.

Vic pointed up. "Where computer data is stored. Not on the machines anymore."

"So the ballots, when cast, would be tabulated somewhere else?" Peggy said.

"You really underestimated this woman," Vic said to Vigil.

"No I didn't," Vigil said. "She just needed to get familiar with the *Times'* system."

Vic looked at Peggy, raised his eyebrows and said, "The *Times* has a system?"

Peggy nodded. "Yeah, they use a different password to log on to their terminals than we used at the *Rocky Mountain Sun*. It took me— what Les?—minutes to memorize it? After that, everything's pretty much the same."

"Enough," Vigil said, holding up both his hands. "This hurts my head. The cloud, please. I've heard of it. What is it?"

"None of the voting software or the vote tabulations would be on the machines," Vic said. "Everything accesses data storage farms through the internet or cell phone systems."

"How would people vote?" Vigil said.

"At polling places like they do now," Vic said. "Or with mail-in ballots like we all use, or by landline phone, cell phone, and the internet, tablets, almost like we do our banking and shopping."

"Sounds expensive," Peggy said.

"Just the opposite," Vic said. "Other than his new cheap machines, the entire Universal Vote system is software based. Riley mentioned setting up an independent foundation to handle everything."

"I can see why the pols wouldn't buy it," Vigil said. "Too many people voting means they lose control. What's next? Direct Democracy?"

"Security seems like an even bigger issue," Peggy said. "Where's all the data going? India?"

"Riley told me each state could have its own server farm if it wanted one," Vic said. "States have them already. This would just be an add-on. But security is the real key. You're right about that, Peggy."

"I think that might be the show stopper," Peggy said.

"That's where *Sundial* comes in," Vic said.

"That ranch?" Vigil said.

"That ranch was where the Universal Vote System was developed, along with *Sundial*," Vic said.

"So what is *Sundial* then?" Vigil said.

"*Sundial* was, or is, the security system for Universal Vote," Vic said. "But it turned out to be far more and I think that may have been what got Riley killed."

Vic explained *Sundial* as best he could, regurgitating what Stone had told him, but not mentioning Stone's name. The math involved was well beyond his comprehension. Peggy got it right away. Vigil was clear-minded enough to grasp the basics.

"So Riley's *Sundial* protects the votes in his Universal Vote thing," Vigil said. "And lets any government or company or terrorist group encrypt data, reports, cables, anything, with a cipher that was virtually unbreakable."

"Unbreakable?" Peggy said.

"Essentially," Vic said. "Not impossible, but orders of magnitude more secure than what exists now."

"It's the perfect cipher," Peggy said. "Everybody would want it. And it keeps the NSA out!"

"Cipher," Vigil said. "I've always wanted to use that word in something. So, I take it this cipher is something that could just get somebody killed."

Ursula topped off their coffees.

"Already has, if I'm not mistaken," Vic said.

*   *   *

"Do the police know about this?" Vigil said.

"They should by now," Vic said, then hesitated. "Well, that's not exactly true. They should have both SD cards by now, but it's hard to say if they've figured out how to decipher the *Sundial* white paper."

"How did you do it?" Peggy said.

"That, I can't tell you," Vic said.

"Like hell you can't," Vigil said.

"That's what I said," Vic said. "I can't."

"Ha ha," Vigil said. "I've got to know your sources. Quartermaine will want to know."

"The paper boy?" Vic said.

"Please don't call him that again," Vigil said. "Oh, he was pissed."

Vic wondered about this yarn he had spun for his new partner and his new boss. Was it pure fantasy? Was the *Sundial* cipher really that valuable? Maybe Riley was nutty enough to kill himself. He wanted to see how plausible his theory was, so he laid it out for these two, and they seemed to have bought it. But was it true? Was it real? To Vic it seemed real enough to pursue.

"No sources," Vic said. "Fire me if you want."

"All right," Vigil said. "You're fired."

"Les, knock it off," Peggy said.

"I just wanted to see what it sounded like," Vigil said. "Okay, you're re-hired. Happy?"

"Delighted," Vic said. "I've got to figure out where to go from here."

Vic wolfed down his breakfast, wanting to get out on his own as soon as possible. "I've got some stuff to do at home," Vic said. "I'll be in tomorrow morning, unless you've got some ribbon-cutting to cover, Les."

"Hardie har," Vigil said. "Stick with this. Keep me in the loop." Peggy and Vic just looked at each other. Vic raised one eyebrows, which was not easy for him. Peggy shrugged.

Outside, after Vigil paid the bill, both tried to give Vic a ride. He had committed his transport to and from the morning breakfast meeting to the transit offerings of the Regional Transportation District. Like many people, both Vigil and Peggy seemed to think Vic might perish if they turned him loose on the streets of Denver, dependent only on the bus for transportation.

"I think on the bus," Vic said. "Light rail too. I stare at the city flying by and just think. If I don't want to think, make a call on my phone, or re-read Great Expectations."

"You're nuts," Vigil said.

"Yeah, but a good kind of nuts," Vic said. "You remember, Les? I was on the light rail when you hired me."

"I was in my office," Vigil said sharply.

"I was in mine," Vic said. "The end car."

"Come on, Peg," Vigil said, as he bolted for his car. Peggy followed and furrowed her brow back at Vic, who just shrugged and launched his block and a half walk to catch the Number 65 bus heading north on Monaco. The hulking transit vehicle took him to Colfax where he jumped off and walked the dozen blocks or so to his house near 19th Avenue and Holly Street. The trip took about forty-five minutes.

All he thought about were Riley's death and *Sundial*.

26

Two doors down from his house, Vic sensed something looked out of place. The round stained glass window in the center of his arched front door had been punched out. A sense of personal violation washed over him. In broad daylight no less, he thought. It could have been a run of the mill thief, but he doubted it. As he approached the house from across the street, he called Driscoll on his cell phone.

"Don't go in there, Vic," Driscoll said. "Keep on walking. Get up the block and keep an eye out. Stay on the phone." Vic complied. The cop was back a minute later. "I'm rolling a couple of squads from District One, lights only," Driscoll said. "Frakes will be out there. It'll take him a while. He's over at Riley's. Where are you now?"

"Walking around the corner at 19th," Vic said. "I want to see if there's anyone in the alley."

"That's too close," Driscoll said. "Walk up to Montview."

"No," Vic said. "I want to see if someone comes out of my house."

"Dammit," Driscoll said. "Watch it then." He clicked off.

In five minutes, two Denver police cruisers wheeled off Montview and sped down Hudson to where Vic was standing on the corner at 19th. They stopped in the middle of the intersection, lights flashing, windows open.

"You Mr. Bengston?" said the dark-haired Latino women piloting the first car. She was nice looking, mid-forties. Dream on, he told himself.

"Yeah," Vic said.

"What's going on?" she said. Another cop, a skinny white guy about the same age was leaning over to hear Vic.

"The window on the front door was broken out," Vic said. "You can easily open the front door just by reaching in."

"Have you been inside?" the guy said. Vic shook his head.

"Okay, you stay here," the female officer said.

"Want a key?" Vic said.

"Sure," she said. Vic unwound the latchkey from a wire ring he kept on a small green carabineer.

"This opens any outside lock," Vic said.

"Thank you, sir," she said. "Now you need to stay over here."

"Yes, mam," Vic said, but he repositioned himself to the middle of the block so he could see a bit of his front yard as well as into the alley behind his house. The female officer was on the radio as she pulled her squad car around to the front of the house. The other squad car pulled into the alley and blocked it.

As the female officer stepped out of her car, Vic glimpsed a fireplug of a man about Vic's height and wearing a hoodie land in the alley. He must have hurtled the back fence, Vic thought. The guy sprinted up the concrete path away from the second squad car.

The alley did not go straight through to 17th Avenue Parkway, where alleyways would not have been conducive to the "parkway" look. Before the last house, it took a ninety-degree turn to the left back to Holly Street.

The driver of the second squad car, defensive backish, African American guy, had made it halfway down the alley in pursuit when Vic saw the hoodie runner throw a hard block into the cop's mid-section. The big guy in blue hit the deck and hoodie sprinted to the alley corner, made sharp left, and vanished. The car's number two occupant, a pear-shaped middle-ager who could have stood a few months in a gym, loped down the alley behind his partner. They met up at the corner where the alley turned back toward Holly Street. Pear-shape's hand went up to the radio mic pinned to his shoulder. Vic looked over toward the front of his house where the pretty cop and her male partner had weapons drawn, arms up, ready to bust in the front door. The pear-shaped cop was still standing at the end of the alley. The lady cop carefully knelt down and unlocked Vic's front door. Her partner rushed through and she followed. Sirens in the distance indicated reinforcements were on their way. But hoodie was in the wind. Pear-shaped cop certainly was not chasing him. Vic could not imagine rushing through a door not knowing what was on the other side. Took guts, he thought.

* * *

"Anything missing?" Frakes said.

Vic beheld the devastation in his study. Every book he owned was on the floor, built-in shelves empty. He looked at Frakes and said, "My 1934 Press of the Pioneers edition of Townsend's Lincoln and Liquor. I don't see it anywhere."

"How can you tell?" Frakes said. "Look at this mess."

"Just a hunch," Vic said.

"You're not much of a house keeper," Frakes said. Vic closed his eyes and shook his head. "Were you hiding anything in here?"

"Yes, my copy of Lincoln and Liquor. It's rare, and it's obviously gone."

Frakes rolled his eyes. "Anything else?"

"No," Vic said.

"You sure?" Frakes said. Vic ignored him. "Where's your computer?"

Vic looked at his desk. It really was not a desk at all. It was just a six-foot hollow-core door that rested on top of a pair of wire basket drawers he picked up at a garage sale for a fraction of what The Container Store charged. The basket drawers were pulled out, all their contents spread on the floor as well. The small four-wheel dolly that held his desktop computer box was empty. The box was lying on its side over in the corner. The case was open, but the hard drive was still there. Vic noticed one of the small silver screws that held it place was on the floor. Hoodie was trying to pull the drive, Vic concluded, as he glanced back at his desk to the spot where he kept a naked backup hard drive inserted into a box that was connected to the computer. The box was there, but no drive.

"One of my backup drives is gone," Vic said. "Big one. Three and a half inch SATA."

"What was on it?" Frakes asked.

Luckily, nothing of value, Vic thought, then said, "A lot of important stuff, but I mostly use this system for internet work and storage. Everything's backed up daily online anyway."

"In the cloud?" Frakes said.

Vic turned to him and said, "We are keeping up with the technology, aren't we, detective?"

"We try," Frakes said.

"Think we could get a copy of your hard drive there in the box?" Frakes said.

"Not without a court order and a pile of crap from the *Times*," Vic said.

"Thought so," Frakes said. "I had to ask."

"Consider your ass covered," Vic said. "Anyway, there is nothing on those drives pertaining to David Riley. I keep that stuff elsewhere." Vic looked up at the ceiling and Frakes nodded. The cloud.

The Riley *Sundial* material was not in the cloud. All of it was on his tiny netbook computer hard drive in the trunk of his car, and on two flash drives, one of which was in his bank safety deposit box. But there was a complete copy of the *Sundial* files on the backup hard drive now missing from his trashed study. Vic had finally listened to his youngest son, Conor, who was the IT security genius that kept one of Denver's massive health care enterprises running and told him many times to back up his data to multiple locations regularly. Vic had possession of all of those locations, except one now.

"Well, Driscoll wanted me to make sure you were okay, and it looks to me as though you're just darn AOK, right?" Frakes looked at his watch. Then he took out his card and handed it to Vic. "Here's my new extension and email. If you see anything else missing let us know, will you?"

"No," Vic said. Frakes smiled.

"We're going to leave an officer here for the time being," Frakes said. "In case this guy comes back."

"How about the other officer?" Vic said.

"Which one?" Frakes said.

"The tall one who ran down the alley. What happened?"

"Guy clocked him," Frakes said. "He'll be all right. Knocked the wind out of him."

"Smart fella," Vic said.

"Who?" Frakes said.

"The scofflaw," Vic said.

"Yeah," Frakes said. "Too smart for my taste."

"How do you mean?" Vic said.

"Your run of the mill burglar just bolts," Frakes said. "He doesn't stop, turn and set up to assault a cop to insure his escape."

"So he was a bit of a pro?" Vic said.

"More than a bit," Frakes said.

* * *

It took several hours to refill the built-in bookshelves with the volumes scattered ankle-deep on his study floor, including Lincoln and Liquor, a gift to him in his college days from the founder of Chicago's Abraham Lincoln Bookstore. Other than the backup hard drive, Vic could not see that anything else was missing, unless the guy grabbed a Tony Hillerman paperback for a quick read on the bus. The two officers, the ones from the first squad car, made themselves at home in the kitchen. They used laptops and Vic's wireless network to file their reports and get an update on the officer who seemed as though he had hit a brick wall.

"Scraped elbows, bruised ego," Officer Jannette Lopez said to Vic.

"His partner okay?" Vic said.

"I think so," Lopez said. "Still catching his breath."

That was about the extent of the conversation. Vic fixed a large pot of French press coffee. The officers polished that off before they attacked the sun tea he kept in the fridge. A repair service arrived and installed a thick round piece of plywood in the front door window. Vic thought he might install something a little more secure than crumbling old pieces of stained glass.

After three hours, the officers got word to leave.

"Call this number if anything happens," Lopez said, handing him yet another card. "We're going to come by every couple of hours at least for the next twenty-four, but call if anything seems out of the ordinary, okay?"

"Sure," Vic said, glad to see them gone, although Lopez was a nice addition to the house.

Baker the dog did not care all that much. He just enjoyed all the excitement.

* * *

Vic descended into his basement. He walked over to a four-foot long chest-high shelf on one wall. A power strip ran along the back. Various types of plugs occupied the receptacles. Wires led to an assortment of battery chargers and small electronic devices. This was his charging station. One of the devices was a basic backup cell phone that Vic simply added call time to when it ran low. He picked up the phone and dialed a number.

"Yes," Nelson said.

"I'm loading the Glock," Vic said.

"All right," Nelson said. "Remember how to shoot it?"

"Yes, I do," Vic said.

"When did you last shoot it?" Nelson said.

"A month ago, at the range," Vic said.

"Clean it?" Nelson said.

"A week ago," Vic said.

Okay," Nelson said. "You're good to go. Be careful. Remember what I taught you."

"Will do," Vic said and hung up.

Despite the training, the gun made him nervous.

27

Vic strung a holster onto his belt and snugged the Glock 19 into it. He put on a light wind breaker to hide the weapon. He also checked his wallet to make sure his concealed carry permit was there. It was. He walked out the back door, down the three redwood deck stairs, across the back yard, along the pathway past his vegetable garden, and out the gate into the alley. He headed toward the turn where the burglar took out the patrolman.

Like his many trips up and down alleys, Vic took in what most people ignored, cracks in the stained and worked over cement, the long outlawed now disintegrating ash pits, and the gates leading to his neighbors' lairs. Maybe he would find something, he thought, remembering how, many years earlier, he managed to track down and recover two bicycles stolen from this same property. He knew that for Driscoll and Frakes playing detective was a tough sixty-hour-a-week job. For him it was fun and magical.

At the right-angle turn of the alley, Vic saw what he assumed was a small spot of blood on the pavement. He made a mental note to have Lopez give him the name of the injured officer, so he could send the guy a card or thank-you note. The patrolman took one on Vic's behalf, a benefit from first responders that most citizens take for granted.

Vic scanned the pavement, then the dark recesses that comprise any alleyway, searching for anything that might have been missed in the confusion. He fanned his hands across the dense ivy that, over the years, had transformed wire fences into impenetrable green alley fortifications. Amidst the brown and gnarly tangles of dry vine stems and shriveled leaves, he spotted a smooth black and silver object that was neither vine nor fence, but was buried deep inside the foliage as though it belonged there. Only it did not. Vic wormed his right arm down through the plant and fence entwinement until his fingertips touched the hard drive. He pushed a little harder until he could grasp it with his thumb and forefinger. Then he pulled it out. The recognizable thick Sharpie pen handwriting designated the drive as "BU01."

"This is good," Vic said aloud. "Hoodie guy does not have a copy of *Sundial*."

Then Vic's heart began thumping again, as he said to the empty alley, "That means hoodie guy will be back."

* * *

Vic grabbed the hard drive, jogged back to the house and raced downstairs to his ham shack. He pulled down a plastic storage box from a shelf above his radios and fished out a gangly cable with some oddball connectors attached to it. He slipped one of the connectors onto the back of the drive and plugged the other end of the cable into the USB port on the side of a tiny netbook computer he used to log stations when he ran amateur radio contests. Then he turned the netbook on.

When the system booted up, Vic opened a special program one of his son's gave him. In a few minutes, he had wiped and reformatted the backup hard drive. He reset the computer clock to the day before and then he copied all the data files he had on his radio station computer to the hard drive. When that was done, Vic reset the clock on his ham radio computer, sprinted back out the door, hurting his already sore left knee, jogged back down the alley and replaced the "missing" hard drive in the vine fence.

What remained in the alley was a small hard drive, maybe with Hoodie's fingerprints on it, along with a complete backup of all his ham radio articles, contest and operating logs, and various ham radio software programs, essentially everything that reflected Vic's geeky interests.

But nothing about *Sundial*.

* * *

As he stared at the now doctored hard drive, Vic questioned what he had done, then forgot about it. Driscoll has *Sundial*, although it might not be decrypted. He scrolled through his cellphone contact list and thumbed a number on the smooth glass face of the phone.

"Driscoll," the detective said.

"Vic."

"My least favorite golfing buddy," Driscoll said. "What now?"

"Can you find Frakes?" Vic said.

"Why?"

"I'm standing right next to my missing backup hard drive," Vic said.

"Don't tell me in was in the alley," Driscoll said, frustrated that his crew missed it.

"It was almost impossible to find," Vic said. "I just lucked out."

"You lucked out more by calling me," Driscoll said. Vic knew he was right. That was why he called him. Still, he felt guilty, wiping the drive.

"I don't see how the guy could have hit the patrolman and then jammed the thing so deep into the vines," Vic said.

"You'd be surprised what happens during an altercation," Driscoll said. "But he probably jammed it down there on purpose."

"This guy's coming back then," Vic said. "Can you send someone over here muy pronto?"

"Hang on," Driscoll said, putting Vic on hold. A minute later he was back. "We're sending a car right over. Hang tight and stay on the line until they get there. Frakes will be along in a while."

The rest was small talk except Vic's fumbling attempt to apologize once again for entering Riley's house, and Driscoll informing him that the matter was still under advisement by his office. Vic asked him if his lab had gotten anywhere with the picture. Driscoll played dumb and said, "As far as they could tell it was a watercolor of the Oriental Theater."

Five minutes after Vic called Driscoll a squad car pulled into the alley and parked just over the sidewalk. Lopez and her partner stepped out and walked toward Vic. He never did get the partner's name, and he still liked the way Lopez looked.

"Mr. Bengston," Lopez said.

"Officer Lopez, and officer?" Vic said.

"Jameson," her partner said.

"Officer Jameson," Vic said.

"Where's the item?" Lopez said, staring right into his eyes. "We searched this spot a couple of times."

"I got lucky," Vic said, pointing deep into a gnarly tangle of ivy mixed with outlaw morning glory. "A corner of it caught my eye. Otherwise I would have missed it too."

"Well, I'll be damned," Jameson said. "That is really wedged down in there."

Lopez called Frakes on her radio.

"Don't touch it," Frakes said through the tiny speaker-microphone pinned to Lopez's right shoulder. "I'm sending the lab over to retrieve it."

"I doubt if the guy left fingerprints," Vic said. "He was a pro."

"Even pros make mistakes," Lopez said, smiling a nice smile. She nodded toward the hard drive embedded in the vine. "We missed this."

28

The Olde Capitol Tavern in "historic" downtown Golden, Colorado, was one of those restaurants that looked great on paper. The stately brick post-Civil War structure housed the Colorado Territory capitol for a few years before it moved eastward to Denver City, where it became permanent after Colorado set up shop as a real state in 1876. The capitol switch still rankled a few in Golden. Sometime in the early 2000s, the tavern building went up in flames. Firefighters saved the structure and restoration was a non-debatable issue. Locals raised funds immediately to clean up, restore, and install a sprinkler system. Upper floors morphed into revenue-generating professional office suites.

The restaurant re-opened at street level and continued to offer mediocre food and mostly beer brewed down the street by Coors, the historic western brewery whose claim to fame was making its thin brews from Rocky Mountain spring water. That actually meant the water came from Clear Creek, a South Platte River tributary often used by Vic and many of his friends in their younger days to relieve themselves after an evening of drinking and dancing further upstream at rustic bars hidden in the foothills.

Vic occupied the booth next to the old vault used to house territorial documents. He nursed a luke warm cup of coffee that was definitely not Designer Joe. Paxton Stone slid into the booth across from him.

"Don't order the salmon," Stone said.

"It looked good," Vic said. "And over wild rice pilaf."

"Liz and I had some last night," Stone said. "It was like cardboard."

"What's good?" Vic said. "I haven't been here since the pre-fire management."

"The burgers are okay, if the meat's all right," Stone said.

"Such a ringing endorsement," Vic said.

"No, I'm joking," Stone said. "The burgers are very good. I know the guy who grass feeds the animals."

"All rightie then," Vic said.

They each ordered the Territorial Burger, which came with all the fixings and, of course, American cheese. In the world of advertising, or branding as it now was called, it mattered little that there were no hamburgers when this place housed what must have been a rowdy government for Colorado Territory. Stone ordered his well done.

"Well done?" Vic said. "Is there more I should know about meat handling in this place?"

Stone laughed and shook his head. The wait guy stood at parade rest, pencil poised.

"You're safe any way you order it," Stone said. "I like hockey pucks."

"If I wind up kissing the porcelain god, I want you and Liz to bring bon bons to my hospital room," Vic said, then to the waiter, "Medium rare."

The two talked about hot rods, model railroads, and ham radio while they ate. Stone ordered a microbrew as an alternative to the Coors on tap. Vic tasted it, and, through the bite of alcohol, he picked up a pleasurable flavor that was probably foreign to most of the brewmeisters down the street. He stuck with the bad coffee.

"Have you gotten rid of the *Sundial* stuff?" Stone asked, a cloud of seriousness masking his freckled face.

"I have," Vic said. "The cops have it all."

"How do you know that?" Stone said.

"I just know," Vic said. "What about the test file you encrypted?"

"I can't un-ring that bell," Stone said. "Once on the net it's there forever."

"Has anyone deciphered it?" Vic said.

Stone picked at his remaining salad, sipped his beer and ignored the question. Vic just stared at him. Two silent minutes crawled on by.

"One," Stone said. "And it was right away."

"What do you mean, right away?" Vic said.

"I mean within a half hour," Stone said.

"None of the rest?" Vic said. Stone shook his head. "So, what does that mean?"

"It probably means the guy has *Sundial*," Stone said.

"Doesn't that also mean he knows you have *Sundial* too?" Vic said.

Stone nodded a pale worried face, and said, "But he's a friendly."

"How do you know that?" Vic said.

"Well, I assume that," Stone said.

"Which will wind up making an ass out of you and me?" Vic said.

Stone just shook his head and raised his eyebrows.

* * *

"Do you have any idea who this person is or where he lives?" Vic said.

"It's really hard to say," Stone said. "These guys hide their tracks. They're the best of the best. Still—"

"Still?" Vic said. He was waiting Stone out again.

"Still, there was something that he wrote, something that made me think I knew him. I think this is a guy named Jared Picune. If it is him, I know him quite well, or I did."

"Did?" Vic said.

"Okay, if it is Jared, we worked together at Genra-IC about six years ago," Stone said. "This guy was a genius at chip design. But it was his hobby, his avocation, that he spent most of his energy on."

"Not ham radio?" Vic said.

"No. Ciphers. Mathematical ciphers. Encryption."

"Wouldn't there be a lot of people, amateurs and pros, all over the world who are into mathematical ciphers?" Vic said.

"There are," Stone said. "But I remember a conversation I had with him back before we both left Genra-IC. He was over for dinner, with his girlfriend. I forget her name. Amy, I think. Anyway, we had finished a couple of bottles of wine and—"

"Wine?" Vic said. "In Golden? I thought that was against the law."

Stone cracked a smile and laughed, the intended effect.

"We don't all hew to the Coors company line out here," Stone said.

"Okay, so you were tipsy," Vic said.

"And I pulled out my fractal patterns," Stone said.

"You pulled them out when I once dined at your table," Vic said.

"You and a hundred other people," Stone said. "Fractals fascinate me. How shapes replicate each other in finer and finer detail, either in nature or by using software programs to generate the images."

"Was Jared equally interested?" Vic said.

"He was more than interested," Stone said. "Mesmerized, I'd say, so much so that I insisted on giving him the code I wrote to generate some of the images, just to play with."

"Did you?" Vic said.

"Did I what?" Stone said.

"Give him the code?" Vic said.

"Oh, sure," Stone said. "He was a colleague."

"So how does that connect with ciphers and *Sundial?*" Vic said.

"He said something to me that, well, at the time I thought was a fairly impractical idea," Stone said.

Vic raised his eyebrows.

"He said he wondered if fractals, either natural or software generated, could be used to breed numbers that would be very difficult to re-generate," Stone said.

"Natural?" Vic said.

"Sure, like snowflakes, crystals, plant structures," Stone said. "All those exhibit fractal patterns, but they come along with nature's imperfections."

"Pax, I remember those pictures you showed me," Vic said. "They looked like psychedelic patterns you'd print on tee-shirts to sell at a rock concert out at Red Rocks."

"Fractals do tend to blow your mind," Stone said. "But, no, there might be some interesting ways to generate numbers that could be used for something else."

"Like a cipher?" Vic said.

"Like a cipher," Stone said.

"A key?" Vic said.

"A key," Stone said.

"So I take it that you don't think the use of fractals to encrypt documents or data is that far-fetched of an idea anymore," Vic said.

"Not since I read the *Sundial* paper," Stone said.

"I still don't see how you generate a number with fractals," Vic said.

"All right, bear with me for a bit," Stone said. "Let's say you have a simple triangle."

Stone pulled out a ball point pen and drew a triangle on a napkin. It was pointing down.

"Are the sides equal?" Vic said.

"Yes," Vic said.

"Isosceles, right?" Vic said.

"Wrong, sort of," Stone said. "An isosceles triangle has at least two equal sides, which this one does. This actually has three equal sides. It's equilateral."

"I was partially right," Vic said.

"And you still claim membership in your high school Math Club?" Stone said. "Disgraceful."

Vic raised his hands in surrender. Stone continued.

"Okay, now you take a third in the center of each side and use that as the base for three more equilateral triangles," Stone said, drawing a smaller triangle on each of the three sides of his initial triangle.

"It looks like a star," Vic said. "With six points."

"Right," Stone said. "It's called a Koch Star, named after a Swedish mathematician, and it gets even better."

Stone then did the same thing with each of the new sides and he wound up with a symmetrical shape that had eighteen points.

"It's starting to look like a doily or a snowflake," Vic said.

"Correct again!" Stone said. "Now, this is known as a Koch Snowflake, because the more you keep doing the same thing the more it begins to look like the stuff that falls from the sky each winter."

"I still don't see how you come up with numbers that can be used to encrypt my bank ATM deposit," Vic said.

"Or a State Department cable?" Stone said. "Or a secret financial transfer from one entity, say a sovereign fund, to a terrorist front?"

Vic was puzzled over the geometry and math, but not the implication of possessing unbreakable encryption technology. He shook his head in resignation.

"Say we want to use computer generated fractals to come up with a number," Stone said.

"Yes, let's say," Vic said, clueless.

"And we picked a triangle," Stone said. "There are an infinite number of shapes that could be used but we'll pick an equilateral triangle. Of course, there is an infinite number of triangle dimensions we could use, and an infinite number of smaller identical fractal shapes that we could generate. Then, within this final shape, there could be an infinite number of points that create the inside of the final shape."

He pointed his pen tip to one of the inside points on the snowflake he drew on the napkin.

"What if we start here and measure the distance between point B," he said, moving his pen tip one point to the right. "And point F." Stone moved the pen tip four points over and drew a line between point B and point F.

"If we picked real numbers for the initial triangle size and the number of fractals we generate, then this line will have a finite length, say sixty millimeters or two point four inches," Stone said. "Multiply the line length by some other number in the cipher and you get a third number."

"A picture is emerging, a fairly muddy one," Vic said. "I think."

"Like I said, the possibilities are endless. Infinite number of shapes, infinite number of fractals, infinite number of internal lines to measure, infinite number of ways to manipulate them, add them, subtract them, divide, multiply," Stone said. "It gives you quite a range."

"So big that nobody in your clique of hackers can figure it out," Vic said.

"Except one," Stone said.

"Jared?" Vic said.

"Jared," Stone said.

"Where do you think he is?" Vic said. "I'd like to interview him."

"I don't have a clue," Stone said. "I haven't seen him for months."

"Do you think he was involved with *Sundial*?" Vic said.

Stone leaned back and smiled his boyish grin, nodded, and said, "That would be my guess."

"How about Jared's family?" Vic said.

"Nothing comes to mind," Stone said. "I'm not sure where his family's from or where they are now. I don't even know if he's married or still has that same girlfriend."

"You said you saw him a few months ago," Vic said.

"I caught a glimpse of him at DIA. Walking onto a jet way."

"What airline," Vic said.

"Southwest."

"What destination?"

Stone leaned back and folded his arms. "Fort Lauderdale."

"How do you know that?" Vic said.

"I was at the next gate, a flight to Seattle," Stone said. "I saw the destination at Jared's gate."

"Talk to him?" Vic said. Stone shook his head. "Wave?" Another shake. "A glimpse then." A nod. "Sure it was him?" Another nod.

"Well, that gives me something," Vic said. "Not much. But something."

The two picked through their food and returned to small talk for a while. Then, Stone halted his fork midway between plate and mouth.

"You know what?" Stone said. Vic looked up. "Jared mentioned a brother. I don't even remember his name."

"What about him?" Vic said.

"He said he was a big time fishing guide," Stone said. "Montana in the summer. I think on the Madison River."

"Winter?" Vic said.

"Key West," Stone said.

29

"Key West?" Vigil said, clearly displeased.

"The trip was planned," Vic said. "Long before you hired me." That was true, Vic told himself. Since he tried to get down to Key West every year or so, a trip there was always planned, technically.

Peggy was within earshot. Closing her eyes, she shook her head.

"What about the Riley story?" Vigil said.

"I'll be gone for what, five days?" Vic said. "I don't want to lose a deposit on a boat." No one would, Vic thought. He did not have a deposit on a boat, but that was not what he had just said to Vigil. He was keeping things generic, open-ended.

"Can you work anything from down there?" Vigil said.

Vic pursed his lips and nodded. "Except if I'm out flats fishing. I'll have my netbook and cellphone."

"What is a netbook anyway?" Vigil said.

"A small laptop," Vic said.

"Why don't they just call it a laptop?" Vigil said.

"Branding," Vic said. "Give it another name. Sell more units."

"Branding," Vigil said. "That's like advertising, right?"

"Same thing," Vic said. "With a little marketing."

"Thought so," Vigil said. Then he sprung the trap. "Did you talk with Logan over in sports?"

"Logan?" Vic said. "What for?"

"For that Key West fishing story you're going to research next week," Vigil said.

Vic stared at Vigil, then said. "The fishing story. Yeah. Sure I'll check in with the old timer before I leave."

"Old timer?" Vigil said. "He's younger than you."

"Remember, we're baby boomers," Vic said. "We're taking over the planet. Be nice."

On his way over to the sports department to find Logan, Vic called his travel agent on his cell phone and asked her to find the best flight deal down to Key West and back.

30

Key West International Airport consisted of a few single story whitewashed buildings, a parking lot, real palm trees, and an east-west airstrip on the Atlantic Ocean side of the island. Outside the main door, Vic stood at the curb, a green daypack slung over his right shoulder. His well-traveled black nylon suitcase, bought twenty years earlier from REI for his very first trip to Europe, occupied a small segment of pale blue stained cement next to him. Vic welcomed the weather swap, Colorado's chilly mile high spring morning for Key West's moist seventy-five-degree late afternoon, tempered with a light Caribbean breeze caressing his face. He never wanted to leave. Within minutes of landing he was on island time.

As Vic savored the sea air and day-dreamed of a tiny writing shack on the island, Barb drove up in her little white Toyota pickup. She pulled in fast, slammed on the brakes and jumped out.

"Well this is one big surprise," she said, hugging Vic.

"Surprise, surprise," Vic said. "You're looking good."

"Dumb luck," she said, crackling her funny little laugh. She walked around to the back of her truck and opened the hatch on the topper that sheltered the pickup bed from the rain. "Toss your stuff in here."

Vic set his suitcase and backpack in an open corner of the truck bed amidst Barb's house cleaning supplies. Nearly three decades earlier, roughly the same time Vic had left the journalism business to navigate the corporate world, Barb and her sister chucked their Midwest lives and moved to Key West. Barb was a department store buyer when she put St. Louis in the rear view mirror. The first thing she did when she hit Key West was to start a housecleaning service, something that paid cash money every day. When most people retire, she was still at it, now only a few days a week, vowing never to give up the job she created and, along the way, enabled her to pick up and fix up a half a dozen Key West rental properties that were probably worth a few million bucks in the current market.

"Kelly's working today down at Nico's," she said, hitting the breaks to avoid a young couple wobbling on a lime green motor scooter. "He's down to three days a week, really just enough to keep his health insurance until Medicare kicks in."

"Skin cancer gone?" Vic said.

"Yes," Barb said. God, she was chipper. "Eighteen months so far."

"How's Kelly doing then?" Vic said.

"He feels great," Barb said. "But he's replaced his baseball cap with a Panama hat."

"Add sunglasses and you've got a good Key West look going for you," Vic said.

Barb laughed as they pulled into her place off George Street. She and Kelly lived in a compact but comfy two-bedroom flat that occupied the upstairs of what once was a two-story island house, clapboard siding, tin roof. A food pantry occupied one end of the kitchen along with the door to their large master bedroom. The kitchen, essentially a galley set-up, was separated from the living room area by a two-sided split-level counter, with the kitchen a half a foot below the living room. Bar stools occupied the living room side of the counter. The kitchen side was a standup work area where Kelly loved to cook.

Vic stowed his gear at the foot of a built-in teak ladder at one end of the living room. It led to a small loft carved into the ceiling area during a recent restoration project. The loft offered everything Vic needed, a large mattress pad, a ceiling fan, and a reading light. And it was free, considerably below standard Key West overnight rates.

Vic thought of his late business partner, Ben, the good times they had in Key West, and of Ben's dead brother, Barry, the cranky artist and set-builder from New York. Both died too young.

"I miss Ben," Vic said. "Barry too. And the company's annual meeting down here."

"We all do," Barb said. "We'll always miss both of them. There's a lot of Barry in this place. He was a good carpenter, when we could get him to work. You know you're always welcome here. You're family too. No one else is here this week. The guest room is available."

"I always took the loft," Vic said. "Barry's loft. He built it and I like it, so long as my knees keep navigating the ladder."

Barb handed him a house key. "Kelly set up the red bike for you," she said. "Here's the key for the bike lock, and take one of the lights over there when you go." She pointed to a bank of six small flashlights plugged into a charging strip. In Key West, the preferred mode of transportation was bicycle. Also, driving a bike at night without a light was illegal, and visitors were often ticketed for bicycling without them as they weaved their way home from some bar, restaurant, Mallory Square, or Duval Street after dark. Then she handed Vic a quarter sheet of paper.

"I found a Jeff Picune," she said. "He wasn't in the phone book, but I asked Jim Turpin if he knew Picune, and he did. By the way, Jim's a good flats fishing guide if you want to go out while you're here. This Jeff, I gather, heads out east past the reef. barracuda and deep sea."

"Where's his boat?" Vic said.

"Fisherman's Row," Barb said. "I don't see how he can do that without a phone."

"Cell phone," Vic said.

Barb chuckled and smiled. "Oh yeah. I keep forgetting about that. I didn't see an ad in the white pages though. Probably has trust fund money."

"All right," Vic said. "I'm going to ride over there and see if I can find him."

"We're going to meet at Nico's around six," Barb said. "We'll figure out dinner from there. Kelly wants to cook tomorrow night, but maybe we'll just go over to the Blue Parrot tonight."

"Anything's fine by me," Vic said. "It's all good. I'm going to change and head over to the boats."

Barb left to go clean some women's condo she'd been cleaning for fifteen years. Vic shed his Denver clothes and tossed on island gear: shorts, polo shirt, ball cap, shades, white socks and his New Balance 608s, currently his preferred cross-training shoe.

He set out on bicycle to find Jared Picune's brother, Jeff, and maybe learn a little more about *Sundial*.

31

Fisherman's Row was about a mile from Barb and Kelly's. Vic cycled down Duncan, through a park, and then walked with the light across Roosevelt, which was U.S. 1, the highway that runs from the Canadian border in Maine along the east coast, through Florida, threading the long ribbon causeway linking all the keys before dead-ending in Key West, about 80 miles north of Cuba. He pedaled up a wide sidewalk that separated Roosevelt from a small bay, passing by houseboats, sailboats at anchor, and a floating crab shack before turning left into the parking lot at the foot of the Palm Avenue Causeway. He stopped, straddled the bike, and pulled the piece of paper Barb had given him from the left pocket of his nylon shorts.

"Jeff Picune," Barb's note read. "FR#23."

He stuffed the paper back into his pocket and re-rolled the bike, giving pedals a few hard thrusts and then coasted past the charter boats, most of them good sized with flying bridges up top and client comfort zones down below. Most of the charters were in for the night. Captains were busy with various chores. A red-faced fishing guide stood over one of the stainless steel cleaning stations efficiently rinsing, scaling, and filleting the day's take-home catch, mostly red snappers, so the clients could carry something back to their vacation condos or local restaurant for a fresh fish dinner. The trophy catches, barracuda off the reefs or the occasional marlin, had been returned to the sea for future charter trips. Crew prepped baits for the next morning, washed down decks, helped lucky and unlucky clients load gear back into their cars, and cracked open beers to wash down the long hot day out on the water.

Vic continued his slow roll down Fisherman's Row, passing boat names like Gulfstream III Fishing, Captain Hook, Red Bull, and Captain Bill's, all designed to give the usually tame tourists a little hint of Caribbean piracy or rakishness. He stopped at number twenty-three, the berth of Hacker Charters. Like all the others, the boat was backed into the dock. It was dark and closed up. He leaned the bike up against a signpost and stepped onto the aft deck.

"Jeff," Vic called. No answer.

He knocked on the rear cabin door. Nothing.

Vic stepped back onto the cement dock and looked down at the stern of Picune's boat. It was named Hacker II.

Wondering where Hacker I was, Vic walked over to the first occupied boat, two berths down from Hacker II. This outfit was named Sustainable Charters, a clear departure from the rough and tumble names Vic has just cycled past. Must be something like catch and release in Colorado, Vic thought. Someone, either crew or captain, was down on her hands and knees scrubbing the stern deck. Vic peered at the smaller stern, round and nicely packed into a pair of teal nylon shorts.

"Excuse me," Vic said.

A swish of light brown streaked shoulder length hair swung around with a mildly weather beaten but beautiful face of a woman Vic pegged as being in her early fifties. She stood up, sponge in one hand, rag in the other.

"Hi," she said. "Need a charter?"

"No, not yet," Vic said, rethinking his plans to go flats fishing on the gulf side of the island, and maybe, instead chartering this boat for a jaunt out into the Atlantic. "I'm looking for Jeff. Have you seen him?"

"Jeff?" she said.

"Hacker Two," Vic said nodding back toward berth twenty-three.

"Oh, the computer nerd," she said, wiping her hands and stepping off the boat. "Naw, haven't seen him all day. Who are you?"

"Vic Bengston," he said. "I'm in town for a few days. Jeff and his brother are old friends."

"That would be Jared," she said, tossing the rag and sponge into a red plastic bucket, then held out her hand.

"Marti Clemons," she said. "Marti with an i—Vic?"

"Yeah, Vic Bengston, with a V," he said, taking her hand and relishing in the warm, moist, and firm grip of a woman. "Marti. This is your boat?"

She nodded and said, "All forty-five feet of it."

"Nice hull," Vic said. She smiled.

"Some of these jerks think we're bad luck," Marti said, sweeping her right arm across Fisherman's Row. "There are three of us here now, girl captains."

"And how are you doing?" Vic said.

"Better than most of the boy captains," she said with a sly grin.

Vic looked down at the boat's name on the stern and said, "What does Durga mean?"

"She's a Hindu goddess. In Sanskrit, Durga means invincible."

"The boy captains probably don't like that," Vic said.

"No they don't," Marti said. "But then again they haven't a clue what it means either."

"You don't know where he might be, do you?" Vic said. "Jeff, that is. What did you call him? A computer nerd?"

"Not a clue," Marti said, nodding. "At night, on his boat there. He's always on the computer. His flats boat is gone, though. He might have gotten a client for permit or bone fish, but I doubt it."

"Why's that?" Vic said.

"They'd have been back by now," she said. "Plus the wind was up today. I don't think anyone went out onto the flats."

Vic remembered the times he and Ben spent their days reading the *Key West Citizen* and the *Miami Herald* on Barb and Kelly's deck waiting for the wind to drop just enough so a guide could take them out into the Gulf of Mexico to fish the flats west of the island. It needed to be calm, so almost any wind kept the fishing boats at the dock and the bars full.

"Did you happen to see a visitor?" Vic said.

"Like his brother?" Marti said.

"Yes."

She shook her head and said, "No, I haven't seen him or anyone else for that matter."

Vic didn't want to push the questioning too far. He thought it would be nice to spend a little more time with this gift from the sea named Marti, but he knew his time on the island was limited, and he did want to track down Jeff Picune and the missing brother, Jared, if Jared was even around.

"Well, maybe I can catch him tomorrow," Vic said.

"If you have any interest in a charter, give me a call," she said, handing him a card.

"Thanks," Vic said. He pulled out his wallet and tucked it into one of its credit card pockets.

"You have a card?" she said.

"No, I don't," Vic said. There were six in his wallet.

"How about a cell phone number," Marti said. "In case I see Jeff. Just write it on here."

She held out another one of her cards. Vic took it and pulled a screw-top fountain pen out of his shirt pocket. He removed the top, wrote his cell phone number on her card and handed it back to her.

"You don't see many of those," Marti said, looking down at the fountain pen.

"I like to write with it," Vic said.

"I like to watch you write with it," Marti said, and then while looking him straight in the eyes, "I'm always here about this time tidying up and chilling out for the evening."

"I'll keep that in mind," Vic said.

"See that you do," Marti said. "I am a captain after all."

"And me a mere swabby."

Vic secured his pen and rode off on his bike to cross the island and meet Barb and Kelly at Nico's, but thinking of Marti.

32

Nico's Steakhouse was a compact frame structure that fought back hard with only wood and white paint at the corrosive sea air and island environment. Some might call it a shack. Whatever it was, it had occupied its space beneath the trees a block off the Key West bight on the Gulf side of the island since 1934. It had opened every single day since then, even during hurricanes when locals stood knee-deep in water, drinking beer and maintaining Nico's continuous opening record.

Vic pushed the heavy wooden front door open and walked through the narrow dining area, flanked by six booths on one side and three round tables on the other. He passed the kitchen where some of the island's best steaks and fish sandwiches were prepared and stepped into a courtyard of sorts occupied by about ten more tables. A tiny L-shaped nine-stool bar occupied the area to the right, along with a few wooden benches, a picnic table, and the pathway to the johns. On the bar-side, patrons consumed adult beverages while waiting for their tables, or until closing time, whichever came first. A glass-doored cabinet along the back wall of the bar featured Nico's clothing line, including sweatshirts, tee-shirts, ball caps and bar towels. Little in the way of a structural roof covered either of these areas, mostly umbrellas and a broad tree canopy.

When Vic walked in, drinkers occupied all nine bar stools. Others stood two deep behind those lucky enough to have snatched a seat. The television above the bar displayed the popular Weather Channel so everyone could see how bad the weather was back in their hometowns.

"Vic!"

It was Kelly, from behind the bar. He held up a Kaliber bottle. Vic nodded. Kelly knocked off the cap and poured the amber non-alcoholic beer into a glass. Vic pushed his way through three layers of bar patrons to grab the glass. It was too loud for real conversation.

"Barb should be here in a minute," Kelly shouted. Vic just nodded. "We're going over to the Raw Bar for dinner, okay?" Vic nodded again and handed Kelly a five. He waved it off. Then Kelly pointed over toward the door back to the restaurant. Barb had just walked in.

"Wait a minute," Kelly said. He poured a glass of white wine and handed it to Vic. "I'm done in about twenty minutes."

"I'll take care of Barb," Vic shouted back.

"Please," Kelly returned. "Someone has to."

Vic made his way over to Barb and handed her the wine. She smiled as she took the wine glass, then laughed, a laugh quickly and efficiently absorbed by the crowd noise. Barb pointed her glass toward the small wooden bench in a corner. It was labeled, "Broker Bob's Office." They sat down shoulder to shoulder, ear to mouth and vice versa to make conversation over the din.

"Is Bob around?" Vic said.

"I saw him yesterday, here," Barb said, taking a sip on her chilled wine. "He had to go up the Keys the help shut down the brewery."

The last time Vic was in Key West, Broker Bob had lined up a few investors to launch a microbrewery, which wound up doing a landmine business selling Key West Brew at places like Nico's. Top Gun star Kelly McGillis had the idea first, parlaying stacks and stacks of Hollywood dollars into a Key West restaurant that featured its own microbrewed beer. Broker Bob, who actually was a Wall Street broker, spent much of his time in Key West at Nico's on his bench with his cell phone cutting deals, figured there was room for microbrew competition.

"Shut down?" Vic said.

Barb laughed.

"Bob got spread a little too thin between his clients, the brewery, and the PT boat," Barb said. "Something had to give."

"So it was the brewery?" Vic said.

"Yup," Barb said, brightly. "He tried to sell it but there was some problem with the lease. Kelly can tell you. Anyway, it went under."

"The boat still runs?" Vic said.

"Oh, sure, but Bob's partners took over its management," Barb said. "Bob captains it every so often."

Vic encountered the PT boat the previous winter when he was half asleep on a sunset sail aboard the Stars and Stripes, a twin-hulled replica of the first catamaran to win the America's Cup under the command of Dennis Conner. The World War Two PT boat, with Broker Bob at the helm, came blasting by the sailing yacht, pointed its guns toward Vic and commenced a fake attack. It was all part of the sunset activities that drew hundreds of thousands of tourists to the island each year.

"I don't see any regulars," Vic said, scanning the crowd.

"Two cruise ships are in," Barb said, giggling. "Can't you feel the island tilting?"

The Key West fathers and mothers had decided to dredge out a much larger area on the Gulf side of the island and expand the dock to handle up to three giant cruise ships, guaranteeing that Key West would forever be a regular stop when many of the floating behemoths made their way out of Miami and Fort Lauderdale toward Mexico, Central and South America, and the Caribbean.

The dock was located so the cruise ship mob swarmed up Duval Street, the main tourist strip filled with the requisite gift shops, bars, restaurants, tee-shirt emporiums, ice cream parlors, electronics stores, and a calamity of other enterprises designed solely for the purpose of separating dollars from vacationing visitors. Some of the vacationing multitudes managed to stumble their way a few blocks off Duval, ending up at the Key West Bight, an eclectic mix of boat works, docks, marine supply stores, eating and drinking emporiums, dive shops, the island's best fish market and grocery store, and the terminal for the high speed ferries from Fort Meyers. Fewer still managed to migrate across the public parking lot next to the bight and made it into Nico's. However, when you start with thousands of souls pouring from the massive cruise ships a mile away, even a small percentage of migrating tourism hordes stumbled into the tiny restaurant and bar, jamming it wall to wall for most of the evening. When that happened, the locals shied away from Nico's and worked their way deeper into the island to consume their evening beers at bars considered even more local by those who lived in Key West year round.

Barb updated Vic on what daughter Karen, sister Pam, and longtime friend Joan were doing. Vic, in turn, filled Barb in on what his four grown-up children, grandkids, and ex-wife. They both teared up remembering her cousins, Ben and Barry. After fifteen minutes, Kelly appeared at Broker Bob's bench.

"Drink up kids," Kelly said. "We're meeting Touch Tone Tim and Karen over at the Raw Bar." Kelly was grinning and happy. He was a retired lawyer who went all in for Key West years earlier and enjoyed tending the tiny bar for his friend, Peter, who happened to own Nico's.

Vic and Barb finished their drinks and the three headed out the front door, dodging a few Nico's-bound tourists. A block away, the Raw Bar guarded the right flank of the entrance to the Key West Bight. Karen and Tim waved them over to a dockside table.

"Hey, Kelly," one of the regular bartenders shouted as they walked past the big horseshoe bar and over to the table.

"Brian, how are you doing this fine evening?" Kelly said on his way around the bar. "Send over some beer and wine." Barb waved. Vic just smiled.

For the next hour, the five sat and ate and exchanged tidbits from their lives and the lives of those close to them, Vic filing away the quirky aspects of the local stories for use in novels he thought he might write someday. He relished the time, dockside with the windows open to the activity of the small harbor, a mild island breeze caressing him. Despite the interesting small talk, especially the latest antics of Key West politicians, Vic reminded himself he was on a tight schedule, and a mission.

"I'd like to book a charter with Jeff Picune," Vic said. "Scare some fish. A friend of mine knows his brother, Jared."

"I've heard of Picune, but don't even know what he looks like," Tim said. Touch Tone was the island's phone guy, one of the few around who actually knew how the entire system worked. As a result, he was always busy fixing one problem or another, especially in the wake of hurricanes and tropical storms, which occasionally wreaked havoc in the keys.

"Well, he wasn't at his big boat over on Roosevelt and his flats boat was gone when I left there about six," Vic said.

"He might have the boat out of the water for work," Kelly said. "That's pretty late to come back from a flats charter."

"That's what I was told," Vic said. "I'll cycle over there in the morning."

"So are you working on a story, Mr. Reporter?" Karen said.

"I'm supposed to be," Vic said. "A fishing story."

"A fishy story?" Barb said. Everyone guffawed and ordered their last round of drinks, Vic sticking with a St. Pauli Girl NA. Everyone except Vic was getting ready to head for the barn. Even in party happy Key West, weeknights were treated differently than weekends since the bulk of the non-trust fund baby locals had to get up early the next day and do real work.

"I'm going to take a walk along the bight first," Vic said. "It might be my only shot at it this trip."

"Did you grab a flashlight?" Kelly said.

"I did," Vic said, patting his pants pocket. "Thanks for getting a bike ready. I was going to rent one."

"No bother," said Kelly. "We've got extras for our visitors, so you saved a few bucks."

"Keys?" Barb said.

Vic held up one of several rings that Barb and Kelly kept on hand for visitors. The ring held two keys, one for the bike lock and one for the front door.

They all hugged outside of the Raw Bar next to the "Eat it Raw" sign, which featured a bikini-clad girl holding a tray of a dozen oysters in the half shell. Her face is cut out so visitors can stick their heads through from behind to have their friends create personalized pictorial mementos from the Half Shell Raw Bar in Key West. Vic had his picture taken years ago and was long past this aspect of Key West tourist rituals.

As the two couples walked toward their respective cars in the parking lot, Vic circled back toward the bight and walked along the boardwalk that fronted a mile or so of the harbor's edge. It was still early, around ten o'clock. Light posts throughout the harbor and along the bight dropped pools of light along the boardwalks and the docks. The temperature was about seventy-five. Light breeze. Sea air. Boats all around him.

For Vic it was heaven.

33

Vic wandered down the wide public wharf that occupied the center of the harbor. A few yachts, mostly sailboats, were tied up at the various long-term and short-term berths. Harbor activity had ceased for the night. Most of those on the live-aboards were inside for the evening doing whatever it was that owners of half-million dollar and up yachts did at night. Various emanations of light escaped from portholes, open hatches, and cracks aboard the vessels.

Since he had thus far owned a half a dozen sailboats in his life, Vic's attention was drawn to those. Each one was rigged to suit the owner's specific requirements. An open aft cockpit might be covered with an expensive custom-made Bimini or with a simple sunlight resistant square of blue or black canvas draped over the boom and secured at the corners and edges with ropes or bungee cords. Rigid solar panels were affixed to stern rails to keep batteries powered up. A few boat owners just tossed flexible solar collectors up on deck to top off their energy cells, which was what Vic did on his boat. An occasional compact wind generator pumped electrons into the batteries as its small blades spun in the light evening breeze. He imagined living aboard one of these leviathans, cruising from port to port, living the life of a novelist, but then questioned whether he could even write book length fiction let alone plot it sufficiently to encourage a few hundred thousand readers to plunk down hard earned cash each year to ingest his literary offerings.

Vic walked back in from the end of the public wharf and turned right toward far off bar music so he could meander among the smaller piers and jetties where the bulk of the boats, both big and small, were tied up for the evening or the season. He did not see the man of average height and dressed in a sky blue poly fly fishing shirt, tan cargo shorts, and deck shoes step from the darkness next to the Turtle Kraals restaurant and bar. Nor did Vic notice the man as he began to shadow Vic's amblings along the Key West Bight.

* * *

His walk took him along the boardwalk on the Gulf side of the island, with the water, docks, and boats to his right, and shops, markets, restaurants and drinking spots to his left. Occasionally, Vic would foray out onto one of the piers that jutted into the harbor, casually observing the boats docked on either side. He made mental notes of rigging ideas he might use with his current or some future sailboat he captained back in Colorado. Mostly Vic enjoyed being around the water. He found the mild sound of the sea and the tinkling of shrouds and halyards against aluminum masts soothing.

The distant music grew gradually louder as his stroll took him closer and closer to the Schooner Wharf, a half inside half outside bar that trucked in its own sand to make a beach for the outside part. As the lyrics focused, Vic heard a gravel-voiced singer and guitar player lamenting about how someone lost his love in the clear blue waters of some Caribbean isle, essentially the island version of a country and western song.

He halted at the edge of bar's fake beach to assess the crowd, mostly tourists and a few parrot-heads. The singer, veiled by a grizzly salt and pepper beard, had squeezed himself onto the tiny stage tucked far into one corner of the beach. Butt on a bar stool, guitar strapped around his neck, microphone before him, and left foot resting on his amp, he sang his lament gruffly and perfectly.

Before entering the Wharf for a kiddie cocktail or a coffee, Vic detoured out onto a long a dock that stretched into the harbor directly across from the bar. A majestic three-masted schooner offered up each evening to tourists for sunset sails occupied most of the space. Vic had taken a few rides on this boat and even piloted the helm on one of the cruises. It was like a massive thoroughbred horse, sleek, muscular, shiny and smooth, hued with browns upon browns and trimmed with greens, yellows and golds. Vic wondered just how long it took to restore this wooden marvel.

A small flats boat, about an eighteen footer, caught his eye. It was tied up on the same dockside as the monster schooner, tucked beneath the giant's protruding bowsprit. Vic walked over to it. He saw no fishing tackle, bait boxes, or anything that indicated its owner had been out on the flats a dozen miles offshore earlier that day.

The stern boasted the name HACKER I.

* * *

Vic pulled a business card from his wallet.

"Jeff—call me—It's about your brother—Vic," he wrote on the card, along with his cellphone number.

He knelt down and stuffed it tightly inside the cleat hitch that secured HACKER I to the dock.

* * *

Jeff?" the bartender said as he poured a Beck's NA beer into a chilled glass and set it down in front of Vic.

"Left me high and dry," the gravelly singing voice intoned and, at the strum of a guitar chord, ended his wailing to the hoots and howls and clapping of a handful of overly imbibed tourists half reclining in lounge chairs on the sand and surrounded by buckets of iced Corona beer.

"Yes," Vic said. "That's his boat out there."

"He was here a while ago," the bartender said. "He had a couple of beers."

"Did you see him leave?" Vic said. The bartender shook his head.

"Just a sec," he said and walked over to his cash register, reached up to a small shelf and removed a stack of credit cards. He pulled a pair of drug store reading glasses from his shirt pocket. Without unfolding the glasses, the bartender just held the lenses up to his eyes while he examined each card one by one. About five cards in, he terminated the inspection, returned his glasses to his pocket, the credit cards to their shelf, and walked back over to Vic. "His card's still here. He'll be back, eventually."

"Eventually?" Vic said.

"Could be tomorrow or a few days from now," the bartender said. "We just stick them into the safe if the owners forget them. Most of them get claimed. Jeff's a regular. He'll be back, but he probably won't worry about the missing card."

The boat was still tied up outside. The credit card was still in the bar, the tab still open. Vic was not sure whether he should, but he did anyway, and pulled a business card from his wallet. "Here's my card," Vic said, handing the bartender his *Denver Times* card. "That's my cell number. If you happen to see Jeff, ask him to call me, would you? I'm a friend of his brother."

"Sure," the bartender said, taking the card and dropping it in the same shirt pocket with the cheap reading glasses. "I didn't even know he had a brother."

Vic sipped his unleaded beer, savoring the taste, missing the alcohol buzz that turned a spot like this into a magical dream. He turned around so, with his back to the bar, he could take in the warm Key West night and the water and the boats and the shimmering lights of the harbor.

He also hoped Jeff Picune might return to claim his credit card.

34

The stocky muscular man stepped from the men's room in the inside part of Schooner's Wharf. He leaned against the edge of a narrow shadowy alcove out of the way of bar and restaurant foot traffic. Nursing a club soda and lime, he watched the back of Vic Bengston on the far side of the circular bar. He could see Bengston take a drink every so often from a beer. Occasionally the reporter glanced around to see who was in the crowd. He was looking for Picune too, the stocky man thought as tinkling ice cubes signaled the end to his soft drink. He set the empty cocktail glass on a nearby table and walked away from Vic, through the rest of Schooners Wharf, out the other door, and back up the bight toward Turtle Kraals.

* * *

A half hour passed. The beer was gone, and still no Jeff. Vic decided to begin his leisurely nighttime bicycle journey back to Barb and Kelly's house and check out Jeff's boat on Fisherman's Row in the morning. He had already paid cash for the drink, so he left a tip and shoved off in the direction of Turtle Kraals and eventually across the parking lot to Nico's where his bike was parked.

As he walked past the tower deck behind Turtle Kraals, Vic heard what sounded like a bar stool or chair falling onto the floor above him, and then heated conversation between two men.

"Get out of my face, asshole," said one voice right after the chair-fall sound.

"Come here, Picune," commanded the other voice.

Then hurried steps across the deck floor, and finally Vic saw someone rushing down the stairway from the top of the Turtle Kraals tower, a popular place to end a workday with a cold beer and a good view of the harbor. Another guy, a stocky guy, followed close behind that someone as the two poured down the tower steps.

"I'm a fisherman!" the someone shouted. "That's it! Get some other damn guide!"

"I said wait," the follower said. "I want to talk to you."

The someone—Jeff Picune, Vic figured—came rushing toward him. Tall, about six one or two, thin, short hair with a receding hairline, Jeff blew right by Vic and headed down the boardwalk toward Schooners Wharf and HACKER I. The second guy, who seemed to be chasing the first guy but at sort of a race-walking pace, was shorter, maybe five-ten, well-built, stocky, in shorts and a fly-fishing shirt, sporting sandy cropped hair.

As this second guy, the stocky one, was about to rush by, Vic pushed off the building he was leaning up against and threw a hard fullback block with his left shoulder right into the guy's upper body. The sandy haired guy immediately left the wooden boardwalk of the Key West Bight and flew ass first into the harbor, landing with a "Hey!" and a loud splash. Vic raced walked to the right, back toward the deck tower and into the rear door of Turtle Kraals. He pushed his way through the drinking crowd and out the front door, double-timing it out into the public parking lot hoping he would see Jeff Picune and not his now water-logged, and presumably madder than hell, pursuer.

Vic jogged along the darkest edge of the parking lot and around the rear of the grocery market, circling back around to the bight. Keeping to the shadows as best he could, he worked his way back to Schooners Wharf. Over the gravelly singer's latest number, he heard what sounded like an outboard motor, but saw no sign of the sandy haired guy. He snaked his way through the Wharf's bar crowd, edged over to the bight side of the bar, and peered as a far as he could up toward the Turtle Kraals. Two piers over, he thought he could make out a few people on the dock pulling someone from the water.

Breathing hard, wishing he were in better shape, Vic stepped out of the bar and walked over to the bow of the big schooner. He looked down at the water beneath the bowsprit. HACKER I was gone.

35

"Are you going out today?" Vic said from the cement dock.

Marti Clemons looked up from the small table secured to the aft deck of her fishing boat. The *Herald* and the *Citizen* covered the table. Steam spiraled from a white porcelain coffee mug on the table. No makeup. Dressed in a teal short sleeve shirt, a pair of tan shirts and ragged canvas deck shoes. She was beautiful, too beautiful for an old wreck like him.

"Not today," she said with a bright smile. "Not even if you had a fistful of cash."

"Why's that?" Vic said.

"I've got to change the oil on my diesel, replace the filters, and hope to hell he runs for another year," Marti said.

"He? I thought everything boats was female."

"Dirty, smelly, and stubborn. What does that sound like?"

"Got me there," Vic said. "So, something is not quite right with the power plant?"

"You could say that," she said. "Stalled for more than an hour yesterday morning. Almost lost a charter."

"That was before we met, right?" Vic said. She nodded.

"Coffee?" Marti said.

"Con leche?" Vic said, raising his bushy gray eyebrows.

She laughed and said, "You tourists! Gotta do everything Cuban down here."

"It's the only time I sweeten and cream my coffee," Vic said. "Honest."

"Honest," she said. "Now there's an interesting word, coming from a journalist."

Vic let the comment go. Marti jumped up and bounced her way down into the galley. She returned in a minute with another heavy white mug, the kind you see at busy breakfast joints frequented by what few blue collar workers there were left in the country.

"Coffee con leche," she said, handing him the cup.

Vic took a sip and let the warm sweet liquid candy wash over his tongue and down his throat.

"My partner and I used to shoot videos down here, "Vic said. "The crew and I grabbed breakfast sandwiches and coffee con leche every morning from a hole in the wall not too far from here."

"That would be Millie's," Marti said. "Literally a hole in the wall."

"Right at sidewalk level," Vic said "Great chow."

"You have a partner?" She said. "What sort of videos?"

"Well, he died," Vic said, squeezing back a tear. "PR agency. We shot a lot of video for our clients. One of them made window shades. Window fashions, they call them. We set up shoots in some of the homes down here."

"But you don't do that anymore," Marti said. "You're a journalist now. Your PR business is gone. And you don't usually drink sweet coffee."

"Black, all the time, at home," Vic said, rubbing his left shoulder. "Honest."

"There's that word again," she said, a bit sarcastically. "What's up with the shoulder?"

"Bumped it last night," Vic said.

"Fall out of bed?" she said, smiling.

"I threw a block," he said. "Haven't done that in years."

"Years?" Marti said.

"Decades."

"What does the other guy look like?"

"He looked wet last time I saw him," Vic said.

She sipped on her coffee, then shot him a stare.

"Okay, let's have it," Vic said. "We barely know each other, and I can tell something's bugging you?"

She turned serious.

"You said you were friends with Jeff and his brother," she said.

"I did," Vic said, sensing what was coming. He saw the flats boat tied up next to HACKER II when he had walked by on his way to Marti's boat.

"Jeff never heard of you," she said. "Says he's never even seen a copy of the *Denver Times* either."

Vic's heart seized up with that feeling he got when someone, especially a woman, was angry with him, confronting him. His therapist told him to ignore the feeling and push through it.

"I spotted his flats boat down at Schooner Wharf last night," Vic said. I left my card for him."

"How nice," Marti said, chilling the Key West breeze. "But you didn't have one for me."

"Well, I thought, instead of trying to explain everything—"

"You'd just make up a story," Marti said. "All you reporters are the same."

"It's a bit more complicated than that," Vic said, not wanting to explain why. At least she did not call him a liar, which he was. "When did you see Jeff?"

"Last night, when he came home."

"What time?" Vic said.

"About eleven," she said. "I couldn't sleep."

"Did he say anything else?" Vic said.

She shook her head, then smiled at him and said, "You're doing it again."

"What?" Vic said.

"Pulling stuff from me against my better judgment," Marti said.

"I have that way about me," Vic said. "Plus you invited me on board for coffee con leche."

"Let's try this again, okay?" she said.

"What?" Vic said.

"This," she said, waving her hand over the newspaper laden table with two coffee cups and two people. "No more lies, okay?"

"Can I stretch the truth a bit?" Vic said. She shook her head. "Omit something relevant?" Another head shake. "All right. I'll give it a go."

They clinked their coffee mugs.

* * *

"Look," Marti said. "There's Jeff."

Vic glanced over at HACKER II. Jeff was on out on his deck rifling through what looked like a backpack.

"I'll go say hello," Vic said.

"Well, he is an old friend," Marti said while refilling her coffee mug. "Right?"

Vic looked up at her, sighed and shrugged his shoulders. "Not really."

He got up and walked down two stalls.

"Jeff Picune?" Vic said.

Jeff looked up. He licked his lips and rubbed his chin with his right hand. He kept his left hand inside a dark forest green backpack.

"I'm not going out today," he said.

"I'm not looking for a charter," Vic said. "I wonder if I could talk to you."

"What about?" Jeff said. He had that unsettled look of a college student strung out on caffeine, all-nighters, rough exams, maybe drugs. Vic plunged in.

"*Sundial*," Vic said. "And your brother."

He jerked the hand from the backpack. The hand did not bother Vic all that much. It was the revolver that was in the hand that gave him pause. It was compact, stubby, a police special, Vic thought. At least that was what they always called them on television. Vic's heart went through that flutter thing again and he wondered how many months or years had just been trimmed from the back end.

"Who the hell are you?" Jeff said.

"I'm a reporter," Vic said. "The *Denver Times*. Bengston. Vic Bengston."

Jeff took in a deep breath and exhaled slowly. His gaze dropped off of Vic's eyes, and he seemed to lose focus.

"It's not loaded," Jeff said. "I thought you were, well, not him, but maybe working with someone else."

"Sandy haired guy, about my height, a shade younger?" Vic said.

"A lot of shade younger," Jeff said, regaining a little composure.

"Was that you last night?"

"Yes it was," Vic said.

"Thanks," Jeff said. "You gave me enough time to get away from him, but he must know where I live."

"Oh, I'm sure he does," Vic said. "What did he want?"

"The same thing as you. *Sundial.*" Jeff pulled a box of shells from the backpack and set it next to the gun on the starboard bench. "The guy was really persistent, wouldn't let go."

"What did you tell him?" Vic said.

"Nothing!" Jeff said. "I didn't know what he was talking about. I don't know what you're talking about."

"You've never heard of *Sundial*?" Vic said.

"Other than the thing in the garden that tells time by the sun?"

"Yeah, other than that," Vic said.

"Never," Jeff said.

"Your brother didn't mention it?"

"Jared?" Jeff said. Vic nodded.

"Not that I can recall—look that's the same kind of question that other guy was pumping me with," Jeff said. He reached for the gun and held it in both hands in his lap. "You work with this other guy, don't you?"

"No, I don't," Vic said. "I'm down here staying with some friends."

"What are you doing here then?" Jeff said.

"I came down here to find you, to see if you've seen your brother," Vic said.

"Is he okay?" Jeff said. "Is he in trouble?"

"I don't know," Vic said. "When did you last hear from him?"

"It's been weeks," Jeff said. "I'll bet it's been a month."

"Have you tried to reach him?" Vic said.

"His cell's turned off or something," Jeff said. "I've called every day for the last week or so. No answer."

"That's too bad," Vic said.

"Why?" Jeff said.

"I need to talk to Jared," Vic said. "About a story I'm doing."

"On this *Sundial*?" Jeff said.

"Oh, I'm not sure about that," Vic said. "*Sundial* could be a part of it."

"What is *Sundial?*" Jeff said.

"I'm not really too sure about that either," Vic said, keeping his knowledge to himself. "A lot of people want it."

"Or, you don't want to tell me about it," Jeff said. "If Jared is in trouble, then I'm in trouble. We're brothers, you know."

Vic looked back over at Marti. She was into the newspapers. Vic had made the honesty deal only with her. He turned back to Jeff and said, "I don't have clue what *Sundial* means."

* * *

Vic decided to give Jeff something to cling to, something that might indicate he was actually chasing down a story, which he was.

"All I know is that there's a ranch in Colorado, or a piece of property," Vic said. "It's not really a ranch. But it's owned, or it was owned by David Riley."

Jeff adjusted himself, straightened his back a bit. The two had moved into the main cabin of HACKER II. Vic sat on one of the vinyl covered benches, Jeff in the captain's chair at the helm, up by the controls.

"So what about this ranch?" Jeff said.

"Oh, I'm not sure," Vic said. "I'm truly fishing on this one. No pun intended. But I think Riley had a special team of computer programmers working up there on some new electronic voting system."

"Who's David Riley?" Jeff said.

"I would have thought you computer types would have known that," Vic said.

"Computer types?" Jeff said. "I'm a simple fisherman."

"With boats named Hacker One and Hacker Two?" Vic said.

"That's what Jared and I did when we were kids," Jeff said. "We took pride in our work."

"Hacking into computers?" Vic said.

"We never did anything malicious," Jeff shot back. "We always sent the exploited code to the computer owner, so they could fix the problem."

"Sort of a Lone Ranger and Tonto, roaming the countryside,

rooting out the bad guys, making things right for the good guys?" Vic said.

Jeff just looked at Vic for a moment, and said, "How old are you?"

"Old enough to be your dad," Vic said. He was. Jeff still seemed like a kid to him. He had to be the age of his son, Conor, maybe younger. Vic stared back at Jeff, like the dog challenge. He had a hunch Jeff was busting to talk. All he had to do was wait him out.

"Jared financed my boats," Jeff said. "I decided to name them in his honor and in the honor of what it was we did when we were together, growing up."

"What was your biggest hack?" Vic said. He thought this might work into an interesting feature, computer hacker turned fishing guide.

"Is this for a story?" Jeff said.

"Sure, why not?" Vic said.

"Then I can't tell you," Jeff said. "Actually, I promised someone else I wouldn't tell."

"Oh, who was that?" Vic said.

"The United States Government," Jeff said.

"Really?" Vic said, picturing Wilford Brimley, the Homeland Security contractor who had rousted him and Dad at the *Sundial* facility.

"Suffice it to say, I, or we, compromised a system or two in our youth," Jeff said.

"That could have been what, six months ago?" Vic said.

"No, it was seven years ago," Jeff said.

"You were caught?" Vic said.

"No, we turned ourselves in," Jeff said.

"Decent of you, old chap," Vic said.

"Actually, it scared us, what we did," Jeff said. "We really do like this place."

"This place?"

"The United States of America," Jeff said.

"Oh that This Place," Vic said. "How did you turn yourselves in?"

"Simple phone call to the FBI," Jeff said. "But we had a present for them, the government."

"I'm not sure I understand," Vic said.

"Well, after Jared and I found this hole in the system I can't tell you about, we decided to figure out a way to plug it," Jeff said. "So we developed a fix for the problem."

"Were they grateful?" Vic said.

"Very," Jeff said. "No charges and a contract to work for them."

"More like no public embarrassment," Vic said. "The feds work hard to keep their dirty laundry out of the public eye. How old were you when this event took place?"

"Eighteen," Jeff said. Vic did the math. He was twenty-five, younger than Conor.

"So, was Jared the older or the younger of you two?" Vic was pleased with this method of determining age, leadership, pecking order between the brothers.

"Oh, he was eighteen too," Jeff said.

"I'm sorry?" Vic said. He was puzzled over this.

Jeff laughed. "You don't know, then?"

"Know what?" Vic said.

"We're twins," Jeff said. "Jared and I."

"Fraternal?" Vic said.

"Identical," Jeff said.

* * *

Identical twins, Vic thought. Stone had not mentioned this. Maybe he did not know either.

"Close?" Vic said, raising his eyebrows.

"What do you mean?" Jeff said.

"You and your brother," Vic said. "Are you close?"

"Very," Jeff said.

"So Jared lives down here too?" Vic said.

"Can't tell you that," Jeff said. "He called me. Jared did. He's scared. Somebody's after him."

"The guy on the bight last night?" Vic said.

Jeff leaned back, folded his arms and nodded.

Then it dawned on Vic. "Did he think you were Jared?"

Jeff nodded again.

"What did he say to you?" Vic said.

Jeff looked up from Vic and then toward the dock. He licked his lips.

"Why don't you let him tell you," Jeff said, nodding toward Marti's boat and slowly reaching for his backpack.

Vic turned around and saw a stocky sandy haired man, medium height, talking to Marti. Standing next to him was a man of similar build, only Vic knew him.

Detective Greg Frakes.

* * *

"Wait a minute," Vic said. "I think you're okay."

"Like hell," Jeff said. He had cracked open the box of shells and started shoving them into the chambers of the stubby revolver.

"Put that down," Vic said. "I know that guy."

"Which one?" Jeff said.

"The one with the dark hair," Vic said. "He's a Denver cop."

"Well, I can't get to the flats boat anyway," Jeff said.

"Stay put," Vic said. "I'll go out."

Marti pointed toward Jeff's boat. Worry masked her pretty face.

As the two men started toward the HACKER II, Vic stepped out of the cabin and onto the aft deck.

"Hi Vic," Frakes said. Sandy hair halted, stone faced.

"Detective," Vic said. "We were just going out for red snapper."

"No you're not," sandy hair said. He flashed a badge. "FBI."

"Crap," Vic mouthed.

"Vic, you want me to call someone?" Marti shouted from her boat.

"No, I'm all right," Vic called back. "Thanks."

"I wouldn't be too sure about that, Bengston," Frakes said, sounding tough, probably for FBI's benefit, but strained. He looked tired.

"We need to talk to you both," FBI said. He had his hand on the butt of an automatic clipped to his belt. "Any weapons on board?"

"Jeff," Vic called.

"Come on out of there and let me see your hands," FBI said. He had drawn his weapon.

"I'm coming, I'm coming," Jeff said. He poked his empty hands out the cabin door and stepped out onto the deck. "There's a .38 in there. I just loaded it. On the backpack."

"I'll get it," Frakes said and he brushed on by Vic and Jeff.

"Turn around, both of you," FBI said.

Vic and Jeff complied.

"Clear in there?" FBI called to Frakes.

"Yeah," Frakes shouted. "Looks like one .38, now unloaded, and a box of shells. He returned to the stern deck with Jeff's gun and the box of ammo. FBI frisked both Vic and Jeff.

"Okay, sit down," FBI said.

"Can I see your badge and ID?" Vic said.

"Come on, Vic," Frakes said.

"Come on, hell," Vic said. "I want to see who this clown is."

FBI pulled out a leather wallet with his badge and ID in it. He handed it to Vic, who examined it carefully.

"Special Agent Brad Rodgers," Vic said. "It looks fake."

"Bengston!" Frakes said.

"Feels damp," Vic said, handing the wallet back to Rodgers.

"No thanks to you, jerkoff," Rodgers said.

"Greg, what in hell are you doing here?" Vic said.

"Cooperating," Frakes said. "With a federal investigation. What are you doing here?"

"Working on a fishing story," Vic said.

"More like fishing for a story," Frakes said.

"Children!" Rodgers said.

"We all seem to be here for the same thing," Vic said.

"Oh?" Frakes said.

"Yes," Vic said. "To find Jared Picune."

* * *

All three looked at Jeff.

"What?" Jeff said, holding up his hands in surrender. "I don't know where Jared is."

"Oh, don't you?" Rodgers said.

"No, I don't," Jeff said.

"I went back to Turtle Kraals last night," Rodgers said to Jeff, then to Vic, "after I was helped out of the damn water."

"You didn't identify yourself as an FBI agent to me," Vic said.

"A regrettable mistake," Rodgers said. "Charges would have ensued had I told you who I was."

"Charges would have ensured?" Vic said, parroting the agent, who just nodded and smiled. Then to Jeff, he said, "I went back and got your beer glass. It retained a nice set of prints. Jeff."

Jeff put his left hand over his mouth, rubbed his chin, and looked down. "Look, I don't know where Jeff is."

"Jared?" Vic said.

Jeff, or Jared, looked up. "Yes."

"Interesting way to hide out," Frakes said.

"If you have a twin brother," Rodgers said.

"Identical twin brother," Vic said.

"Nice wrinkle for your story," Frakes said.

"What story?" Vic said. "My red snapper fishing story?"

"No, the *Sundial* story," Rodgers said.

"I don't know what you're talking about," Vic said.

"All of us here know what *Sundial* is," Frakes said. "I followed you down here while Agent Rodgers interviewed Paxton Stone."

"Stone?" Jared said.

"Yes, Stone," Rodgers said. "He did say you were the only hacker who cracked his test encryption. And you did work for David Riley at the Sundial Ranch, didn't you?"

"That doesn't mean I—"

"What?" Frakes said. "Murdered him?"

"Well, I didn't," Jared said.

"I thought it was suicide," Vic said.

"No," Frakes said. "Medical examiner finally released her homicide conclusion. She sure took her sweet time. I talked to Driscoll a little while ago."

"So was it you?" Vic said to Rodgers, who flashed red.

"What do you mean?" Rodgers said.

"You're not just working for the FBI, are you?" Vic said, casting a fly.

Frakes looked at Rodgers, then back to Vic.

"This has got to stay off the record, way off, Bengston," Frakes said. A strike.

"What, that you guys are chasing your tails?" Vic said.

"We caught you, asshole!" Rodgers shouted, sticking his face right into Vic's.

That was it. Vic rose up and jabbed the heel of his left hand hard into the bottom of Rodgers' jaw. The upward blow caught the agent by surprise and sent him teetering backwards. His feet tangled up in a coil of rope lying on the deck and the man just flipped over the starboard gunnel.

"My God!" Frakes said, rushing to the side of the boat.

At the splash, Vic yelled, "Man overboard!" and grabbed the life ring affixed to the stern. He stepped over, looked down at the floundering FBI agent in the water, and gently tossed the ring so it would bounce off Rodger's head. The agent grabbed the ring and using the attached line Vic walked him over to a ladder at the edge of the dock.

"He's going to shoot you, Bengston," Frakes said.

"Well, make sure that he doesn't," Vic said. "He deserved what he got."

Vic stepped off the back of the boat and onto the concrete dock. Rodgers had a hand on one of the ladder rungs and was setting a foot so he could climb out. Vic reached down with a hand. Rodgers batted it away. The agent pulled himself up, turned around and flopped down on the dock. He had that rain-soaked dog look. Rodgers reached for his holster. It was empty.

"Dammit!" he said. "Lost my gun."

"I'll get it," Jared said. He had already popped on a face mask and snorkeling tube, which seemed a bit odd to Vic, and was slipping on some fins. In another minute Jared was over the side with the second splash of the morning.

"All right," Rodgers said. "I lost it. I'm gonna count to ten on this one, Bengston. But dammit, man, twice in twenty-four hours?"

"I didn't know who you were last night," Vic said.

"Well, you damn well know who I am today," Rodgers said.

"Do I?" Vic said.

* * *

"Where's Jared?" Vic said.

"Oh no," Frakes said, jumping off the boat and onto the dock. He looked down in the water. Nothing. "He's gone."

"Car Fifty-four, where are you?" Vic said.

"Cut the crap," Frakes said. "And stay here."

Frakes and Rodgers headed off in opposite directions looking between each of the boats tied up at the dock. Vic stepped off of HACKER II and walked back over to Marti who was surprisingly calm as she observed the show. She smiled.

"You seem to lead an interesting life," she said.

"I always wanted to try that," Vic said.

"What?" Marti said.

Vic motioned the upper cut with the heel of his hand.

"Are you a brawler?" Marti said.

"No," Vic said. "I once saw one of my brawler buddies from high school use the heel of his hand to finish off a fight. It makes a lot of sense, the physics of it, I mean. Pretty hard punch there at the base of your palm, and you don't break your knuckles."

"But you're not a brawler?" Marti said.

Vic saw her sizing him up. His face flushed.

"No, really," Vic said. "I'm a writer. I live it all vicariously. Writers, journalists, we all become experts at things we've never done. Then we write about them."

"No wonder the media's so screwed up," Marti said.

"That, and the superficial readers, viewers, and listeners who believe all that garbage," Vic said.

"You write garbage?" she said.

"No I don't," Vic said. "I investigate stories or research a feature and then write it as close to the truth as I can."

"Win any awards?" She said.

"A couple," Vic said.

"What do you think about this WikiLeaks thing?" Marti said.

"It's ruffling a lot of feathers," Vic said

"Isn't it putting reporters out of business?" she said.

"Reporters have been going out of business for decades, ever since the media began consolidating and the internet showed up," Vic said.

"Well, I like to read newspapers," Marti said. "There's something about them."

There sure was, Vic thought as he watched her sip her coffee and browse through the local rag.

"Besides ruffled feathers," Marti said. "Is it right? WikiLeaks?"

"I'm a purist when it comes to the First Amendment," Vic said.

"Meaning?" she said.

"I err in favor of free speech and a free press," Vic said. "WikiLeaks is peeling away the outer layer that politicians, nations, businesses, even celebrities use to keep the truth from the public."

"Celebrities?" Marti said.

"I think there are some celebrities on that list of Swiss bank records Wikileaks released," Vic said. "Tax evasion, off shore accounts, all that, while they rant against the establishment fat cats."

"But celebrities?" she said, smiling again. "Must they endure such embarrassment?"

"How about prosecution?" Vic said. "They're already fake people, and we, that's the editorial we, seem to hang on their every word. Displaying their bank record to the world just peels off another one of those layers. Pierces the facades."

"The government documents bother me," she said.

"Why?" Vic said.

"Well, some of that stuff needs to be secret," Marti said.

"Does it now?" Vic said. She was right, but he wanted to push her a bit.

"You don't agree?" she said.

"A small percentage, maybe."

"A chink in your resolve, your pureness?"

"Just a little one, I guess," Vic said. "Still, Julian Assange is a bit too creepy for me, sort of a self-appointed arbiter of the truth."

"Somebody has to do that, arbitrate," Marti said.

"Let the public do it," Vic said. "Anyway, I still err on the side of revealing the truth. Everybody already knows most of the politicians are dumb asses, hypocritical at best, corrupt at worst."

"Most?" Marti said.

"Not all of them," Vic said. "I worked for one once. He was a straight shooter. There actually are many who are not idiots like the ones the media covers. But there are a lot of jerks, and WikiLeaks just confirms our suspicions by providing by providing us with some details."

"Doesn't leave much for you reporters to do," Marti said.

"There aren't enough of us left to do any good, anyway. Plus, a lot of reporters just suck up to the scofflaws and agree to keep their secrets to maintain access."

"Such a cynical view of your own profession," Marti said. "Why do you do it?"

"Because it's fun," Vic said.

"What about Snowden?" Marti said, wading in deeper.

"A lot more complex," Vic said. "I waffle on Snowden."

"I thought only politicians waffle," she said.

"They invented waffle," he said.

"But you. You said you waffle."

"I know," Vic said. "A blow hot and cold on Snowden. He stole all those documents. That's probably a crime. But there's no other way to reveal them."

"Like Ellsberg," Marti said.

"If he hadn't taken the Pentagon Papers and copied them, no one would have known," Vic said.

"There's another 'but' in there somewhere," Marti said.

"Terrorism," Vic said. "Sophisticated global crime. Money laundering by mobsters and tribal jihadists. Businessmen, wealthy, stashing money offshore."

"Connect the dots, Vic," Marti said. "You're losing me."

"They're all using the internet and cellphones to scam the rest of us, or in the case of terrorists, kill us," Vic said.

"Snowden spilled too much?" Marti said.

"He may have," Vic said. "I don't know. If you look at what the NSA did, I don't see how they can track down this stuff without intercepting everything they can get their hands on."

"But we citizens don't like the government listening in," Marti said.

"I know," Vic said. "The NSA probably knows my brand of toilet paper."

"Triple sheet?" Marti said.

"No," "I'm a single sheet man."

"And what it is you're after—this story—has something to do with, Snowden? Wikileaks? What?"

"Can't say," Vic said. "Not sure."

"Won't say?" she said.

Vic nodded.

* * *

By the time Frakes and Rodgers returned, Marti had removed her clothes, revealing a nice bikini-clad body, donned her snorkel gear and jumped into the water to search for Rodgers' gun. The FBI agent boarded HACKER II like he owned it and started rifling through Jared's backpack. Frakes walked over to Marti's boat and stumbled aboard like a landlubber, hands outstretched, balancing himself on the slightly rolling vessel.

"See him?" Frakes said.

"No," Vic said. "Have a coffee con leche. Take a load off."

Frakes sat down at the small table across from Vic. While the detective shuffled *Herald* sections around, Vic poured the last of the coffee into a clean mug and added the warm cream and sugar. He handed it to Frakes.

"Here," Vic said. "I think you're going to like this one."

"Yeah, I need it," Frakes said.

"You okay, Greg?" Vic said."

"No sleep last night," he said. "Caught a redeye."

"You look like you caught more than that," Vic said.

Frakes lifted his head a bit, like a punch drunk fighter. "Where's your girlfriend?"

"For the record," Vic said. "She's not my girlfriend."

"Whatever," Frakes said. Vic pegged the cop as the same age as his oldest son, about forty. "Where is she?"

"Down searching for Rodgers' gun," Vic said.

"You're kidding?" Frakes said.

"I'm not kidding, Greg," Vic said, mocking seriousness. "I'm dead serious. You were about to tell me who else Rodgers represents."

"DHS," Frakes said. "He's tasked to them."

"For the Riley murder investigation?"

"That's part of it," Frakes said. "The other part you can guess."

"*Sundial,*" Vic said.

"Never heard it from me," Frakes said, sipping the sweet creamy coffee. "This is good."

"Here come the newlyweds now," Vic said, twinging a bit seeing Marti walking with Rodgers, talking comfortably with him, she a good decade or more older than the agent, but knowing many women did like younger men, not old farts like him. As she shook water from her hair, Rodgers shook water from his automatic.

The two boarded the Durga. Marti said, "Make yourselves at home. I'll brew a fresh pot of coffee."

"Can I have the classified section?" Rodgers said, sitting down. Frakes handed it to him.

"Did Homeland Security clear you to read the classifieds?" Vic said.

"Very funny, asshole," Rodgers said. The FBI agent ejected the clip, racked the barrel to eject the round in the chamber, and placed everything in front of him onto the paper, the classified ads.

"Does your girlfriend have a cloth I can use," Rodgers said.

"She's not my girlfriend," Vic said. "I just met her yesterday."

"Whatever," Rodgers said. "You've gotten awfully cozy awfully fast."

"That's what happens when you band together against a common enemy," Vic said. "Marti! Do you have a towel or rag that can be destroyed?"

"There's a light blue bucket up there with a couple of rags hanging on the lip," she shouted up the companionway. "Take what you need."

Rodgers got up and walked over to one corner of the deck where the bucket lived. He fished through the rags and selected one. It looked like a piece of an old tee shirt. He returned to the table, sat down and began cleaning his gun.

"Fresh coffee, more heated milk, and cane sugar," Marti said as she emerged from the cabin carrying a tray with the coffee con leche essentials. She set it on the port side bench seat.

"Mr. Agent?" Marti said.

"Sure," Rodgers muttered as he shook his gun and wiped away the seawater. "You wouldn't have any thirty-weight motor oil on board by any chance?"

"Coffee con Exxon?" Vic said. Rodgers just glared at him. Frakes shook his head.

"Look in the port lazarette, just afore the stern," Marti said.

"Huh?" Rodgers said.

"In the back of the boat," Vic said, pointing. "Lift that lid."

Rodgers got up again, opened up the lazarette and retrieved a yellow quart of Pennzoil.

"Correction," Vic said. "Coffee con Pennzoil."

Marti smiled at Vic and he winked back.

Frakes read the sports section and sipped his coffee while Marti prepared a mug for Rodgers, who was now blowing through the open chamber on his gun. The agent tore off a small piece of clean cloth, poured a little oil on it, and then began covering as much of the weapon as he could with a thin coat of the protective lubricant.

Vic had never seen island time subsume two human beings so rapidly.

36

Rodgers had finished cleaning his gun. Frakes tried to read the paper but kept nodding off. Vic and Marti small talked.

"Aren't you guys in a hurry to find Jared?" Vic said to Rodgers.

Frakes snorted himself awake and said, "Jeff too, don't forget."

"How could I?" Vic said.

"I've already talked to the Key West police," Rodgers said. "They'll find him. Or them. They've already alerted the taxi drivers. Airport's covered. Fort Meyers shuttle. Fort Jefferson boat."

"When did you call the locals?" Vic said.

"Few minutes ago," Rodgers said.

"Your cell phone didn't get trashed by the water?" Vic said.

"Used this," Rodgers said. He held up a small handi-talkie.

"Can I see that?" Vic said. "I'm a certified ham radio operator."

"As well as a certified jackass," Rodgers said. "Leave it off though."

He handed the small radio to Vic, who turned it on immediately. Key West police traffic blared from the tiny speaker.

"Give me that," Rodgers said reaching for the radio. Vic shot his arm skyward, keeping the radio out of reach.

"I've got one sorta like this, but for the amateur bands," Vic said.

"Don't hit the transmit button," Rodgers said.

Vic pressed the red button and, holding the handi-talkie near his mouth said, "Key West police, this is Hacker Three."

"Hacker Three, identify yourself," the dispatcher said. This time Rodgers' strike hit the mark and he snatched the radio from Vic's hand.

"Key West, this is agent Rodgers," the agent said. "Forget that last transmission. Sorry."

"It's forgotten, agent Rodgers," the dispatcher said. "The Chief was about to call. We have your bogey."

"That was fast," Rodgers said. "We'll be down in a little while. Ice him, will you?"

"Will do," the dispatcher said. "Car seventeen—"

Rodgers turned the radio off.

"Does that have DTMF?" Vic said.

"It does," Rodgers said. "Saves battery life."

"What's that?" Frakes said.

"It lets agent Rodgers here leave his radio off, but a signal from the cop shop can turn it back on to send a message," Vic said.

"Whatever," Frakes said.

Rodgers and Marti were just looking at Vic.

"I have a recessive nerd gene," Vic said. They continued to stare. "What? I like radio."

"I'll say," Marti said.

"So he's in custody?" Vic said to Rodgers, who just nodded. He continued drying, cleaning and oiling his gun.

"Can I go question him with you?" Vic said.

"No you cannot," Frakes said.

"Am I going to be arrested?" Vic said.

"I'm considering it," Rodgers said. "Assaulting a federal agent is, well, an ugly charge."

"Would an apology help?" Vic said.

"It might," Rodgers said.

"Then I apologize," Vic said.

Rodgers looked up from his gun cleaning and said. "Didn't help much. Anyway we've got to focus on Jared and Jeff and not you, so long as you stay out of our way."

"Agreed," Vic said, mentally crossing his fingers.

* * *

Two Key West squad cars pulled up and parked by Jeff's boat. That might be half the force, Vic thought. He wondered if the Monroe County sheriff was involved in the case.

"Here's our ride, Frakes," Rodgers said.

Frakes dropped the sports section and gulped down the last of his coffee. Rodgers left a half full mug.

"Why two cars?" Vic said.

"One for us," Rodgers said. "And one for the boats. We're impounding them."

"I guess that makes sense," Vic said.

"Look, I'm not going to arrest you right now, Bengston," Rodgers said. He wrote a phone number on his card and handed it to Vic. "I will get even, however. This is my backup cell phone. I'll have it within a half hour. I'd appreciate a call if you leave Key West, but I would like to interview you at some point. I've got your number."

"So do I," Frakes said, puffing up a little behind the prowess of the FBI.

"One question," Vic said.

"What!" Rodgers said.

"Did Paxton Stone tell you about *Sundial?*" Vic said.

"No," Rodgers said, with a bit of an edge. "He didn't tell us anything about *Sundial*. Nor did he have a copy of it anywhere."

"You don't have a clue what *Sundial* is, do you?" Vic said.

"No comment," Rodgers said. A definite "no," Vic thought, liking the sound of that.

"By the way," Rodgers said flatly, flipping the comment over his shoulder as he left. "Your buddy Paxton Stone is dead."

37

After Frakes and Rodgers left, Vic silently sipped his sweet coffee and stared at the sunlight dancing on the water of the small harbor. He focused on a forty-foot sailing yacht anchored near the other side, thought about Pax's wife. They had no kids. Paxton, gone. He pinched the tears off the bridge of his nose and let the island and the sparkling water and the boats swaying with the gentle breeze crowd out the thoughts of his now dead friend.

"Did you know him?" Marti said.

"Who?"

"The dead man, who else?"

"Sorry," Vic said. "For a long time."

"I'm sorry, Vic," she said, not pushing, just letting him work it out at his pace.

"I'd better get a hotel room," Vic said.

"Are you in danger?" Marti said. He looked at her. "Am I in danger?"

"I don't really know," Vic said. "But I need to move my stuff out of Barb and Kelly's and get into a hotel. I don't want to get them caught up in this. You either."

"I can take care of myself," she said, in a confident way, not confrontational. Vic hoped she was right.

"Something nearby?" Marti suggested.

"Holiday Inn's not far," Vic said. It was just across the harbor and a few blocks up Roosevelt. "They have a good Sunday brunch."

The two looked at each other and smiled.

38

Vic sat on the edge of his bed. It was a late rising for him, about ten-thirty. The night before, after he left Marti's boat and went back over to make apologies to Barb and Kelly, he checked into the Holiday Inn. He unpacked his small travel case. Inside was a circuit board, electronic parts, a small soldering iron and some hand written notes. It was a filter circuit for a radio he was building. Working on electronic projects, like fly fishing, took his mind off everything. He futzed with the project until about two in the morning before he could keel over and fall asleep.

He cradled the phone between his cheek and shoulder while going through his notes and punching numbers on the phone. Finally, he got through the *Times*' automated telephone push button maze.

"Nice to hear from our Florida Keys correspondent," Peggy said. "How's the fishing?"

"I've got a Denver cop down here, and I've already assaulted the same FBI agent—professed FBI agent—twice," Vic said. "Jeff Picune has vanished and Jared is in jail down here. I'm told an old friend is dead, and I might be in love."

"So no fish, as yet?" she said, all business.

"As yet," Vic said.

"You found Jared?" Peggy said.

Well, actually, I found Jeff, but he turned out to be Jared," Vic said. Silence on the other end.

"I'm confused, Bengston," Vic.

"Jared and Jeff are identical twins," Vic said. "Jared was here posing as Jeff. You can't tell them apart. Jared's in custody now so I can't talk to him about *Sundial*."

"Cool angle, Dude," Peggy said. "The twins thing. By the way, Homeland Security made its regular stop today, looking for you."

"Did you talk to them?" Vic said.

"No, Les said you were on vacation. Personal leave, he called it. You're scheduled back tomorrow aren't you?"

"Yeah, but I won't be there," Vic said. "Better let Les know. Look, there's something more important I need you to check out."

"Okay," Peggy said.

"See if there is a special agent named Brad Rodgers working for the FBI out there," Vic said. "Call Al Robinson at the Denver office. Tell him you work with me and that you're asking on my behalf."

"Work for you?" Peggy said.

"Work with me," Vic said. "Cut me a little slack."

"Never, old man," Peggy said. Okay, Al Robinson."

"This is off the record, tell him," Vic said. "Way off."

"Is he going to go for this?" she said.

"He will," Vic said. "There's something else."

"There's always something else," Peggy said.

Vic could not speak.

"Vic?"

"Yeah," Vic said, swallowing hard. "I also need you to check out a death of a Golden resident, Paxton Stone."

"Fire," Peggy said. "In Golden. Some hot rod shop, full of paint. Stone listed as the sole victim. I'm working the story. I've got notes right here. You know him?".

"Yeah, I knew him," Vic said. "He was a friend."

"Gosh, I'm sorry, Vic," she said. "Didn't make the connection."

"When did this happen?" Vic said.

"Late yesterday," Peggy said.

"How late?"

"Lemme see, uh, here it is, around three-thirty," Peggy said.

"Your time," Vic said

"So about five-thirty out here," he said.

"You're getting pretty good with your time zones there Vic," she said. "I'm really sorry about this. I had no idea he was a friend."

"Are you sure about the time?" Vic said.

"Oh yeah, we've already got some freelance art on it," Peggy said. "The place was a total loss."

"Criminy," Vic said.

"I don't like it when you cuss like that," Peggy said. "Can't you do better?"

"Golly gee willikers. I don't want to turn those dainty ears too pink on Sunday morning."

"Should I know something more about Stone?" Peggy said.

"He was just an old friend," Vic said. "Write it up like you were going to. Leave me out, okay?"

"Is he connected to *Sundial*?" Peggy said.

"No, he's not," Vic said. "Find out about Rodgers. Don't mention this to anyone else, okay? Especially Vigil or the cops."

"Okay, Boss," Peggy said.

"I'm not your boss," Vic said.

"I know," she said. "I just wondered what it would sound like."

"And?" Vic said.

"It sucks," Peggy said. "I prefer to be the boss."

"I figured as much," Vic said. "Discrete inquiries, okay?"

"Okay, pard," Peggy said.

"That sounds better. Now I've got to prep for a brunch date."

"Oh?" Peggy said. "Someone I know?"

"No, you do not," Vic said. "Remember to tell Vigil I won't be back tomorrow."

"Have fun," Peggy said, then paused. "I'm sorry. You won't have fun, because of your friend. Stone."

"I'll do what I can," Vic said. "Byeulater." He threw his cellphone onto the bed. The phrase, "byeulater" came from one of his grandsons. Vic liked it. For a moment, the thought of his grandsons took his mind off Stone. He smiled, thinking of the young boy uttering his own made up phrase when they would part after a visit, and then wondered which of his children would produce the first granddaughter. He thought of Paxton Stone. Dead. Burned up in a fire. He was not happy anymore.

Vic slid the tips of his right hand fingers up and down his sternum to sooth the throbbing heart. Then he rubbed his left shoulder a bit and pin wheeled the left arm to loosen it up. Three aspirins usually numbed the morning shoulder ache. He walked into the bathroom to get the pills, and he just stared at himself in the mirror as he did almost every day. The aging man peering back looked tired and overweight. Each year more of his father stepped into the mirror with him. Vic wondered what a beard would do for him. Maybe a Don Quixote goatee. That might be appropriate, he thought.

So far two people he had recently interviewed were dead. Both were connected to *Sundial*. Riley had invented it. Stone had figured it out. And what about Picune brothers? Just lucky hackers or was there something more?

A crystal ball might help.

39

It is hard to find bad food in Key West. As a destination highly dependent on the tourist dollar, good food is vital for any traveler, rich or poor. The restaurant at the Holiday Inn was no exception. Barb and Kelly had always dragged Vic, and whoever else was visiting, over to the hotel for its Sunday brunch. This time it was only Vic and Marti, but that was plenty. They engaged in small talk, where did you come from, family, where you married, kids, divorce is crappy, how long have you been fishing, I can understand why you returned to journalism and writing, her daughter was an MIT graduate, the discovery that Marti was an MBA who also had fled corporate America, why did you stop drinking, when are you returning to Denver, and, finally, the invitation to dinner that night on her boat. Vic's cell phone interrupted the conversation.

"Are you with Rodgers?" It was Frakes. He sounded groggy.

"No, I'm with a friend," Vic said.

"Can you meet me?" Frakes said.

"Where?" Vic said.

"You call it," Frakes said. "You know this place. I don't."

"A joint?" Vic said.

"A joint's fine," Frakes said.

"Nico's." Vic looked at his watch. "Hour and a half?" He looked at Marti, raised his eyebrows, and nodded his head. She nodded back.

"Right," Frakes said, then hung up.

"The story?" Marti said.

"The story," Vic said. "Only I'm not real sure just what the story is."

"No matter," she said. "This has been a nice chapter, right here."

Vic paid up, and the two bicycled back over to Marti's boat. She leaned her bike against a white lamppost and walked over to Vic who straddled his transportation machine. She stretched out her arms, laid them across Vic's shoulders and clasped her hands behind his head.

"You be careful, Vic Bengston," she said, kissing him lightly on the lips. "I'll see you later tonight."

* * *

Vic's casual bike ride over to Nico's took him to the other side of the causeway where he could wander among the live-aboards and houseboats. His cellphone summoned. He stopped the bike in front of an aqua seafoamy looking two story houseboat. A brown pelican posed on the deck rail.

"Bengston."

"Vic," Peggy said. "I've got the low down on Rodgers."

"The low down," Vic said. "Going through my picks of best noir flicks?" No response. "Okay, give me the low down, chief."

"Shut up and listen," she said.

"I'm all ears," Vic said.

"Rodgers is FBI but he seems to be a specialist," Peggy said.

"In what?"

"Counter Terrorism."

"That makes sense, in a way," Vic said. "If *Sundial* is what it appears to be, I could see the feds not really wanting this in the hands of you know who?"

"The Colorado Legislature?"

"Well, you've got a point there," Vic said. "Anyway, you know who I mean. I don't want to say it over the cell phone. According to Snowden, the NSA hears all."

"Last week's news, bub," Peggy said. "Robinson said the guy's assigned to the *Sundial* Task Force."

"Oh, so we're elevated to a task force now?" Vic said.

"Not exactly 'we'," Peggy said. "This has been around for a while, about eight months."

"Really?' Vic said. "Riley must have made quite a few people nervous."

"That's what I thought," Peggy said.

"So Rodgers is for real," Vic said. "And I, in fact, have assaulted a federal officer twice in two days."

"That's got to be some kind of a record," Peggy said. "For a reporter, at least."

"It's my personal best," Vic said.

* * *

Sunday afternoon was always busy at Nico's. Cruise ships were preparing to depart. Locals were drinking Bloody Marys to take the edge off the previous night and hunker down for the workweek ahead. Seasonal residents, tamer and far wealthier than the locals, were in for a Sunday meal.

Vic walked into the open bar area, around the short waist-high wooden railing and positioned himself on a stool right next to what once was the exterior wall of the restaurant. The Weather Channel was running a retrospective of scenes showing weather reporters being ripped off the planet surface by wind while covering some hurricane.

The bartender was a tall middle-aged guy, probably a refugee from a former life up north. Vic did not recognize him. He finished serving up a round to a passel of blue-haired ladies who clearly would be wobbling their way back to a cruise ship at the end of the day. He leaned in toward Vic. "What'll it be?"

"Coffee fresh?"

"Just fired it up," he said, wiping his hands on a Nico's bar towel, one of which could be purchased as a souvenir. "Give me a minute or two."

Vic nodded, and Bartender was off to serve another hand waving a twenty.

"Bengston," came the voice from behind him. Vic turned. It was Frakes, on the other side of the railing.

"I've got some fresh coffee coming," Vic said. "You look like you could use some."

"Why don't we go outside or something," Frakes said. "Find someplace where we can talk."

"We can talk here," Vic said. The din was just high enough to provide cover for anything but a loud-mouthed drunk. Vic sensed movement next to him, the picking up of the tab, the reach for the wallet, the signs of someone, in this case a forty-something couple who seemed not to be rushing for a cruise ship, but indeed preparing to disembark from the bar. Vic nodded toward the couple and said to Frakes, "Come on back here."

Frakes walked around the railing and stood next to Vic. The guy sitting next to him laid three tens on the bar along with the tab and cleared the stool. Frakes slid onto it when the couple left. Bartender arrived with steaming coffee in a clear glass mug.

"One more for my father, here," Vic said.

He reached down and came up with a second mug. Another reach and the round glass Bunn coffeepot was in his hand. He filled the mug for Frakes.

"You boys eating?" Bartender said.

"I'm good," Vic said. "What about you, Greg?"

"I haven't eaten," Frakes said.

The bartender handed him a small menu. Frakes looked it over and ordered the catch of the day fish sandwich.

"You won't be disappointed," Vic said.

"Got that right," Bartender said, and he walked off to put the order in.

"They're both gone," Frakes said.

"Who?" Vic said.

"Who do you think?" Frakes said. "Rodgers and Jared."

"Did you check the boat?" Vic said.

"We've been there all night, or most of the night," Frakes said.

"We?" Vic said.

"Key West cops," Frakes said. "And me."

"I thought they only did reality TV shows," Vic said.

"Ha, ha," Frakes said. "They're actually a pretty good cop shop."

"They lost Jared, Greg," Vic said.

"Not really," Frakes said. "Rodgers went in there last night, flashed Homeland Security, and walked out with him."

"That seems too easy," Vic said.

"He's FBI, Bengston," Frakes said.

"Is he?" Vic said.

"What do you mean by that?" Frakes said.

"I mean, is he FBI?" Vic said.

"Driscoll said he was," Frakes said.

"Frank should know," Vic said.

"That's what I thought," Frakes said. "Rodgers and I seem to be playing to different maestros, though."

"You're trying to solve a murder, and he's got the national security thing going, right?" Vic said.

Frakes nodded and took a sip of his coffee. Bartender placed a set-up in front of the detective.

"We've got to go back this evening," Frakes said.

"There's that 'we' again," Vic said.

"Yes, we," Frakes said. "Driscoll wants to see you."

"What about?" Vic said. "Jared?"

"Jared is gone," Frakes said. "With Rodgers. So I'm not really sure."

"Jeff?" Vic said.

"No clue where he is," Frakes said.

"Rodgers?"

"Definitely flown the coup," Frakes said.

"Did you check the outbound flights, Greg?" Vic said.

"Do I look that dumb?" Frakes said, testy.

"I'll invoke the Fifth on that," Vic said. "No, you look tired, or extremely relaxed."

"The latter," Frakes said. "One more day down here and I'm headed to the Cuban barbershop for a haircut, a leisurely lifetime of coffee con leche, and condo shopping. Anyway, Rodgers probably flew in on a black jet and no doubt left the same way."

"So much for interagency cooperation," Vic said. "Anyway, I can't go tonight. I've got a date. First one in about three years."

"Cancel it," Frakes said. "I've called American, changed your reservation and we're out of here on the seven-twenty."

"Oh, thank you very much," Vic said. Marti's image began to blur.

Frakes hesitated, looked down at the floor, then said, "There's something else."

"What?" Vic said.

"I don't know," Frakes said. "A feeling."

"About what?"

"Rodgers."

"Rodgers what?" Vic said.

"The fire," Frakes said.

"Greg, I feel like I'm stuck in a swamp here," Vic said. "What's your point?"

"Don't mention this to Frank," Frakes said. "I know he's your buddy, but you can't mention this, not yet. Not till I talk to him first."

"Mention what, Greg?"

Frakes looked down at the coffee in front of him on the bar. "Well, when I told Rodgers about the fire, he seemed to know something about it that he shouldn't really have known, or couldn't have known."

"You sound like Donald Rumsfeld," Vic said. "When did you talk to him, about the fire that is."

"I called him when I was driving out to DIA to catch the plane down here," Frakes said. "Right after it happened."

"What's the choice morsel here, Greg?" Vic said.

"I started to tell him about the fire," Frakes said. "I mean it couldn't have been an hour, hour and a half afterwards, and he, well he interrupted me and said 'yeah I know. Arson. Probably a medium speed fuse. We're on it.'"

"We're on it?" Vic said. "Maybe someone from the task force told him."

"Look, I'm on the task force," Frakes said. "Nobody called or texted me. I found out about the fuse ten minutes earlier, through one of my contacts."

"And that would be?" Vic said.

"A pal on the Golden Fire Department," Frakes said.

"He called you?"

"No, I called him."

"This was when?" Vic said. "Midnight? Some pal. You always call to chit chat in the middle of the night?"

"No," Frakes said. "I got a tweet on my cell phone. Golden fire. I follow fires."

"A tweet?" Vic said.

"Yeah, we all use Twitter now, Bengston," Frakes said. "Where have you been, Mars?"

"Okay, you saw a tweet," Vic said. "Why call?"

"I don't know," he said. "I was driving to the airport, wanted to stay awake. I knew he'd be up."

"And he already knew the cause?" Vic said.

"He was already at the fire," Frakes said.

"Does this 'he' have a name?"

"Yeah, but you're not getting it," Frakes said. "Doesn't matter anyway. They knew the guy, Stone. They knew about his hot rod shop. Went straight to paint locker and found the fuse residue. Went right into a can of mineral spirits."

"We used to buy these little fuses when we were kids," Vic said. "Jetex. To ignite tiny jet engines we tied to cars."

"Well, this was a little more sophisticated than that," Frakes said. "But it probably was just a hobby fuse. Medium speed. Burns about ten seconds a foot."

"That's fairly precise, Greg," Vic said. "You some kind of pyro freak on your days off?"

Frakes just shook his head. "No. My pal told me."

"You know it won't take much for me to find out who this pal of yours is," Vic said.

Frakes leaned back and said, "Go for it."

"Are you sure no one else could have told Rodgers?" Vic said.

"I suppose it's possible," Frakes said. "But this guy told me I was the first one he'd talked to by phone."

"Seems weird, Greg," Vic said, "that Rodgers knew how the fire started so soon."

"That's what I thought," Frakes said.

Bartender returned with Frakes' order. "Haddock," he said. "It's great. Enjoy." He spun off to pull draughts for two college kids. The Weather Channel now ran clips of flooding and tornadoes all happening everywhere but Key West. Vic sucked at his coffee, pondered what Frakes had just told him, watched the cop inhale his meal, and thought about the date he would not have that evening.

40

Airliner hum usually put Vic to sleep, but not this time. Frakes looked clinically dead, leaning against the window, even drooling out the lower side of his mouth. Vic thought of Marti and what might have been. Maybe on a future trip. He knew little about her, but what he did know, he liked. Frakes snorted once, then quieted down. A female flight attendant had already doled out rations of four pretzels and a club soda. Vic resisted swiping Frakes' tiny packet.

He did not feel like writing, so he dug into his briefcase and pulled out a Tony Hillerman novel, *Fly on the Wall*, which he was re-reading. Vic enjoyed Hillerman's mysteries, many of which involved tribal police on the Navajo Indian Reservation. But *Fly on the Wall* was all about the news business. It took place in some mythical Midwestern state capitol where a reporter was murdered. The prime investigator was a fellow reporter and columnist. Much of the action takes place inside the fictional statehouse. Vic had no difficulty visualizing the polished brass elevator doors, the sconces, the portraits of governors on the walls, the cave like lighting, the elegance of the governor's office, the dizzying height of the rotunda, the broad granite steps, the smooth shiny marble trim, or imagining the sounds of the clattering press room, the echoes of political deals, and the loud raps of gavels in the House and Senate chambers where state policy was made.

Then he thought about writing novels one day, read two more paragraphs, and passed out.

41

Musty scents of living soil breached Vic's nostrils as his hands burrowed through the soft friable planting medium created over years by adding compost, sand, and kitchen waste to an ecosystem devoted solely to growing tasty fresh vegetables. Vic expressed his fondness for pure clean soil and the living planet that provided it by growing food in a maze of raised beds that had replaced most of the Kentucky blue grass in his back yard. As he piled compost around the base of recently planted heirloom tomato bushes, he thought about stories he wrote decades back about those Earth-lovers who chained themselves to trees in forests so loggers could not cut them down, who chased whaling ships in the northern seas to save the whales, or raised money to buy land so it could be set aside as wilderness. A few even murdered to protect animals, plants and ecosystems. Vic felt content to write about those people, but not be one of them. Building fertile soil in his back yard sufficiently scratched the itch to save the world from humanity. Running his hands through the dirt helped him forget the death of Paxton Stone and enabled him to procrastinate the call to the Widow Liz.

"Mud pies for dinner?" the voice said.

Vic shot skyward, spun around, and, arms flailing, fell backwards into freshly seeded lettuce bed.

"A little jumpy are we?" Nelson said, reaching a hand down to pull Vic out of the foot-high garden bed.

Vic did the best he could at brushing the dirt off his backside and the rest of his gardening grubbies.

"I'm glad the cold frame wasn't set up yet," Vic said.

"That could have been ugly," Nelson said. "Shattered glass, severed arteries, all that."

"You want some coffee?" Vic said.

"Why do you think I drove forty-five minutes out of the foothills and halfway across Denver?" Nelson said. "The price I pay for a free cup a joe."

"So you went home last night?" Vic said. "Wife ecstatic?"

"Then some," Nelson said.

The two walked across the back yard and three steps up onto the composite deck that ran across the back of Vic's Park Hill home in northeast Denver. Before he and Erin had divorced, they popped the top and added a second story to make room for the kids. Theirs was a little different from most other Denver pop tops. One thing they wanted to do was retain the street side look of the place, a white stucco bungalow with a red tile roof. Instead of going straight up, their contractor, a friend from the neighborhood, designed an offset second story that took off from the peak of the roofline and ran straight back toward the alley. Steel posts supported the overhanging second story. Vic and two of his sons, when they were in elementary school, built a wooden deck beneath the overhang. The house left the family in the divorce, but a few years ago, when his public relations business boomed, he had socked away enough to buy the Holly Street house back at fifteen times the price he and Erin had paid for it in 1970. Vic loved the house then and he loved it now, especially the bookcase lined study he had built in what once was the front bedroom on the first floor. Parts of the wooden deck had rotted away so he rebuilt it with composite lumber. The same two sons who had helped him build the first deck, along with his third son and daughter, worked with him on the new deck. Grandsons played in the yard during the reconstruction.

"Let's go inside," Vic said.

They settled into easy chairs in the study. Steam rose from their Colorado QRP Club coffee mugs. Nelson held his up in front of his face.

"What does QRP mean?" Nelson said.

"Basically, low power amateur radio," Vic said. "We use a maximum of five watts of power when we transmit either Morse code, digital or voice."

"As opposed to what?" Nelson said.

"Anywhere from a hundred watts to a kilowatt or more," Vic said.

"Why the low power?" Nelson said.

"More of a challenge," Vic said. "Communicating with another ham on the other side of the globe with five watts or less."

"Is that hard?" Nelson said.

"Sometimes," Vic said. "Skill comes into play. It's a lot like fly fishing."

"I don't know why you do that either," Nelson said.

"It relaxes me," Vic said.

"As I recall, last month you actually fell into the South Platte River rather than fishing it," Nelson said. "Filled your waders. Caught a cold. Lost some pricey polarized glasses. Barrel of fun."

"Well, there is the occasional stumble," Vic said. "Speaking of stumbles, how are your chickens?"

Nelson just glared at Vic. In a move toward self-sufficiency, Nelson and his wife, Midge, had decided to raise chickens behind their foothills home. They invested in some sort of a high-tech coup, fencing, bedding, feed, and many books before they even bought the birds. Nelson even installed one of his surveillance systems.

"At this point, I think I've got the overall cost down to around five or six dollars an egg," Nelson said.

"How self-sufficient of you," Vic said. "You know, chickens have free reign down in Key West."

"Well, there aren't any foxes or coyotes or big cats to feed on them," Nelson said.

"Have you ever seen an angry cruise ship traveler?" Vic said. "When they hit town, the chickens split. It's not a pretty sight."

"I can only imagine," Nelson said.

The two men sipped coffee in silence for a few minutes. Quiet never bothered them. They had hiked together, backpacked together, camped together, and the need to be talking all the time was simply not in their genes. They were about as comfortable with each other as two men could be, even during times of stress.

"I've got a problem," Vic said.

"I got that from your phone message," Nelson said.

Vic laid out everything he knew about David Riley's murder, *Sundial*, the Picune twins, special agent Brad Rodgers, Paxton Stone's death, and Frakes' suspicions about Rodgers. Nelson listened intently, chewing the inside of his cheek, as Vic ran down the events since the two had slipped into Riley's home. Finally, Nelson recapped. He shot his left hand up, spread the fingers, and grasped the pinky.

"So only the cops and you, and maybe Jared, have an actual copy of the *Sundial* white paper," Nelson said. Vic nodded. "And you're not sure if the cops have even figured out what it is," he said, grabbing the ring finger. Vic nodded again. "Stone said he erased everything." Nod. Middle finger. "You're puzzled over who Rodgers really works for?" Nod. Index finger. "You think Rodgers may have killed Riley?" Vic raised his eyebrows and tilted his head. Nelson grabbed his thumb.

"If you go any further, this becomes a six-finger problem," Nelson said. "I've never really liked six-finger problems."

"Can they be that much worse than five-finger problems?" Vic said. "It's just one more finger, another twenty percent."

"But it takes up my gun hand," Nelson said. "That's why I don't relish six-finger problems."

"Well, I'm wondering about—"

"Please don't say it," Nelson said. "I implore you."

"I'm wondering about the death of Paxton Stone," Vic said. "Rodgers seems to have known too much about it too quickly, maybe—"

"Don't say it, please," Nelson said.

"Maybe even before it happened," Vic said.

Nelson stuck the pinky of his right hand into Vic's face, then grabbed the digit.

"That's six," Nelson said. "Somebody working with Rodgers killed Stone, right?"

Vic shrugged and said, "Maybe."

"I hate six-finger problems," Nelson said.

42

Vic fidgeted in the drab ten by ten police department waiting room, appointed with dull paint of indeterminate industrial color, stains on the cement floor, a shabby composite ceiling, lined with green and gray metal chairs, very Mid Twentieth Century Cop.

He shared the space with a handful of other "guests," some of whom stunk of dope, now a common odor in all sorts of public places since the medical marijuana craze swept the state followed by voter legalization of recreational pot. There were more dope shops in Denver than Starbucks. Potheads were ecstatic. So were local and state governments, drooling over millions in new tax revenue. It was not like the old days, Vic thought, recalling how he would meet a boyhood pal between flights at the old Stapleton International Airport to snag a Fritos bag filled with pot he had cultivated for five years in the back woods of Washington State. There was something far more romantic about that, he concluded, now that buying dope was like going to Target.

An officer stuck her head into the room. "Okay, Bengston, the boss will see you now."

As Vic walked through the detectives' bullpen, he noticed that all the blinds on Driscoll's windowed office were down and closed, the door closed. The officer grabbed the doorknob to Driscoll's office and swung the door inward to let Vic in. She closed it swiftly behind him. Vic stood inside the office like a deer in the headlights.

Nobody said a thing. Driscoll sat behind his desk. A white document lay before him. The cover sheet had a large logo on it, a *Sundial*. To Vic's left sat agent Brad Rodgers and Jared Picune. Or, maybe it was Jeff, Vic thought. To his right, detective Greg Frakes squirmed and bounced his right leg. Next to Frakes, to Vic's astonishment, sat Paxton Stone.

* * *

Vic just stared at Stone, who returned the look but then glanced down. A small white patch, a bandage, covered what appeared to be a shaved spot on the back Stone's head.

"I think everyone here knows each other," Driscoll said. His big black face revealed nothing. Vic looked at him, and he looked straight back. Still nothing.

"Pax, I, uh," Vic said.

"Exaggerated," Driscoll said. "The report was exaggerated. Just sit down, Vic."

"Is this Jared or Jeff?" Vic said.

"Jared," Rodgers said.

"Are you sure?" Vic said. "How can you tell?"

"We can tell," Rodgers said.

"As well as you can stay out of the water?" Vic said.

At that, Rodgers stood up and squared off with Vic, who squeezed his sphincter to avoid wetting his pants.

"Sit down, both of you," Driscoll said. It was an order.

Rodgers resumed his earlier position. There was only one unused chair, tucked into the corner next to the closed door. Vic pulled it out a foot and sat down. Then he stood back up.

"Vic?" Driscoll said.

"Dammit!" Vic said. "I've known Stone for twenty years and I'm told he's been killed in a fire. We even run a story about it, and here he is. Anyone want to let me in on the joke?"

"I'm really sorry, Vic," Stone said. "I had—"

Driscoll raised a big linebacker's hand to cut him off.

"Vic, sit down and relax," Driscoll said. "The fire happened. Stone got out, but we, well—"

"Faked his death?" Vic said.

"More like took advantage of the situation," Driscoll said. "I'm sure you can understand that, Vic. You do it all the time, you clowns in the media." Vic gave him the dog stare. "Look, we had some intel. From Agent Rodgers here. He indicated something might come down at Stone's, and we were watching the place anyway. After the fire, Agent Rodgers' office persuaded Stone to play along with the death thing for a while, maybe trip up our target."

The detective's lead in was perfect, so Vic unloaded. "I have a source that says Rodgers maybe lit the fuse. Planned it. Any comment?"

Rodgers shook his head, then looked at Driscoll. "Frank?"

"I don't know what the hell he's talking about," Driscoll said to Rodgers, then to Vic, "What are you talking about, Vic?"

Vic did not respond. Instead he assessed the little gathering. Obviously steamed, Rodgers perched on the edge of his chair. Stone examined the floor tiles, but looked up and said to no one, "What?" Jared folded his hands in his lap, no expression on his face. Frakes shuffled his feet, bounced the other knee, and drilled his glare at the wall behind Driscoll, who looked like he was about to explode.

"Who's your source?" Rodgers said.

"A guy named 'informed'," Vic said.

"I am going to put your ass in jail, Bengston," Rodgers said. "I swear." Vic flipped him the bird. Frakes shook his head again and looked away.

"Greg," Driscoll said. "Anything to add here? Greg?"

Frakes broke off his staring contest with the wall and said, "I seem to be out of the loop. I thought Stone was dead too, until this meeting."

"This is all off the record," Rodgers said, glancing at Driscoll. "No more discussion of it, okay?" Driscoll nodded. "Frakes?" Frakes nodded. "Stone, Jared?" They followed suit. Then he turned to Vic. "Bengston?"

"You already got my salute on that one, Agent Rodgers."

None of it made sense to Vic, who decided to forget about chasing whatever "it" was here in this room, but track "it" down later. He could not imagine Driscoll buying the lame fire story.

Vic continued training his eyes on the chief detective who reined in his frustration and just returned the stare. Then there was something from Driscoll, a slight shrug, a raised eyebrow, a trivial thumb gesture, something Vic sensed. Something that told him yet one more game was being played in this crowded office.

* * *

"You knew quite a lot about this fire when we were in Key West, right after it happened," Vic said to Rodgers. "Maybe before it happened. You told me my former friend here was dead." Rodgers said nothing.

"Vic, I'm really sorry," Stone said. "I thought it might help." Vic ignored Stone and continued with Rodgers.

"It sounds like a really stupid idea," Vic said.

"But it's a classified stupid idea," Rodgers said. "I need to remind you of that. No news stories."

"I'm not bound by any rotten federal regulation," Vic said.

"Vic!" Driscoll said.

"Frank, is there anything in this little scheme that makes sense to you?" Vic said.

"He's got a point, Brad," Driscoll said.

"Irrelevant," Rodgers said. Then he wagged an index finger at Vic. "The U.S. Attorney has a lot to say about this."

"The assault thing?" Vic said.

"The assault thing," Rodgers said.

"But only the one, right?" Vic said.

"One is enough," Rodgers said. "We need time to figure this out."

"Which part of 'this' are we trying to figure out right now?" Vic said.

Rodgers just sighed and looked up at Driscoll's dirty ceiling. Then he said," We had a tip—"

"Frank's 'intel' here?" Vic said. "Intel sounds so much more, well, intelligent."

"Yes, intel," Rodgers said. "We had intel that someone was going to hit Stone's place to look for *Sundial*. If we caught the guy—"

"Or gal," Frakes said.

Rodgers turned slowly toward Frakes and said, "Or gal." Then back to Vic, "We thought if we caught someone, we might at least be able to close out one possible group that might be after *Sundial*."

"And maybe solve your murder, huh, Frank?" Vic said. "So you went along."

Driscoll nodded.

"We needed a strong lead," Driscoll said. "This was a possibility."

"So where is the guy, or gal, in a colored jail jump suit, hand-cuffs, charged with Riley's murder?" Vic said. "Certainly not in this little room. You really need a bigger office, Frank."

"Well, there was a problem," Driscoll said.

"And what was that?" Vic aid.

"Guy showed up an hour and a half early," Driscoll said, then looking at Frakes, "Or gal."

"The surveillance team was late getting there," Driscoll said.

"Where were they?" Vic said.

"Going away party for one of their team," Frakes said.

"They were partying?" Vic said, winding up. "Now there's one heck of a story. What is this, the Secret Service? Party while the government burns to the ground?"

Driscoll raised both hands. "He was being deployed to Afghanistan!"

Vic held his tongue, then said, "All right, Frank, deployment. Okay, I get that. Still, late to a stake out? What about the fire?"

"Firebombed the place on the way out," Frakes said.

"We thought Stone might be safer if we confirmed that he was 'consumed' in the fire," Rodgers said. "At least for a few days, while we work through all this."

"Oh what a tangled web we weave," Vic said. "When first we practise to deceive!"

"I told you this stuff was dangerous, Vic," Stone blurted out.

"Pax, our conversations were privileged," Vic said.

"Like hell they were," Rodgers said.

* * *

"Where's the firebomber?" Vic said.

"Gone by the time anyone got there," Frakes said.

"Nice work, team," Vic said, then to Stone, "Pax, did they get *Sundial?*"

"No," Stone said. "I told you I destroyed my hard drives."

"I guess they wanted to make sure no one got it," Vic said, thinking that whoever torched the place might not have *Sundial* at all, which meant they were still after it. Vic wondered about the report in front of Driscoll on his desk, wondered if the pages inside actually contained the *Sundial* white paper or were blank.

"What about you, or your pal, Nelson?" Driscoll said.

"What about us?" Vic said.

"Do you have a copy of *Sundial*?" Frakes said.

Vic shrugged.

"Do you or don't you?" Rodgers said.

"It certainly would be a grand retirement plan," Vic said.

"This is no joke," Rodgers said.

"What?" Vic said. "*Sundial* or this investigation of yours?"

"Stop!" Driscoll said in a booming elevated voice. Frakes stuck his fingers through the metal blind slats and pulled them down to look into the big room.

"Easy, boss," Frakes said. "They'll be in here weapons drawn in a minute."

"All right, all right," Driscoll said. "Let's get down to business."

Vic sensed an arduous meeting ahead and the prospect of another one when he walked a few blocks back to the newspaper for his meeting with the *Times'* top brass.

* * *

"Where's Jeff?" Vic said.

"We don't know," Rodgers said. "We're looking for him. Discreetly."

"How nice," Vic said. "Are you really with the FBI?"

"I am," Rodgers said. "Well, yes, but I'm tasked to another agency."

"I know," Vic said. "Homeland Security."

"Could be," Rodgers said.

Vic looked at Driscoll and raised his hands like a wide receiver imploring the ref to throw a flag for pass interference.

"Yes," Driscoll said. "He's Homeland Security. On background only. A special little group within it."

"And that would be?" Vic said.

Driscoll looked at Rodgers who reluctantly nodded. The detective held up the white paper and said, "*Sundial*. The *Sundial* task force."

"And these two guys here," Frakes said pointing to Stone and Jared and then looking right at Vic, "maybe you too, figured it out."

"Really, it's little more than that, detective," Rodgers said.

"What do you mean?" Frakes said.

"Jared here came up with *Sundial*," Rodgers said. "But Stone, over there, helped him."

"Helped him?" Vic said to Stone, who looked up at Vic a little too sheepishly.

"I'm sorry, Vic," Stone said. "I was sworn to secrecy. I thought maybe if I could put you onto Jared that you might be able to get the story from him rather than me. I'm not really sure what I was thinking. The encryption discovery was spooky enough. We saw how valuable the technology was, and, well, it scared the hell out of us."

"That hacker test?" Vic said.

"Never happened," Stone said. "I would never put *Sundial* out onto the net."

"But you would give it to me?" Vic said, not knowing whether he was being helped or sandbagged. "I'm still a bit unclear as to your motives, Pax."

"I wanted it out, in some fashion," Stone said. "The story about the technology. But I wanted us to have the technology, and only us."

"Us?" Vic said.

"Us," Stone said. "U.S. The United States."

* * *

"Just a wild guess here," Vic said to Rodgers. "You want to make sure we keep the technology, but you don't want a story written about it."

"That's always the position of the United States government," Rodgers said.

"Unless it serves the government's needs," Vic said.

"Unless it serves our needs," Rodgers said. "Yes."

"Well, it is our government, Brad, remember?" Vic said. "Mine,

Driscoll's, Stone's, Frake's, Jared's, his brother's, and a little bit of yours."

"Spare me the civics lesson," Rodgers said. "Real world's a little different."

"Jared," Vic said. "Aren't you worried about your brother?"

"Yes I am," Jared said.

Vic returned to Driscoll. "Frank, what the hell do you want from me, besides a stroke a hole?"

"We want you to hold the story," Driscoll said.

"What story?" Vic said.

"The *Sundial* story," Rodgers said.

"I'm not talking to you," Vic said to Rodgers.

"You'll have to eventually," Rodgers said.

"Like hell," Vic said. "Frank, what story?"

Driscoll nodded toward Rodgers. "What he said."

"Do I even have a story?" Vic said.

"What do you mean?" Driscoll said.

"I mean that what I have is a pile of crap," Vic said. "You guys finally get around to saying what we knew all the time, that Riley was murdered. By the way, Frank, thanks for releasing the ME's report in time for one of the TV reporters to trip over it and get it on the air well in advance of our first edition."

"Look, the ME had to do a lot of forensic work to finish up with Riley," Driscoll said. "We had to be sure it was a murder. Timing the release of Touhy's report was out of my hands."

"Are you sure now about the murder?" Vic said.

"Yes, we're sure," Driscoll said. "We suspected it from day one."

"But are you really sure that you're sure?" Vic said. "You know, if you're not sure about the things you need to be sure about, well—"

"We've taken enough heat already from your rag about it," Driscoll said. "We just wanted to be thorough."

"And throw a head fake at any possible suspects?" Vic said.

"No harm in that," Frakes said. "Gives us a jump on them."

"If only the crooks would call in their plans ahead of time," Vic said. "Like filing a flight plan. That would help too."

Driscoll glared at Vic. Their next golf game would be brutal.

"So, you drag your feet on Riley's death, why I don't know, really," Vic said. "Then my old buddy here gets killed in a fire at his home. Only he wasn't killed. Now it's a deliberate fire, arson, I guess, but that's after we misreported his death, which we now have to un-misreport without getting into *Sundial*."

"Life's tough," Rodgers said.

"How do I explain all this to my editors without going into *Sundial*?" Vic said. "That's just some of the garbage I've got to go clean up over there on my side of Civic Center when I meet with my bosses. Then, after successfully navigating my years from high school until now without engaging in a single fist fight, I have, in a matter of a few days, assaulted an FBI agent twice!"

"Cry me a river," Rodgers said. "Remember, it's only the one assault."

"Oh thanks," Vic said to Rodgers while miming the Jack Benny hand wave, then back to Driscoll, "Look, Frank, I think I know what *Sundial* is all about. I've got unused notes from a Riley interview. We covered it indirectly."

"We're going to want to see those notes," Rodgers said.

"Bite me," Vic said. "I've got the empty Sundial Ranch guarded by Homeland Security. I've got my now undead friend, Paxton Stone, who first plays like he has no clue about *Sundial*, and then it turns out he was really a part of it with Jared the mysterious hacker here, who really didn't break the code in Pax's fake test, because he actually created the damn thing."

"Don't forget the breaking and entering at Riley's," Frakes said. "And tampering with evidence."

"Yeah," Vic burst out. "And the federal assault charge."

"There's the obstruction of justice thing too," Rodgers said.

"Hear him?" Vic said to Driscoll. "The obstruction of justice thing too? The Denver Police Department handed me the key to Riley's house along with the security code. That'll provide a nice wrinkle in our coverage of this fire drill."

Driscoll said nothing.

"Like I said," Vic said. "Where's the story? How do I sort all that out? And by the way, Frank, who did kill Riley?"

They all stared at him now. He was in front of his high school speech class struggling to overcome stage fright, remembering one of the tricks his speech teacher offered. So, mentally, Vic stripped everyone in the room down to their skivvies.

"See?" Vic said. "You don't have a damn clue. Maybe that's the headline. 'No Damn Clue'. You don't know who killed Riley. You faked a citizen's death. And you don't know who has *Sundial* or who's after it, do you?"

"About *Sundial*," Rodgers said.

"Yeah, I'll tell you about *Sundial*," Vic said, glaring at Rodgers, wanting to assault him for a third time. "You don't want me to just hold the story. You want me to spike the story."

"Well, that's sort of what we had in mind," Frakes said.

"Another state heard from," Vic said turning to Frakes. "I suppose in return for no charges being filed against me, right?"

"Vic, I think you now have a firm grip on the obvious," Driscoll said.

Vic looked around the room. Jared and Stone kept watch on the floor. All three cops were smiling.

43

Vic walked a few extra blocks after he left Denver Police Headquarters to lower his breathing rate and give him some time to sort things out before he met with Vigil and Quartermaine over at the paper. He strolled around the corner and walked up Delaware Street past the string of brightly painted brick Victorian homes that housed the city's bail bond industry, past the Aloha Wellness Center, which sold medical dope right across the street from the cop shop, then east on 14th Avenue past the U.S. Mint and City Hall. Civic Center Park offered up a green living break from the city cement, brick, granite, glass, asphalt, and steel.

He sat for a bit on a stone bench next to Seal Pond, a tiny body of water flanked on each side by bronze statues of naked children riding the backs of seals, art objects that would most likely be frowned upon by growing numbers of the intolerant. The concrete pond had not been fired up for summer, the central fountain quiet, the seals not spitting their usual streams, empty of water, and devoid of the coins park visitors tossed into it during the warmer months. Staring out across Colfax Avenue at the Denver Times building, Vic contemplated his quandary.

At the cop shop, he had agreed to nothing, but had pled the need to speak with his editors and his lawyer. Vic thought neither the Denver cops nor the FBI would do anything to him, concluding they were just blowing smoke, but he did not want to let them know that. Enough of the Riley investigation had already been screwed up. After falsely billing the death of the one of the country's top high tech innovators as a suicide, cops allowed at least three people to enter Riley's house easily and rifle its contents. Then there was the fire at Stone's.

The lax security at Riley's house would make a pretty funny story, if only Vic could explain why he chose to explore the house as well. The *Times* management probably would not be too excited about one of their reporters exercising his breaking and entering expertise, especially in the wake of the international flap over the Rupert Murdock cell phone hacking scandals, even if someone from the cop shop technically let him in. There was the Key West caper, Rodgers letting himself get potted twice by a rank amateur, Stone's police-inspired death, the Jeff and Jared mix-up, and *Sundial.*

The cops had him in a corner. He writes a story about the investigation foul-ups, and they arrest him on one of several charges. End of journalism career, for a second time. Yet Vic knew that he had them in a corner too. The fake suicide investigation, fabricated fire death, sloppy police work, any of these could torpedo his friend, Driscoll, and get Rodgers reassigned to the North Dakota FBI office. In this investigation, there seemed to be only one subject that could raise Vic above the possibility of police retaliation, only one subject that was so big that even breaking and entering, copying evidence, or assaulting an FBI agent might be forgiven.

And that was *Sundial,* Vic's trump card.

44

Even though the adrenalin in his system kept his heart racing, Vic was pleased with his performance in Driscoll's office. Maybe his wandering right eye that tilted a bit toward the ceiling made his outburst seem slightly more psychotic than the cops had expected. It used to scare his kids when they were little. Could it rattle cops?

Vic actually did have a story, but it was one that mostly raised questions. He roughed it out in his head as he crossed Colfax and entered the Times building.

"Hi, Vic," came the voice from behind the empty marble-topped lobby counter. Vic walked over and saw the guard-greeter flipping through various security cameras on his screen.

"Joe," Vic said. "Word?"

"It's 'Wassup?' now," Joe said.

"What about 'How're Ya Doin'?" Vic said.

"Just fine, just fine," Joe said.

"I've got a rush meeting with the brass," Vic said.

"I know," Joe said.

"You know?" Vic said.

"They asked me to let them know when you hit the door," he said.

"Word travels fast," Vic said heading for the elevator. Delay my arrival announcement as long as you dare."

"Actually, Vigil used the term 'sorry ass' when he called me," Joe said as the elevator door closed.

On the fifth floor, Vic passed by another counter, this one empty. He badged his way into the newsroom, glad to see that still worked, and trotted to his desk to quickly knock out a lead.

* * *

VOTE
Draft/Bengston

Voting system entrepreneur David Riley, murdered in his east Denver home earlier this month, had developed a data encryption method considered by some experts to be virtually unbreakable.

So powerful, this encryption system is highly sought by U.S. federal agencies, foreign governments, financial institutions, other corporate interests, criminals, and terrorists, according to knowledgeable industry sources.

Riley's company, Millennial Vote Systems, created the security protocol, codenamed *Sundial*, to safeguard election ballots cast with a new, but still secret, Universal Vote System designed to enable any eligible voter to register and vote in an election from anywhere using the internet, cell phones, landline telephones, tablet computers, satellites, cable television, and even gaming systems. Astronauts could vote from the International Space Station or the moon under Riley's vision.

Riley revealed the existence of the Universal Vote System during an exclusive interview with the *Denver Times* shortly before his murder.

While Universal Vote would likely revolutionize elections, computer encryption experts say *Sundial* would provide virtually unbreakable security for electronic financial, government, military, and other communications or computer data.

The existence of the *Sundial* encryption technology was not disclosed during the Riley interview, but uncovered during an investigation by the *Times* following the entrepreneur's death.

In his final media interview, Riley told the *Times* that because his Universal Vote System would "rapidly and extensively spread the vote franchise," it was met with stiff resistance from the nation's top political leaders, who feared the loss of party control over their respective voter bases.

While the Universal Vote concept seemed to rattle political operatives, Riley's *Sundial* data encryption protocol seems to be real diamond in the rough.

A virtually unbreakable encryption method would be a "highly sought after prize by any enterprise demanding the highest levels of security for data and communications," one industry expert told the *Times*. "Military and government secrets would be infinitely more secure than they are today."

Such an encryption scheme likely would have prevented the embarrassing leaks of domestic and foreign spying programs revealed by former NSA contractor Edward Snowden, or the disclosure of U.S. State Department cables, Swiss banking documents, and corporate insider information that have been made public by the controversial Wikileaks.com website, according to sources familiar with the technology.

Riley, who made several billion dollars with his widely used Millennium touch-screen voting machines, planned to use the encryption technology only for his newly developed Universal Vote System, according to *Sundial* documents obtained by the *Times*. The documents indicate Riley planned to keep the encryption system proprietary rather than share it with any public or private enterprise.

During the interview, Riley said he wanted to expand the vote franchise to "every eligible man and women, first in the United States, and then globally, to make sure all people have a voice in what governments do on their behalf."

One of the ideas to protect the *Sundial* encryption system was to create a foundation or public trust to handle the security aspects of his Universal Vote System, according to the *Sundial* documents.

"Democracy demands participation by every citizen," Riley said during the *Times* interview. "If voting eligibility is going to be limited by age, then I'll accept that. However, I want voting to be as easy as brushing your teeth. I don't even like voter registration, but if I must put up with it, then I want to be sending citizens emails, text messages, robo-calls, and tweets to register them on the spot. Then they can vote. Can you imagine casting an encrypted ballot over a social media network like Twitter or Facebook? My team has made that possible."

Riley told the *Times* he was "shocked" when he laid out his plans for the Universal Vote System before the heads of both major political parties.

"I felt like a real naive son of a bitch," he said, adding that both party leaders, in separate meetings, expressed "virtually identical" reactions.

"They turned beet red and said this concept was totally unacceptable," Riley said. "The Republican chairwomen said there would be widespread voter registration fraud by the Democrats. The Democratic chairman said Republicans would manipulate the technology to keep poor people from voting."

He said he was "disgusted" by their response.

"They didn't even hear my explanation that the built in security solved both problems," Riley said. "They weren't pretty meetings."

-30-

* * *

That was enough for now, Vic thought. He was giving all his notes to the *Times* even though the interview took place before the newspaper hired him. The paper would get the glory. Vic wondered if he overdid the mention of the *Times* in the story, but he wanted to make it clear to Vigil and Quartermaine it would be the newspaper's coup. They can always be edited out.

In return, he trusted the paper would defend him in court if it came to that.

Vic ordered two sets of his lead paragraphs printed, walked down to a nearby laser printer, grabbed the copies and hoped Quartermaine and Vigil were big enough to overlook the felony charges that might be coming his way from the local cops and the feds.

* * *

Vic found Vigil in his fifth floor office. The two of them walked out of the newsroom in silence. As they stepped onto the elevator to head up to the ninth floor and Quartermaine's cave, Vigil said, "What's in the folder?"

"Just something I want both of you to read before we talk," Vic said.

"Letter of resignation?" Vigil said. "That might be appropriate."

That would make it easy, Vic thought, but he said, "I just need your take, both of your takes, on this."

"God almighty, Vic, give me something here," Vigil said, almost pleading. "I am the damn editor after all."

Vic handed Vigil the copies. "One's for you, the other one for Quartermaine." They stepped out of the elevator and stood right outside it as Vigil read what Vic had written.

"How good are your sources?" Vigil said.

"Solid," Vic said, "But—"

"But there's a problem," Vigil said, shaking his head.

They started for Quartermaine's office.

"Well, they say they want the story held," Vic said. "But I think they really want it spiked and buried forever."

"Who's 'they'?" Vigil said.

"The United States Government," Vic said.

""Oh, that 'they'." Vigil said. He looked out the window at Denver's skyline, then back at Vic. "It'll get out somehow. Why not us?"

"You know, if this were the *Sun* twenty-five years ago, even the *Times* back then, I'd agree," Vic said. "But the *Sun* is gone and this rag is hanging on by a thread. It's more susceptible to outside pressure when there's no real competition."

"We've run plenty of good stories," Vigil said.

"One of your best columnists just quit because the brass told her she wrote too many nicey nicey pieces about illegal immigrants," Vic said.

"There was more to it than that," Vigil said.

"No there wasn't," Vic said. "Where did the pressure to lean on her come from? Not the business community. They like illegals. They help their bottom line. Not agriculture. Those kids down at Cherry Creek High School aren't going to bend over all day and pick onions to pay for their four dollar lattes."

"Hey, my kids go there," Vigil said. "So did yours."

"Les, that's not my point," Vic said. "Farmers need the Mexicans in the fields. It certainly wasn't the Democrats who complained about her columns. They want them to become citizens and vote. It was the loud mouthed tea party crowd who think we can get along without any government."

"Quartermaine wanted more balance," Vigil said.

"From a columnist?" Vic said. "That's the whole point of a column, to grind an axe. Quartermaine's got his local righty columnist. They can balance out the political ledger. Hire more people, Les. Quit laying off journalists."

"I don't control the columnists," Vigil said, pleading again. "Quartermaine and his editorial page does."

"I know that, but the point is that Quartermaine seems to buckle under pressure from the right," Vic said. "If a few tea party zealots and conservative Republicans in this state can influence the fate of a leftie columnist, just imagine what kind of pressure the FBI, Homeland Security, and who knows who else can bring to bear on this story?"

"Give the man a chance, Vic," Vigil said, both hands outstretched.

They stood outside Quartermaine's office, finishing the discussion. Vic surmised that Vigil was thinking about his family and his mortgage again, and he could not really blame him.

"Okay, he'll see you now," said Quartermaine's combination secretary, receptionist, and ninja.

"Thanks Geraldine," Vigil said.

The two walked into publisher's office.

45

Quartermaine's sprawling office occupied the southwest corner of the building. With windows on two sides, it gave him a commanding view of the state capitol, Civic Center Park, city hall, the snowcapped mountains of Colorado's Front Range, police headquarters, and much of Denver's urban skyline. Sitting behind his vast mahogany desk, empty but for a copy of the day's *Times* and a telephone, the man looked like a gnat positioned squarely on the fifty-yard line at the football stadium, which he could see from his window.

"Let's go over here, guys," Quartermaine said, waving toward a small round conference table surrounded by four chairs. The use of the word "guys" sounded a bit forced, as though Quartermaine was trying to be one of the "guys." It was the same feeling Vic got when he heard National Public Radio do a sports story.

"I'd like you to read this before we talk," Vic said, looking at Vigil. "Les?"

Vigil handed his boss a copy of what Vic had written.

"Would you now?" Quartermaine said.

"Sure," Vic said. "It thumbnails what I'm looking at. Then we guys can shoot the breeze about it, okay?"

The satire was lost on Quartermaine. Vigil shot him a glance. Vic shrugged and smiled.

Quartermaine sat down and read the top of Vic's story. He set it on the table in front of him.

"I got a call from Homeland Security," Quartermaine said.

"Are you sure it was Homeland Security?" Vic said.

"I know the secretary personally," Quartermaine said.

"And it was the Secretary of Homeland Security?" Vigil said.

"Yes it was," Quartermaine said.

"Then it was probably a call from Homeland Security," Vic said. "They don't want any of this to see the light of day, do they?"

"No they don't," Quartermaine said.

"And you caved," Vic said.

"Vic!" Vigil said.

"No," Quartermaine said calmly. "No, I didn't."

"Yet," Vic said.

"Yet," Quartermaine said. "I said we'd hold the story."

"Well, it's still not complete anyway," Vic said. "Les thought I should rough this out for you to show you where I'm headed."

Vic, feeling Vigil looking at him, kept his eyes trained on Quartermaine, dog-staring him, waiting for him to finish reading the story.

After a minute, Quartermaine broke. He glanced up at Vigil.

"Les," Quartermaine said. "Are these sources good?"

Vigil looked at Vic, nodded and said, "Yes."

This astonished Vic. Vigil had just gone all in on the *Sundial* story.

"Keep it moving forward," he said, handing the copy back to Vic. "And keep me updated. Les?"

Vigil nodded.

"I'm going to need something from you first," Vic said.

"What's that?" Quartermaine said.

"A promise," Vic said.

"For what?" Quartermaine said. He sounded perturbed.

"A promise that you will not disclose anything about this story to anybody for any reason," Vic said.

"Or what?" Quartermaine said.

"Or it will appear in the *Huffington Post*," Vic said.

"Aw, Vic, will you knock this off," Vigil said.

There was another thing that Vic knew, or was told about Quartermaine. The man liked the sound of Pulitzer Prize, the way it rolled off the tongue, a fact he picked up during his monthly poker game down at the press club. One of his card playing partners mentioned that Quartermaine really liked the big journalism prizes even though the stories they represented were often antithetical to his business aspirations. Journalists do not win Pulitzers for writing puff pieces about business, government, or media consolidation. They won them for writing stories that embarrass the kind of people Quartermaine normally hung out with.

So here was Quartermaine, owner of a Pulitzer Prize winning newspaper sitting across the table from a Pulitzer Prize winning reporter with a story that might win yet another Pulitzer Prize. Seeing this story, the one on the table before him, appearing first on the Huffington Post website was a bit more than even Quartermaine's bottom-line oriented make-up could stomach.

"I don't like threats," Quartermaine said.

"All I am saying is that I had this story before I went to work for the *Times*. My notes are my notes, and this story is from my notes."

"Vic, we know that," Vigil said.

"And I'm offering my notes to the *Denver Times*," Vic said. "That's all. If the fruits of my labor aren't welcome here, then they'll be welcome somewhere else. That's the business of journalism, Mr. Quartermaine."

"There's more to this business than the stories," Quartermaine said.

"The next time you're riding your Schwinn in some neighborhood and tossing your product up onto the porch of one of your customers, you damn well better have something in it worth reading, or you'll just be peddling a shopper rag full of ads," Vic said.

Vigil fidgeted as Vic got up to leave.

"You've got my word," Quartermaine said. "Just stay in touch with Les."

One thing everyone at the poker game said, or at least the ones who knew the backstory on Quartermaine was that he kept his word.

"Right, chief," Vic said. He had always wanted to say that. Then he headed for the door with Vigil tagging behind.

* * *

Vic strolled through the city room and stopped at Peggy's desk. Her fingers flew across the keyboard as letters, words, sentences and paragraphs splatted onto her screen.

"Do we still work here?" she said, without looking up.

"For now," Vic said.

Peggy continued plapping on her keyboard.

"Your friend called," she said.

"Which one?" Vic said. "I have so many."

"Speedster," Peggy said. "He said he was sending over some instructions."

"Instructions?" Vic said. His pulse beat against his temple. "And?"

"Who the hell is he?" Peggy said. This time she paused her flashing fingers and looked up at him. Since the first time Ellison called, and Vic thought it was an old statehouse press room buddy poking fun, he nicknamed the source after the guy's favorite plaything, a fully restored 1957 Porsche Speedster. Vic had not told Peggy who the source was.

"I can't tell you," Vic said.

"And why, old man?" Peggy said. "Still protecting the young damsel?"

"I don't know," Vic said. "It just doesn't seem right, yet."

"That's crap and you know it," Peggy said. "Anyway, it's Stew Ellison."

"How did you figure that out?"

"Well, let me see," Peggy said. "I rifled your desk. I had a friend break into your house and toss the place. I hacked your laptop. I asked Quartermaine and Vigil. Oh, and then when Speedster told me who he was, I put it all together."

"Nothing gets by you," Vic said as he pulled his chair over from his Dilbert cubicle and sat down next to Peggy.

"He actually identified himself?"

"Oh, I had to pull it out of him, but then he spilled his guts," Peggy said.

"What did you do?" Vic said.

"I said hello, and then he said this is Stew Ellison. Is Vic Bengston available?"

"You're tough as nails," Vic said. "And to think the *Times* wanted to waste those talents on the Features department flogging unsuspecting celebrity chefs."

Peggy handed him a sealed envelope.

"Some geeky looking guy dropped this off while you were upstairs sumo wrestling with Quartermaine and Vigil," Peggy said.

Vic sat down, the envelope in his hand, and updated her on the meeting with the cops, Stone, and Picune, as well as the short session in the front office. Then he made the zipped lips gesture which Peggy aped back at him.

"What's the local story, besides complete confusion in the wake of Riley's death?" Peggy said.

"We could have some fun with that," Vic said.

"I think Vigil wants a little more than a humor piece," Peggy said. "Where are you on *Sundial*?"

Vic dug out the folded copy of the story lead he gave to Quartermaine and Vigil. He handed it to Peggy who quickly scanned it. "This is promising."

"You'll be an editor here yet," Vic said.

"And once again you'll be getting me coffee," Peggy said.

"The story would have a little more gravitas if I could tie in the politicos' universal hatred for Universal Vote with Riley's murder," Vic said.

"How universal," Peggy said.

"Extremely universal," Vic said.

"That's like very unique," Peggy said. "It's either universal or it's not."

"It's universal," Vic said. "Or it was intended to be so. The Republicrats might put the kibosh on it."

She nodded toward the digital clock on the wall. "Aren't you going to read Speedster's message?"

Vic ripped open the envelope and read the single sheet inside. He folded it up and stuffed in his shirt pocket.

"Were you ever going to mention Ellison?" Peggy said.

"Eventually."

"Eventually when?"

"When the time is right," Vic said.

"Like now?" Peggy said.

"Well, he is in my pre *Times* notes, Peggy," Vic said. "And he was all about the Universal Vote System, not *Sundial*."

"But the vote system is how we get into the *Sundial* story."

"We met out at Centennial Airport in the Landing Strip," Vic said.

"Over fine wine and cheese? Candle light?"

"No, over eggs and sausage. He called me right after I got my non answers from the RNC and DNC chairs. He works every side of the aisle."

"I thought he was strictly GOP," Peggy said.

"He's strictly Stew Ellison," Vic said. "He works the Dems through another outfit. But the big chiefs talk to him directly."

"Did you two boys talk about *Sundial*?" Peggy said.

He pulled out the folded envelop send tossed it to Peggy. "Not till this."

She opened the note and read it aloud, "11:30 tonight. Pavilion near Ferril Lake. Vital Info on SUNDIAL. Alone please. Speedster." Peggy looked up at Vic. "The politicos didn't know about *Sundial*."

"Well, I can only infer that from what Riley told me," Vic said.

"I suppose a follow up interview with Riley's out of the question," Peggy said.

"It'd be a bit one-sided," Vic said.

"Stinky too," Peggy said.

"Ellison's like Chickenman," Vic said.

"Chickenman?" Peggy said.

"Oh, a radio spoof on superheroes," Vic said.

"From the Stone Age, no doubt," Peggy said.

"Chicago radio," Vic said. "The Sixties. Chickenman—He's everywhere, he's everywhere!"

"Half century," Peggy said. "Wonder if my grandpa heard of him."

"Probably," Vic said. "He was everywhere."

"Like Speedster," Peggy said.

"You're quite mad, you know," Peggy said with a terrible British accent. "City Park, just before midnight. Right out of your film noir flicks."

Vic shrugged. "In a way. What could go wrong?"

"Got an hour?" Peggy said. "I'll fill you in."

46

Vic parked his Jeep at the north side curb on 21st Avenue just west of the entrance to City Park right in front of the century-old building where Vic and his former business partner housed their video production studio and public relations firm. The building was a stately brick and stone number that covered half the block. Street level space was mostly retail, except for one small apartment in the center of the building. Eight apartments occupied the second story. Vic and Ben's studio took up the center of the building, about two thousand square feet on the main floor and another thousand in the dank basement. Decades earlier, the space was a Piggly Wiggly grocery store. Then it was an appliance store, followed by a theatrical scene shop, and finally Vic and Ben's headquarters for public relations and corporate video production.

The old studio space was still vacant, but the two other businesses were still there. To the west, a retired African American architect ran a small gift shop, everything imported from Africa, except the Vermont maple syrup. Most days it was closed. But Mr. Henderson was always there on Fridays and Saturdays, mostly to hang out and chew the fat with old friends. Vic usually wandered over there when he took a break from writing a script, building a publicity plan, or directing a video shoot. Mr. Henderson did not sell much except at Christmas time, but he did not really care. "Gets me out of the house," he would say with a twinkle and a grin. "Better than hanging out in a bar." The corner store, facing the park at 21st and York, was a flower shop run by an African American woman who grew up with the Carbone boys, who owned the building. Their parents, Italian immigrants who ran a bakery in north Denver, erected the building in 1908, and it had been in the family ever since. Vic expected it would be there for another century.

He crossed York Street and entered the park, about a half mile from the designated meeting place, the outdoor concert stage on the western shore of Ferril Lake, one of three small bodies of water inside the park. As he passed the dark and silent tennis courts, Vic heard the roar of a lion from the Denver Zoo on the northwest corner of the park. Birds screeched. Monkeys howled. Even animals suffered from insomnia, Vic thought. Then he thought what he was doing was pretty stupid, took a deep breath and muttered, "In for a penny, in for a pound."

He paused near the statue of Martin Luther King. It was actually the second statue of King erected on the same site. The first one looked hideous and was eventually replaced after many complaints. The civil rights leader, now illuminated by a mottled combination of moonlight and shadows from nearby trees, looked much better.

From the King statue, Vic cut across the lawn and slowly approached the rear of the large stucco and tiled roof pavilion that overlooked Ferril Lake to the east, and, further away, the Denver Museum of Nature and Science and the Gates Planetarium.

He walked beneath one of the porticos of the open pavilion and hesitated in the shadows. From there he could see the moonlit concert stage at the water's edge. While he watched for movement, he wished Nelson was with him. Off in the zoo, the monkeys continued their riotous noise for a few more minutes before settling down. That was when Vic heard the sound of someone walking, then low talking, but he could not make out the words. It sounded like two men. Outnumbered already, he thought, by a couple of guys who did not seem to be too concerned about the noise they made. As the voices grew louder, Vic could see two men on the trail along the northern shore of the lake. He stepped a few feet to the left and deeper into the shadow of a massive pillar. The duo crossed the wide concrete plaza and walked straight toward him. Vic felt the familiar thumping of his heart.

The two men argued about which rookie the Colorado Rockies should sign to elevate the overall mediocrity of the team's pitching staff. Vic held his breath. The men walked through the portico and passed within a few feet of him, continuing their discussion, walking right on by and out the rear of the building toward the bronze Dr. King. Their voices trailed off as the City Park night swallowed them whole, leaving behind the aroma of Colorado's newest cash crop, dope.

Vic turned his attention back toward the lake and the concert stage. A figure stepped out of the darkness.

"You can come out now, Bengston," a muffled voice said.

Vic squinted to see him, but it did not help. "Ellison?"

"Yes," the voice said.

Why would Ellison disguise his voice, Vic wondered, unless to defeat an audio recording? Only the digital recorder was on his desk at the paper.

"Step out!"

The heart raced faster. Vic eased his way from the shadow into the moonlight and walked slowly across the plaza between the concert stage and the pavilion.

A click.

"You've got a gun?" Vic said. He really missed Nelson now.

"I know how to use it too," the voice said. It was not Ellison, but he could not make out who it was.

Vic froze, and said, "I'm pissing in my pants at the moment."

"I don't care if you're crapping on the patio," the voice said. "Get over here."

Why closer? Vic wondered. He was only twenty feet away.

"I thought you just worked with numbers, election returns, all that," Vic said. "Not this tough guy stuff."

"If I come over there, I'll be shooting," the voice said. "Pissing will be the least of your worries."

It definitely was not Ellison. Still, nothing rang a bell. Vic took a few slow steps backward, hoping to recede into the black shadows of this real life noir encounter.

"I'm coming, but only if you promise not to shoot," Vic said.

"This isn't a movie," the voice said. "Just get over here."

So the voice could not yet tell that Vic was edging backwards, he thought. Maybe his guy just wanted a guaranteed shot.

"All right," Vic said, hoping his faltering short-term memory had mapped everything outside the portico he had entered a few minutes earlier.

"Stay in the light, where I can see you," the voice said.

Vic spun and accelerated toward the portico entrance. He summoned the memory of an indoor hurdles race against a boyhood pal in high school as he pushed as hard as he could against the cement. His brain begged for speed, wishing he could fly, as he leaped two steps back up onto the portico. He fought the memory of his run for a fly ball that year he spent in Alaska when he pulled both hamstrings. Would that happen again, hobbling him like a lame horse, followed by a bullet to the head? It mattered little. Whoever it was behind him, he had a gun. Vic seemed to hit his old high school speed. The hamstrings held. He sailed out the rear of the portico. His heart was not happy.

The gun popped, and he cut around a dense juniper that ripped at his legs. Vic planted his left foot and cut again, this time to the right, sending him down a gentle grass covered slope. Now he was on that eighty-yard touchdown run in sophomore football when he burst through the hole in the line. Out in the open now, Vic ran as hard as he could toward a parking lot north of the pavilion. He heard a zip, then a crack. More shooting. Pain seized his chest. Memory told him Duck Lake was straight ahead. He saw his children, young and innocent, with him as they fed bread to the ducks and geese, then hit the asphalt walkway around the lake.

Vic cut to the right and flew along the southern edge of the tiny pond. The end of the walkway came rapidly, suddenly, and painfully as Vic smashed into a tall chain link fence and crumpled to the ground. His body hurt all over. His face numbed. Hot blood trickled from his nose. Salty tears stung his eyes. Curled up at the base of the fence on a small patch of gravel, Vic groaned. His heart still seemed to be functioning, but his lungs scraped at him with searing pain.

A bullet hit the water of Duck Lake. Vic grabbed the chain link and pulled himself up. He kept going, climbing skyward. The fence was taller than any fence he had ever scaled in his life, but he just kept clawing his way up and over the top, thanking someone for not bothering to top this one with barbed wire. Vic wished he had mastered that trick of hitting the top of a fence, reaching over with one arm and flipping the rest his body over. His high school buddy, Al, had figured out how to do it, but he never did. Instead he was stuck with the wobbly straddling move at the top, swinging one leg over and then the other, losing all speed, opening himself up as an easy target.

But there were no shots. Vic wondered if his luck would ever run out in this life. Both legs over, he half fell and half climbed back down to Earth. Keep moving, he screamed at himself silently. He sprinted in the same direction for another ten yards, then cut to the left, a handy pass pattern he used to run out of the backfield. Only he had not counted on the big linebacker stopping him cold just before his cut. It was a massive soft something that he ran into right after he heard another gunshot. Whatever it was it had a little give to it but not all that much, like a giant firm mattress, bouncing him backward a few feet with a loud grunt, more like a low growl. Vic reached out and his hands felt the leathery skin, rough, smelling of dust.

The elephant was probably as surprised as Vic was. It moved off with a couple of hops, big hops. And then a loud toot. Vic took a step. His left foot sank into a soft stinking mound. Then he began to run again, toward a single light that illuminated what looked like a gate. A gunman behind him and elephants around him, Vic trotted quickly across the zoo's simulated patch of Africa hoping he could avoid being shot or trampled. The locked gate did not help, but it was part of the same fence he had negotiated earlier. So up he went again. This time, at the top, he swung his left arm over the precipice. His hand grasped the chain link and he pivoted his body over with it, somehow managing to maintain his grasp on the other side, avoiding a ten-foot fall. He seemed to have finally mastered the over-the-fence flip in his sixth decade of living. Vic climbed down the fence, quickly and in control, landing on a walkway between the animal pens.

He followed the pathway into a large central open area where zoo visitors gathered. Only there was no one around except the rumbling of moving elephants, screeching, chirping, and growling of the now restless inmates. Vic knew where he was, not far from the concession stands and the main entrance. In a few minutes, he found an emergency exit and pushed his way out of the Denver Zoo.

He jogged and walked straight north, crossing 23rd Avenue and then City Park Golf Course until he got to 26th. He headed west, crossed York Street, and then turned south on Gaylord, doubling back to where he had parked near his old studio. Along the way, his heart rate returned to normal and the pain in his chest subsided, only to be replaced with agony from his face and screams from nearly every joint in his body.

All this was scented with the musty aroma of pachyderm waste.

47

"What the hell happened to you?" Peggy said as Vic walked up to her cubical the next morning. He had two grandé Starbucks in his hands. He handed one to Peggy.

"French kissed a Mack truck doing ninety miles an hour," Vic said.

"What's a Mack truck?" Peggy said.

"Never mind," Vic said, flopping down into a small folding chair Peggy kept in her cube for visitors. "I went to see Girard this morning. Nothing broken."

"Girard?" Peggy said.

"A doctor friend," Vic said. He sipped his coffee through the tiny hole in the top. It had cooled enough to suit him.

"You going to tell me what happened or will we be playing Mr. Macho this week?" Peggy said. "I tole you, Lucy, not to venture into that park at night."

"Yeah," Vic said. "But did Lucy ever listen?"

Vic flinched as he reached forward to set his coffee on the corner of Peggy's desk. He leaned back and told her what happened. "Half my night was spent with the cops. They spent most of the time trying to figure out how to use their new cop tablet computers. Typing on a touch screen takes forever."

"You sure it wasn't Ellison?" she said, examining his face. "Just looking at it makes me hurt."

"I'll trade places in a heartbeat," Vic said.

"Are you going to tell Driscoll?" Peggy said, nodding toward Vigil's office. "And the brain trust over there?"

"Yes and no," Vic said.

"I think they should know," Peggy said.

"Oh, so they can fire me and send you back to writing nice little puff pieces about some horse jumping event down in Greenwood Village?"

Peggy said nothing.

"I've got a contact number on my laptop," Vic said, gingerly pushing himself out of the chair. He grabbed his coffee and moved toward his desk, slowly. "I'll see if he's in D.C. He couldn't have gotten back there this quickly if he was shooting at me last night in City Park."

"Unless he had a private jet waiting out at Centennial Airport, Vic," Peggy said.

"Good point," Vic said. "That's all he flies."

* * *

Vic dialed the number.

"I was thinking about calling you today," Ellison said.

"Why didn't you?" Vic said.

"Well, I was just thinking about it," he said. "I wasn't sure if you'd take the call."

"Or whether I could take the call?"

Silence. Then, "I'm not sure what you mean."

"I'll bet you don't," Vic said.

"Look, I don't know what you're getting at. I did want to talk to you about Riley's Universal Vote System," Ellison said. "I'll be back out in Colorado next week. Can we get together then?"

This seemed far too amiable to Vic, far too casual, as though nothing had happened the night before. "I missed you at the zoo," Vic said. Silence again. "Rather, you missed me."

"You're going to have to bring me up to speed, Bengston," Ellison said. "I'm not really following you."

"Were you following me last night?"

"Honestly, where are you going with this?" Ellison said.

"You should know," Vic said.

"No, honest," he said. That word again.

"That's a strange response, Stew," Vic said.

"What?" Ellison said.

"Honest," Vic said.

"Perfectly legitimate word," Ellison said.

"I missed you last night," Vic said. "On cable."

"I wasn't on the air," Ellison said. "I flew back to Washington in the afternoon from LA. Didn't feel too good."

"I can't trust you, Stew," Vic said. He did not want to blurt out an accusation that if proven incorrect would put his own credibility in jeopardy.

"Sure you can," Ellison said. "We can talk about it next week."

"Next week again," Vic said. "Let's talk now."

"Not here, not on the phone," Ellison said. "Next week, in person. You pick the place."

"Call my cell phone," Vic said. "You've got my number."

"Better give it to me again, just in case," Ellison said.

Vic gave him the number and they hung up, ending what Vic thought was an odd conversation with the brains behind countless election victories throughout the country.

* * *

Peggy sat quietly next to Vic's desk. She sipped her coffee and just looked at him. Finally, she said, "Are we in some parallel universe? Should I call the Fringe Unit?"

"You might as well," Vic said. "I swear, this guy might be telling the truth."

"Somewhat of a relative term to guys like Ellison," Peggy said.

"I don't know, Peggy," Vic said. He leaned back after pulling the plastic top off the paper coffee cup. He took a gulp of the now cooled liquid. "Wants to see me next week. He didn't rise to the zoo bait at all. Feigned astonishment? I just don't know."

"He never struck me as much of an actor," Peggy said. "But I've only seen him on cable."

"He's a brainiac. He works with numbers and ideas and does most of it behind the scenes, although he's on the tube more and more."

"Hate to burst a bubble, Vic, but there are no more tubes," Peggy said.

"Well, on the flat, then," Vic said. "What should we call it? The slab?"

"I like slab," Peggy said. "Let's go watch the Superbowl on the slab."

"On the slab," Vic said. "Has a better ring to it."

"Well, if you're not sure about Ellison, stay conservative," Peggy said.

"What do you mean?" Vic said.

"I mean don't default to your slobbery bleeding heart liberal assumption that everyone is good inside," Peggy said.

"Just keep assuming he's a typical political slime ball? Evil incarnate?"

"Essentially, yes," Peggy said.

"He did say he represented both parties in this matter," Vic said.

"And doesn't the Ninth Law of Political Thermodynamics tell us that for every Republican slime ball there is an equal and opposite Democratic slime ball?" Peggy said.

"This is true, Frau Professor," Vic said. "Are there independent slime balls?"

"Oh yes," Peggy said. "In politics, all players are slime balls."

"And, yet, it's the best system on Earth," Vic said.

"Only because we can vote out the slime," Peggy said. "Theoretically."

"So cynical," Vic said. "And you're not even thirty-something yet."

"I'm thirty-one," Peggy said. "And that's Freulein Professor, okay?"

48

Vic left the city room before Vigil caught a glimpse of his mashed up face. He walked over to the library to see if Miss Raglin might be able to shed a little more light on *Sundial*. As he passed through Civic Center Park's semi-permanent throng of homeless, impoverished seniors, druggies, and street people, Vic felt more like one of the crowd, bashed in as he was.

Inside the hall of books, he tip-toed past a few dozing patrons, and wove his way through the interior, around corners, up the stairs, past the dimly lighted stacks and into the research section. A slice of light escaped from Miss Raglin's cracked open door. Vic peeked through and saw her from the back sitting upright before her computer terminal.

"Door's open," she said. "Come in."

Vic pushed the door open and stepped into her small neat office. She plapped a few more computer commands and spun around to face Vic. She smiled. It was a small round mouth, full lips. Vic put her about a decade his senior. Her crystal blue eyes sparkled with intelligence. Her unwrinkled skin savored a life never damaged by smoking.

"Vic!" she said.

"Miss Raglin," Vic said.

"You need more help," Miss Raglin said.

"You need more gasoline."

"I always need more gasoline," she said. "It keeps my plane in the air. By the way, what does the other guy look like?"

"It was a door," Vic said.

"And I'm Therese Peltier," she said, spinning back to the screen.

"Huh?"

"First woman to fly a plane," she said. "At least, according to the male historians. So what do you need? *Sundial*? More of the David Riley thing?"

Vic nodded, then realized she could not see him. "Yeah."

She turned toward him again. "I can just chum and see what I catch off the back of the boat, or I can cut a precise bait, tie it onto the perfect hook, run it across the right reef and take a record barracuda for a real fun fight," she said. "How do you want to proceed?"

"Was that from book learnin' or is there even more to you than I really know?" Vic said.

"Oh, there's a lot more to me than what you know," Miss Raglin said with a devilish grin. "With that little plane, I can fly to all sorts of exotic places."

"Let's go for barracuda," Vic said.

"I thought that might be your response," she said, whirling back around toward her terminal. Her fingers quickly plapped text into a note card window she had opened up on her screen. Then over her shoulder, "Give me more info. I've already dialed in David Riley."

Vic gave her a few key words and phrases, nothing in context, just search words that could be used for cross referencing. She filled the little electronic note card with her notes. Voter security. Republican Party. Democratic Party. Stewart Ellison. Cryptology. Encoding. Voting machines. Voting software. National security.

"That's enough, don't you think?" Vic said.

"Only the one name?" she said. "Ellison? There must be others."

Vic was reluctant to start with the names. She turned back toward him and peeked over her computer glasses.

"Vic," Miss Raglin said. "We've known each other for years. Your words are safe with me."

Vic looked at the note card window in the upper right corner of her screen. "But are they safe on the internet?"

"Vic!"

"Jared Picune and Jeff Picune," Vic said. "Jeff has a fishing boat in Key West. It's called Hacker Two, or Roman numeral I-I. Another boat, a smaller one, is called Hacker One or I. I'm not sure where Jared actually lives, but he spent some time in Colorado. And Paxton Stone. He lives in Golden, hot rods and software. He ran a dragster at Bandimere Speedway. The other names are cops and one fed. I don't think they're of any real use."

"The Stone in the fire?" Miss Raglin said.

"How did you know that?" Vic said.

"Newspapers, my dear boy," she said. "You work for one, remember? Give me the fed."

"Brad Rodgers," Vic said. His heart thumped.

"Police officer," she commanded.

"Gregory Frakes," Vic said.

"Greg?" she said. "I know him. Decorated. What's up with that?"

"I don't know," Vic said. "Just curious."

"What about your golfing buddy?" Miss Raglin said. "Not curious there?"

"Okay. Driscoll too."

"Now get out of here," Miss Raglin said. "I've got a lot of barracuda to haul in. I'll call you. Go do something with that face."

* * *

Vic walked over to a bench between the central library building and the art museum. The searing pain tortured the entire left side of his head. As he sat down, he reached into his shirt pocket and fumbled for the two aspirin tablets he tossed in before he left home that morning. Swishing his tongue across the insides of his remaining teeth made his mouth water a bit. He popped the pills and dry swallowed them, doubting whether even the aspirin would curb the pain. He hated drugs.

Across 14th Avenue, on Broadway, a few dozen people, mostly downtown workers and a handful of backpacked street dwellers, cued for the buses leaving the downtown area. His tired eyes drifted across Civic Center Park and its daily inhabitants. A lone cop—Vic recognized him—casually worked the crowd conducting welfare checks on the homeless and the kids who set up shop on the streets during the day before retreating to their safe suburban homes at night. No one seemed to be in real conflict, but many out there were in distress. A picture of urban diversity. The sun felt good on his cheek. Or was it the aspirin?

Vic pondered Stew Ellison, recalling passages from a political biography written about him that revealed his Machiavellian nature. He was an inside man, a behind the scenes lever puller, a Republican strategist, a numbers cruncher, a small government zealot. His admitted connection to Democrats puzzled him. Then again, Vic thought, maybe the apparent inconsistencies did make a bit of sense. Get enough conservative Democrats in the House and Senate, line them up with the Republicans, and maybe Ellison could engineer a veto-proof Congress on a few key issues.

There is only one way that could happen, Vic concluded, through the election process and further manipulation of the vote. That means Ellison probably wants Riley's Universal Vote System crushed and *Sundial* buried, or he wants to completely control it himself. Either way, that might be worth killing him in City Park. A chill ran up Vic's spine.

49

Vic jumped when his cellphone rang. In about a second, he determined he had crashed on his living room sofa.

"Bengston."

"Sanchez."

"Hello Lucas. I haven't been arrested."

"No, but Jared Picune has," Sanchez said.

"On what charge?" Vic said.

"Material witness," Sanchez said. "A junk charge, but the feds can park him in jail for a few days until they figure out what to do. He wants to talk to you. Against my advice."

"Driscoll or Rodgers won't let me near him," Vic said.

"Do you have a suit?" Sanchez said.

"What?" Vic said.

"A suit," Sanchez said. "We used to wear them when you covered the statehouse and I covered the cop shop."

"One, I think," Vic said.

"Does it still fit?" Sanchez said.

"It might," Vic said.

"Can you be at my office, wearing that suit, by one-thirty?" Sanchez said.

Vic looked at his watch. It was just after ten.

"Sure, but I'd like to know what for," Vic said.

"Just do it. I've got to go," Sanchez said and then he hung up.

* * *

Vic made it to Sanchez' office exactly at one-thirty. No Sanchez.

One of the paralegals said the lawyer was on his way. Vic scrolled through *Washington Post* headlines on his cellphone.

"You clean up well," Sanchez said to Vic when he strolled in twenty minutes late.

"You're late," Vic said, not looking up from the notes he was writing in his official slim line reporter's notebook.

"You're not a judge," Sanchez said. "And it's my own office."

"Points taken," Vic said.

Lucas Sanchez had worked with Vic at the *Rocky Mountain Sun* nearly thirty years ago. Sanchez left journalism to go into law. He teamed up with the legendary Mitch Geller and the two became the city's top criminal defense team. Their offices occupied a narrow, Victorian three-story red brick house less than two blocks from where the *Rocky Mountain Sun* building once stood, that building having been replaced by the lavish Justice Center, actually a pair of buildings separated by a wide plaza but connected by underground tunnels. The west building housed the courtrooms for District and County judges and a series of high security holding cells for the boys and girls appearing in court on any given day. The east building was a state-of-the-art jail that housed mostly locals awaiting final adjudication of their cases.

The nattily attired lawyer stood in front of Vic, who looked up and said nothing.

"What happened to you?" Sanchez said.

"Bicycle crash," Vic said.

"Still riding?" Sanchez said.

"Still crashing too," Vic said. "Where's Jared?"

"He's in jail," Sanchez said. "We're going to see him. You're my associate."

"You're passing me off as a lawyer?" Vic said.

"All journalists wish they were lawyers," Sanchez said. "I did."

"Most lawyers wish they were doing something else," Vic said.

"Until the check clears," Sanchez said. "They love the money."

"You?" Vic said.

"I like the money too," Sanchez said. "I like the spotlight even more. And I like the law business, the defense business, even more than that."

"I suppose it has its moments," Vic said.

"Oh, it does, it does," Sanchez said. "And this is one of them. Let's go counselor."

"Just don't call me a lawyer in front of anyone, okay?" Vic said. "I'm an investigator."

"I can't pass you off as a lawyer, Vic," Sanchez said, smiling. "It's against the law."

* * *

The lawyer and the reporter crossed Colfax Avenue and entered the Justice Center plaza, guarded by a massive clump of odd looking structures pointing skyward.

"Are those wings or leaves?" Vic said.

"I think they're about three million dollars' worth of gossamer wings, but you can't be too sure with public art," Sanchez said.

"I'm sure the taxpayers are delighted," Vic said.

"Not to mention the artist who was given carte blanche to display her dream for all of Denver to see," Sanchez said.

"Or his," Vic said.

"I don't think a guy could make that," Sanchez said. "Maybe weld it together, operate the crane to set them in place, that sort of stuff, but not create it."

"You're probably right," Vic said. "Guys come up with object de arte like the devil horse out at the airport."

"Yeah, and that one fell on its creator and killed him," Sanchez said.

"It still scares my grandkids," Vic said.

"Killer art," Sanchez said.

The two walked slowly toward the jail, the Van Cise-Simonet Detention Center. Behind them stood the courthouse, the Ralph L. Carr Colorado Justice Center. Carr was a former governor who treated the Japanese interred in Colorado during World War Two with a little respect. Vic had no idea who Van Cise or Simonet were.

"They need to make these buildings huge just to hold their names," Vic said.

"Like Sports Authority Field at Mile High?" Sanchez said.

"It's still Mile High Stadium for me, and forever," Vic said. "Plus the new thing looks like a giant bedpan."

They had arrived at the massive doors to the jail, Vic feeling they were about to enter the Land of Oz. Sanchez hefted one and held it open for Vic. Vic then held one of the inside doors for Sanchez, who nodded and said, "Just give the guard your driver's license. Remember you are a civilian helping me."

The two cued up in a line for "Professional Visits." Four people stood in front of them. Non-professional visitors stacked up to their left in a much longer line comprised mostly of families and friends of those whose bad luck, stupidity, or criminal lifestyles landed them inside the jail. None of them looked as though they had just driven their BMW in from Cherry Creek North, the Polo Club or any other of Denver's more tony neighborhoods.

A half dozen people lounged in chairs permanently affixed to the floor in the center of the spacious stone lobby. Tellers behind bullet-proof glass on the north wall handled bond payments. Visitation booths, small built-in desks with sidewalls, video screens and phones occupied the west side of the lobby. Two lanes of electronic screening systems on the south side of the cavern separated the main lobby from the elevators and a sweeping spiral staircase that led up to a pair of arraignment courts, the only courtrooms actually inside the jail.

"Lucas," said a stocky Latino deputy processing the professional visitors.

"Ed," Sanchez said. "How's Juan doing?"

"We're hoping for a baseball scholarship to CU," the deputy said. He took Sanchez' driver's license, pulled a clip-on visitor badge off a wall rack behind him, dropped the license into the empty slot, and handed the badge to the lawyer.

"Tossing a one-hitter in the state championship sure didn't hurt," Sanchez said.

"You got that right," the deputy said. "Is the gentleman with you?"

"Yes," Sanchez said. "An associate, helping out with the interview."

"I'll need your driver's license, sir," the deputy said. Vic opened his decomposing leather wallet. The license fell out and onto the narrow circular counter in front of him, along with his old Colorado press card. Vic covered the press card with his right hand and picked up the license with his left. He reached over the top of the thick chin-high glass security window and handed it to the deputy, who gave Vic a visitor badge.

"We're seeing Picune, Jared," Sanchez said.

The deputy adjusted his reading glasses, stabbed at his keyboard with a pair of rigid index fingers, and then wrote some information on a half-sheet of white paper.

"Here ya go, Lucas," the deputy said, handing the paper to Sanchez.

"Maybe we'll see you on the way out," Sanchez said. "Take care."

Sanchez led Vic over to one of the screening lines where they dumped everything they had on them, including belts, into a plastic tub that was conveyored through an X-ray scanner. Sanchez waltzed through the metal detector unscathed. Vic set it off.

"Just pull up your pant legs, sir, so I can see your shoes," the young female deputy said. Vic complied and the two were allowed to retrieve all their personal items. They walked up to a thick steel door in a small alcove just beyond the screening lines. Sanchez pressed a button on a three-by-three chrome steel plate that looked like it had a tiny speaker in it. The door clicked and Sanchez pushed it open.

"How did they know who it was?" Vic said.

Sanchez pointed to the ceiling and said, "There are about a million cameras in here. They see everything and everyone."

"We hope," Vic said.

"Flip your badge over so they can see the front," Sanchez said. Vic did so as Sanchez pushed another button. The speaker emitted an electronic tone and another click preceded the mechanical movement of an inner door, which slid open to the right. The two men stepped into one more lobby that housed four elevators. "This one's for non-prisoners," Sanchez said, pointing to the door on the far right.

"But the other three are for inmates?" Vic said. "All of us together?"

Sanchez nodded. "Saved money. Mayor's idea."

"And now he's the governor," Vic said.

"I'm sure we'll be treated to many more fabulous ideas before his reign of terror ends," Sanchez said. "He's not much of a Democrat."

The elevator door opened and they stepped in. Sanchez pressed the button for the fourth floor.

"An associate?" Vic said.

"An associate could mean anything," Sanchez said. "A lawyer, a paralegal, a secretary, an investigator."

"A reporter?" Vic said.

"A reporter," Sanchez said. "There are still a few freedoms left in this country."

"Well, for criminals maybe," Vic said.

"The only reason you're not a criminal, Vic, is that you've never been charged," Sanchez said.

"Wise guy," Vic said.

"Yes, I am," Sanchez said.

* * *

The elevator door opened on Four and deposited them into mirror image of the elevator lobby down on One. They stood near another heavy steel door. Looking through the thick wire-mesh security window, Vic could see two deputies standing in the hallway on the other side next to what looked like a three-pane bay window jutting into the hallway. The windows were mirrored so no one could see in. A deputy rapped on one of them. A moment later, the steel door clicked and opened up. Vic and Sanchez stepped into the main hallway.

"Counselor," said the deputy who had knocked on the mirror. He was tall, thin and looked like he was in his late 50s. A sculpted gray handlebar mustache set his nose off from his mouth.

"Deputy," Sanchez said, handing him the slip of paper issued on the first floor.

"I told Picune you were in the building," the deputy said. "He with you?"

"He is," Sanchez said.

"Okay, Lucas," the deputy said, sounding a little less officious. "I've got you set up in the first interview room down there." He pointed down the hallway to their left. "I'll bring Picune down."

Sanchez and Vic walked halfway down the hall, past a small medical examination room, before stopping in front of the interview room. Click. Sanchez pulled open the door and the two entered. The door closed from behind and sealed them in. The room was about ten by ten, corralled by cinderblock walls painted off white with a glossy finish like the rest of the jail. Hard floors, hard ceiling, hard time, Vic thought, even when you are waiting for arraignment.

They sat down in cheap green plastic chairs on one side of a cheap plastic table with folding metal legs, the kind of four-foot by two-foot table available at any office supply box store for fifty bucks. There was nothing else in the room except a third green plastic chair on the other side of the table. Click. The door opened. In came Picune with the deputy holding one arm. No cuffs, chains or leg irons. No weapon in the deputy's holster. When Picune sat down across from them, Sanchez said, "Billy, why is he in gray?"

"That's how he was classified, Lucas," the deputy said. "Special case."

"So you've got him in with all the perverts," Sanchez said, showing a little frustration.

"You know we don't classify up here," the deputy said.

"Can you see if he can get yellow?" Sanchez said.

"I doubt if that will happen, but I'll ask the captain," the deputy said. "Buzz when you're done."

"All right," Sanchez said. "Thanks." The door closed behind the deputy.

"It's private in here," Sanchez said to Jared, then to Vic, "No video. No audio."

"How do you know?" Vic said.

"I just know," Sanchez said.

"So we can talk, freely?" Jared said.

"Freely," Sanchez said. "Jared, are you having any problems in your pod?"

"No," Jared said. "I hang out near the guard, at least today I did. He's kind of a computer nut so we just talked about that. I think I'm okay, but I don't want to be here."

"We're working on bail," Sanchez said. "It's going to be high."

"I've got a lot of money," Jared said.

Vic looked across the plastic table at Jared. He seemed puny and insignificant in his gray jail garb, at least two sizes too big for him. Vic pulled out his narrow notebook and a fountain pen.

"How did that get through screening?" Sanchez said as Vic unscrewed the top and revealed a sharp weapon-like nib.

"Must have been the first one they have ever seen," Vic said as he wrote "boyish" on a blank notebook page. Jared looked like a high school kid caught up in a prank gone bad.

* * *

"Let me set some ground rules, okay?" Sanchez said. He did not look Latino. He looked Irish, pasty white. But he was Latino to some degree and grew up on Denver streets with the toughs of the city's southwest side. His gray suit matched his whiteness. His attitude matched his Latino surname. Vic skipped his suit and wore tan wash pants, a light blue oxford button down shirt, no tie, open at the collar, a dark blue blazer, dark blue socks and Bass Weejuns, all standard issue. "Ask anything so long as it has nothing to do with the murder of David Riley."

"Bullshit," Vic said.

"I mean directly with the crime, not what Riley was into, okay?" Sanchez said, raising his eyebrows.

"All right," Vic said. He clicked on his small digital recorder, which occupied its usual spot in his shirt pocket.

Sanchez looked at Jared and said, "I'm guessing you won't have much time in here, so you'd better get to it."

Jared turned to Vic and said, "My brother and I invented *Sundial.*"

"I know that," Vic said. "Well, that you had a hand in it." He surmised it, but now it was confirmed. Vic's heart did a happy dance. "The two of you did? You and Jeff?" He felt like Diane Sawyer, wide-eyed, faked astonishment. That's what he just told you, dummy. To calm himself, he flipped a notebook page and fiddled with his pen. He had to do something with his hands, anything, to minimize the sweaty palm problem. Taking notes was the most useful method of using his hands. The nib made a dark note on the paper. "My brother and I invented *Sundial*—JaP."

"Just the two of you?" Vic asked.

"The encryption scheme? Yes. We were fishing. On Jeff's boat. And talking."

"About what?" Vic said.

"Ciphers, encryption," Jared said. "We thought there had to be a way to protect—everything. Jeff was in the cabin. He had a picture, and old drawing, of a nautilus. You know, the mollusk, kind of grows in a spiral. He was looking at it, and he just blurted out 'fractals'."

"And, to that, you said?" Vic said.

"Nothing for a while. I was hauling in red snapper for dinner. I just thought about it." Jared just looked at Vic.

"Okay," Vic said. "You thought about it. What came next?"

"We got back to the dock and were cleaning the fish and it just hit me," Jared said.

"What?" Vic said.

"How we could use fractals and patterns of nature to make an encryption tool."

"That was it?" Vic said.

"No. We spent the next week docked, working on the problem. It actually kind of scared us. It seemed so powerful. It needed to be tested."

"When was this?" Vic said.

"Oh, about three years ago," Jared said.

"Did you tell anyone?" Vic said. "I mean at the time."

"No. We wanted to test it."

"You were working for Genra-IC then?" Vic said. "With Stone?"

"Yes."

"Did you have a contract with Genra-IC about—"

"Ownership," Jared said. "Yes, I did and I didn't want them to own it."

"Why?"

"They had contracts with companies all over the world," Jared said. "Governments too. I felt—we felt—only our government should have this, or, at least someone or some company we could trust."

"And that took you to Riley?" Vic said.

"Well, Pax did," Jared said. "He left Genra-IC a few months before I did and went to work for Riley on the touch screen vote system. I reached out to him when I saw a small article about the vote machines and the need for solid security."

"So you thought your fractal theory might work for electronic voting?" Vic said.

"Oh, more than that," Jared said. "Jeff and I already had the encryption scheme figured out. It was time for an application."

"So you went to work up at Sundial Ranch?" Vic said. Jared nodded. "How many others worked with you?"

"On *Sundial*?"

"Well, yes, on *Sundial*," Vic said, wondering what Jared thought he was talking about. Another secret project?

"There was a lot more going on up there," Jared said.

"In Loveland," Vic said.

"Yes," Jared said.

"Like what?" Vic said.

"Well, there was the laptop team," Jared said. "They were working on the new laptop voting app. Actually that one was going to be ported over to the iPhone, iPad, and Androids too."

"So you could vote on your cellphone?" Vic said.

"Yes," Jared said. "And on tablets. We were fighting with Microsoft about getting it on all their devices."

"Any luck?" Vic said.

"No," Jared said. "Microsoft wanted to own too much."

"What else went on at the ranch?" Vic said.

"The Universal Vote Initiative, UVI we called it," Jared said. "That was mostly design. Meetings. White boards. Flow charts."

"Were you in on the UVI meetings?" Vic said.

"No, I was *Sundial*," Jared said. "That's all I did. Day and night."

"Do you know anything about the UVI meetings?" Vic said.

"Not really," Jared said. "Except there was this one."

"One?" Vic said.

"There was one meeting," Jared said. "Three suits. I mean, I just knew they were suits. They weren't wearing suits, but I knew they were suits, you know? I've seen too many. Like they come out west and wear cowboy clothes. Get out of Dodge, you know. These guys were all suits, from Washington I think. Dr. Riley really didn't say. Some of them looked pretty stupid in their duds." Then he laughed, his only sign of letting go a bit.

"What did you tell the suits?" Vic said.

"I told them about *Sundial*," Jared said.

"You used that term, *Sundial*?" Vic said.

"Yes, I told them that Dr. Riley's team had worked up a security system, a new cipher algorithm that allowed us to encrypt data with super high security."

"Algorithm?" Sanchez said.

"A series of steps that perform a task on a computer or in a mathematical equation," Jared said.

Vic and Sanchez looked at each other. Sanchez raised his eyebrows.

"Just high security?" Vic said to Jared. "Is that all you told them."

"Well, actually, I used the term 'highest security'," Jared said. "Then one of the guys stood up asked 'you mean unbreakable security?'"

"What did you tell him," Vic said. "What did you answer?"

"I told him, yes, unbreakable," he said. "Actually, I said virtually unbreakable."

"How did the suits react?"

"Well, the one who stood up looked pissed, I mean really pissed," Jared said. He sat down and said something to the guy next to him. Then he made a cell phone call.

"Did you go into any details?" Vic said.

"Oh gosh no," Jared said. "Dr. Riley didn't want to give out any details. He just ID'd me as one of the *Sundial* Trio, the three key human components to the system."

"Who were the three?" Vic said.

"Me, Dr. Riley and Elvis," Jared said.

"Who's Elvis?" Vic said.

"I don't know," Jared said.

"You don't know?" Vic said.

"No," Jared said. "Only Dr. Riley knew."

"I thought Paxton Stone worked on the project?" Vic said.

"Well, I know he said he did but he never really worked directly with me," Jared said. "Except to answer a few questions about the Genra-IC chips.

"Genra-IC was involved with this?" Vic said.

"Over on the UVI side, the integrated circuits that went into the voting machines," Jared said. "Stone didn't help me all that much on the encryption stuff. It was pretty much done anyway. We just needed to refine and test, and—work out the kinks."

"Okay," Vic said. "So there were you, Riley and Elvis, whoever Elvis is. So, how did you three work together?"

"Occasionally I'd get some code to test from Dr. Riley or from Elvis," Jared said. "You know to put it together with mine, test it, make notes, and give it back. I used to get two distinctive batches of code from Dr. Riley. One was mathematically based, generating prime numbers, stuff like that."

"And the other?" Vic said.

"Fractals," Jared said. "It was all about fractals. How to make them. How to use them. How to replicate them. Even how to render them from biological observations. It was sweet."

"Do you think the fractal stuff came from Elvis?" Vic said.

"Pretty sure," Jared said.

"How did you know?" Vic said.

"Just guessing, but Dr. Riley got his PhD in higher math from MIT," Jared said. "His dissertation was on generating hyper prime numbers, giant prime numbers, nothing to do with fractals. So I just assumed the factual stuff came from Elvis."

"But you have no idea who Elvis is?" Vic said.

"Not a clue," Jared said.

"Why was the plug pulled at Sundial Ranch?" Vic said.

"Dr. Riley thought we had a security breach," Jared said. "He wound down the place pretty fast after that. He paid us for the rest of the year and told us all to scatter. He said he'd be in touch."

"Did that happen before or after the meeting with the suits?" Vic said.

"Right after," Jared said. "I mean right after. Within a few weeks, the place was a ghost town."

* * *

Three knocks on the door indicated time was up.

The jail reversed the entire process to disengage Vic and Sanchez from Jared, return him to his holding cell, and spit the two men from the building. They stood on the front steps with driver's licenses in hand.

"What happens next?" Vic said.

The lawyer looked at his watch. "Appearance in the arraignment court, in about an hour. Sticking around?"

"Should I?" Vic said.

"No," Sanchez said. "It'll just be a formality. Read the charges. If there are any, enter the plea. Start the bail argument. If no charges, try to bust him loose."

"Murder?" Vic said. "Jared? He called him Dr. Riley, a term of respect. This seems like a stretch."

"Cops, prosecutors, they tend to stretch things at times," Sanchez said. "Especially in high profile cases. Nothing surprises me, but this time I don't think there will be any charges at all. I'm more worried about the feds penning up Jared just to keep him off the street."

"Or safe?" Vic said.

"More like on ice while they try to figure this whole thing out," Sanchez said.

"Can I call you?" Vic said.

"Sure," Sanchez said. "Still got my cell number?"

"I do," Vic said.

"Then go do what you reporters do between life altering events," Sanchez said.

Vic shook his hand. He planned to walk down to a coffee shop at 12th and Speer. He hesitated.

"Lucas?" Vic said.

"Yes, dear?" Sanchez said.

"How's Betsy?" Vic said.

"She's crazy, Vic," Sanchez said. "Stay away from her."

"Is she all right?" Vic said.

"I told you, she's crazy," Sanchez said.

"Will there ever be a trial?" Vic said.

"I doubt it," Sanchez said.

"Is she still in Pueblo?" Vic said.

"Vic!" Sanchez said.

"I'm just curious," Vic said. "Thinking of a follow-up."

"No you're not," Sanchez said. "And yes, she's still in Pueblo. Probably for a long time. Leave it alone."

"They're going to want a follow up story," Vic said.

"She can't talk to anyone right now, Vic," Sanchez said. "If Vigil bugs you, tell him to get somebody else do the follow up. She's protected, in treatment, and not giving out stories to the press."

"I just thought," Vic said. He stared off unfocused and rubbed his left shoulder.

"Leave it alone, Vic," Sanchez said.

Vic couldn't leave it alone. The woman almost killed him.

50

Vic actually preferred Hava Java's coffee to Starbucks'. It was a little less burnt, lighter, easier on his system, and it was an indie coffee shop, not a corporate coffee shop. The caffeine really did him no good. Occasionally, when he felt his heart racing and wondered if this was the start of some health crisis, Vic had to mentally retrace his steps for that day. Invariably he realized he had consumed too much caffeine, either an extra cup of coffee or a half a gallon of iced tea at lunch. He was stoned, jazzed up on caffeine, and he just had to wait for it to work its way out of his system. Then came the resolve again. Drink decaf. Limit the number of cups of the hard stuff to one a day. The bottom line was that he had to quit and stick to decaf or herbal tea. Today he was drinking caffeine.

Vic took his cup of Designer Joe outside to one of the three wrought iron tables set on a tiny patio overlooking Speer Boulevard, a tree-lined ribbon park and thoroughfare that ran southeast to northwest through central Denver. The boulevard was named after a former mayor known for his beautification projects. Cherry Creek carved its way through a shallow canyon that ran down the center of Speer as it flowed toward the South Platte River in the lower downtown area. The city had re-excavated the creek, adding landscaping, boulders, and bike trails, converting it into a lush facility used for recreation and wildlife habit. From where he sat, Vic could see some of the other parkway habitants, two homeless men lounging on the grass up at street level. They appeared to be eating lunch. Traffic thundered by on each side of the wide boulevard. Occasionally, one of the greenbelt dwellers would take a cardboard sign and occupy a nearby traffic-lighted intersection to replenish their meager coffers.

Vic's cell phone rang. He set his coffee down and stood up, digging in his pants pocket for the phone.

"Bengston."

"Clemons."

"Marti," Vic said. "This is a nice change of pace."

"I wanted to let you know," she said. "Wait. First, how are you?"

"A little worse for wear," Vic said.

"What does that actually mean?" Marti said.

"I don't have a clue, but you know what I said, right?" Vic said.

"Yes, you've been better," Marti said.

"I'll have to look that old phrase up," Vic said. "It really doesn't make any sense, does it?"

"No," Marti said. "But I'm sure it did when it was first uttered. Okay, so you've been better. Cold? Lost a thumb-wrestling match? What?"

"Just got banged up a bit," Vic said. "Ran into an elephant, but that was after I ran into a fence."

There was a pause.

"Don't ask," Vic said.

"All right, I won't," she said. "You can fill me in the next time your down here."

That sounded inviting, Vic thought.

"I'm not sure when that will be," Vic said.

"Well, your guy is back here, back in town at least. The Hacker boats are over at the Coast Guard dock." Marti said.

"My guy?" Vic said.

"Yeah," Marti said. "Jared Picune. I talked to him this morning. I still haven't seen his brother."

* * *

"How do you know it was Jared?" Vic said.

"I knew you'd ask that," Marti said. "Jeff has a small scar. It's really tiny, embedded in his right eyebrow."

"Well, at least is not a birthmark on his behind, and how do you know this?"

"When they both turned up on the back of Jeff's boat one day I sat them down and told them I wasn't too interested in games and wanted to know the best way to tell them apart," Marti said. "Jared pointed to his micro scar."

"Maybe that was Jeff," Vic said.

"Jeff?" Marti said.

"Who pointed to his scar," Vic said.

"And said he was Jared?" Marti said. "Why would they do that?"

"Just to keep everyone a little off balance," Vic said. "It seems to be working."

"So I do need to see if he's got a birthmark on his butt," Marti said.

"No," Vic said. "But do yourself a favor and stay away from Jared, or Jeff, or whoever it is." Should he tell her? he thought. Yes. "Look, I got shot at the other night, the night I ran into the fence."

"And the elephant?" Marti said.

"Yes, the elephant too," Vic said. "I mean no one shot at the elephant. I sort of bumped into him."

"Or her," Marti said.

"Or her," Vic said. "I didn't stop to look. Anyway it was dark and someone was trying to kill me."

Silence again. Then she said, "You're starting to get a little too high maintenance for me."

Vic's heart seemed to stop. A cold front blew through.

"I don't want you getting hurt," Vic said.

"I don't want me getting hurt either," Marti said.

"High maintenance?" Vic said.

"I'm wary," Marti said.

"You've run into a few elephants and fences too?" Vic said.

"A few," Marti said. "But I've never been shot at."

"I'm not one of those adrenaline freaks, Marti," Vic said.

"That was my impression," she said. "I'm done with those. But—"

"But you didn't expect gunplay," Vic said.

"No, I didn't," Marti said with a tone of finality.

"Would you mind calling me if you notice anything odd with Jared, or Jeff?" Vic said.

"Well, if I spot him, I will," Marti said. "With the boats gone, I don't know where he is staying. Look, I gotta go. A charter client just showed up. Be safe."

She hung up. Vic doubted whether she had a charter. It was mid-afternoon in Key West, a little late to start a half-day fishing trip.

* * *

As Vic finished his coffee, he wondered who it was that he had interviewed down at the jail. He thought about calling Sanchez, but he doubted whether he was going to get anything more out of Jared, or Jeff, at this point. He dialed Frakes. His direct line went to voicemail. Vic hated voicemail so he did not bother leaving a message. He dialed Frakes' cell phone number.

"Frakes."

"Bengston."

"Oh, you," Frakes said. "We're not happy with you, and the zoo says you gave their animals diarrhea."

"Har har," Vic said. "Something's come up, something important."

"Why don't you call your golfing pal?" Frakes said.

"Because I'm calling you, Greg," Vic said. "This is your case, isn't it?"

"After a fashion," Frakes said. "So what is it you're finally willing to tell us?"

"You might not have Jared Picune in custody," Vic said.

"I'm sure we have Jared in custody," Frakes said. "I just saw him."

"How do you know it's not his brother?" Vic said.

There was a slight hesitation. Then Frakes said, "We just know."

"I don't think you do," Vic said. "I just got a call from my fishing friend in Key West. She said she talked with Jared this morning.

"How does she know it's Jared?" Frakes said.

"Her guess is as good as yours, Greg, if you think about it," Vic said. "She said Jared has a small scar just above his right eyebrow."

"How can she know that?" Frakes said.

"She was on their boat with the two of them and Jared pointed to his scar," Vic said. "At least that's what she told me."

"Or Jeff pointed to his scar," Frakes said.

"Finally, Greg, you're getting the point," Vic said. "Nobody is really too sure who's who."

"We're running prints," Frakes said.

"And if they don't have any prints anywhere?" Vic said. "Then what are you going to do?"

"Punt, I guess," Frakes said. "Have you told Sanchez this?"

"Not yet," Vic said. "But I'm going to have to."

"I hate this case," Frakes said.

"For once we agree," Vic said.

* * *

His phone rang again.

"Bengston."

"Raglin here."

Vic flipped to a fresh page in his notebook. He wrote "Raglin" and the date.

"What-a-ya-got?" Vic said.

"Where should I start?"

"Let's go with Jared and Jeff," Vic said.

"The Picune brothers," she said. "Little geniuses all the way back to high school. After getting busted for hacking into their school's academic and personal files, they developed a computer game that made them instant millionaires their junior year."

"Where was this?" Vic said.

"Key West," Miss Raglin said. "Born and raised there."

"I didn't even think that they might have relatives down there," Vic said.

"They don't," she said. "Parents died in a plane crash, a commercial plane crash, in Iowa, nineteen eighty-nine. It was that tumbling out of control landing in Sioux City. Mom and Dad were barely adults. No siblings. Grandparents dead."

"Who raised them then?"

"Wolves," she said.

"Not funny."

"Sorrrrry, Vic," Miss Raglin said. "A couple by the name of Nussbaum. Tom and Guinevere. Spelled more the old English way, G-U-I-N-E-V-E-R-E, but pronounced like King Arthur's squeeze."

"That's quite a handle," Vic said.

"What? Tom?"

"You are full of them today, aren't you?"

"Sorrrrry. Close friends of the boys' parents," she said. "They have homes in Key West, Denver, and Aspen."

"Paupers, then," Vic said.

"Hardly. But money wasn't an issue. The dead parents were worth a bundle. When they died there was a trust fund valued at about two hundred million dollars."

"And they started making boatloads on their own with their own software with their own brains," Vic said. "At least they're not louts."

"But these guys are free and unfettered, relative-wise."

"Except from the Nussbaums and friends, maybe, from high school or college," Vic said.

"Maybe," Miss Raglin said.

"No criminal record?" Vic said. "Something that might involve fingerprints?"

"Not as adults," Miss Raglin said.

"What do you mean?" Vic said.

"There was an incident, just before they turned seventeen," she said.

"And incident?" Vic said.

"A shooting," Miss Raglin said. "They were minors."

"You have their juvenile records?" Vic said.

"Let's say I have a description of the incident," Miss Raglin said.

"All right," Vic said. "I won't ask you how you got that."

"No, you won't," she said. "Their birthday is August fourth. On August third, two thousand and one, Jeff shot Jared."

"Shot him?" Vic said.

"That's what the cops wrote," Miss Raglin said. "They were horsing around with a pellet gun and Jeff clipped Jared."

"Where?" Vic said.

"Just above his right eye," she said.

"Fingerprints?" Vic said.

"I couldn't find any reference to any," Miss Raglin said. "They were minor celebrities by then. The cops just filed a pro forma report and nothing happened."

Vic wondered if Frakes and Driscoll could get their hands on the same juvenile records. There was more on the Picune twins. Miss Raglin ran through it fast and efficiently. The brothers grew up fishing so as soon as they were done with high school, they bought a forty-five foot fishing boat and a small flats boat, Hacker I and Hacker II. They lived on the boat up near Miami while they zipped through the university in three years.

"Majors?" Vic said.

"Jeff was computer science," Miss Raglin said. "Game development. Jared, computer science, with an honors thesis on ciphers and cryptology. Found one story from the local rag in Coral Gables about the twins, a bit about their background, the game, the hacking, and the mini computer lab they set up on their boat.

"Did you ever read that library check out list?" Miss Raglin said. "Riley's?"

I glanced at it," Vic said. "Why?"

"Well, read these things, young man," she said, with that schoolmarm look of hers. "The thesis Riley inter-libraried in was Jared Picune's honors thesis on cyphers."

"Ooops," Vic said. He shrugged. "What else?"

"Jeff just went back to Key West," Miss Raglin said. "With the boats. Started a small consulting company, J and J Consulting, and ran a charter fishing operation. Jared moved to Colorado, did two years with Genra-IC and then went to work for David Riley."

"Genra-IC was where Jared's path intersected with Paxton Stone's," Vic said.

"Well, I'm glad I'm not the only one in your little Pulitzer world doing some real research," Miss Raglin said. "Both of them were in Genoa-IC's system and software security division. You didn't know that, did you?"

In his worst Johnny Carson, Vic said, "I did not know that."

*   *   *

That was all she had. Nothing yet on Brad Rodgers. Vic had no idea what to do next, so he called Peggy.

"Mayer."

"It's me," Vic said.

"It certainly is," Peggy said. "What's going on?"

Vic told her what Miss Raglin told him. He didn't mention his source.

"Do Driscoll and Frakes know they have the wrong Picune?" Peggy said.

"I don't think so," Vic said. "I don't think Sanchez knows either."

"Well, Paxton Stone has officially risen from the dead," Peggy said. "AP moved a story that said he was treated and released for smoke inhalation, and that the police had been mum on his status in order to, I'm quoting here, 'further the investigation into the fire.'"

"Quoting whom?" Vic said.

"The FBI," Peggy said.

"Rodgers?" Vic said.

"No, just the FBI," Peggy said.

"Well, we knew Stone would be back," Vic said. "It was just a matter of how they phrased their cover story. And his real connection with Riley and Jared is interesting."

"Interesting how?" Peggy said.

"I'm not exactly sure," Vic said. "But Stone—Pax—probably had his reasons for keeping his association with Riley quiet, and I think what he told me about his hacker network was on the square. I've been re-running all the meetings with Pax in my mind. I might have missed something."

"Is there much left?" Peggy said.

"Of what?"

"Your mind?"

"I walked right into that one, arms wide open," Vic said.

"That you did," Peggy said. "Back to Stone."

"I don't think he ever told me anything that was untrue."

"He omitted a few points," Peggy said. "Big ones."

"Yeah, but it wasn't as though he was dodging anything," Vic said. "I went to him for help and he helped me."

"Maybe he just acted like he helped you," Peggy said. Vic said nothing. Then she said, "Have we got anything to write yet?" Both of them were feeling the heavy breath of Vigil on the backs of their necks.

"I don't think so," Vic said. "Unless we just go with the *Sundial* stuff." He paused for a moment. "I'd really like to bust something loose on this, but I'm not quite sure how to do it. Why don't you see if you can flesh out this nexus among the Picunes, Stone, Genra-IC and Riley. See if you can verify employment, what they were working on, anything, although I doubt if anybody will talk about that. Just try."

"How good is your source on the Picunes and the pellet gun thing?" Peggy said.

"Gold dust," Vic said. "And from two entirely separate people."

"All right," she said. "I'll run down as much as I can and keep Les off our backs. You know the drill. Act like we've got all wrapped up and just need a good quote or two."

"Atta girl," Vic said.

"Girl?" Peggy said.

"Atta woman?" Vic said.

"Atta boy," she said, and hung up.

51

It was only a short round, a nine hole warm up for a weekend charity scramble Vic and Driscsoll had golfed in for the past nine or ten years. The first few holes were a little uncomfortable, in near silence, fallout from the charged meeting in Driscoll's office. Then Vic's pitch stunned Driscoll.

"You what?" Driscoll said.

"I pushed them," Vic said. "With the deadline thing, editors on my back, all that."

"Who did you tell?" Driscoll said.

"Well, you, Rodgers, Frakes, Stone, Ellison, and Jeff, through his attorney," Vic said.

"You mean Jared," Driscoll said.

"No, you've got Jeff in jail, Frank," Vic said. "Or had him. Sanchez got him out when you boys came up short."

Driscoll rolled his eyes. "You've already done this? Set it up?"

"Sure," Vic said. "It was fairly easy. I just said my editors want the first piece by the weekend and that I like to work on the boat. Then I dropped Thursday night."

"And you are doing this, why?" Driscoll said. "I know I won't like the answer."

"To smoke out Riley's killer," Vic said.

Driscoll looked up at Vic. "Who are you, Hopalong Cassidy?"

"It worked for Hoppy," Vic said.

Driscoll walked across the green toward Vic, then said, "You've got to unring this bell, Vic. This is not amateur hour, no time to play policeman."

Vic's jaw jutted to the right. Driscoll saw that and he knew no manner of finger-wagging, threats of arrest, or anything would deter this idiotic plan.

* * *

"You know how I am about boats," Driscoll said. Then he sunk a long putt on the ninth green for a bogey.

"The same way you are about snakes," Vic said, watching the cop lumbering up to the cup to retrieve his ball. "We aren't even leaving the dock."

"But why Thursday night? What the hell's so special about Thursday night?"

"Boat races," Vic said. "The bigger sailboats. It's a nice evening out. They grill burgers up in that monstrosity of a building the marina manger built. A little wine. A change of pace from your ghetto life."

"Vic, we live in the Highlands," Driscoll said. "Coffee is four bucks a cup."

"You know what I mean," Vic said.

"No, I don't know what you mean," the detective said.

"We can watch the races, pig out, relax in the boat—"

"I never relax in boats," Driscoll said. "I can't swim."

"The boat'll be tied up," Vic said.

"Sailboat races?"

"They can be thrilling," Vic said.

"I could stay at home," Driscoll said. "And watch the paint dry too."

"Frank, I need you there," Vic said. "After dark, I'll walk down from the marina to the boat to work on the story."

Driscoll looked up from his scorecard. "He'll see me too, Vic."

"No, because you'll be there already," Vic said.

"What do you mean?" Driscoll initialed his score card.

"I need you to be there early, in the afternoon," Vic said. "No one'll see you then."

"I have to sit in that floating coffin of yours all afternoon?" Driscoll said. "What about the thrilling sailboat races? Wine? Burgers?"

"Yeah," Vic said. "I guess that'll have to wait. You need to get there, say, at five. I'll give you the code to get you through the gate on the pier. Just slip into the cabin. I'll have plenty of water and snacks in there for you. Pringles?"

"Originals," Driscoll said. "I'd walk off a cliff for Pringles Originals. Vic, you're nuts. Call this off."

Vic, jaw jutting to the right, shook his head.

* * *

"Will you have *Sundial* with you?" Driscoll said, fishing.

"I don't have a copy of *Sundial*, Frank," Vic said. "I'll have a phony copy like the one you had on your desk the other morning."

"Good prop, wasn't it?" Driscoll said.

"I expect it will be for me as well," Vic said. "I'll have a thumb drive too, with some dummy files on it."

"Who is your Mister X?" Driscoll said. "Or Ms. X?"

"There is no Ms. in this mix," Vic said. "That nonsense is bouncing between Frakes and Rodgers."

"Your suspect, then?" Driscoll said.

"You know as well as I do," Vic said. "It makes the story even heavier."

"FBI and DHS killing people to get their hands on *Sundial*?" Driscoll said. "Seems far-fetched to me."

"Wrong initials," Vic said. "Try CIA, DIA, or NSA."

"Or none of the above?" Driscoll said. "This could be a freelance job. Stone? The Picune brothers? Even Ellison. *Sundial* is worth a lot."

"Well, Ellison's too pudgy to be player like Rodgers," Vic said. "He's a string-puller. Maybe he hired Rodgers."

They had gotten to their cars, parked next to each other near the pro shop at Kennedy Golf Course.

"I'm going to have to say we got a last minute tip," Driscoll said. "And I want Greg there."

"I thought you might," Vic said. "Like I told you, I told Greg. Not the 'smoking out' bit, just that I'd be working on my boat. He gave me a gun, you know, and told me not to tell you."

"Don't bring that gun," Driscoll said. "I'll put Greg in the picture, but do not bring that gun, understand? Your kids, and your grandkids don't want you dead, Vic."

"I don't want me dead either," Vic said. Then he did a Kings-X. "No gun. Promise."

"Where's your putter?" Driscoll said.

"In my bag," Vic said. "Where's your weapon?"

"In my bag," Driscoll said.

"Will you be armed Thursday evening?"

"I'm always armed," Driscoll said.

52

Vic had thought about his gun. He dragged it around that one day, but the idea of a reporter packing heat bugged him. He could shoot fairly straight but was not used to handling it, so he left it at home. Too late now anyway, he thought. The sailboat races were over. He had consumed a burger that had to be sent back for more cooking, twice. It was either the beef rumbling about inside of him, or it was his nerves. He could not tell which.

At eight forty-five, he gathered up his small dark green backpack filled with fake *Sundial* files, a thin laptop, and a water bottle. He left the post-race gathering and sauntered down toward the docks. The flaming orange and yellow sunset had collapsed into an ashen gray evening as the shadows crept in to consume the rest of the day. The late afternoon wind, which was nearly too heavy even for the big boats, had dropped to a feeble breeze just strong enough to clang and tinkle the halyards and hardware against the aluminum masts. The only useful light came from the pools dropped into the docks by the marina lampposts.

As Vic pushed against the combination keys on the lock at the main entrance to the docks, the tall chain link gate swung open. The spring never fully closed the thing in the first place, but Vic's heartrate bumped up a bit anyway. He walked down past the small floating dock office, sealed up and dark, past the two picnic tables and gas grills next to the portapotty, and turned right onto the smaller dock that led to his boat.

His Catalina 25 was dark, the mainsail flaked atop the boom, tied, and covered with its ocean blue protective cover. The jib was furled and covered with the same blue ultraviolet resistant cloth. Looking around, first at the other boats, then across the docks, and finally back toward the marina building, Vic saw no one as he stepped aboard his boat. The restored teak companionway doors were closed, but not latched. The small brass padlock lay open on the sliding hatch, where Vic had left it that afternoon.

Vic opened the doors and stepped down the companionway into the darkness of the cabin. In for a penny, in for a pound, he thought. Then he saw all the faces of his lovely children and their children in his mind as he tossed his backpack toward one of the bench seats he knew would be there. He reached to his right and flipped on a small light.

"Frank?" he whispered.

"Up here," came a quiet reply from the head.

"Enjoying your squat?" Vic said, still whispering. "You'll pay for this."

"Leg cramps are fun too," Driscoll said.

Vic's pulse subsided to a pounding roar. He pulled the laptop and a file folder from the backpack. In a few minutes, he was sitting at his tiny table, computer open, thumbing through a stack of phony papers, and plapping fake notes on the small computer.

* * *

Vic heard something on the dock, a quiet muffled sound, barely audible, but different from clanging halyards, far off boat motors, and water lapping sounds of the marina.

"Someone's here," Vic said. "I'm going up."

"Stay to the right if you can," Driscoll said quietly.

That would be the port side, Vic told himself as he stepped out of the cramped little cabin.

Behind him, in the dark, and silently, Driscoll pulled his weapon from his holster.

"Keep coming. We need to talk." It was Stone. Then Vic heard a metallic click.

"And then what?" Vic said, his heart desperate to flee from his chest.

"And then nothing. We just need to talk. Calmly. Rationally."

"With a gun on me? How rational and calm is that?"

"I'm protecting you, but you need to listen and follow my commands," Stone said.

Vic stood in the cockpit of his boat. He glanced aft at the dark cold water highlighted by glitzy, dancing reflections of marina lights.

"Okay if I sit?" Vic said.

"Easy and slow."

"I'm not armed, Pax," Vic said as he eased down next to the tiller on the port side.

"Or, maybe Elvis is more appropriate," Vic said.

"It's a code name," Stone said. "That's what I need to talk to you about."

"Can't say I like the gun thing," Vic said.

"This is for your protection," Stone said. "Trust me."

"Those words give me no solace," Vic said. "They usually mean the opposite."

"Not in this case, Vic," Stone said from his position amidships but still up on the dock. "Like I said, this is for your protection."

"Yeah, right," Vic said. Then he leaned back and fell over the transom into the water.

53

Vic heard a dull thump. Stone must have jumped from the dock onto the boat. But no zings or pings or whatever bullets sounded like as they searched you out in the water. He kicked off his deck shoes, scrambled, and pushed his way under water beneath Dan's MacGregor 26 berthed next to Vic's Catalina. Thank you for water ballast, Vic thought, as he eased his way under the rounded belly of the Mac's hull. No deep keel to swim around. He surfaced briefly on the other side of Dan's boat, gasped for another load of air, then pushed himself down and went for the dock. Vic swam all the way underneath the floating matrix to the other side, where some joker had parked his Benetau 35, much too big for Cherry Creek Reservoir, while he had it up for sale. When he thought about how nice it would be to live aboard the Beneteau down in Key West, Vic's head slammed into something hard enough to make him think twice about swimming under any sort of dock. Head throbbing, air giving out, he reached up to feel the bottom of the dock and pulled himself, hand over hand, in the direction he thought he was supposed to go. In a year or so, his right hand curled around an edge that might indicate the other side of the pier. He wondered about Driscoll as he hauled himself around and surfaced, forcing himself not to make noise as his oxygen starved body gulped in a fresh supply.

Vic had resurfaced, but this time into the middle of some other conversation. Stone was talking to someone.

"What makes you think I have it?" Stone said.

"Who else would have it if not you?" It was Rodgers. Was it the good Rodgers, the cavalry? Vic thought. Or was it the Rodgers serving a government, our government, or some other entity at any cost? And where was Driscoll? He wondered.

"You destroyed it in the fire," Stone said. "When you tried to fry me."

"We came in after that, Stone, and saved your ass," Rodgers said. "Not before. I'm having trouble following you."

"Like hell you are," Stone said.

"Look, we need it back," Rodgers said. "You've got a copy, and I want it."

"I don't have a copy, Brad," Stone said. "You saw to that. And who is this 'we' we are talking about?"

"I work for the FBI now, Stone."

"My ass, you do," Stone said. "You should have killed me when you had the chance."

"You've gone off the deep end," Rodgers sad. "I didn't try to kill you."

"That, unfortunately, was an oversight on my part." It was another voice, from further away. "Please, neither of you move," said Detective Greg Frakes. "Where's Bengston?"

*   *   *

Oversight? Vic thought. Since when would a botched murder attempt be considered an oversight by a Denver cop? Vic's heart took off again. Driscoll should have heard that, or Vic hope he had heard it. Vic quietly pushed himself back underwater and clawed his way back underneath the dock, thinking he might be able to get to the stern of his boat and get his hands on the flare gun in the lazarette.

Vic surfaced again on the other side of the dock, but on the port side of Dan's Mac 26 which was between him and his Catalina. Just as he was about to duck back down and swim under Dan's boat, a hand grabbed his left shoulder hard and pulled him back into the dock. "Shhh" was all Vic heard. The hand turned him around. It was Nelson. His weapon was in his other hand. He held the barrel up to his lips. Vic motioned him to come closer. Nelson leaned in.

"Frank is on my boat, inside the cabin," Vic whispered. "Try not to shoot holes in it below the water line."

Nelson just shook his head. With his free hand he motioned Vic to stay put. Then he faded into the darkness. Vic pushed himself silently away from the dock and over to the side of Dan's boat. He made his way around to the stern so he could see Stone, Rodgers, and a shadow of Frakes in a standoff that reminded Vic of the showdown scene in The Good, The Bad and The Ugly. Three men set in a triangle, each with a gun, Stone on Vic's boat, Rodgers on the dock, and Frakes off in the darkness.

"Does Bengston have *Sundial?*" Frakes said.

"I doubt it," Stone said. "The police probably have it."

"Not all of it," Frakes said. "Just the public key. We want both parts of it. You know that."

"We, meaning whom, Greg?" It was Driscoll, emerging from the cabin. He stood still in the companionway, half in and half out of the cabin. "You mean Denver police, or someone else?"

Stone slowly lowered his weapon, then threw it in the water.

"Stone's disarmed," Rodgers said. "Do you have a weapon, chief?"

Driscoll did not answer.

"Fellas, I want *Sundial,*" said Frakes.

"For whom?" Driscoll said.

Rodgers asked again. "Do you have your weapon, chief?" Again, no answer from Driscoll.

"Who's this 'we', Greg?" Driscoll asked. "I know about Brad's 'we'," but tell me more about yours."

"A client," Frakes said. "That's all."

"Moonlighting again, are you?" Driscoll said. "Security systems?"

"You could call it that," Frakes said. "The crap in the safe was worthless."

"Riley was your client?" Rodgers said.

"One of them," Frakes said. "I installed his system."

"There's another client," Driscoll said.

"Yeah, the one who wants *Sundial,*" Frakes said.

"You disappoint me, detective," Driscoll said.

"I know, but it couldn't be helped," Frakes said. "The fee, you see. The fee was, well, too big to ignore."

"To kill Riley?" Driscoll said.

"No, to get *Sundial*," Frakes said. "The Riley thing. That was impromptu. Threw things off for a few weeks, the suicide theory."

"Not a very good idea," Rodgers said. "Theft is one thing. Murder's quite another."

"There's enough in this for all of us," Frakes said.

"You are joking?" Driscoll said.

"Worth a try," Frakes said. "Brad?"

Rodgers remained silent.

"Stone?" Frakes said.

"If I have the private key," Stone said. "Killing me will insure you never get it. I always take steps."

"I'll bet you do," Frakes said. "That leaves Bengston, then."

"Frakes, You don't have a clue who's got it," Rodgers said. "We all have it."

"I don't think so," Frakes said.

The gunshots merged into one giant explosion. Stone tumbled off the boat into the water. Rodgers hit the deck. Driscoll dropped to his knees, his bullet tearing through the fiberglass of Vic's boat toward the darkness of Frakes' voice. A thud came from the dock near the front of Dan's Mac 26, followed by a splash. Vic held onto the rudder.

*   *   *

"Rodgers?" Driscoll said. "Stone? Vic?"

"On the dock," Rodgers said.

"I've been hit," Stone said from behind Vic's boat. "Right arm. I think it's broken."

"Greg?" Driscoll said. "Vic?"

Nothing.

Vic edged around the rudder again. He saw Rodgers scramble across the dock to Stone and pull him up from the water. "I've got Stone," Rodgers said.

Vic began moving back around to the port side of the Mac 26 when his head smashed into something floating in the water. This second unexpected water collision triggered a reflexive intake of less than pure marina water down the wrong pipe. Vic's body erupted with a loud wet cough that expelled the dirty liquid from his insides. Blindly flailing for a hand hold, he struck a solid piece of the dock with his right and grabbed it. Coughing and spitting in one direction, gasping for air in the other, Vic's left hand fell upon Frakes' body, bobbing next to the dock. Instinctively, he had grasped Frakes' clothing to steady himself. Vic glanced at the body. Marina light danced across what was left of the detectives' face.

"Vic!" Driscoll said. "You all right?"

"I think so," said Vic. "I can't say the same for Frakes."

54

"I trained him," Driscoll said as they walked up to the first green at Kennedy Golf Course.

"Apparently, not well enough," Vic said. Driscoll stopped and glared at him. "Sorry."

"He was good. Commendations. Then he got greedy, I guess. How do you spot that early on?"

"I don't think you can, Frank," Vic said. "You can't blame yourself."

"Well, I do," he said. Then he chipped his ball to within a foot of the pin.

"Remind me not to play with you if you really get down," Vic said. He addressed his ball, waggled the club, then shanked it off to the left and into the rough.

The rest of the round was just small talk. Family updates. They always did the family updates. Regularly. Then a bit of sports. And some politics. Vic knew there was something Driscoll wanted to talk about, but the detective held it back for eighteen holes.

* * *

Vic sat on the edge of the wayback in his Grand Cherokee, a bucket of bolts that was now eating him alive with overly-priced repairs. The only thing he now liked about the car was that the rear hatch door shaded him from the sun while he changed from golf shoes into a good pair of New Balance cross trainers he had picked up for ten bucks at a local thrift store. Driscoll stood next to the popped trunk lid of his new Chrysler. The detective pulled each shoe off with the toe of the opposite foot and slipped into a pair of beat up old Keds. He stuffed the golf shoes into a side pocket of his golf bag, then dropped his clubs into the trunk. Vic just tossed his golf shoes into the back of the Jeep next to his clubs. He pulled the tattered plastic, brass, and wood golf trophy from another zipper compartment and handed it to Driscoll, who had won the regular Saturday round. Then he pulled the hatch closed.

"Why Chrysler?" Vic said, nodding toward his Jeep. "They maimed this bucket of bolts."

"They're retooled," Driscoll said. "American-made."

"It was the Superbowl ad wasn't it?" Vic said.

"Actually, my brother-in-law works for a car broker," Driscoll said. "He needed the sale. Got a great deal. It was a program car."

"My son-in-law is looking for an old Subaru for me," Vic said. "I'm done with Detroit."

Driscoll lifted his half-full water bottle. "Let's hear it for in-laws."

"Here here," Vic said, grabbing a full bottle from his golf bag.

"Vic?"

"Frank?"

"There's a bit of a problem with closing the case," Driscoll said.

Here it comes, Vic thought. "And that would be?"

"Well, two things."

"Start with one," Vic said.

"Okay, the autopsy," Driscoll said. "There's an open door."

"Door?" Vic said.

"An unresolved point," Driscoll said. "This cannot go public." Vic gave him the Who Me? Look. "I'm serious. Off the record? Completely?" Vic nodded. "Neither Rodgers nor I killed Frakes."

Nelson, Vic thought. He was not surprised. "Oh?"

"Was Nelson there?" Driscoll said.

"I didn't invite him," Vic said. That much was true. "What are you getting at?"

"My bullet, they found lodged in a lamppost," Driscoll said. "It wasn't even close."

"Close enough to wreck my cabin hatch," Vic said. "Can I put in for reimbursement?" Driscoll just shot him the glare. "Nuff said."

"Rodgers hit him in the lower jaw," Driscoll said. "It wasn't fatal."

"And his second shot killed Frakes," Vic said. "It was in the ME's report."

"Rodgers only shot once," Driscoll said.

This time Vic stared.

"The fatal round came from the other direction," Driscoll said. "Hit Frakes in the back of his head. It wasn't from us."

"You knew this when we went over the ME's report in Quartermaine's office?" Vic said.

"Yes. It was part of our arrangement with the Feds."

"Arrangement?" Vic said.

Driscoll nodded and said, "The whole case went black. Feds landed on us with all three feet. Everything is sealed."

"Somebody else killed Frakes?" Vic said. "The Third Man. This changes our deal."

"It does not," Driscoll said. "But I haven't slept much the last few days. This is national security."

Us again, Vic thought. U.S.

"There's a killer out there," Vic said.

"No, it's some other agent, someone else, doing his or her job," Driscoll said. "For us."

"That's fairly cynical," Vic said.

"That's the way it is, Vic," Frank said. "Still I'd like to know—I'm wondering—just who does your friend work for?"

"Pax or Nelson?" Vic said.

"Nelson."

"He's a handyman, a freelancer," Vic said. "I don't know who his clients are. And I don't want to know. What about Pax? He's no slouch either. I know he's got a dark background."

"Stone had no gun and was floundering in the water with a busted wing," Driscoll said.

"He did have a gun, and he knew how to use it," Vic said. "He pulled it on me, then tossed it in the drink. I'm sure you boys recovered it."

"There's no way unless he's a magician," Driscoll said. "It wasn't loaded."

"I can't help you, Frank," Vic said, glad the detective had not asked him if he had seen Nelson at the marina.

* * *

"There's the other thing too," Driscoll said. "The *Sundial* thing."

"It'll be in Sunday's paper," Vic said. Driscoll took in a sharp breath, then dropped his head. "Well, what did you expect? We're a newspaper."

The detective looked up, eyes tired. "You're not going to print the whole *Sundial* paper are you?"

"I can't print what I don't have," Vic said, which was true, technically.

"That could apply to the Dead Sea Scrolls, Vic," Driscoll said.

"Caught me," Vic said. "No, only a general description, but no real details. Nothing about prime numbers or fractals. Mostly gibberish, but that's on orders from on high. It's still out there, Frank. Where are the Picune twins? They have it in their heads."

"They are in the wind," Driscoll said. "Rodgers says he knows where they are. They're safe, and on our side."

"Did you guys ever figure out who you had in custody and when?" Vic said. Glare from the big cop. "Will I still be invited for Christmas dinner?" More glare.

"We're already taking major heat over Frakes," Driscoll said. "When *Sundial* breaks—" He just shook his head.

"Frank—you and Rodgers will be credited with preventing *Sundial* from falling into the wrong hands," Vic said, although he was not quite sure which hands were right and which ones were wrong.

"And getting credit for a kill we did not make," Driscoll said. "Especially one of our own. I don't like that."

Vic looked at his friend, source, and adversary. Driscoll slumped more than usual, bearing the weight of the case, and the lies. He looked up at Vic and said, "Will you at least ask Nelson if he was there?"

"No I will not," Vic said.

"What about the public's right to know?" Driscoll said.

"Who have you spoken to in the last three days about this?" Vic said.

"Off the record?"

"Sure."

"Homeland Security, DIA, FBI, CIA, NSA, and my contact at the White House."

"Alphabet soup," Vic said.

"With guns," Driscoll said. "Big ones."

"What did they say about Nelson?" Vic said.

"Leave him alone," Driscoll said.

"Well, that's my plan too," Vic said. "I've got to run."

"Hot date?" Driscoll said.

"Not exactly," Vic said.

"She must be crazy," Driscoll said.

"That's not the half of it," Vic said.

They drove off, Driscoll to paint a bedroom in his house, Vic to meet Stew Ellison at Centennial Airport.

55

The Perfect Landing always served up a good plate of food. Vic ordered coffee and, after he added the half and half to cut the beverage's sometimes abrasive effect on his insides, turned to gaze out the window to observe the activity at the general aviation facility in the south Denver suburbs. A white tri-pacer practiced touch and goes, Vic wondering how healthy its pilot really was. He avoided small planes at all costs. A non-descript white Learjet of some variety occupied the tarmac below him. The pilot seemed to be conducting a final walk around while a two-person ground crew wrapped up refueling and moved back from the plane. From beneath him, a pudgy gray haired guy in a Hawaiian shirt and gray pants waddled out toward the plane. It was Stew Ellison.

Vic tossed a ten, all he had in his wallet, onto the table and bolted from the restaurant. He raced down the stairs, tripping once but regaining his balance by jumping into the tiny main terminal waiting area below the restaurant. He got to the glass doors leading to the tarmac as the sealed up Learjet began its taxi toward the runway.

"So much for that interview," he said to the door.

"Excuse me?" said a young girl behind a check-in counter.

"Oh nothing," Vic said. "Who was that? I thought I recognized him."

She looked down at her desk. "Mr. Ellison. Flight plan to D.C."

That was easy, Vic thought, then wondering how easy it would be to grab one of these planes. "I was late for our meeting."

"Well, they met over there," she said, pointing toward a small seating area. Empty coffee cups, two of them, occupied the uncleared coffee table.

"Where's the other guy?" Vic said. She pointed toward the parking lot.

"Thanks," Vic said, deciding that security, or lack thereof, at general aviation airports might make a nice piece for the paper. He doubled timed it out the door, across the drop off pavement and to the edge of the parking lot only to see a dark SUV wheel around toward the lot exit. The driver's side window was down. Brad Rodgers was at the wheel.

*   *   *

Vic's cellphone rang.

"Bengston.

"Ellison."

"You stood me up," Vic said.

"Pressing business," Ellison said.

"I'm sure," Vic said.

"You can be."

"I caught sight of Rodgers, though," Vic said.

"Brad's a good man," Ellison said.

"Is he?" Vic said.

"He is," Ellison said. "He spoke highly of you."

"I'll bet. I assaulted him twice."

"He respects your work," Ellison said.

"No he doesn't," Vic said.

"No," Ellison said. "He doesn't, but he respects its impact."

"Better than nothing."

"Sorry I missed our meeting," Ellison said.

"Somehow I'm not convinced," Vic said.

"We got want we wanted," Ellison said.

"*Sundial?*"

"That too."

"Who is 'we'?" Vic said.

"The interests I represent," Ellison said.

"Us? "Vic said.

"You and me?"

"No, us. The U.S."

"Well, that's one of them," Ellison said. "The rest are—confidential—but safe."

"Oh, I'll sleep nights now," Vic said.

"You should," Ellison said. "At least as a journalist. You have a source. Sources, actually, in me and Rodgers."

"We're you Frakes' client?" Vic said. "He tried to kill me. He killed Riley."

"Off the record?" Ellison said.

"Off the record."

"No."

"Who was his client then?" Vic said.

"No comment."

"A government?"

"No comment."

"A company?"

"No comment."

"How can I trust you?" Vic said. "You're no commenting me to death."

"You have no choice," Ellison said. He was right. Vic knew that. Reporters played sources. Sources played reporters. "The good guys won, Vic. The good guys have *Sundial*."

Only Vic was not sure just who the good guys were.

* * *

Vic, Peggy, and Vigil spent the bulk of the two days sorting out what was on the record and what was off. The Picune twins and Paxton Stone were off the record under a deal struck between the *Denver Times*, the feds, the local cops, and Vic. Credit for the creation of *Sundial* would go to Riley's "team" which he set up in the foothills west of Loveland to devise a method to safeguard ballots cast with his Universal Vote system. Vic relished writing the copy about the heads of the country's two major political parties and how they reviled the concept of the Universal Vote. In print, Denver police detective Frank Driscoll and FBI agent Brad Rodgers were the ones who took down the good cop gone bad, Greg Frakes, and there was no mention of a third man. Quartermaine hated the deal, but relented when he determined in his head, even confirming it with the federal agents, that *Sundial* was uncovered during an investigation of Riley's suspected murder by *Denver Times* reporter Vic Bengston. *Sundial* was described in general terms, no mention of prime numbers or fractals, but Vic felt the story was strong enough to convey the importance of the encryption scheme.

56

It was Vic's favorite part of the day. The sun was low, casting long shadows and a yellow light that made warm days with green leaves seem even warmer and more inviting. He knew hundreds of people were in Mallory Square or lined up on the hotel decks facing the Gulf side of Key West, all waiting to toast the sun as it made its last gasp for the day.

On the east side of the island, trees and buildings blocked much of the sunlight, which would vanish a few minutes earlier, turning the Atlantic into a grayish moving landscape capped with a sky of sunlit clouds fading to mute pinks, purples, oranges, and, eventually, night.

Vic stood on the cement walkway of Fisherman's Row, looking across the lagoon and out into the ocean from the now empty stall number twenty-three. The charter sign was gone. Hacker I and Hacker II were still over at the Coast Guard dock, red tagged by the Department of Homeland Security.

Jeff Picune was gone too, nowhere to be found. A local banker told him over a beer at Nico's that when the feds got around to freezing Jeff's assets, there were none to freeze. Jared's twin brother had moved them all, one step ahead of the sheriff. Peggy and Vic had searched for Jared in Colorado, but he vanished as well. The reporters speculated, but not in print, that the Picune assets were probably well hidden, cloaked by internet protocols that hackers like the Picunes knew how to use—for good and for evil.

* * *

Agent Rodgers offered little help. He actually volunteered to drive

Vic to Denver International Airport two days earlier. "I could use a vacation too," Rodgers had said in his own car, also a dark SUV.

"May I recommend southern California," Vic said.

"I'm not going to follow you to Key West," Rodgers said. "At least, I owe you a lift."

Sure he did, Vic thought, and then some. "I appreciate it." He did too. He wanted to find out why Rodgers offered the ride.

"Picune and Stone helped us untie the *Sundial* knot," Rodgers said. "My bosses tell me it will keep us ahead for a few more years."

"Ahead of what, or whom?" Vic said.

"The bad guys, Vic," the agent said. "You can't imagine how bad they are."

"Or how rich they are," Vic said.

"Meaning?"

"Meaning the price for *Sundial* is high, super high," Vic said. "Eventually, money will change hands in one direction and *Sundial* in the other."

"Jeff?" Rodgers said. "Or Jared? They've got more money than they'll ever need."

"What about your pal, Ellison?" Vic said.

"He's your pal," Rodgers said, faking innocence.

"Give me a break, Agent Rodgers," Vic said. "That was you leaving Centennial the other day."

"Moi? No way." He paused a beat or two. "What about you"

Finally, Vic thought, he gets around to why the ride offer. "What about me?"

"*Sundial* could provide quite the little nest egg," the agent said. "For an aspiring writer."

"I would have to be an aspiring writer," Vic said. He had thought often of writing novels, if only he could muster the confidence. "I already am a writer. A reporter, Brad. And I would have to have *Sundial* in my possession to cash in on it. We've been over that a few dozen times thus far. Also, I have to correct you."

"Where did I go wrong?" Rodgers said.

"*Sundial* would be quite the large nest egg," Vic said. "Massive."

"Then a big nest egg," Rodgers said.

Vic's cellphone rang. He swiped a security pattern across the smooth screen. "Hello? Hi there. Oh I'm fine. Just driving out to the airport with your friend Agent Rodgers. Oh, okay." Vic turned to Rodgers and said, "She wonders how your gun is doing." Rodgers shook his head. "He said the bullets still are a little salty. Yeah, I'll be in around six-thirty. Byeulater."

"You've searched my house twice, Nelson's place once," Vic said. "I gave everything I had to Driscoll and he give it to you."

"It's software, Bengston," Rodgers said. "It could be anywhere."

57

For two days, Vic walked around Key West thinking about *Sundial.* He was not good company. He was distracted. He excused himself from dinner at Barb and Kelly's house to wander the island at night, just thinking. Marti was growing tired of his moods, but she seemed to understand.

Vic thought about President Kennedy and Adlai Stevenson when they unmasked the Soviet attempt to base nuclear missiles in Cuba. He was in high school then, having been molded in the duck and cover fear of nuclear annihilation throughout his grade school years. He thought about the mish-mash of Vietnam that erased the lines between good and bad, right and wrong, war and peace. He thought about Nixon and detente, the attempt to delicately balance off world powers against each other, Watergate, and finally of President Reagan when the Gipper suggested that the near mythical Star Wars technology should be given to all major powers, again to maintain that balanced power. He recalled images in Berlin as the wall fell with the evaporation of the Soviet empire that had so dominated his generation's fears. Then came the horrifying memory that fall morning when his oldest son awakened him with an urgent phone call and a command to turn on the television. As the massive tube at the end of his bed spewed images of a burning tower in Manhattan, Vic relived his shock as a tragic accident morphed suddenly and without warning into something dark and sinister when the second plane pierced tower two in blistering rage. As he watched the towers collapse, entombing thousands in a fiery rubble filled sepulcher of hate, Vic recalled the stark realization that if they would do this, they would do more. There was no limit. In the years since then, he observed that as the new wars emerged, some hot, some cold, all of them involved computer and encryption technology.

Before he left Denver, he almost sent *Sundial* to WikiLeaks, thinking of the Reagan concept of giving the technology to everyone, but he held off to think it through a little more, and because Julian Assange was such a smarmy creep. Would the powers be equally balanced against each other if they all had *Sundial*, like detent? Vic just shook his head at the question. Detente depended on a sense of civilization, a respect for institutions, concepts of social and economic cooperation that seem to be disappearing.

"More like Hobbes' State of Nature," he said to a brown pelican gliding low in the waning light along the surface of the teal lagoon. "The war of all against all."

* * *

Vic knelt to the cement next to the empty Hacker I and II berth in a pool of light now provided by a lamppost, the sun having done all it could that day. He reached into his shirt pocket and pulled out his cellphone, then peeled off the back and with a fingernail removed the tiny micro SD card he had slipped into the phone before he left Colorado. It was not the one he had swiped from Driscoll's desk, but it contained the same powerful secrets, the keys to *Sundial*.

From the pocket of his shorts, he retrieved a butane lighter purchased for this eventuality. He opened the short blade of his vintage Swiss army knife, the one his father recently passed on to him, and stabbed the little black chip. Holding it up, he lit one corner with the lighter. The plastic casing began to smolder and sputter with a sickening stench. Vic had to relight it twice before the flame reduced the card to a shriveled up glob of plastic with a few glints from the distorted gold electrical contacts. Vic dropped the memory card remains to the cement, let it cool for a minute, then ground it into a tiny charred pile of rubble with his left foot.

Vic scraped the remnants of the SD card onto one of his business cards. He dumped the bits into his right palm, walked to the water's edge, stuck out his arms, and brushed both of his hands together as though he were ridding himself of leftover crumbs from a particularly dry and powdery scone. Gravity, with a little help from the gentle island breeze, delivered the leftovers to the lagoon, where Vic assumed salt water would do the rest. The pelican circled back and landed on the cement a few feet away, thinking it might have been food.

"I have no idea how many others have *Sundial*," Vic said to the curious bird. "I do know, for sure, that we have it. We. Us. The U.S." The pelican cocked her head.

"Good luck with your hunt," Vic said. The bird flew off as Vic knelt, looked at the soothing water, and flashed on that aging face he saw every day in the bathroom mirror. Then he stood up and headed toward the quiet and inviting lights of Marti's boat.

"Coffee con leche?" Marti said, stepping up the companionway from the main cabin. Her hair was unfettered, freshly washed and dried, her body concealed by loose jeans and a baggy oxford shirt. He could make an excuse and leave. He was so good at that. And just head back to Barb and Kelly's.

Vic's eyes adjusted to the night. "Is that my shirt?" Vic said. The mirror image of the aging face dissipated and the normal mental view of himself returned, the ten year old looking out in wonder.

"Yeah." She smiled. "Your jeans too."

"Coffee con leche sounds great," Vic said, stepping from the concrete dock onto the gently rocking deck of the Durga.

Acknowledgments

The author would like to gratefully acknowledge those who have helped in the research and writing of this novel. They include Denver Sheriff Deputy Lowell Moore; Elissa Tivona; Dave Elsner; IT and computer security gurus Liam Schneider and Trygve Schneider; my whip, Kevin Schneider, who keeps me focused; my fabulous photographer, Clarissa Schneider; Mike Mason, whose interest in fractals triggered bizarre thoughts in my mind, and Simon Singh, author of The Code Book, an invaluable and extremely interesting history and explanation of secrecy and cryptography. The music of the Dave Brubeck Quartet also served up ongoing inspiration. Many thanks to all.

A special thanks to Gene Bengston, who taught me American history in Junior High School. He was tough but fair. I swiped his last name for my ongoing baby boomer character, Vic Bengston. More important, he made the story of this nation interesting, eventually leading me to my undergraduate and graduate studies of American government, which, despite its shortcomings, is the best on Earth.

And a very special thanks to my readers. If they do not know by now, I am an "Indie" author. I research, write, edit, and publish my creative work—much like the painter, the musician, and the independent filmmaker. The readers, their comments on and reactions to my work, keep me going.

In this new world of publishing technology, placing your creative work in front of the public has become easier. Yet marketing is still a challenge, so if you like what you read—if it entertains you or triggers a fun memory to two—pass it on to your friends and networks. By all means, post a review on Amazon. It just takes a few minutes.

I am working on the next Vic Bengston Investigation now, as you are reading this.

–RJS / November 2015

Suggested Reading and Viewing

Books

The Code Book: The Science of Secrecy from Ancient Egypt to Quantum Cryptography by Simon Singh

Alan Turing: The Enigma by Andrew Hodges

Codebreakers: The Inside Story of Bletchley Park. Edited by F. H. Hinsley and Alan Stripp

Feature Films

The Imitation Game. Biopic about mathematician Alan Turing, credited with cracking the German Enigma code during World War II. Benedict Cumberbatch stars.

Breaking the Code. An earlier biopic on Turing, which is a tad better than The Imitation Game, but both are excellent. Derek Jacobi stars.

The Bletchley Circle. A post WWII mystery miniseries featuring four women who served as codebreakers at Bletchley Park. All but forgotten after the war, they team up to solve complex mysteries. Brilliant!

Documentaries

YouTube. Search on words like enigma, Alan Turing, Bletchley, cryptology, encryption, codebreakers, etc. for a wealth of documentary programs on these fascinating topics.

About the Author

Richard J. Schneider is the author of the popular Vic Bengston Investigation mystery novels. He is a former wire service and newspaper journalist, scriptwriter, and media producer who has won numerous awards for his work. He lives in Colorado. *For more information, visit: www.richardjschneider.com.*